SPIRITS ADOPTED

ALSO BY ALICE DUNCAN

The Daisy Gumm Majesty Mystery Series

Strong Spirits

Fine Spirits

High Spirits

Hungry Spirits

Genteel Spirits

Ancient Spirits

Spirits Revived

Dark Spirits

Spirits Onstage

Unsettled Spirits

Bruised Spirits

Spirits United

Spirits Unearthed

Shaken Spirits

Scarlet Spirits

Exercised Spirits

Wedded Spirits

Domesticated Spirits

Library Spirits

Spirits Adopted

Rosy Spirits

The Mercy Allcutt Mystery Series

SPIRITS ADOPTED

A DAISY GUMM MAJESTY MYSTERY
BOOK 20

ALICE DUNCAN

ePublishingWorks!
love what you read.

Disclaimer for Fictional Works

This is a work of fiction. Names, characters, places, and incidents are products of the author's imagination or are used fictitiously. Any resemblance to actual persons, living or dead, businesses, events, or locales is entirely coincidental.

AI Use Restriction

Without limiting the author's and publisher's exclusive rights under copyright, any use of this publication for training generative artificial intelligence (AI) technologies is prohibited. Unauthorized use for this purpose may result in legal action.

Piracy Warning

The scanning, uploading, or distribution of this book without permission is illegal and punishable by law. Please purchase only authorized editions and avoid participating in or encouraging piracy. Your support of the author's rights helps protect their work.

Released March 2025
ISBN: 978-1-64457-728-8 (pb)
ISBN: 978-1-64457-729-5 (hc)

ePublishing Works
644 Shrewsbury Commons Ave, Ste 249
Shrewsbury, PA 17361, USA
www.epublishingworks.com
Phone: 866-846-5123

The future ain't what it used to be.

YOGI BERRA

AUTHOR'S NOTE

A sincere thank-you to the members of the Facebook group, DAISY DAZE, founded by Iris Evans and Leon Fundenberger. If it weren't for the Daisy Dazers, I'd still be struggling to come up with a plot for this book. Special thanks to the following folks:

- Jon Ludwig
- Lyndele von Schill
- Andie Paysinger
- Iris Evans
- Margaret Cronk
- Kris Lawson Carabetta
- Su Holland
- Nancy Arellano
- Chris Randel
- Mary Roraff

Honestly, there wouldn't be a Daisy #20 if it weren't for the people listed above. I hope I'm not leaving anyone out!

ONE

I sat at the kitchen table on a pleasant Saturday morning in October of 1926, pondering the merits of eating another orange versus eating another slice of buttered toast slathered with Aunt Vi's plum preserves, when the telephone's ring shattered my peace. Looking down upon my beloved dachshund, Spike, I said, "Crumb, Spike. I think the universe is telling me I shouldn't eat more of anything at all."

Spike wagged his tail at me, but I knew he was on the side of buttered toast.

With a grunt, I shoved myself up from the kitchen table. The only reason I grunted was because I was eight-plus months pregnant and feeling unwieldy. I kept repeating to myself, "Only another month or so," but it didn't help a whole lot.

To be fair, my pregnancy thus far had been uneventful. I hadn't even been sick in the mornings. My husband, Sam Rotondo, a detective with the Pasadena Police Department, remained overly protective, but that's better than him not caring at all.

According to people who claim to know such things, I was carrying the baby low instead of high—whatever that means—and this proclaimed the child to be a boy. I already knew the sex of my baby because a Tongva shaman, Mr. Emilio DeLoera, had told me. Therefore, I just thanked people and went on about my business.

I lifted the receiver and said, "Hello?"

When a bellowed, "*Daisy!*" came through the receiver, I yanked it away from my ear. The only person who shrieked at me over the telephone was Mrs. Algernon Pinkerton, and I thought she'd gone to Santa Barbara for the next few months. Surely she didn't need me in Santa Barbara. Did she?

Alarming notion.

Daring to put the speaker end of the receiver to my lips I repeated my sedate, "Hello?" because I doubted the Mrs. Pinkerton theory.

"Daisy, it's Harold! You've got to *help* us!"

"Harold," I said, surprised. "Why are you in such a lather? I thought lathering was your mother's job." Harold Kincaid was the product of Mrs. Pinkerton's first and lousy marriage to a ring-tailed polecat named Eustace Kincaid.

Hmmm. I'll explain the "ring-tailed polecat" comment later, along with Harold, who also needs some explaining.

"You'd be in a lather too if someone dumped a baby in a basket on your doorstep!"

"What?"

"Are you deaf as well as pregnant?" Harold demanded. "You heard me!"

"Somebody left a baby in a basket on your doorstep?"

"Isn't that what I just said?"

Harold was clearly in a touchy mood. "Yes, you did say so. It's just…difficult to imagine."

The wail of an infant drifted to me through the receiver, and I revised my opinion.

"Do you hear that?" Harold bellowed.

"Yes. It sounds like a baby, all right. But who'd leave you a baby?"

"How the devil should *I* know? But what the heck am I supposed to do with it now?"

A poser, to be sure. "Um…I'm not sure. Would you like me to call Sam and ask him?"

Silence greeted my question.

I tried again. "Harold? Do you want me to ask Sam what to do with a baby left in a basket on your doorstep? I'm sure he knows."

"But…it's just a baby. I mean, I don't know anything about babies, but I think this one is about as newly born as a baby can get and still be out of the womb."

"Yes?" I wanted to ask, *So what?* but restrained myself.

"If you tell Sam, he'll get the authorities involved, and the poor kid will go to an orphanage or some other God-forsaken place."

"Do they send babies to orphanages?" I asked, never having considered the matter before.

"I don't know!" said Harold, who was back to shouting. "But I don't want this tiny red-faced thing to go someplace where nobody will care about it. It's only a *baby*! It deserves better than that."

"You keep calling it 'it,'" I said. "Is it a boy or a girl?"

Again, silence floated through the wire. Then Harold said, "Um…I don't know. Roy?" I deduced he'd turned his head away from the receiver because I only faintly heard the name of Harold's houseboy, Roy Castillo. Coming close to the speaker end of the receiver once more, Harold said, "Roy's looking. It hardly looks human at this point."

"That's not very nice," I told him.

"Tell me that when someone drops a baby on *your* front doorstep," he growled. "Ew, good Lord, Roy, that's disgusting!"

"Harold," I said. "It's a baby. It can't help it."

"I know, I know, but it's still disgusting. Oh. Yes, I see. Thanks, Roy." To me he said, "It's a girl."

"Oh my goodness. Can you take care of her for a little while until we figure out the best thing to do for her?" I said. "I'll call Flossie Buckingham. If anybody aside from Sam knows what to do, she will."

"That's better than Sam," said Harold. "At least Flossie won't send her to Siberia or an orphanage or anything."

"We don't yet know what will happen," I warned him. "There may be laws about this sort of thing."

"What sorts of things? Leaving babies in baskets on doorsteps? I imagine there are laws." Harold had taken to snarling. "But I still don't want to send the kid to an orphanage."

"Are you equipped to care for a baby?" I asked, thinking Harold, who lived with his companion Delray Farrington, probably wasn't loaded down with the paraphernalia required to care for a newborn.

"No. No, I'm not. I'm going to call Hazel Greenlaw and hire her to be a nurse to the thing until we come up with a permanent solution to the problem."

"The problem? Poor kid," I said.

"She *is* a problem, dammit!" said Harold.

"Yes, I know, but she's a human problem. You don't want to adopt her yourself, do you?"

"*No,* I don't want to adopt it. Her. Whatever it is. But I don't know what I'm going to do with it…I mean her, either," said Harold. "The only thing I know for sure is that the kid's not going to end up in an orphanage if I have anything to say about it."

"What do you have against orphanages?" I asked.

"If you'd ever visited one, you wouldn't ask."

His answer surprised me. "Do you visit orphanages on a regular basis?"

"No, but I used to tag along when Mother was being Lady Bountiful and visited the Pasadena Orphanage for Children and the Los Angeles Orphan Asylum. Not sure why she made me go with her, but those visits gave me a horror of orphanages. I don't know who this kid is or where she came from, but she doesn't deserve a fate like that. Think about *Oliver Twist* and triple it."

"Good Lord."

"The good Lord has nothing to do with places like that, even though half of them are run by religious organizations. But yes, please call Flossie. I'm going to get in touch with Fred and Hazel Greenlaw. I expect the kid should have a medical examination. And what am I supposed to feed her? Oh God, Daisy. Help me!"

"I'll drive down to your place as soon as I call Flossie. I'll stop at a store and get some infant formula, too."

"What the devil is infant formula?"

"Food, Harold. For the baby. I'm assuming you don't plan to nurse her yourself."

"We can't just feed her milk from a cow?" Harold sounded almost desperate.

"No, plain cow's milk isn't good for babies. I'll bring you a book about babies, too. I have about a thousand of them thanks to your mother, Mrs. Bissel, Mrs. Hanratty, and every other Pasadena matron I know."

"Hurry," said Harold. "Please hurry."

"I shall. Good luck."

"Thanks."

Harold hung up his telephone, and I gently replaced the receiver on mine. A baby. Somebody had left a baby on Harold Kincaid's doorstep. Even thinking the words sounded insane.

Insane or not, however, it had happened. Shaking my head in something akin to dumbfoundment (I'm almost positive that's not a word), I picked up the telephone's receiver again and dialed the number for the Pasadena chapter of the Salvation Army. My pals, Johnnie and Flossie Buckingham, were in charge of it.

The telephone rang twice before the receiver was picked up on the Salvation Army end, and a voice said, "Pasadena Salvation Army."

Dang. It wasn't a voice I recognized. I said, "May I please speak with Mr. or Mrs. Buckingham? This is Mrs. Rotondo calling."

"Neither the captain nor Mrs. Buckingham is here at the moment. May I take a message?"

After thinking about it for maybe three seconds, I said, "No thank you. I'll call later. Actually, you might just write a note asking either of them to telephone me. Daisy Rotondo." I probably wouldn't be home, but I wasn't sure what else to do.

Harold had sounded truly desperate, and I needed to get some baby formula and some bottles and other baby things to him as soon as I could. When I heard the back door open and the ka-*thump* of

Mr. Lou Prophet's leg and peg entering the house, I almost groaned aloud.

"Spike," I said to the loyal hound sitting at my feet. "What am I supposed to do now?"

Apparently Spike didn't know what I should do any more than I did because he only gave me a happy wag. I didn't see anything to be happy about, but that's because I'm not a dog. Dogs are far superior to people when it comes to moods and so forth.

"Miss Daisy?" came Mr. Prophet's voice from the kitchen.

"I'm at the telephone table," I called back.

Spike, who loved company, raced to greet Mr. Prophet in the kitchen.

"Howdy, Spike," I heard Mr. Prophet say.

Then he ka-*thumped* through the kitchen, pantry, dining room, and to the hallway where the telephone table sat. There he loomed over me. A tall man, bowed slightly by age, Mr. Lou Prophet, in spite of having lost one of his legs, presented a formidable appearance. If you were to meet him in a back alley at midnight, for instance, you might drop dead from pure terror, but he wasn't really all *that* bad. In actual fact, he'd been more helpful than not since he suddenly showed up in our lives a couple of years ago.

Perhaps I'd better explain Mr. Prophet now and get it over with. You see, Mr. Lou Prophet was a relic of the Old West. When he was but a lad, he'd fought in the Confederate Army during the Civil War. There wasn't anything left of his Georgia home after the war ended, so he drifted west. There he became a bounty hunter.

Bounty hunters are thin on the ground in the refined and dignified city of Pasadena, California, and Mr. Prophet doesn't precisely fit in here. Sam and I had met him when he'd saved me from being killed by a knife thrown by Sam's horrid nephew, Frank Pagano. Frank was an idiot. Mr. Prophet was an oddity.

Sam and I had sprung him from the wildly misnamed Odd Fellows House of Christian Charity and had more or less adopted him. He now lived in a little cottage at the back of our home on South Marengo Avenue in Pasadena and had adopted a cat named

Yuyu (short for Yuyutsu, which is an Apache word meaning "loves to fight").

Anyhow, Mr. Prophet is a fount of quaint Old-West sayings. He's where the "ring-tailed polecat" mentioned earlier came from. And now he loomed over me, and I was in a crisis and didn't need to be bothered by him.

"Why are you looming over me?" I snapped.

"What're you talkin' about? I ain't loomin'."

"It feels like you are."

"Well, I ain't."

"Very well, you're not looming. Did you want something?"

"A ride to the library if you're goin'," he said.

"Crumb," I said, wilting on my chair.

"What's the matter with you?" he asked with pardonable grumpiness.

To tell or not to tell; that was the question. After considering options for a few seconds, I decided to tell the old coot what the matter was. Of all the people I'd met in my almost twenty-six years of life, Mr. Prophet was the least judgmental, except when it came to the lovely city of Pasadena, which he claimed to hate because it was too cultivated for him. He preferred dirt, snakes, scorpions, natives, incalculable desert wastelands, booze and loose women. Never mind that it was booze and loose women that had led to his downfall. Literally. He and a couple of ladies of the night, along with a crate of booze, were in a car that drove off a cliff in Malibu and crashed into the Pacific Ocean. Mr. Prophet was the only survivor, although he'd lost one of his legs.

"Well?" he snarled. I guess I was taking too long to answer his rude question.

So I told him.

Silence followed my explanation.

Then Mr. Prophet said, "Hellkatoot."

TWO

"Yes," I said.

"Well, ya goin' to his place, or you gonna sit here all damn day?" he growled.

"I was about to get up and go when you came in and stopped me," I growled back.

"I ain't stoppin' ya," he said. "I'll go with you. You're gonna take him some of your baby things, right?"

"Yes," I said, heaving myself to my feet once again. "And a book about babies."

"Kee-rist, there're books about babies every damn place in this house these days. Where ya gonna get the…what'd you call it? Formula?"

"I'll stop by the Bennetts' store and get formula," I told him. "Hope they have baby bottles too. I have diapers and other baby necessities upstairs in the nursery."

"I'll go with you and help carry stuff," he said.

"Thanks."

"What about Spike?"

"What *about* Spike?" I asked, surprised by the question.

"You ain't takin' the dog, are you?"

"No. Harold likes Spike, but I fear Spike might get bored with the baby or annoy the doctor or something."

"He's got a doctor there already?" asked Mr. Prophet.

"He's telephoned for both a doctor and a nurse. Don't know if they're there yet."

"I kin figger out how he might know a doctor, but how's he know a nurse?" Mr. Prophet wanted to know.

I opened my mouth to tell him, decided it was too long a story and said, "I'll tell you in the car."

He shook his grizzled head. "I'll take Spike outside to do his business while you start roundin' up baby shi—stuff."

"Good idea." He might be rough around the edges, but he tried to be helpful.

Anyhow, I hurried—as fast as I *could* hurry—up the stairs to the nursery. Once there, I grabbed one of the seventy-five bags I'd been given by various wealthy women in Pasadena. Most of the ladies had called them "baby bags" or "diaper bags," but they could be used for anything. However, today the one I chose would be a diaper bag. I began filling it.

In truth, I just committed a gross exaggeration. There weren't seventy-five bags, but there were an abundant plenty, for sure.

Hmm. Perhaps another explanation is due here. You see, I know most of the wealthy women in Pasadena because, for more than half my life, I'd earned my living and that of the rest of my family as a spiritualist-medium. A fake one. Except for one or two memorable occasions I'd just as soon forget, I couldn't summon anyone's dead relations from the Other Side—whatever that was—for a chat with a grieving relative.

I piled diapers, diaper pins, rubber baby pants, some homemade cold cream (for the baby's bottom), and some homemade powder into the bag. For the record, I wasn't the one who'd made the cold cream or powder. A lady named Mrs. Rattle came to the house and cleaned it for us Monday through Friday. As this was a Saturday, she wasn't here. However, she'd made some amazingly soothing creams and powders that she claimed were purer than commercial ones. I figured both Harold's baby and mine deserved purity.

I looked on the shelf over the crib and grabbed a book about child-rearing that Harold might find useful. I popped in a set of Beatrix Potter books because they were small. I threw in *Healthyland* because it had information about what to read to a baby as well as what to do with a baby. Kate Greenaway was next, and my fingers were poised to clutch a copy of *Grimm's Fairy Tales* until I remembered the humans always lost in Grimms' stories and most other fairy tales.

Honestly, have you ever *read* those things? Those so-called "fairy tales" are disgusting. In place of Grimm, I dumped in *Happy Heart Stories*, a copy of *A Child's Garden of Verses* by Robert Louis Stevenson, along with the 1922 and 1923 issues of *Playbook*. I figured, life being what it was, the kid would have plenty of time to learn about pain and suffering when it was out of diapers.

"You done up there?" a rusty voice asked from the foot of the stairs.

"Yes!" I said, closing the diaper bag and almost falling over when I tried to pick it up. Oh dear. Sam would be really angry if he knew I lugged anything so heavy down our flight of stairs. He worried about me, bless the man. "I can't carry everything. Can you come up and help me?" This was not an idle question, nor was it ungrammatical. He might be able to help me, or he might not be able to. It depended on how secure he felt using his leg and peg on the steps.

"Yeah," he said and ka-*thumped* up the staircase.

I decided to make life easier on both of us, grabbed another one of my many diaper bags and put half of everything into one and left the second half in the first one. When Mr. Prophet appeared at the nursery door, I thrust one bag at him and took the other. "Here you go. Thanks for helping. I'd have had to make two trips otherwise." Mind you walking up and down the stairs a couple of times a day would, according to our wonderful family physician Dr. Benjamin, only be good for me. However, even he would frown on so-pregnant a lady carrying such a heavy load.

"Yeah," he said, gracious as ever.

Joking! He might not be gracious, but he was definitely helpful.

"You gonna take the Chevrolet?" he asked as he got to the bottom of the staircase. I noticed he had to hold onto the banister as he took the stairs. So did I. Neither of us wanted to fall down all those steps.

"Yes. I don't want to tell Pa about the baby and Harold yet, though. Is that all right with you?"

"Don't have nothin' to do with me. I'm only curious, is all."

"Thanks."

"No thanks needed," he said in a growly voice.

"Well then, when I get the Chevrolet, I'll just tell Pa we're going to the library," I said.

"That's no good. We won't be comin' back with any books, and how're you gonna explain these stupid bags with baby junk in 'em?"

"Oh dear," I said. "You're right."

"Durned right I'm right," he grumbled.

"Very well, you stay on the porch and I'll go across the street and get the machine."

"That'll do."

"I'll just tell Pa I want to take the car to the store." That wasn't even a fib. I *was* going to take the car to a store.

Therefore, I left Mr. Prophet sitting on a chair on the porch. Sam had gone into work for a couple of hours to do paperwork, so his Hudson wasn't in our driveway. I always left my car, the Chevrolet, across the street in my parents' driveway. The arrangement worked well for all of us.

When I arrived at my folks' pleasant bungalow, I hurried up the drive to the side door and knocked as I turned the handle and walked inside. "Anybody home?" I called. My mother had to work half-days at the Hotel Marengo on Saturdays. She was the hotel's chief bookkeeper.

To my surprise, my entry into my parents' home wasn't met by a series of deafening barks from my father's darling but undisciplined black-and-tan dachshund, Rosebud. Because Spike had lived with my parents until my marriage, and because I didn't want my father to be lonely when Spike moved across the street to live with Sam and me, I finagled Rosebud from one of my wealthy clients,

Mrs. Bissel, who bred and showed dachshunds. I'd never even heard of a dog show until I met Mrs. Bissel. She lived in Altadena rather than Pasadena, but they were almost the same town. Altadena flourished in the San Gabriel foothills, and Pasadena flourished a little farther south. Both were beautiful communities in which to live.

Unless, of course, you were Mr. Lou Prophet, but since you aren't, you needn't worry.

"Daisy!" Vi walked out of the kitchen and to the dining room, into which room the side door opened. "Are you all right?"

A word about my aunt, Viola Gumm. She worked as cook for Harold Kincaid's mother, Mrs. Pinkerton. Because Mr. and Mrs. Pinkerton were spending time in Santa Barbara, Vi didn't have to go to work for a while. I doubted I'd ever understand the pleasure Vi took in cooking, because cooking isn't one of the domestic skills I'd mastered to date—although I kept trying. Vi, though, is probably the best cook in the whole Pasadena area, if not the entire state of California. She had been attempting to teach me to cook since I married Sam. Well, she'd attempted the same thing before we married, but this time, I was paying attention.

"I'm fine Vi, but I want to borrow the car to go to the store."

"*Borrow* the car?" said Aunt Vi with a laugh. "It's your car, Daisy. Take it any old time you want to."

This was true, but I didn't want my father, who used to be a chauffeur for rich Pasadenans, to feel as if he had no choices left in his life. He had a weak heart, and I wanted to keep him on this side of the sod for as long as possible. Just as Vi is the best cook in Pasadena, my parents are the best parents in Pasadena, if not the world.

"Well, I know that, but I thought I'd ask anyway." I glanced around the dining room. "Where are Pa and Rosebud?"

"Taking a walk. I think Joe tried to telephone you earlier, but the line was busy or nobody answered it or something."

"Ah. Yes, I was on the 'phone for quite a while this morning." I didn't tell her why.

"I see. Well, because the weather's getting chilly, I thought I'd make some butter beans and ham for supper. This is an easy meal to make, Daisy. Would you like me to give you a lesson?"

Crumb. "Thanks, Vi, but I have to hurry this morning. When I get home, I'll get the recipe from you, is that all right?"

"There's not much of a recipe to follow, but I'll write down the few simple steps for you. It's a good thing we had that ham last week because I can use the bone and the last of the meat with the butter beans. You can use any kind of bean, really. I just had some butter beans."

"Thanks, Vi!" I said, aiming for enthusiasm. "But I need to get going now. I was probably on the 'phone with Harold when Pa called, because he asked me to hurry to his house. Guess he wants to show me something."

With a huge smile, Vi said, "Dear Harold. He's such a nice fellow."

"He is," I agreed.

Then I scrammed out of the house as if my heels were burning. When I got to the car, I managed to squeeze my bulk behind the wheel. My feet barely reached the pedals on the floor. I'm *so* glad I'd bought the Chevrolet. Before I bought the Chevy, we used to own an old Model-T Ford that had to be cranked into life.

Oh, and the reason I'd had enough money to purchase the brand-new car was because I rid Mrs. Bissel's basement of a ghost (or it might have been a spirit). The Bissel basement had contained no ghost (or spirit), but a runaway girl. I swear, my spiritualist job got me into pickles all the time. I was attempting to cut back on my spiritualist workload now that I was a married woman and would soon be a mother. Neither Sam nor I needed any more ghosts in our lives.

I drove the Chevrolet across the street and into Sam's and my home's driveway. Mr. Prophet carried one of the diaper bags to the car, and I hopped out and got the other. Again, perhaps "hopped" isn't the correct word. Lumbered maybe. I not only lumbered, but I huffed too. Being pregnant wasn't a lot of fun in reality, although I was looking forward to when the baby came.

Provided both the baby and I survived his birth.

Gadzooks. I should stop thinking things like that.

"What's this baby Harold got left?" asked Mr. Prophet as we went south on Marengo.

"What do you mean, 'got left'? It's a baby. A girl baby," I told him.

"That's what I wondered. If it was a boy or a girl," said Mr. Prophet.

I turned on Bellevue and pulled the Chevrolet to a stop in front of Bennetts' Grocery and Dry Goods Store. "I'm going to get some infant formula if you want to come with me. Or even if you don't," I said.

"Eh. I'll wait here," said Mr. Prophet.

"Be right back," I said as I grunted myself out of the car.

"Good morning, Mrs. Rotondo!" said the jolly Mrs. Bennett. "What can we do for you today? We have some lovely lamb chops."

"Thank you," I said. "But I'm not in the market for chops today. Actually, I need some infant formula and some baby bottles if you have any. It's kind of an emergency."

"An emergency?" said Mrs. Bennett. Her glance fell to my protruding belly and then found my face again.

"Well, yes. You know two of my very best friends run the Pasadena chapter of the Salvation Army?"

"Yes, you've told me. A great organization, the Salvation Army." Many people didn't share Mrs. Bennett's approval of the Salvation Army but I did with, as Bertie Wooster might say, knobs on.

"Well, they've recently taken in a young woman who is in a desperate situation."

"Huh. A desperate situation, is it? She should have kept her legs together, is what she should have done."

Mrs. Bennett's disapproval irked me. Yes, I'd just lied to her, but hundreds if not thousands of young women were burdened each year by unplanned pregnancies. My experience, tangential though it was, had taught me that most of the poor things had either been seduced and abandoned by rotten men or had been out-and-out ravished by rotten men. In other words, nine times out of ten, the baby wasn't the woman's fault but she bore the total responsibility.

I didn't say so to Mrs. Bennett.

What I said was, "In this case, the poor girl was assaulted." I tried not to sound as angry as I felt about the store owner's stinky attitude. "And she needs bottles and infant formula. If you don't carry—"

"Oh, no," said Mrs. Bennett hastily. I think she might have noticed the pointy edges to my words. "We have formula and Evenflo bottles. Evenflo are the best, and we have Sobee baby formula too. The poor thing."

I supposed the "poor thing" was my imaginary young woman who'd been raped. I swear, life got so complicated sometimes.

Nevertheless, I smiled sweetly at Mrs. Bennett and said, "Thank you so much. I probably should stock up on some of these things for when my own bundle of joy arrives."

"That's true," said Mrs. Bennett, now firmly on my side. "You never know what will happen, do you?"

"You sure don't," I said, for once that morning telling the truth.

THREE

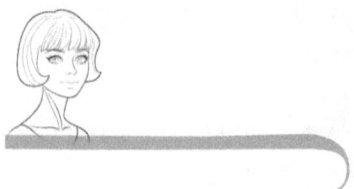

As soon as we left the Bennetts' store, I re-started the Chevrolet, drove to Fair Oaks Avenue and turned south. When I got to California Street, I turned left and traveled on California clear across town to Allen, where I turned south. One couldn't drive too far south on Allen Avenue when one began at California Street, because one would run smack into the gigantic Castleton Estate and gardens, founded by former railroad magnate E.W. Castleton. I knew Miss Emmaline Castleton, daughter of the rich man, but my aim that day wasn't to visit Emmaline but Harold. I turned left on Orlando Street, therefore, made a couple more turns and got to Harold's glorious mansion.

"Kee-rist, is this where Harold lives?" asked Mr. Prophet, staring at Harold's home with something akin to awe. Maybe it was awe mixed with disapproval. As mentioned earlier, Mr. Prophet wasn't a fan of civilization, and Harold's home and the surrounding estates were nothing if not civilized. Affluent, even.

"This is it," I affirmed. "Quit gawking and help me get these things to the door, will you?"

"Yeah," said Mr. Prophet. "I'll help."

Neither the peevish old codger nor I had to wait long for help from Harold's household. I suspect Harold had stationed Roy Castillo at the front door, because almost as soon as I'd parked the car, Roy ran out of the house and up to the Chevrolet.

"Mrs. Majesty," he said. "So glad you could help. This has been a tough morning."

"I'm sure it has been," I told him. "Mr. Prophet and I brought a couple of bags full of baby things, and I got some baby bottles and baby formula at the store. Has Miss Greenlaw arrived yet?"

"She should be here any minute," said Roy. "Dr. Greenlaw couldn't come because he was called out for an emergency earlier in the morning, but another doctor will be here with Miss Greenlaw soon. I think his last name is Vialargo, although I'm not certain."

Mr. Prophet grunted himself out of the passenger side door, so I introduced the two. "Mr. Lou Prophet," I said, gesturing at the craggy elderly person who'd just exited the Chevrolet, "please allow me to introduce you to Roy Castillo. Roy works for Harold and was taught how to cook by my very own Aunt Vi."

"Pleased to meet you, sir," said Roy, hurrying over to Mr. Prophet and holding out his hand.

After looking askance at Roy's hand for a few seconds—he wasn't accustomed to people calling him "sir"—Mr. Prophet conde-scended to shake it. "Likewise," he grunted.

"I put the baby things in the backseat, Roy. There are two padded bags full of diapers, pins, lotions and so forth. The grocery basket has the bottles and formula in it."

At that moment, another automobile came to a halt at the curb in front of Harold's house. As it was a lovely red Marmon Wasp, I knew to whom it belonged: Dr. Fred Greenlaw. Dr. Greenlaw's sister Hazel sat in the driver's seat. I was extremely glad to see Hazel the nurse. Although I'd brought a lot of stuff for Harold to use on the baby, it would be Hazel who taught him precisely how to use it. And I imagined the other doctor, whose name I'd already forgotten, would give the wee tot a thorough examination as soon as he arrived.

As Roy leaned in to fetch parcels from the backseat of the Chevrolet, I rushed to the Marmon Wasp and opened the door.

"Hazel! It's so good to see you again. I have a feeling Harold's going to need you and the doctor for at least a few days."

"I expect he will," said Hazel with a laugh. "Fred's and my father"—the father of Hazel and Fred was also a Dr. Fred Greenlaw —"added Dr. Lawrence Vialargo to the staff six months or so ago because he and Fred are so busy. I think you'll like him. He's a little stiff at first, but he's a good doctor and he loosens up after he knows a person for a while." She fetched her own bag of tricks from the Wasp's tonneau. She also lifted out a pile of soft flannel fabric, thereby jogging my limp brain to attention.

"Oh, my, I didn't even *think* about baby blankets," I said, feeling stupid. "I brought diapers, formula and bottles."

"We can definitely use those," said Hazel. "Poor Harold was nearly incoherent when he rang Fred and me." Hazel chuckled, but I had a feeling it would be a long time before Harold found anything funny about his present predicament.

Another automobile—it looked like a new Chevrolet Roadster to me—joined the line in front of Harold's house. A tall blond man emerged from the driver's side of the machine and turned to retrieve his bag from the passenger seat. A good-looking fellow, he still couldn't hold a candle to the younger Dr. Fred Greenlaw when it came to masculine handsomeness. I wondered if this newcomer was of Harold and Fred's persuasion when it came to women. Without being incredibly rude, I didn't know how to find the answer.

Not the least bit shy, I walked over to the newly arrived doctor and held out my hand. "Awfully glad you could come, Doctor. My name is Daisy Rotondo, and Harold is a great friend of mine. This morning's delivery came as a huge shock to him."

Taking my hand after only a moment—don't know if he was shocked by my boldness or what—he said in a deep voice, "Good to meet you, Mrs. Rotondo. I'm Dr. Lawrence Vialargo. I'm fairly new to Pasadena, but I've been a physician for several years."

"Glad you've joined us," I said. "Please allow me to introduce you to the rest of the folks here. Well, you know Hazel."

"Yes. Indeed," said Dr. Vialargo with what looked like a genuine smile.

I introduced Hazel and Dr. Vialargo to Mr. Prophet. After first shaking hands with Hazel, Mr. Prophet turned to the doctor. As soon as he did so, he gave a small start of what appeared to be shock then shook the doctor's hand. He didn't speak to either one of them. In other words, the doctor and nurse were gracious and Mr. Prophet was the way he was, although the doctor's smile didn't last through their handshake.

Then we all traipsed up the walkway to Harold's front door. Mr. Prophet brought up the rear. When I glanced back at him, Mr. Prophet had a frown on his weather-beaten face. I don't think it was for any particular reason other than that he found himself in a rich man's paradise, and he was far from being a rich man. In truth, I believe he disapproved of wealth.

As a woman from a family in which the breadwinners were all women, I could see his point to a lesser and different degree. For instance, neither my mother nor my aunt earned as much money as did a man with similar skills. As for me, I'd invented my job out of thin air, so I charged whatever the market would bear. Luckily for my family and me, it bore a lot.

When Hazel got to the front door, she turned the knob and held the door for the rest of us to enter. Baby wails greeted us.

"Is that you, Daisy?" a fretful Harold called from an upstairs room.

"It's not only I, but Hazel and Dr. Vialargo. Mr. Prophet is here too," I called back.

"Lou?" Harold's voice squeaked at the end.

"He wanted to meet the baby," I said.

Harold muttered something I couldn't make out. I suspect it was just as well.

"We'll carry the things we brought you upstairs, Harold," I said. "Try not to panic."

"Too late," said Harold. "I'm already panicking, and this kid won't stop screaming. I'm afraid it's starving to death or has the plague or something."

Roy carried both baby bags up the stairs at a run. Dr. Vialargo followed with his black doctor's bag, Hazel carried her own bag of tricks and I brought the grocery basket containing formula and baby bottles. Mr. Prophet was on his own.

As we walked I asked Hazel, "Is the baby in the same room where Mrs. Bannister stayed?"

"Sounds like it," said Hazel.

"Yes, it's the same room," Roy confirmed. "Mr. Harold has ordered a bassinet and other items to be delivered by Nash's Department Store."

"Good," I said. "Does he know when they'll be delivered?"

"Some time this morning," said Roy. With a grin, he said, "Mr. Harold was most insistent."

"I'll just bet he was." Nobody, not even successful store owners, dared defy the wishes of their extremely wealthy clients.

"Oh my God you're here! Thank God!" Harold said when we approached the door to the sickroom. Well, this time the room wasn't being used to house a sick person but a newborn baby.

When I stepped into the room, it was to find Harold looking haggard, his hair standing on end, his face mottled pink and white. He held a swaddled bundle. "Roy tried to clean it up," he said. "But it needs to be examined and fed and so forth. I have *no* idea what to do with a baby." He glanced at the tall, handsome, blond doctor. "Are you Fred's replacement?"

"Not precisely," said the doctor. "But I'm here to give the baby an examination. I'm Dr. Lawrence Vialargo. You're Mr. Kincaid?"

"Yes," said a frazzled Harold. "Thank you for coming. I know nothing about babies!"

"What a surprise," I said.

"I'll teach you," said Hazel, amused. "Here. Let me take the poor thing before you smother it to death."

"Oh God, I didn't *smother* it, did I?" said Harold. "Well, I couldn't have, because it's been screeching for a couple of hours now. Dead babies don't screech, do they?" After Hazel relieved Harold of his burden, Harold's hands went to his head and he tugged at a couple of tufts of hair on each side.

I put my bag of baby accoutrements on top of a nearby dresser and laid a hand on one of Harold's shoulders. "Calm down, Harold."

"Calm *down?*" he yelled. "How calm would *you* be if somebody left a baby in a basket on your front doorstep?"

"Not very," I admitted, "but perhaps while Dr. Vialargo and Hazel tend to the wee one, we can go downstairs. I'll fix you a cup of hot cocoa. That should be calming."

"I'll bring up some Ovaltine or hot chocolate, Mr. Harold," Roy offered.

"No," said Harold. "Let's all stay here until the doctor and Hazel say the poor thing is going to survive. I can't *believe* this!" He glared at me. "But if you bring up the subject of orphanages one more time, I swear I'll never speak to you again."

"Orphanages?" Hazel, who had put the baby on the bed and was unwrapping it, shared a glance between Harold and me. She'd filled a baby-sized tin basin with warm water from a nearby bathroom, and it now sat on a table she'd pulled up so it was close to the bed. In case of splashes, she'd set the basin on a piece of oilskin. "Who was talking about orphanages?"

"Daisy wanted to send it to an orphanage," said Harold.

"I did not! I only said Sam would know what to do with a baby left on a doorstep," I said.

"That means it would have gone to an orphanage. Or some kind of baby farm somewhere."

Dr. Vialargo, who had washed his hands in the same nearby bathroom in which Hazel had fetched her water, said. "I don't believe we have baby farms here in the USA, Mr. Kincaid. Orphanages, however, are all too common." He had an interesting accent I couldn't place. He also sounded as if he spoke from experience and perhaps shared Harold's opinion of orphanages. Again, I couldn't very well ask without being rude.

"I *know* orphanages are too common, because I've seen them. And I don't want this kid to be brought up in an orphanage."

"You might begin calling the baby 'her' instead of 'it', Harold," I suggested gently.

"Oh hell," muttered Harold. As if he didn't want to but was compelled by a force greater than himself, he tiptoed over to the bed and peered down at the naked baby. "Good God," he said. "It looks like a naked pink frog. And it doesn't have any hair."

"She will grow hair, Harold," said a serene Hazel. "Dr. Vialargo hasn't examined her yet, but she looks the picture of health to me." She picked up the naked infant and, still holding her carefully, laid her in the basin of water and proceeded to bathe her. I noticed she used Ivory Soap.

"Do you recommend Ivory Soap for newborns?" I asked.

"It's a good soap to use," she said. "It isn't full of harsh chemicals or fragrances."

"Ah," I said, deciding I'd stock up on Ivory Soap for my own baby boy.

The infant was tiny, and it didn't take Hazel long to bathe her. She lifted her out of the basin and grabbed a towel she'd set handily by on the dresser.

"You're an expert at this aren't you, Hazel?" I said with admiration. I knew for a fact she was unmarried and had no children.

"I've been hired to care for several newborns in the years since I qualified as a nurse," said Hazel, smiling at me. She dried the infant with soft toweling and held it to her shoulder, tenderly patting her back. "Where do you want to check on her, Larry?"

After gazing at the room for a few moments, Dr. Vialargo said, nodding at Roy, "If you can please move the basin—just dump out the water in a bathtub or a sink—I'll examine her on the dresser. Put some towels down to provide a cushion, will you, Mrs. Rotondo?"

"Sure," I said as Roy hurried to follow the young doctor's instructions. I laid several of Harold's cushy soft towels on the dresser, and Hazel laid the infant on them.

The doctor said, "Thank you both. Young man, would you mind preparing a bottle for the baby now? There are instructions on the formula package. Mrs. Rotondo, you brought the formula and baby bottles, right?"

"Right," I said.

"Excellent. And you...I beg your pardon. What is your name again? I missed it," he said to Roy.

"Roy Castillo, Doctor. I'm Mr. Kincaid's houseboy."

"I see," said the doctor. "Roy, if you could please prepare a bottle—make sure the formula doesn't feel hot on the inside of your wrist—we might make this poor little girl comfortable at last."

"Thank God," muttered Harold.

Lest you think these conversations were taking place in a silent atmosphere, they weren't. The baby shrieked during its unswaddling and didn't shut up until Hazel set her in the warm water. My ears still rang.

During the unwrapping, bathing and drying of the infant, Mr. Prophet had stood like the statue of a cigar-store Indian against a far wall of the bedroom. When Dr. Vialargo began his examination of the new human on the dresser, Mr. Prophet crept a little closer. I'd forgotten all about him. Nevertheless, I stepped aside so he could get a better view of the child.

"So that's a newborn, eh?" he said in a rusty whisper.

"That's a newborn girl child," I affirmed.

"Tiny little thing, ain't it?"

"Yes, she is," I said.

"But it looks mighty big to come out of a female. Is it brand new, or has it been around for a while?"

I turned to stare at him. His gaze seemed glued to the baby girl squirming on her bed of towels on the dresser. "She's brand new," I said. "And yes, it hurts to give birth. If men could get pregnant, they wouldn't be so free about spilling their seed here, there and everywhere."

Mr. Prophet and I had discussed this topic before. He'd been cavalier about the flagrant womanizing he'd done in his youth and middle years. I'd scolded him for being irresponsible. He'd pretty much told me I was making a mountain out of a molehill. Made me want to cry as well and rant and rage.

He said, "Huh."

But he didn't argue.

"In fact," I went on because I didn't want the old sinner to misunderstand, either by accident or on purpose, the point I was making, "Many women and children die during the birthing process. These days, what with better hygiene, science, and medical care, death doesn't happen as often as it used to, but it still happens."

"Huh."

"Also," I said. "I'm sure you've heard of homes for unwed mothers. What I want to know is: where are the homes for unwed *fathers*? There aren't any, because so many men are irresponsible fiends."

"Huh."

Dr. Vialargo continued checking the infant, listening to her heart and lungs with his stethoscope, and palpating her limbs, belly and other body parts. Hazel stood aside, ready to help the doctor. Mr. Prophet and I only watched. So did Harold, who stood at the end of the dresser. He looked terrible, poor guy. Worn out and tense, he stared at the proceedings as if he were watching a delicate operation.

"Well?" Harold said after a minute or two. "Is it going to live? Did I kill it?"

"Harold!" Hazel exclaimed. "You certainly didn't kill this precious girl. You saved her life."

"You did," Dr. Vialargo agreed. "You took her in and you're attempting to care for her." The doctor glanced at me. "And you're correct, Mrs. Rotondo. Orphanages are full of children who are either unwanted by both parents, or who were born to unmarried women. I've often speculated about how things might change if there were homes for unwed fathers. Or at least penalties."

"My goodness," I said, surprised that a male doctor had agreed with me about what sounded like an outrageous point of view to many other people.

"Goodness has nothing to do with most of the orphanages and homes I've seen," said Dr. Vialargo dryly. "Mr. Kincaid, you're doing a good deed by caring for this infant and not instantly giving her over to the authorities."

"Oh," said Harold, surprised and (I'm pretty sure) gratified by the doctor's words.

"In fact," I said. "You're a hero, Harold Kincaid."

"You are indeed," said Hazel.

"Hero, hell," Harold said after a long pause. "I sure as blazes can't keep it. I'm against the law, remember? I doubt the community would be pleased if it knew a baby had been delivered to my door."

And now I suspect is the proper time to explain Harold Kincaid.

He was correct when he said he was illegal. That's because Harold was attracted to members of his own sex and not females. Being the way Harold was is a crime. This makes no sense to me, as people of Harold's sort don't choose to be the way they are. I've been told there are women, too, who are attracted to people of their own sex and not to men. I don't understand it, but I know the truth, and the truth is that Harold had no choice in the matter of his sexual persuasion. Doubt me if you wish, but you'll be wrong if you do.

So put that in your pipe and smoke it.

And if you want to know *why* this is true, ask God. I don't have a single clue.

Oh dear. Sorry. I didn't mean to be crabby.

FOUR

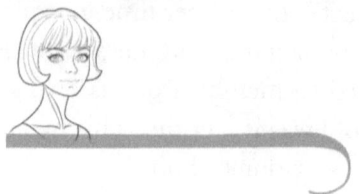

D r. Vialargo glanced from Harold to me and back to Harold.
He said merely, "Ah. Perhaps we can find a good home for
this infant that won't scandalize the neighborhood." His voice was
about as dry as the Mojave Desert.

"Excellent idea," said Hazel. She proceeded to pin a new diaper
onto the infant, lifted one of the soft flannel blankets she'd brought
with her and picked up the baby, wrapping the flannel around her as
she did so.

Not sure about anyone else in the room, but I stared in fascina-
tion at the way Hazel handled the kid. Her movements were sure
and fluid and she never jerked or bumped the baby. The baby, while
still peevish, was expressing her disapproval softly as if she was worn
out. She probably was, poor little thing.

"I've prepared a bottle for the baby," said Roy, returning to the
room. "I followed the instructions on the formula bottle but you
might want to check it first, Miss Greenlaw."

"Thank you, Roy. I'll do that." Hazel gave Roy a sweet smile,
took the Evenflo baby bottle and dribbled a few drops of formula on
her wrist. "It's perfect," she said, wiping her wrist on the pinafore
apron she wore over her nurse's uniform. Then she sat in the chair

in which she'd spent far too many hours during the earlier sick-room affair and put the bottle's nipple to the baby's puckered mouth.

You could feel the oxygen being sucked from the air as those of us watching drew in expectant breaths. At first the tiny thing's mouth didn't open. It remained puckered like a prune, and its hands had formed fists that kind of flapped beside its bald head. After several fraught seconds, the kid finally caught on to what Hazel was attempting to do and she drew the rubber nipple into her tiny mouth and started slurping.

Those of us who'd held our breath when Hazel first began the nursing process, let it out again in something of a "whoosh."

After several more seconds of sucking sounds, Harold whispered, "Is it eating?"

"She's eating," Hazel confirmed.

"Thank God," said Harold. "Will you stay here with the infant, Hazel? I need a drink. Roy, can you come downstairs with me? Or us? You can get refreshments for everyone." He turned to Dr. Vialargo. "Thank you *very* much, Doctor. I don't know what I'd have done if you weren't able to accompany Hazel."

"I'm sure Miss Greenlaw would have been as efficient a monitor as I," said the doctor, not sounding modest but merely practical. "The baby's healthy, so you shouldn't have much trouble caring for her."

"But I can't keep caring for her," said Harold as if he aimed to begin panicking again any second.

"Don't worry about that yet, Harold," I advised him. "Roy said you've ordered a bassinet and other paraphernalia from Nash's, and Hazel will be remaining for as long as the baby is here, won't she?"

"Yes," said Harold, letting out another chuff of breath. "Yes, she will, bless her."

"Well, then," I said, "all we need to do now is try to find who her parents are. Or who her new parents will be." Everyone in the room stared at me. "Um, that might not be as easy as it sounds, mightn't it?"

"Probably not," said the doctor, whose tone was again dry if not desiccated. "However, I should get back to the office." He stuck a few things back into his doctor's bag, being careful to organize them.

"Oh, please don't go yet," said Harold, holding out a hand. "I need to pay you or at least give you some coffee and a doughnut or something. Roy made some excellent apricot-nut bread for breakfast, and there's bacon. Tea, even, if you prefer tea. I *must* at least feed you. I know I haven't had my breakfast yet."

After a significant hesitation, Dr. Vialargo said, "That's most kind of you, Mr. Kincaid." He shook down the arm of his suit coat and checked his wristwatch. "I believe I could use some coffee and...did you say apricot-nut bread?"

"Yes. It's delicious. Roy claims it's so easy to make even Daisy can do it," said an enthusiastic Harold. "But let me visit the powder room and make myself decent. It's been a...difficult morning. Roy?"

"Right here, Mr. Harold," said a grinning Roy Castillo. "Want me to visit the kitchen and prepare some coffee and other edibles for your visitors?"

"Yes, please," said Harold. "And make a good breakfast for Hazel too, please."

"Thanks, Harold," said Hazel. "I have to admit that your call interrupted my breakfast."

"I'm sorry," said Harold pitifully.

"It's all right." Hazel chuckled.

"I'll prepare the food right now," said Roy. He hurried out of the baby's room and scuttled down the hall to the magnificent staircase. Harold's home was beautiful, although it did take some odd turns here and there.

Then it was I noticed the ancient man in the corner of the room. Mr. Prophet didn't speak, but he was watching everything that went on with a furrowed brow as if he were attempting to make sense of something. I had no idea what, but I decided to save him from embarrassment. Providing he ever got embarrassed, and I'm not sure he did.

"Come along, Mr. Prophet. You can have some of Roy's bread and some coffee."

He allowed silence to fill the room until it was almost uncomfortable. Then he said. "Yeah. Thanks. Think I will."

Okey-dokey then. I gave Hazel an eye-roll relating to Mr. Prophet. She only laughed quietly and continued feeding the baby.

Harold had already gone to the powder room. I didn't think he'd take much time over his morning ablutions because no matter what the occasion, Harold practiced excellence when it came to hospitality, even unexpected hospitality—if that makes sense.

Because Harold was otherwise occupied, I said, "Mr. Prophet and Dr. Vialargo, please come with me. I'll lead you to the breakfast room. This house is big enough to get lost in."

"Thank you, Mrs. Rotondo," said Dr. Vialargo.

"Please just call me Daisy, Doctor. Mrs. Rotondo lives in New York City, wears black, speaks Italian, and attends Mass every day."

He grinned at my attempt at humor. "I see. And did Mr. Kincaid mention something about your cooking skills?"

After heaving a sigh, I said, "Yes, he did. That's because I don't possess any cooking skills. I'm endeavoring to learn, but I don't enjoy cooking."

"Daisy is an excellent seamstress, however," came Harold's light voice from in back of us. I turned to see that he'd tidied himself up and combed his hair. He'd also donned a crisp new shirt. "Cooking is another thing altogether, although her aunt is one of the best cooks in the world."

"True," I said. "My Aunt Vi is a great cook. She doesn't mind spending hours in the kitchen and having the resulting masterpiece consumed in a half-hour. At least when I sew something, it lasts for more than a day or two. Usually."

"I see," said the doctor.

"But here, let me lead you," said Harold rushing up to me. He and I forged ahead, showing the doctor and Mr. Prophet the correct direction in which the food lay.

Only I was wrong. Instead of the breakfast room or Harold's big fancy dining room, he conducted us to a sun porch with large windows giving a great view of Harold's magnificent yard. Because the riot of spring and summer blooms had passed their peak, it wasn't quite as gorgeous as it might have been, but it was pretty darned spectacular. Cascades of yellow, orange and rust-colored chrysanthemums decorated the perimeter of a rose garden whose blooms were pretty much gone.

A table had been set in the middle of the room complete with plates, bowls, saucers, cups and silverware. The china was a pattern I'd never seen before. Harold had hauled me to Bullock's in downtown Los Angeles and forced me to select an "everyday" china set and a "best" china set. This set wasn't one of the ones I'd seen at Bullock's.

"What a nice, airy room," said the doctor. "And your garden is beautiful."

"Thank you." Harold smiled and rubbed his hands together. "Have a seat at the table there. I'll go hurry Roy up."

"He's already put in a day's work this morning," I told Harold. "Don't be hard on him."

"I'm never hard on Roy," Harold snapped. "You know me better than that, Daisy Gumm Majesty Rotondo."

"Sorry, Harold. I do know better."

"Good thing too," said Harold, regaining his better mood. I suspect he wouldn't be in a truly *good* mood until the baby problem was solved permanently.

Mr. Prophet didn't sit at once, but he walked to one of the windows and gazed out over Harold's manicured yard and well-tended flower gardens. "Nice," he muttered.

"Here, Mrs. Rotondo," said Dr. Vialargo, holding a chair for me like a gentleman.

"Thank you," I said, sitting as well as I could. He hadn't pulled the chair out quite far enough and my protruding stomach got squished a bit, but not much.

"Mr. Prophet?" said Dr. Vialargo. "Will you be joining us?"

When I glanced at the window where Mr. Prophet still stood staring out at the yard, I saw him slowly turn. He said, "Yeah. I'll join you." He ka-thumped over to the table, drew out a chair directly opposite Dr. Vialargo's and sat.

Harold came back to us pushing a cart upon which sat a

gorgeous silver coffee pot, creamer and sugar bowl. He put the sugar bowl and creamer on the table and said, "Ah, Roy's all set. He'll serve us in a minute. The coffee and tea are ready, so I'll pour."

He did pour. Harold and I were great pals, so he already knew I preferred tea to coffee after I had my morning's one cup of coffee. He had also deduced—I presume from trial and error—that I preferred Indian tea to most of the Chinese teas I'd sampled, although there hadn't been many of either type in my life to date. I mean, I was a middle-class kid from a middle-class family. When we went to a grocery store and bought tea, we just bought a package labeled "Tea."

Harold served me first out of a beautiful silver teapot. "Darjeeling," he said as he poured.

"Thanks Harold. You're so nice to me."

"About time you noticed," he said and stopped at Dr. Vialargo's left side. What a great waiter he'd make. "Tea or coffee, Doctor?"

"Coffee is fine, thanks."

Harold poured coffee into the cup at Dr. Vialargo's place and moved on to Mr. Prophet. "Lou?"

"Coffee. Thanks," said Mr. Prophet.

It seemed to me that Mr. Prophet wasn't behaving as he usually did. Not that he had bad table manners or anything—evidently his mother or an aunt had taught him manners when he was a child in Georgia—but he appeared almost ill to me. I hoped he wasn't. I didn't want him to be sick and, more, I didn't want that tiny baby girl to catch whatever germs he might have on him. A couple of guns and a knife strapped to his one remaining ankle were plenty; germs would be too much.

That's supposed to be a joke. He did, however, carry a pearl-handled Colt .45 Peacemaker tucked into his waistband, a Derringer up his sleeve, and a large knife in a sheath inside his boot. He nearly always wore a boot. Told me boots were easier for him to get into, and that he'd become accustomed to wearing boots during his army and bounty-hunting days. During those latter days, he rode a horse he'd named Mean and Ugly. And now he had a cat. Who'd'a thunk it?

Anyhow, Harold filled Mr. Prophet's cup. Those of us who like adjustments to our cups' contents began using sugar and cream as we wished. I like a little of both in my tea. Mr. Prophet liked a lot of sugar in his. Dr. Vialargo, I noticed, took his coffee black. Made me shudder to think about it. Not a big coffee fan here, although I always had a cup in the morning to wake me up.

"And I'll join you now," said Harold, setting the coffee and teapots on a large trivet in the middle of the table. Then he sat in the chair opposite me and picked up his coffee cup. "To the new baby," he said, toasting the infant.

We were too far apart to clink, but we lifted our cups in a toast. "May it prosper and be healthy," I added.

"And may it find a good home," said Dr. Vialargo.

Mr. Prophet said, "Huh," and toasted the baby with his own coffee cup.

Once we'd all sipped from our cups, I lifted mine again and scrutinized the pattern on it. "This is gorgeous, Harold. I don't recall this pattern when you dragged me to Bullock's to select china."

"That's because Bullock's doesn't carry it. The Crescent China Company makes it, and the pattern is Siennaware Tulip."

"Oh. It's beautiful. I really like it," I said.

"As do I," said Harold.

"If you didn't get it at Bullock's, where did you get it?"

With a small frown for me, Harold said, "Persistent person, aren't you? I'm surprised you don't remember. I bought them in Paris. France is where Crescent China is made. You were there with me at the time of the purchase."

"Oh. No, I honestly don't remember." I also decided I didn't like the pattern so much any longer.

The trip to which Harold referred was supposed to have been a recuperative one for me. When my first husband Billy died, I went into a terrible slump. He was a delayed casualty of the Great War. In other words, he didn't die "Over There," as the George M. Cohan song proudly proclaimed.

No. My Billy came home to me a little over a year after he'd joined the army to "make the world safe for democracy" along with thousands of other gullible young men. By the time he got back to Pasadena, he was a shell-shocked wreck of his former upright, happy and healthy self. He'd been shot and gassed, couldn't walk well and could barely breathe. He'd finally ended his life by taking an overdose of the morphine syrup he drank to ease the pain in his ravaged body.

After Billy's death, I sank into a depression as deep as the sea. I couldn't eat and lost so much weight that Harold told me I looked skeletal. Whatever I looked like, I still couldn't eat. Or work or laugh or pay attention to books or much of anything else. Harold planned what he conceived of as a grand trip to Egypt, taking in England, France and Turkey along the way. I managed to be sick during the entire trip, although by the time I got home again, I'd climbed out of the deepest pit of melancholy and was almost myself again. I never did become quite *all* of myself. I never have—until my pregnancy—gained back all the weight I'd lost, but I didn't mind. I wasn't precisely fat before Billy died, but I was no string bean.

"It's not the cup's fault, Daisy," said Harold, accurately reading my reaction. "It was Kaiser Bill's, remember?"

Impolite though I knew it to be, I heaved a gigantic sigh. "I know," I said.

We had no more time to thrash out our various woes, because Roy entered the sunroom just then. He bore four plates in the same Siennaware Tulip china pattern. All contained bacon, pieces of Roy's apricot-nut bread and a small bowl. Each bowl, which sat on each plate, contained sautéed apple slices with, if my nose was to be believed, cinnamon and nutmeg.

"My goodness, this is a feast fit for kings," said Dr. Vialargo, gazing at the plate Roy had laid before him. He appeared the least little bit overwhelmed. I suspect he'd thought he'd get a piece of nut bread and a cup of coffee and then escape back to his practice.

After giving myself a hard mental shake and lecturing myself to buck up, I said, "Harold is the perfect host."

"Darned right I am," said Harold.

43

FIVE

W e didn't linger over breakfast, even though Dr. Vialargo was correct that it was a feast fit for kings. But Nash's delivery van showed up shortly after we'd begun eating. Both Harold and Roy hurried to the door.

He'd ordered more than a mere bassinet. I swear he'd bought an entire baby's bedroom suite, all in bright white. He'd selected baby sheets and blankets in shades of pink from blush to burgundy. You'd think he anticipated rearing the baby himself forever, but I know that wasn't the case. Harold was an extremely kind person with a big heart. He told me later that he didn't intend for that newborn baby girl to lack for anything if he could help it. As it happened, he could help it. So he did.

Dr. Vialargo left before the furniture people carried everything upstairs, politely bidding us all a rather formal *adieu*. "Thank you, Mr. Kincaid. It was nice to meet you, Mrs. Rotondo, Mr. Prophet and Mr. Castillo."

"Thank *you*," said Harold. "I was petrified when Roy found that basket on my doorstep."

Lifting an eyebrow and smiling slightly Dr. Vialargo said, "My goodness. I've heard of things like that happening, but not for a long time and certainly not here in Pasadena."

"Technically, I'm in San Marino," said Harold as he started up the stairs.

"I see," said the doctor.

"San Marino is almost Pasadena," I told Dr. Vialargo.

With a nod, he said, "I see."

Then Roy opened the door for him, and he left with his black bag. Tilting my head a bit, I watched him. He was a long, lean fellow. Very tall and with pretty blond hair that most women would envy. I know I did, although being a redhead wasn't too bad I guess. His eyes were a beautiful blue color and his eyelashes were long and lush. I envied him those too. He'd struck me as a man with secrets. Then again, who doesn't have secrets? I don't know. He just seemed a little odd to me but not in the "he's insane" way. Oh heck, I'm not even sure what I'm saying here.

Standoffish? Naw. He wasn't standoffish. Maybe aloof. Yes, I do believe that's the sense I received from Dr. Vialargo. Not that my opinion matters but I always give it anyway. At least he was polite and professional. He'd taken excellent care of the baby. And Hazel had called him "Larry," so I guess he wasn't aloof after you got to know him.

Mr. Prophet and I went to take one last look at the baby and Hazel before I drove us home. The newcomer was asleep in her bassinet, although she wasn't sleeping on the sheets, etc., Harold had ordered for her. He'd taken them out of their brown-paper wrappings and requested that Roy wash them at least once to soften them up before allowing the newborn to sleep on them. I tell you, Harold's heart was as big as the sky. Fortunately for him and the baby, so was his pocketbook.

"Do you mind if I stop by the Salvation Army before I drive us home?" I asked Mr. Prophet after I pressed the starter button on the Chevrolet. Then I recalled germs. "Do you feel all right? I mean, you aren't sick or anything, are you?"

"Why'n the hell you askin' me that?" said the old grump.

"Because you didn't act like yourself at Harold's."

"Who'd I act like if it wasn't me?"

"Bother! You know what I mean. You stood in a corner and didn't speak, and then you looked out at Harold's garden until coffee arrived. I thought perhaps you weren't feeling quite well."

"Huh. I feel fine."

"All right then. Do you mind if I stop by—"

"I don't give a good goddam what you do," he said.

His answer was so abrupt and snarly, it startled me. I hadn't begun driving yet, so I sat behind the steering wheel and stared at him.

"I'll take you home first," I said after contemplating his hunched posture and grouchy face for a second or two.

"Huh," he said.

I drove him home. Sam's Hudson was in our driveway, so I parked the Chevrolet behind it. Mr. Prophet exited the car, but he didn't walk up the porch steps to our house. Instead, he made a bee-line up the rest of our drive to the back gate. Guess he was going to his cottage behind our house.

Something was askew with the tetchy old scoundrel; of that I was certain.

Nevertheless, I recalled that I hadn't even left a note for Sam to explain why I wasn't at home on a Saturday morning. Explaining things to Sam was the first thing I should do. Lordy, life could sure get complicated.

When I'd left the car, walked up the porch steps and across the porch to the front door, it opened before I could turn the knob. Sam, a large man, stood in the door and glowered down upon me. This startled me too, and I jumped a little. Spike, who had come to the door with Sam, danced out and gave me a happy greeting. At least someone in my life was behaving as usual.

"I'm sorry I forgot to leave you a note, Sam," I said after I'd given Spike the greeting he deserved.

"Flossie Buckingham has called three times. Where were you? And did you take Lou with you, or is he down the street?"

Down the street was code. Sam had just asked me if Mr. Prophet was visiting his lady friend, a beautiful Chinese woman named Li

46

Ahn, whom he'd known in his Tucson days. The two of them had reconnected when they both discovered themselves (and each other) in Pasadena.

Did that make sense? I'm sure you can figure it out.

"Come on in the house, Sam, and I'll explain everything."

But would I? Did I want to involve Sam in Harold's problem? Sam would want to get the authorities involved, and that meant taking the baby away from Harold and putting it…somewhere.

I didn't have a single clue what happened to abandoned babies who weren't lucky enough to land on Harold Kincaid's doorstep. I did, however, decide to tell Sam the absolute truth. He not only deserved it, but he might even have a suggestion or two. With any luck at all, he wouldn't suggest putting the kid in an orphanage.

We went into the house and, as usual, walked to the kitchen. Even though I wasn't a mistress of the cooking arts, the kitchen was a comfy room, and it was generally where we gathered to chat.

Before I sat I asked Sam, "Want anything to drink? I know there's orange juice in the ice box, and there's tea or coffee or milk."

Sam placed a bakery box on the kitchen table.

"You brought pastries? How nice!" I said. Then I gave my husband as big a hug as I could, given my girth. "Thank you, Sam!"

"A new bakery just opened on Colorado near the police station, so I went in there and got some goodies." He pulled out a chair and sat. "How about a glass of milk and a cookie or two while you tell me what was so all-fired important that you had to leave the house without even a note for me. You clearly had time to call Flossie, because she's been trying to call you back."

"I'm so sorry, Sam. I know I should have left you a note." I felt guilty about it. Guilt was a familiar emotion, but I still didn't like it.

"Go ahead and spill it," he said.

After taking a large breath for courage and bracing myself mentally, I spilled it. Sitting across the table from Sam, I saw his beautiful brown eyes open wider and wider as I spoke. He interrupted a couple of times.

"A *baby*? On *Harold's* doorstep?"

"A little girl. A newborn."

"Good God." He shook his head hard, then said, "Go on."

I went on and explained about packing diapers and books and going to Bennetts to pick up baby bottles and formula. From what I could see, Sam's degree of astonishment didn't abate as I spoke.

"He's furnished a room for the baby?" Sam asked after a short spell of silence when I stopped speaking.

"Yes."

"He can't keep the baby. He knows that, doesn't he?"

"Yes," I said. "He knows that. He said he doesn't want to keep it. He's just a sensitive, caring soul who is trying his best to make up for the unfortunate child's first hours on this earth."

Sam squinted at me. I saw doubt on his face.

"It's true, Sam," I said in steadfast defense of my best friend.

"If anyone finds out what he and his roommate are, he'll probably be arrested after the authorities snatch the baby away from him," said Sam.

"That's a hideous thing to say, Sam!"

"It's also true. You know it, and Harold knows it. Right?"

I sighed. "Right. But honestly, Sam, when I only just mentioned the idea of an orphanage, Harold hit the ceiling. He said his mother used to drag him to orphanages in his youth."

"What the devil for?" Sam asked.

"I asked him that. He said his mother used to like to play the Lady Bountiful, and she'd haul poor Harold along with her. He said he'd never allow the baby-in-the-basket to go to an orphanage because they're..." I had to think for a minute. Thinking wasn't the easiest thing to do if you were me. "Oh, yes. Because they're worse than they are in *Oliver Twist*."

Again Sam sat still for several seconds. Then he heaved a sigh of his own and bowed his head. "He's right. In New York City, the lucky ones go into orphanages. The rest of them try to live on the streets. Most of them don't make it long on the streets. Or in the orphanages, for that matter."

"That's sad, Sam."

"Yes," he said. "It is."

"He's hired Hazel Greenlaw to be a nurse for the baby. He can make up a story if anybody finds out about the infant and asks whose it is." I heard the hopeful tone to my voice and prayed that Sam would approve of me making up a story to account for a baby.

"I can't be a party to what you're doing," he said at last. "From what you tell me, Harold was well and truly stuck. It's lucky the baby's mother—or maybe it was its father—left it where she or he did. You're right about Harold being kind and generous."

Well, glory be! "Does that mean you won't get the authorities involved?" I asked, still hopeful.

With his head still bowed, Sam began drumming his fingers on the table. Oh Lord, what did this mean?

When I couldn't take the drumming any longer I said, trying to be bright and cheerful, "Would you like milk with your cookies?"

He stopped drumming and glanced up at me. "I don't think I want milk any longer. How about some tea?"

"Sounds good to me." I rose from my chair, filled the kettle, went to the pantry, and got down the lovely Aynsley Mikado tea set one of my clients had given me as a wedding present. Sam and I were stocked to the gills with various sets of china. After our son was born and I felt up to it, I aimed to pack up some and give them to people I knew and loved. My parents and Flossie Buckingham were first on my list.

Lifting down the pretty tin of Darjeeling tea from the cupboard, prying open the lid, scooping out a couple of teaspoonfuls of tea, and saving the loose tea on a saucer, I grew more and more tense as Sam failed to speak on the subject of Harold and the baby. The kettle started blowing its top at me, so I turned the burner off, grabbed the teapot and dumped boiling water into it. Then I swished the water in the pot for a few seconds and tossed the water into the sink. Only then did I put the tea into the pretty little pot and add boiling water. I might not know much, but I knew how to brew tea, thanks to Aunt Vi. She'd told me more than once that tea isn't fit to drink until it's strong enough to climb out of the pot by itself.

I poured milk from the bottle in the Frigidaire into the creamer and poured some sugar cubes into the sugar bowl. Then I set two small plates, two teacups, the teapot, the sugar bowl, and the creamer on the gorgeous tray from the tea set and was about to pick it up when Sam loomed up behind me. Startled, I let out a little screech.

"Shoot, Sam, don't creep up on me like that!" I said. "I almost dropped the tray."

"You shouldn't be carrying the tray," said Sam, picking it up from the counter and carrying it to the table.

"It wasn't all that heavy," I said.

"Still," said Sam.

Very well, then. I opened the white bakery box and saw an abundance of lovely pastries in it. I sure hoped Sam wasn't going to have a fit about Harold and the baby because I wanted one of those jelly-filled doughnuts! I put four doughnuts and several of what looked like shortbread cookies on one of the sandwich plates that came with the tea set and carried the plate to the table.

I sat again, handed Sam a small plate, and put one in my place. Then, unable to take the suspense any longer, I said, "Well? What are you going to do about the baby?"

He glanced up from inspecting the contents of the pastry tray and seemed surprised. "Me? Why should I do anything?"

His answer so amazed me, I darned near dropped a teacup. "You mean you aren't going to get the authorities involved?" Because the charming teacup had clanked on its tray, I checked it out and was relieved I hadn't broken it.

"It's not my problem," said Sam, selecting a couple of pieces of shortbread and a jelly-filled doughnut and putting them on his little plate with the pretty silver tongs I'd also been given as a wedding present. He glanced at me after he'd chosen his goodies. "It's not your problem either, but I don't suppose that'll stop you from getting involved."

"I'm already involved," I said, feeling even guiltier than usual. Sam was *such* a good man, and I hated doing things of which he didn't approve.

"Is the tea ready?" he asked calmly.

"Tea? Oh! Tea. Um, let me look." I lifted the teapot lid and decided it was dark enough. "Yes, it is. I'll pour."

"Thanks." Sam sounded sardonic.

I poured each of us a cup of tea, using a fancy tea strainer yet another person had given me. Aunt Vi said you're supposed to pour milk into the cup before you pour in the tea, but that morning—was it still morning?—I didn't bother. Sam wouldn't know the difference anyway. Truth to tell, neither would I.

The back door opened, and Sam and I both lifted our heads and saw Mr. Prophet enter the house. Of course, Spike had noticed him before either Sam or I did. Spike had even announced Mr. Prophet's approach with a short "woof." He was such a good watchdog. He was also a food hound, so he didn't leave the table area until Mr. Prophet put either his foot or his peg—not sure which—on the kitchen floor. Then Spike dashed over to the stooped, gray-haired old man, gave him a couple of happy-you-joined-us barks, and returned to the table.

"Want a doughnut, Lou?" Sam asked.

"There's shortbread too," I said.

Mr. Prophet looked as if he'd just witnessed foul murder when he grabbed a chair, tugged it out and sat. Then he frowned at me and said, "No. Thanks. Where'd that doctor come from?"

SIX

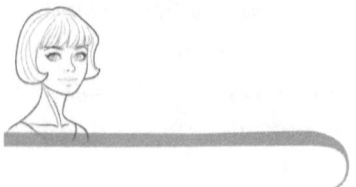

Sam and I both stared at Mr. Prophet for a second or two. Then I said, "Which doctor?"

"The doctor who examined the damn baby," he barked. "Hel-lkatoot, who'd you think I was talkin' about?"

I already knew there was nothing to be gained by showing the old sinner how offensive I found the delivery of his question. He was usually nicer than this. I said, "You mean Dr. Vialargo?"

"That his name?" growled Mr. Prophet.

"The one who examined the baby? Yes, his name is Lawrence Vialargo."

"Where's he from?" he asked again.

Baffled, I shrugged a couple of shoulders. "I have no idea. Why? Is he the reason you've been so cranky and upset today?"

"Ain't upset," he fibbed. "Just want to know where the doctor's from."

"I'm sorry. I don't know," I said.

He huffed and uttered a soft "Damn."

"Why? What difference does it make where he's from?"

Shaking his head he said, "Nothin'. Makes no difference. Just wondered."

I tried to recollect the events of the morning. I vaguely remembered Mr. Prophet appearing startled when he met Dr. Vialargo. "When you met him, you were surprised. I recall it vividly," I said. Okay, so I'd just fibbed a little too. Wasn't as large a fib as his had been.

Childish little thing, wasn't I? Big thing. Sort of medium. Never mind.

Mr. Prophet grabbed a piece of shortbread from the platter and stuffed it into his mouth. After he swallowed, he said, "Looks like somebody I used to know, is all."

"Who? You mean the doctor?"

"Yeah."

"Oh? Whom does he look like?" I asked politely.

He shoved back his chair, rose from the table, grabbed a jelly-filled doughnut from the plate, turned to go back to his cottage again and said, "None o' your damn business, nosy."

Neither Sam nor I reacted to this rude declaration. Well, I drew in an irritated breath. Sam just looked after Mr. Prophet as he stomped back out of the house. After the back door slammed, he turned to me. "What was that about?"

Baffled, I said, "I have absolutely no idea. Dr. Greenlaw was busy with an emergency when Harold called him and Hazel. Given Dr. Greenlaw's unavailability, Dr. Vialargo, who's been with the Greenlaw practice for a few months, came out to examine the baby. I'm not sure because Mr. Prophet hasn't condescended to tell me, but I'm sure he was surprised when he met Dr. Vialargo. Shocked, even."

"Huh," said Sam. He sipped his tea.

I'd just picked up a piece of shortbread when the telephone rang. "It's probably Flossie," I said as I rose to go to the telephone table in the hall.

"I expect it is. Don't take too long. I'm hungry, and these things are good."

"You wouldn't eat my doughnut, would you?" I was only kind of joking. I *wanted* that doughnut.

"You never know," said Sam, sounding mysterious as I walked

out of the kitchen.

Darn. I considered dashing back into the kitchen and grabbing my doughnut but figured a mature woman who was about to become a mother wouldn't be so rash and silly. It was only a dough-nut, after all. Dang, I wanted it!

"Hello," I said after I picked up the receiver.

"Daisy? This is Flossie," said Flossie.

"Hey, Flossie. Thanks for calling me back."

"You're welcome. Sam didn't sound pleased when he realized you hadn't come home from wherever you went. Is everything all right?"

By the way, Flossie and Johnnie had two children of their own: a little boy named Billy (after my first husband) and a little girl named Daisy (after me). Billy was a darling little lad. Daisy was...well, she was a trifle fussy. Little Billy called her a "bwat."

"He wasn't even a little bit pleased. I forgot to leave him a note, and that was inexcusable of me. But listen, Flossie, something odd happened this morning." I relayed the morning's details to her.

"Good heavens!" said Flossie. "Poor little baby."

"And poor Harold," I said, thinking this morning had been harder on Harold than on the infant.

"Yes. Poor Harold too." Flossie stopped speaking for a second as if gathering her thoughts. Even though that jelly-filled doughnut called loudly to me from the kitchen, I didn't butt in on her thinking process. "But what is he going to do? I mean he can't keep the child. Can he?"

"No. If the authorities found out about the baby, I expect they'd step in and take her away from Harold. And then they'd probably arrest Harold. But Harold is adamant that he doesn't want this child to go to an orphanage."

"I don't blame him, but what can he do?"

And there it was, in easy English words. What the heck was Harold Kincaid, bachelor for life and basically a living, breathing crime, supposed to do with an abandoned baby?

"I don't know. Harold doesn't know. Sam doesn't know. Nobody knows. But he's outfitted the infant with a superb nursery and has hired Hazel Greenlaw to be its nurse. That, however, isn't a long-term solution."

"No," said Flossie. "It isn't." She sounded troubled, which made sense to me.

"You don't have any parishioners who have recently given birth, do you? Or who were expecting a baby any second now? That's probably a stupid question, isn't it?"

"No, it's not. We do take in waifs and strays, including the occasional woman who is pregnant, desperate and doesn't know what to do with herself. Sometimes she's just lost her way in the world. More often, she's been seduced and betrayed by a man who claimed to love her. Often the girl's family has kicked her out because they're ashamed of her, and—"

I interrupted her. I know, how rude can one person be, huh? "I hate that attitude!" I said rather loudly in Flossie's ear. "It's not the woman's fault, darn it!"

Flossie didn't speak for a second.

"I'm sorry, Flossie. I didn't mean to interrupt. Or yell at you."

"It's all right," said the kindhearted Flossie. "I agree with you. As does Johnnie."

"But it's always women who pay the price," I grumbled.

"Generally, yes," said Flossie. "Anyway, we take in the occasional unwed pregnant girl, but I haven't seen any lately."

"Golly, I wonder where Harold's baby came from," I said, then amended my statement. "I mean where the baby left on Harold's doorstep came from."

"There wasn't a note in with the baby?" asked Flossie.

"What a good question! I didn't even think to ask Harold if there was anything besides the baby in the basket. I'll do that right"
—I remembered my jelly-filled doughnut—"as soon as I can."

"Thanks, Daisy," said Flossie. "I'll ask Johnnie if he knows what to do about an abandoned baby as soon as he gets home from walking the streets."

We both laughed. That's because Johnnie *did* walk the streets of Pasadena—along with the rest of the Salvation Army Band. He played the trumpet really well. In those days, you could hardly walk down a sidewalk in Pasadena without meeting the Salvation Army Band somewhere on Colorado Street.

"I'll let you know as soon as Harold lets me know, Flossie."

"Thanks, Daisy. And I'll ask people on my end if they know of a girl who was in trouble."

"Thank you very much, Flossie." A moment clicked past (that is to say, the clock on the hall wall clicked a couple of seconds) as I hesitated. "And one of these days, we're going to have to figure out how to find the baby a good home. It's a little girl, and she's as sweet as pie unless she's hungry, poor thing."

"Yes. I'll ask Johnnie about how we might get her adopted too," said Flossie.

We bade each other good-bye, and I hurried to the kitchen to find that Sam hadn't touched my doughnut. Bless his heart. My Sam was a good man.

"Thank you for not snatching my doughnut, Sam," I said as I again sat across the table from him.

"You're welcome. I don't suppose doughnuts count as a proper lunch, though. Is there anything to eat in the Frigidaire?"

After I heaved a smallish sigh, I said, "Probably not. There's bread and cheese. There are a few jars of preserved chicken in the basement. And I know there are still tomatoes on the vines I planted in June."

"Amazing," said Sam. I feared for a moment he was going to criticize my homemaking skills, which he'd be justified in doing, but he didn't. "In New York, we had to plant tomatoes in May, and they'd be gone by October. Earlier sometimes."

"Another good reason to live in Pasadena," I said after swallowing a bite of my doughnut. It was *so* good.

"Do we have bread?" asked Sam.

"Yes. In the bread keeper. Um, would you mind slicing it, Sam?"

"Nope. Don't mind at all. What are you going to do with it?"

"I thought I'd made a couple of toasted cheese and tomato sandwiches. Thank you very much for slicing the bread."

I hate to admit this, but I was a total failure at bread-slicing. Couldn't slice a straight piece of bread to save my soul. Generally

I'd start cutting from the top of the loaf and by the time I got the knife to the bottom of the slice, it would either be three inches thick or a skinny little see-through sliver. Sam was a good bread slicer. I dearly wished someone would invent a *real* bread slicer, however.

"I'll slice some cheese too."

At the word "cheese," Spike's ears went on the alert. He'd developed quite a vocabulary, and he *loved* cheese.

"Don't give Spike too much cheese," I admonished Sam. "Mrs. Bissel will kill me if he gets fat."

With a laugh, Sam said, "I'll only toss him a couple of little bits. I'll even make him work for them."

For the record, my (our) dachshund, Spike, was smart as a whip. He could not merely bark and sneeze on command, but he could do arithmetic! That latter skill was a wonder, since his mommy (me) stank at math. I'll let you in on the secret to Spike-arithmetic later.

"I'll go out and pick a couple of tomatoes," I said as I polished off the last of my doughnut and pushed my chair back from the table.

"Sounds good to me," said Sam.

Lest you think I'm completely useless as a housewife, let me say that I love gardening, kept the kitchen clean and didn't leave things scattered around the house. Well, with one exception to that last item. My sewing room had stuff scattered everywhere, but it wasn't a disorganized mess. I knew precisely where each of my projects was stacked or folded or draped over a piece of furniture. In other words, I was a crackerjack seamstress. Cooking remained a challenge.

Therefore, I picked up everything from the kitchen table, put the remaining pastries back in their box, set the dirty plates, etc. in the sink, wiped down the oilcloth on the table and grabbed a basket from the utility room before going outside to see what could be found in the kitchen garden.

An abundance of tomatoes met my gaze, along with some Kentucky Wonder Beans, carrots, turnips, yellow squash, and even a couple of radishes. I pretty much filled my basket, thinking I could make a nice chicken-vegetable soup with one of the basement's jarred chickens and a bunch of vegetables. Not even *I* could ruin soup. Usually. When it comes to the kitchen and me, there are no hard and fast certainties. I've been known to get distracted and burn coffee, for instance.

As long as I was outside, I decided to pick a few oranges. We had orange, grapefruit, and tangerine trees in our small orchard. The trees in our grove lined the gravel path to Mr. Prophet's cottage. I'd stopped thinking about him after he'd clumped out of the house earlier. As I plucked two oranges and moved along to the tangerine tree—my basket was too full for another large-ish orange—I heard someone muttering.

It was wrong of me, I know, but I set my basket on the ground and walked softly on the grass verge and tried to hide behind citrus branches. As I got nearer to Mr. Prophet's cottage, I recognized by the tone of his voice that he was griping to his cat, Yuyu. Not sure if I've described Yuyu before, but if ever a cat belonged to a man, Yuyu was the cat and Mr. Prophet was the man. Yuyu had a tattered ear, part of a fluffy tail, one eye, and a twisted leg. He was mostly orange, and his one yellow eye was enough to frighten the most stout-hearted person. I wasn't all that stout-hearted, but I wanted to know what the old bounty hunter was whining to his cat about.

"Dammit, Yuyu, it can't be," Mr. P. said to Yuyu in his rusty voice. "Not possible."

Yuyu gave his human a rusty purr.

"Hellkatoot, I wish I could find out where he come from. He ain't from around here, I know that much. And he don't sound like he come from Arizona or New Mexico."

Another scratchy purr.

"Sure as hell, he ain't from Georgia. I know I heard that accent o' his before, but it wasn't from Louisa. She didn't sound like that. Jaysus, I think I'm goin' crazy."

More purring from Yuyu.

"Cripes, I just remembered," said Mr. Prophet, sounding as if he'd just heard the Angel of Death knock at his door. "Louisa's damn aunt. God damn, that sumbitch doctor sounded just like Ol' Starchy Pants." He actually let out an audible groan, although that might have been because Yuyu had dug a claw into his flesh. Claw holes happened sometimes, but generally only when Yuyu was startled.

As I heard Yuyu give another purr, I guessed Mr. Prophet's aged brain had recalled something else of a hurtful nature. Interesting.

"But I swear to God, cat, he looks just like her, only he's a man. He don't act like a pansy, neither. Cripes, wouldn't that be something? Louisa and me producing a Nancy boy? Shit. Damn. Hellkatoot."

I wasn't so fond of eavesdropping that I fancied listening to more profanity, so I tiptoed back to my basket and picked it up. Darned thing was heavy, but not so heavy that I couldn't carry it. I did, however, believe I now knew why Mr. Prophet had been so startled when he'd been introduced to Dr. Lawrence Vialargo.

Sam would have been proud of me. Even though I'd just heard an astonishing piece of gossip, I didn't try to run. Probably couldn't have run if I'd tried, but still...

SEVEN

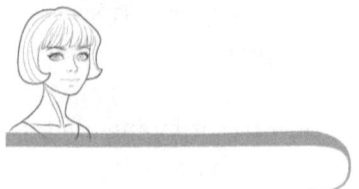

I fairly burst through the back door shouting, "Sam!"

Only then did I notice that my Aunt Vi had come to call. She'd evidently carried with her a large pot because I saw it on the stovetop.

"Vi!" I cried. "I didn't know you were here. It's good to see you." And that wasn't a fib. I loved my aunt and my parents. Her presence, however, would force me to keep my choice piece of news to myself a little longer.

"Daisy dear, I brought you and Sam some of my butter beans and ham. But my goodness, look at that basket of bounty you just harvested!" She beamed at my basket and me.

"Lots of vegetables," I agreed. "Thanks for the soup! Want a toasted cheese and tomato sandwich? I was just going to fix Sam and myself one. There's plenty."

"Thank you, dear. That would be a lovely lunch, I'm sure your father would like a sandwich and soup too. Would you like me to telephone him?"

Dang. I really wanted to tell Sam my news. But I treasured my family more than I wanted to spill gossip, so I said, "Sure. The more, the merrier. He can bring Rosebud over too."

"Oh, he'll love that. Your mother should be getting out of work soon, too. Want to wait until she gets home?"

"That would be nice," I said, thinking as I did so that I'd never get to tell Sam my fascinating nugget of surmised information.

Nevertheless, Vi called Pa and Pa accepted our invitation to lunch.

Because so many of us would be taking lunch at our house, Vi and I set the dining room table. All the leaves had been removed from it, so it wasn't long, but it was a heck of a lot larger than the kitchen table. I got a fresh tablecloth from a drawer in the hutch and flapped it over the table. Vi and I straightened it out, and I set out flatware at five places.

Then I wondered if we should invite Mr. Prophet. After recalling how he'd left Sam and me earlier, however, I decided not to. If he wandered into the house while we ate lunch, I'd set a place for him.

"I love this china, Daisy," said Vi as she set out plates.

"It's Spode Wickerdale," I told her. "Harold made me look at a thousand or so china patterns. I think I finally chose this one out of desperation."

With a laugh Vi said, "It's beautiful."

"I like it too," I said. "And the handles aren't squinchy, so Pa, Sam, and Mr. Prophet can get their big fingers through them."

"Squinchy?" said Vi, puzzled.

"Yes. Lots of the patterns we saw had pointy tops to the handles, making the vacant space too small for big hands."

"My goodness, I had no idea."

"Neither had I until Harold took over my life and wedding preparations. Then I had to pass up several beautiful china sets because of the teacup handles." I shook my head. "I had no idea being rich would be so much trouble. Not that Sam and I are rich, but Harold sure is."

"Bless the boy," said Vi, who loved Harold nearly as much as I did.

Vi and I grinned at each other across the table. When we went back into the kitchen, it was to discover that Sam had not merely cut bread and cheese for me, but he'd also sliced some tomatoes. He turned to smile at us when he heard us.

Vi said, "Joe and Rosie will be here soon. They're going to trek up to the Hotel Marengo and walk your mother here for lunch."

"Excellent," said Sam. "I'll cut some more cheese and another tomato."

"Thanks, Sam," I said, loving him with all my heart.

Sam could be trusted with confidences, as could I. Sam's training as a policeman had taught him not to reveal other people's secrets. My job as a phony spiritualist medium had taught me the same thing. And yes, we'd have been good secret-keepers even without special training, but can you imagine how long either of our jobs would have lasted had either of us spilled top-secret information? Not long, is how long. Telling Sam my suspicions about Mr. Prophet's conversation with Yuyu didn't count as breaking a confidence, by the way.

"I'll fix the sandwiches," said Vi. She'd put the pot of beans and ham on a burner turned down low before she'd helped me with the table.

"I can do that, Vi," I said, thinking she probably didn't trust me not to burn them all.

"I know you can, sweetheart," she said. "Sam said you've been preparing lovely meals recently. But you shouldn't be on your feet for too long in your condition."

Although I wondered what poor women did in the olden days when they had big families, no servants, and life necessitated that they cook and clean for everyone, I didn't ask. Every now and then, I can hold my tongue.

Suddenly, Spike took off to the front door, barking in glee. Aha. Must be my father, mother and Rosebud. I decided to leave lunch preparations to everyone else and walked to the front door. Sure enough, Pa had unsnapped Rosie's leash from her collar and she bounded inside the house and leaped upon Spike with what sounded like a ferocious snarl. It wasn't. It was a play-time growl, and the two black-and-tan hounds raced in a circle around our feet about three times then zipped into the living room. There they tugged on each other's ears, knocked each other over and had themselves a fine old time.

"Good Lord, I didn't know the dogs acted like that," said Ma, watching the disappearing dog butts with something akin to disapproval.

"All the time," I told her. "They have a great time together."

"They're not really fighting, are they?" Ma asked.

"Peggy," said Pa, "don't you think Daisy or I would have stopped them if they were trying to kill each other?" He laughed.

"It's true, Ma. Spike and Rosie play like that every time they get together. When Spike and Yuyu play, they kind of roll around like a black-and-orange ball. Rosie and Spike just bounce on each other, gnaw each other's ears and growl. They sound deadly, but they're really only playing."

"My goodness," said Ma.

My mother was possibly the kindest person in the world, aside from Harold Kincaid, but she was extremely literal. She also possessed little sense of humor and didn't understand nuances. I figured this was because she'd been working with numbers in her accounting job for so long. My experience with math had taught me there's no bending the rules. There's an answer and if you don't figure it out, you're wrong and the teacher gives you a bad grade. I'll *never* feel anything but deep loathing for algebra, but Ma was a mathematical marvel. I admired her, loved her, and didn't understand her any more than I'd understood algebra. Only I adored my mother.

Which is more than you wanted to know, I'm sure.

"Here, Ma," I said, reaching for the scarf she'd just removed from her head. "I'll hang this on the hook here, and you can hang your sweater on a hanger in the closet if you want to."

"Thanks, dear," she said. Then she sniffed the air. "Something smells good."

"It's probably Vi's butter beans and ham," I said. "Sam and Vi are making toasted cheese and tomato sandwiches to eat with the butter beans."

"Sounds delicious," said Ma.

"Let's go and say hello to everyone," said Pa.

He took my mother's arm, and they walked to the kitchen. I heard happy greetings and entertained a moment of gratitude for my family. Then I entertained the fervent wish that they'd all leave as soon as lunch was devoured so I could rat out Mr. Prophet. Not nice of me, I know.

Things didn't go precisely as I anticipated. This isn't a new phenomenon in my life. We'd been sitting at the dining room table, eating and yakking for maybe twenty or thirty minutes, when the telephone rang. It sounded so loud and shrill, I jumped in my seat. Then I rose to answer it. I hoped like thunder nothing had happened to Harold's new baby. I mean to the baby he'd discovered.

"Be right back," I told the assembled diners as I hurried to the telephone table in the hall. I took a seat in the chair, lifted the receiver and said, "Hello?"

"Daisy!"

Good heavens! At first I couldn't figure out who'd be screeching at me over the telephone wires. Then I recalled my first telephone call of the day.

"Harold? What's the matter?"

"*Everything*," he said.

"Understandable, but not enlightening," I told him. "Is the baby well?"

I heard him take in about three gallons of air and whoosh it out again. Finally he said—and calmly too—"The baby is fine. I just got a telephone call from the Castleton Hospital." I heard him take another deep, deep breath.

"About the baby?" I asked, surprised.

"Shut up and I'll tell you," said Harold.

"All righty then," I said and shut up.

"A young woman has been taken to the hospital. Apparently she was discovered, bleeding, near the corner of Walnut and Fair Oaks. She was presumed dead at first, but she's still breathing."

"How horrid!" I said, forgetting to shut up for a second.

"It's not merely horrid," said Harold in the voice of doom. "It's also the answer to one of our questions about the baby."

"It is?"

"Yes. According to the person who called me from the hospital, the poor girl was brought in by a good Samaritan who didn't leave his name. He said he found her bleeding near the corner, picked her up and drove her to the hospital. She was unconscious at the time. He thought she might be dead. The reason they called me is that my name, address and telephone number were scribbled on a piece of paper in one of her pockets. The hospital folks don't know her name or anything about her——"

"Oh my word," I said, shocked.

"Hush," said Harold.

"Sorry," I said.

"As I was saying, the hospital people don't know anything about her *except* that she'd recently—like in the last day or so—given birth."

"Good Lord," I whispered.

"The hospital asked me to visit and see if I could identify the girl. They called her a girl, although when I asked how old she was, they said they didn't know."

"I guess *girl* covers a lot of ground," I said, hoping I wasn't interrupting him again.

"Daisy, you *have* to come to the hospital with me," Harold said, sounding desperate. "I can't do it alone! Hazel has to stay here to tend to the kid and Roy has gone to Jorgenson's for groceries. *Please* come with me."

"Um…" Good Lord, what should I do now? My entire family (well, except for my brother, sister, and nieces and nephew) were taking lunch at my very own dining room table at that precise moment. "Um…I don't know if I can, Harold."

"What do you *mean* you don't know if you can?" he bellowed.

"That's the second time today you've nearly broken my eardrum, Harold Kincaid," I told him. "You're as bad as your mother."

"I am not." He spoke decisively.

"You're right. You're not," I admitted. "But my whole family is

65

here right now. I can't just say I have to rush out and help you visit the hospital, can I?"

After a short pause, Harold said, "I suppose not. But can't you get Sam alone for a minute and ask him to let you go? Did you tell him about the baby?"

"Yes. I told him the whole story, and he's not going to send the infant to an orphanage."

"Thank God," breathed Harold, who has often told me he doesn't believe in God. "Then maybe you can tell him there's an emergency, and you're wanted at the hospital. Or maybe *I'm* in the hospital and asking for you?"

"Hmm. Let me think," I said.

I expected Harold to say something about how hard it was for me to think, but he was plainly too rattled to be snippy, for he said nothing except, "Fine. Think."

I thought. My brain was fuzzy, and I didn't instantly come up with anything logical to explain why I had to rush to Harold's side. I could almost hear Harold's anxiety twanging over the wire to my ear. I'm not sure how long I sat there attempting to think, but it was long enough to bring Sam into the hallway.

He said, "Daisy?" He spoke softly but alarmed me so much I very nearly screamed.

"Sam!" I cried.

"Sam what?" asked Harold in my ear.

"Wait just a minute, Harold. Sam just came out to see what the telephone call was about. Let me talk to him for a few seconds. He'll probably know what to do."

"Oh, gawd," said Harold. "Please hurry."

"I'll try," I said. Then I put my hand over the speaker part of the receiver and whispered to Sam, "Harold was just called by someone from the Castleton Hospital. They want him to help identify a young woman who was dropped off there by an anonymous stranger who said he found her, bleeding, near the corner of Walnut and Fair Oaks."

"Cripes," said Sam. "They don't know who she is?"

"No. But Harold's name, address and 'phone number were

found on a slip of paper in her pocket. She'd only recently given birth, which I guess is why she was bleeding."

"Damn," Sam whispered.

"Harold would like support when he goes to the hospital. He has no idea who the…well, the hospital called her a girl, but who knows what that means? Anyway, he doesn't know who she is, but he'd like me to go with him."

Sam put a hand to his mouth and stood in the hallway looking like a granite statue for several seconds.

"Well?" said a nerve-wracked Harold.

"Sam's thinking," I told him.

"Tell him to think faster," Harold said.

After what seemed like an eternity or two, Sam's hand dropped from his face and he said, "Tell Harold we'll meet him at the hospital. I should go with you, given the circumstances."

I relayed Sam's message to Harold.

"This baby girl isn't going to an orphanage!" Harold hollered loud enough to burst yet another eardrum if I'd had an extra.

I yanked the receiver from my ear, and Sam took it from me. "Relax, Harold. Daisy's told me everything and nobody's going to send the baby to an orphanage. But we might get an idea about her if we can identify her mother."

"No orphanages," Harold said. I know he said it because I heard him say it even though Sam still held the receiver.

"No orphanages," said Sam, grinning. I wasn't sure a grin was appropriate, but what the heck. "Daisy and I will meet you at the hospital. Is that all right with you?"

I didn't hear Harold this time, but Sam said, "Good. It'll take us a few minutes to clear out the house, and then I'll drive us both to the Castleton. See you then."

Sam gave me back the receiver. I held it to my ear. "Harold? Are you there?"

"I think so," he said in a shaking voice.

"Sam doesn't fib, Harold. Don't worry about an orphanage. He just wants to get details and see if we can figure out who the woman —or girl—is."

"All right." Harold sounded reluctant.

"Buck up. We'll see you in a little while."

"I'm too far gone to be bucked," said Harold, but he hung up the receiver on his end.

Sam said, "He's a wreck, isn't he?"

"Yes."

Shaking his head, Sam headed back to the dining room. "See you in a few. We may be able to help Kincaid and the kid."

I said, "I hope so," as I watched his back. I was so lucky to have such a good husband.

EIGHT

I'm not sure what Sam said to my family but, except for Vi, they all left a few minutes later. Including Spike, who went home with Ma and Pa. Well, and mainly with Rosie. When I went to the kitchen, it was to see my wonderful aunt doing the washing up.

"You needn't do that, Vi. I can wash the dishes when we come back home."

"Nonsense. You need to keep off your feet, Daisy," said Vi. "Trust me, you don't want to stand for an hour or two when you're as pregnant as you are."

"Thank you, Vi," said Sam. He took my hand. "Daisy and I will be back as soon as we can be."

"Take your time. I'm so sorry about Harold."

She was sorry about *Harold*? I glanced up at Sam. He shook his head so I didn't say anything except, "Thank you very much, Vi."

"Give the lad my love," she said.

Sam and I exited the kitchen. When we got to the hall, Sam put a finger to his lips. "Need to go to the bathroom before we start for the hospital?"

"Yes. Thanks, Sam." So far the only unpleasant things I'd noticed about being pregnant were the constant need to pee and being tired all the time. Well, and losing my shape. I mean, I was still a shape, but it was round and not curvy as it used to be.

"You'll need a sweater or jacket too, because it's chilly outside. Do you need me to go upstairs and get you one, or do you have one in the downstairs closet?"

"Pretty sure there's one in the hall closet," I said.

"I'll get it for you," said Sam.

"Thank you, Sam." He was *so* good to me. When we'd first met, we hadn't liked each other at all. It took a few years before he stopped squinting at me as if he suspected me of committing criminal acts. Although I'd resented him at first—because I actually *had* been hiding a runaway girl—I'd finally come to appreciate him a whole lot. I headed for the powder room.

The Killebrews, who'd built the home in which Sam and I now lived, had the builders install a full bathroom upstairs and a small powder room, consisting of a toilet and sink, at the end of the downstairs hallway. It was convenient, so I used it and rejoined Sam at the front door. He helped me on with my sweater.

We didn't speak as we left the house and crossed the porch to get into Sam's Hudson. He opened the front door for me and went to get behind the wheel.

When Sam had backed out of the drive and turned south on Marengo, I asked, "What did you tell Vi about Harold?"

"Just that he was at the hospital and had called you to come and visit him."

I thought about his words for a couple of seconds. "Golly, that's not even a lie. Good job, Sam!"

He shot me a grin.

Then I told him about the conversation I'd overheard between Mr. Prophet and his cat. Actually, I suppose it was more like a monologue.

"You think Lou has a son who's a physician and has conveniently and only recently shown up in Pasadena?" Sam sounded incredulous.

"Yes," I said. "I do. I know he was shocked when he was introduced to Dr. Vialargo. He gave a real, physical start."

"He didn't fall down, I hope."

"Of course he didn't," I said, faintly irked. "For heaven's sake, Sam."

"I guess what I mean is, might he not have hit his peg or the toe of his boot on a crack in the sidewalk or anything?"

"Harold lives in San Marino, Sam. San Marinans don't allow cracks in their sidewalks. Anyhow, he was standing still when the doctor was introduced to him."

"Hmmm," said Sam.

"And when I went out to pick tomatoes and grab some oranges, I heard him talking to Yuyu. He was talking about Dr. Vialargo, Sam. I know he was."

"He didn't call him by name?"

"No. Not to his cat. I think Yuyu is his familiar and they communicate via esoteric channels."

Silence filled the interior of the Hudson for a second or two.

"I was only joking, Sam," I said at last. "But I do think he was talking about Dr. Vialargo."

"Interesting," said Sam. "What does this doctor look like?"

"Quite tall. Two or three inches taller than you"—my Sam is a six-footer—"blond hair, lean, pretty blue eyes with long eyelashes, which just isn't fair. Why do men always get beautiful long eyelashes when it's women who need them?"

"Beg pardon?"

I heaved a sigh. "Just a pet peeve of mine. I know so many men, including you, who have long, lush eyelashes. It's we women who need long, lush eyelashes."

"Why?"

"To attract *men*, of course!"

"Oh."

"Anyhow, Dr. Vialargo is tall and has blond hair and pretty eyes. And I distinctly heard Mr. Prophet talking to his cat about Dr. Vialargo possibly being a child Mr. Prophet sired with someone named Louisa. The only Louisa I've ever heard of in connection with Mr. Prophet in his salad days is Louisa Bonaventure, the woman the dime novelists called the 'Vengeance Queen'."

"The 'Vengeance Queen'?"

"That's what they call her in the yellow-back novels."

"And the folks who write those books never stretch the truth or make things up?" Sam's incredulity hadn't abated.

"I don't know if they do or they don't but according to the stories, the only woman Lou Prophet ever truly loved was Louisa Bonaventure. Not that loving her stopped him from dallying with a hundred or so other women."

"Bonaventure. Interesting name," said Sam. "I can't see it translating into Vialargo, though."

"No," I said dissatisfied. "It doesn't. But Mr. Prophet said his accent—"

"He has an *accent?*" said Sam.

"We all have accents, Sam," I said, frustrated. "I sound like a person from Southern California. My father, mother, and Vi sound like their relatives in Massachusetts. You sound like you're from New York."

"I do?"

"Sam Rotondo, if you'll cast your mind back a few months, you might recall that the folks in New York and Massachusetts didn't sound like people from, oh, say Georgia, where Mr. Prophet comes from."

"Huh," said Sam.

"And Mr. Prophet said the doctor not only looks like Louisa, but he sounds just like someone he called Ol' Starchy Pants."

With a small chuckle, Sam said, "Colorful name."

"I don't know who Ol' Starchy Pants is or was, but I doubt if she herself was colorful. Louisa was the colorful one. It would make sense that Ol' Starchy Pants was related to Louisa in some way."

"Why would that make sense?" Sam's eyes narrowed.

"If Louisa had Mr. Prophet's baby and was the kind of woman as described by the dime novelists, she wouldn't want to be saddled with a baby, and I doubt she'd have told Mr. Prophet about the kid. She might have handed the baby over to a family member after it was born. An aunt or a sister or someone like that."

"Hmmm. Louisa wasn't the motherly type?" asked Sam, still sounding doubtful.

"No, she wasn't. From the few stories I've managed to read in Robert Browning's dime-novel collection, she was an unusual woman. Roped, stabbed, and killed folks as easily as she breathed." Robert Browning (not the poet) was a friend of ours. He married my favorite librarian, Regina Petrie Browning.

"Charming," said Sam.

"I can't help but wonder if perhaps Dr. Vialargo came to Pasadena in order to find his father. I mean, adopted children sometimes do that, don't they?"

"I have no idea," said Sam. "Most adoption agencies don't allow children the right to discover their real parents."

"Huh," I said. Not a word I used a lot, but this was a special case. "*I* think a child's so-called 'real' parents are the ones who reared him or her, not the ones who abandoned him or her or gave the kid away. Of course, it's possible the poor mother had no other option. Heck, look what happened to Harold this morning! I doubt a mother would put her newborn in a basket and leave it on someone's doorstep if she had any other option, do you?"

After a short silence, Sam said, "I don't know. I suspect not."

"And," I said, reverting to a topic painful for me, "It's *always* the women who pay for unwanted pregnancies. Always, Sam!"

"Not all men abandon their children," said Sam in a gentle voice. I think he was attempting to soothe my feelings before we got to the hospital, or I continued my lecture. He'd heard it often enough already.

"No. Not all men," I admitted. "And I doubt Louisa Bonaventure was ever a helpless female according to what I've read about her. If she got pregnant, she'd most likely attempt to abort the baby. If that didn't work, she'd hand it off to somebody else."

"She doesn't sound precisely amiable," muttered Sam.

"No, she doesn't," I said. "But she might have been damaged by her childhood. I read that her family had been killed by some gang somewhere. Wish I could remember the state. It wasn't Arizona."

"There are forty-seven states in the Union that aren't Arizona," Sam pointed out.

"Yes, I know that. I just can't recall which one Louisa came from."

"Can you look it up in Browning's collection again?" asked Sam.

"I suppose so, but I'm going to attempt to get Mr. Prophet or Dr. Vialargo to tell me where the doctor was born and reared."

"Don't you think that if Lou wanted you to know his suspicions about the doctor, he'd discuss the matter with you? I doubt he'll relish you digging into his past life."

This time, it was again I who created the silence in the car.

Then I said, "Crumb."

"We're here," said Sam, pulling to the curb in front of the Castleton Hospital.

While Sam exited the automobile and came around to my side to open my door, I looked around for Harold's machine. Until earlier in the year, he'd owned a splendid and large Hispano-Suiza, but it had been wrapped around a huge old oak tree by a villainess. The villainess had died along with Harold's car. The accident scene had been ugly and messy.

Since I'd first met Harold, he'd had several autos. The first I recall was his bright red Stutz Bearcat. Then he'd traded his Stutz for a bright yellow Kissel Gold Bug. That car had also met its end via a criminal, to wit, Sam's deplorable nephew Frank Pagano. Then came the Hispano Suiza, about whose demise I've already told you. That auto too had been red.

He'd replaced the poor dead Hispano Suiza with a Mercedes-Benz Model K 260 (at least, I think that was its full name). Harold had also decided against going for a bright color like red or yellow this time. His new Mercedes-Benz was a sober-hued blue. He'd told me he hoped villains (and villainesses) would be less inclined to steal and wreck a blue car. I hoped he was correct.

"I don't see Harold's Mercedes," I said as Sam helped me out of his Hudson. I regretted the audible grunt I made as I stood. Our young child, while as yet unborn, was causing its mother no little discomfort when it came to getting in to and out of automobiles.

"I don't either," said Sam, also taking a look around the street. "Maybe he went to the parking lot in the back of the building."

"What parking lot?" came Harold's voice behind me as I tugged down my skirt and smoothed my sweater. When one is shaped as I was then, one's clothing tended to ride up one's belly.

"Oh, hey there, Harold," said Sam, turning to hold out his hand.

"Dang, Harold, you scared me," I said, frowning at him.

"It's the new machine," he said. "It blends in with the scenery."

"The scenery around here is green, Harold," I said. I patted my chest in the hope of getting my heart to slow down some.

"And brown," said Harold. "At least my new Mercedes isn't bright red or yellow, and nobody's stolen it yet. Now that you're here, of course, all bets are off."

"Just because you've had two of your automobiles smashed while you were helping me is no reason to think I'm cursed or anything," I told him, trying not to sound miffed. The truth was that I felt totally guilty about Harold's mangled motors.

"You used to be," said Harold with a sniff. "But come on. I need to see who this girl is the hospital called me about. Why would anyone have my address and phone number in their pocket?"

"You couldn't be the father, could you?" I asked.

It wasn't easy to see in the last afternoon on a cloudy fall day, but I think I saw a look of horror on Harold's face.

"*Me?*" he squeaked. "Daisy Gumm Majesty Rotondo, *how* long have you known me?"

"Sorry, Harold," I said.

Not entirely sure, but I think Sam was attempting to repress a chuckle as he took my arm, and we joined Harold's march across California Street to the hospital entrance.

The hospital was shiny and up-to-date, and I'd been there before. Although Sam and I had considered having our baby at the Castleton, we'd ultimately decided on using the Woman's Hospital of Pasadena as our birthing place of choice. Dr. Benjamin, our family doctor, had actually urged me to visit a woman doctor for my pregnancy check-ups. I hadn't even known Pasadena *had* any female

doctors, but I approved wholeheartedly. Because of his recommen-
dation, I'd been seeing Dr. Eleanor Steindorf, and I thought she was
swell.

When we walked into the hospital's lobby and up to the reception desk, I suddenly wasn't sure how to ask my question. Fortunately, Harold didn't suffer from my problem.

When the lady at the reception desk asked what she could do for
us, Harold said, "A member of the hospital staff told me a girl had
been brought in unconscious. She had my name and address in her
pocket, and I was asked to come in and see if I could identify her."

"Oh, yes. Hold on for one second." The reception lady, a silver-
haired old person who might have been a volunteer, picked up a pile
of papers on her desk and shuffled through them, squinting at each
one as she uncovered it. About an hour and a half after she'd begun
searching through the documents, she squinted up at Harold over
her spectacles. "Are you Mr. Kincaid?"

"Harold Kincaid," said Harold promptly. He'd begun twitching
during the approximately forty-fifth minute of the woman's search.
I'm kidding about the time. It only *seemed* to take her a long time. "I
am Harold Kincaid, yes."

"Please wait one moment," said the extremely slow elderly
person. She picked up the receiver of a telephone on her table
clearly marked "Staff," and pressed a button on the foot of the
'phone. Someone on the other end of the wire must have spoken
loudly because she jumped in her chair and yanked the receiver
from her ear, thereby reminding me of my many telephonic
encounters with Mrs. Pinkerton. "Mr. Kincaid is at the front desk,"
she said after sticking a finger to her afflicted ear, grimacing,
removing her finger and replacing the receiver against the poor ear.

As soon as she hung up the receiver, the woman said, "Nurse
Monica Dandridge will be here in a moment, Mr. Kincaid."

"And she'll take me to the girl who had my name in her pocket?"
asked Harold as if he didn't quite believe the woman.

"Yes," said the woman.

"Thank you, Miss Silver," said Sam, startling both the woman
and me.

Only then did I notice she wore a name tag, clearly declaring her to be "Miss R. Silver." My Sam was a superlative detective.

The three of us stepped away from the reception desk and stood for a while in front of it. As more people came into the hospital lobby and no Nurse Dandridge appeared, Sam led us to some chairs lined up against a wall. I was glad of his thoughtfulness as my feet were starting to ache. Vi was correct about standing for long periods being hard on a pregnant woman.

We sat against the wall for another several hours—exaggeration —until finally an efficient woman in a white nurse's uniform and cap marched into the lobby. Without looking around, she said, "Mr. Harold Kincaid?"

"Here," said Harold, standing.

The nurse nodded sharply and said, "Please come with me, Mr. Kincaid."

Sam and I rose from our chairs too, and the nurse frowned at us.

"Only Mr. Kincaid is allowed into the room," she said icily.

"Detective Rotondo, Pasadena Police Department," said Sam, holding out his police identification for her to see. "Mr. Kincaid asked that my wife and I be present when he attempts to identify the woman."

Nurse Dandridge gave the three of us a censorious frown. Then she seemed to ponder the yeas or nays of allowing Sam and me to accompany Harold. At last, and I'd say against her will, she nodded and said crisply, "Come with me."

We went with her.

NINE

I think Nurse Dandridge's shoes had rubber soles because the only clacking I heard came from Sam, Harold, and me. Almost wished I'd strapped rags to the bottoms of our shoes, they sounded so loud against the wooden floorboards.

Nurse Dandridge led us upstairs and down a second-floor hall. When she stopped in front of a closed door—marked 215, if anyone cares—she put a finger to her lips and said, "Please be as quiet as you can be. The poor girl has endured a lot of grief and pain in recent days. We don't want to awaken her if she's sleeping."

"Very well," I whispered. I noticed Sam and Harold merely nodded.

The nurse opened the door to room 215 and walked in before us. Sam and Harold gestured for me to follow the nurse. They were being gentlemanly. I'd as soon they saw the poor girl first. Oh well. Manners were manners. And I was as sneaky as anyone else, so I stepped aside as soon as I'd entered the room and pressed my back against a wall so Sam *had* to see the poor woman on the bed before I did.

Then there was Harold.

Standing beside the bed, the nurse waited for Harold to walk to it. Poor Harold clearly didn't want to look at what was in the bed. He glanced around, saw me pressed against the wall, and reached out a hand and tugged it so I'd have to stand beside him. Curses. Foiled again.

I tried to tiptoe as well as possible, but my bulk made me teeter some so I decided I'd make more noise if I fell over than I would if I just took slow steps. The floor to the room had been overlaid with linoleum—I know because I looked—and my shoes didn't clomp as much as they had on the wooden flooring of the hallway. While this didn't make me happy, it lessened my worry that we'd awaken the girl in the bed. The nurse had turned on a table lamp so at least we could see the bed's occupant.

She didn't make much of a lump under the covers. Harold sort of sidled up to the head of the bed. I softly walked up behind him. The only feature I saw when I peered at the body under the covers was a lot of brown hair.

"Is she lying on her stomach?" I asked, thinking the position would be mighty uncomfortable if it were so.

"I don't know," said Harold in a tentative-sounding voice.

"Here," said Nurse Dandridge officiously. She walked silently to the bed—those rubber soles of hers allowed her to be silent even though she seemed angry with us for some reason—reached down to the girl in the bed and pulled her hair away from her face. I was faintly horrified until I saw that she was being gentle with the patient.

Harold was definitely horrified when he looked at the drawn and pallid face of the girl on the bed. And she did indeed look like a girl. It was Harold's good luck that allowed him to utter an audible gasp, stagger backward, and not bump into anything or topple over. That's because Sam had sneaked up behind the two of us and caught him by the shoulders.

"Do you recognize her?" whispered Sam.

After nodding his head several times, Harold ultimately murmured, "Y-yes. At least I think I do." He turned to Sam and said, "I need to sit down."

Sam helped Harold to a chair and left him there. Then he joined me at the girl's bed and squinted down at its occupant.

Several breaths came from Harold, then he managed to get himself upright and walk back to the patient. "I can't believe it," he said softly.

"You know her?" I asked him.

Harold nodded.

I heard a rustle of starched cotton, and Nurse Dandridge inserted herself between Harold and me. Turning to Harold, she said, "You know this girl?"

"Yes."

"Come with me," ordered the nurse. She marched silently to the door, opened it and glared at Sam and me until all three of us straggled out of the room. Then she carefully closed the door and strode down the hall to what I suppose was a nurses' station. There she spoke in whispers to another couple of nurses—I guess they were nurses—then turned and gestured for us to follow her some more.

So we did.

The militant Nurse Dandridge walked with a stiff back and a ferocious countenance, looking back from time to time to make sure we were obeying her order. We were. She led us to a suite of offices, ending up at the one whose window declared it to contain "Records." She shoved the door open and held it as we filed past her.

"What do you want us to do?" asked Sam. He didn't sound awfully friendly. I didn't blame him, and I fervently prayed that I wouldn't meet up with a nurse like her when it came my time to deliver my baby. Our baby.

The chair behind the desk held a startled-looking gentleman who'd been perusing a gigantic ledger I assumed contained hospital records. Nurse Dandridge turned and crossed her arms over her chest. The man blinked at the nurse over a pair of half-glasses and said, "What is this, Miss Dandridge?" He transferred his gaze to the three of us interlopers and said, "Good afternoon."

Before Sam, Harold or I could wish him a good anything at all, the nurse spoke again, raising her voice so it would drown out anything one of the three of us might say. "That man there"—she pointed at Harold, who gave a start of alarm—"is responsible for the poor girl who was brought here after she was found unconscious and abandoned on the street."

"*I*," squeaked Harold. "I'm not responsible for anything!"

Narrowing her eyes to dangerous slits, the nurse said, "You claimed you know her."

"Yes, I know her," stammered Harold. "But I haven't—"

Sam stepped into the fray, interrupting everyone, bless him. "Excuse me. I'm Detective Samuel Rotondo with the Pasadena Police Department." Again he whipped out his identification card. I noticed the man seated at the desk was still blinking in what I presumed to be confusion. Didn't blame him either.

"And," said Sam stampeding over whatever the nurse had opened her mouth to say, "Mr. Kincaid only knows the woman in room 215. He's not responsible for her condition. Nor does he know why and how she was abandoned at this hospital."

"He said he *knows* her," declared the nurse.

"I do know her, if only slightly," said Harold. He seemed to be regaining his fortitude because he went on in a louder, harder voice, "She's my niece, Melanie Robinson. I haven't seen her since last Christmas. What are you implying anyway? I'm in no way responsible for anything about her. As far as I know, she and her parents and siblings live in Eagle Rock."

"I don't believe you," said Nurse Dandridge.

"Excuse me," said Sam in a dangerous voice. "It's not your business to believe or disbelieve anything anyone in this room says. You or someone connected with this hospital telephoned Mr. Kincaid and asked him to come in, look at that girl, and tell the hospital staff if he knows her name. He did just that. I've known Mr. Kincaid for years, and I can vouch for his honesty. Perhaps you should take us to a person on the hospital's administrative staff."

"Nonsense," said Nurse Dandridge.

Very well, I was fed up with her too. I took two steps, which brought me to the desk behind which the fellow hid. "Be quiet,

Nurse Dandridge," I demanded. To the man I said, "Who are you, and why did this nurse bring us here?"

"I…I'm Francis Hedges."

"And what is your position at this hospital?" I barked at him. Poor man flinched. Guess he didn't care for assertive females because he seemed to shrink further into himself. He'd started shrinking when Nurse Dandridge barged into his office.

"I…I'm in charge of patient records," he said feebly.

"All right," I said and turned to the nurse. "You, Miss Dandridge, can go take a hike, and we'll speak to Mr. Hedges. You have no business accusing anyone of anything. I thought nurses were supposed to take care of people, not condemn them."

"Well!" she said indignantly.

"Oh, go iron your shoelaces," I snarled at her. "Harold is trying to do a good deed here. He doesn't need you making up stories about him."

"Well!" she said again.

"Deep subject," Sam pointed out. "But not relevant. Miss Dandridge, please leave us alone with Mr. Hedges."

And, with one last "Well!" she did. At last.

"My gawd," said Harold in a shaky voice. "I wouldn't want *her* as my nurse. I'll take Hazel Greenlaw any day over that creature."

"Me too," I said.

"Ahem," said Mr. Hedges. "I gather you came in to identify a patient?"

"Yes," said Harold, his voice attaining strength at last. "I received a telephone call from someone in this hospital. Whoever it was told me a girl had been found unconscious and bleeding near a street corner. For some reason beyond my ken, my name, address and telephone number were discovered on a piece of paper in one of her pockets." He shook his head hard. "Drat it, I have the name of the person who called me on a tablet at home, but I didn't think to bring the tablet with me."

"Ah," said Mr. Hedges. "Yes, I believe I know what and whom you're talking about now." He looked and sounded relieved.

"That makes one of us," I snapped.

"Ahem," said Mr. Hedges. "Er, yes. One moment please." He flipped a page or two in the ledger before him and stabbed the bottom of the page with a forefinger. "Here we have it. Indeed. A young woman was transported by"—he squinted at the paper—"um, she was taken to the emergency area. A man brought her in, but no one jotted down his name. She's listed here as Anonymous." He cleared his throat again. "You said her name is Robinson?"

"Yes," said Harold. "Melanie Robinson. If she has a middle name, I don't know what it is."

After he wrote the name in his ledger, he said, "Thank you. And you are?" He gave Harold a nervous twitch of his mouth that I think was supposed to be a grin.

"Harold Kincaid," said Harold.

"Ah. Thank you, Mr. Kincaid." Mr. Hedges jotted Harold's name (I presume) in his ledger. "Do you have any idea why or how Miss Robinson came to Pasadena?"

"Not a clue," said Harold.

"Did you know she was…with child?" Mr. Hedges was clearly an old-fashioned fellow.

"No! I don't keep up with my family. I'm busy and have friends of my own with whom I'm closer than I am with any members of my family. I haven't seen Melanie since—well, I think it was last Christmas. Her family lives in Eagle Rock. That's not far away as the crow flies, but it's far enough away that we don't get together often."

"I see," said Mr. Hedges. "Do you happen to have an address or telephone number for Miss Robinson's family? Or perhaps she got married?"

"I might have the address of the Robinson family at home. If I don't have it, I'm sure my mother does. Mrs. Robinson is a cousin of hers, I think."

"That would make Melanie your cousin, not your niece," I said. "At least I think that's what she'd be. Maybe it's a cousin once removed."

"Daisy," said Sam in a tense voice. "Their precise relationship doesn't matter at the moment."

"I see," said Mr. Hedges, poking the cross piece of his specs so they slid back up his nose. "May I have your mother's telephone number?"

"Sure," said Harold, "but she's in Santa Barbara for another three or four weeks."

"Oh dear," said a fretful Mr. Hedges. "Do you know if your cousin...niece...If Melanie Robinson married since you last saw her?"

"If she did, nobody told me about it," said Harold. "If she got married, I don't know her new last name."

Sam spoke next. "There were *no* identifying documents on the girl's person when she was dropped off here?"

Mr. Hedges blinked several times, adjusted his specs once more and peered closely at the ledger. Naturally, this allowed his cheaters to slide down his nose again. "No. No, according to this, nothing was found on her person except a slip of paper with Mr. Kincaid's information on it."

"Strange," I said.

"Very," said Sam.

"I agree," said Harold. "But I don't know what the hospital expects me to do about poor Melanie and her medical problems."

Curious, I asked Mr. Hedges, "Precisely what *are* her medical problems?"

Mr. Hedges frowned, shoved his glasses up his nose, and seemed to stare at a far corner of his office for a few seconds. At last, he said, "I...Well...Um, we can't disclose personal information to anyone but family members."

"I *am* a family member," Harold reminded him.

"Well, yes, I understand that. But...Well, this information is extremely personal to the young woman. I don't believe these other two people"—he waved a hand at Sam and me—"should be in the room when I divulge her status."

"I'm an officer of the law," Sam said, his words falling like stones and making Mr. Hedges flinch again. "It sounds to me as if at least one crime had been committed, either by Miss Robinson or against her. As an officer of the law, I want to know precisely what her condition was when—I believe it was an anonymous young man?" He lifted an eyebrow at Mr. Hedges.

Making himself as small as possible, Mr. Hedges murmured, "Uh, yes. A man. He didn't give his name. Or his age."

"All right," said Sam. "Miss Robinson was dropped off at the emergency section of the hospital by a man who didn't leave his name—or hers. Do I have that right?"

Slumping yet further, Mr. Hedges almost had to peer over the top of his desk to read his ledger. "Yes. Yes. Yes, you have that right."

"Then there has definitely been at least one crime committed either against Miss Robinson or by Miss Robinson. Now tell us what her condition was when she was abandoned at the hospital."

It appeared for a moment as if Mr. Hedges meant to object again, but Sam took another step toward the record keeper's desk and loomed over him.

"Very well," Mr. Hedges blurted out at last. "She'd been pregnant and lost her child. We don't know how or why."

TEN

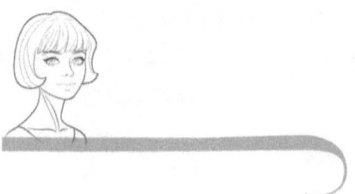

"What do you mean, 'She lost the child'?" I demanded. "What does 'losing' a child even mean?"

"I'd like to know that too," said Harold coldly.

"Um, what I meant was that…well, she had recently given birth, but the child wasn't with her."

"Did the hospital call the police department and tell them about this young woman and her missing baby?" asked Sam, who sounded grimly official.

"The police?" squeaked Mr. Hedges. "The police?"

"Yes. The police," said Sam.

"Uh…um, no. I see no record here of anyone telephoning the police department." Mr. Hedges stared at his ledger as if it might save his life.

"And why not?" I demanded, stepping up to stand beside Sam. Harold joined me at Sam's other side. "A bleeding woman is abandoned at your hospital after having given birth, but there was no baby with her. You don't even know her name *or* take the name of the man who brought her in, yet you don't telephone the police station? I should think that would be the first thing you'd do after seeing to her medical needs."

"Exactly," said Harold.

"Indeed," said Sam. "The hospital might be liable for failure to report a felony."

"A *felony?*" shrieked Mr. Hedges.

"Yes," said Sam.

"Oh dear, oh dear," said Mr. Hedges. "B-but we know nothing about the young woman. Miss Robinson. All we know is that she'd recently given birth, was found unconscious and bleeding—"

"Or so your anonymous depositor of the woman said, according to your ledger," corrected Sam.

"Well, yes, but—"

"Frankly, I'm surprised and appalled," said Sam.

"So am I," said Harold.

"And I," I chipped in.

"Well, but we didn't know what had happened," said Mr. Hedges.

Harold, Sam and I exchanged a disgusted eye-roll.

"This is a debacle," I said. "There's no use in questioning this individual any longer, Sam. He doesn't know anything. Perhaps we should talk to the hospital's administrator."

I heard an audible gulp from Mr. Hedges. "Please, Detective… I'm sorry. I don't recall your name."

"Rotondo. Detective Sam Rotondo. Pasadena Police Department."

"Yes, Detective Rotondo. I can't speak for the administrator of the hospital, but I believe our staff was diligent in pursuing the correct course of action for poor Miss Robinson. They got in touch with the only person they knew of." He pointed at Harold. "Mr. Kincaid there. Please bear in mind that our hospital is dedicated to assisting our patients. This woman was abandoned here only about three or four hours ago. I believe the thinking was that we didn't want to add to Miss Robinson's problems, so a call to Mr. Kincaid before we got the authorities involved seemed the prudent path."

Sam didn't respond to this excuse which, to tell the truth, sounded pretty good to me. I didn't say so.

Harold and I must have telepathically shared our thoughts

because Harold said, "Sam, he's right. I doubt Melanie or her family would be pleased to have the police involved unless it becomes absolutely necessary." He turned to Mr. Hedges. "Do you know if Melanie has been able to tell anyone what happened to her?"

Breathing a sigh of what sounded like relief, Mr. Hedges again consulted his ledger. "No. No, she hasn't regained full consciousness. Or at least she hadn't when I got the report and filled in this ledger page."

The room filled with a tense silence. I swear I could hear people's nerves snapping around me. Naturally, I needed to piddle again. I wouldn't necessarily recommend pregnancy to anyone unless they *really* wanted a family.

Finally I decided I needed the bathroom more than Sam needed to attack Mr. Hedges, so I said, "Let's go, Sam and Harold. The hospital may not be at fault here. We'll have to see what happens henceforth."

"Right," said Sam, who took my arm and turned toward the door.

Harold whispered, "Henceforth?"

"Thank you, and please call again," Mr. Hedges' voice held a hopeful note. I don't think he meant the part about please calling again.

As soon as we'd left the Records office, I said softly and desperately, "Does anyone see a comfort station? I *really* have to go!"

"Henceforth?" Harold repeated, this time audibly.

"She likes words," said Sam, good humoredly. "You require a comfort station?"

"Yes! I can't help it," I said. "You get pregnant and see how often *you* need to use the bathroom!"

Sam, who had been scanning the hallway, laughed and said, "I see one farther on down this hallway. I think it's a restroom, although it might be for staff only."

"Piddle on the staff," I said and hurried as fast as I could to the restroom. It did have a sign telling everyone this particular comfort station was for hospital staff only, but I figured I wouldn't be bothering anyone. Better to use a staff restroom than have an accident in the hospital's corridor, thereby truly piddling on the hospital, if not its entire staff.

I was, however, glad to note I was alone in the room. After I did my business and washed my hands I rejoined the two gents in the hallway.

"Feel better now?" asked Sam.

"Much," I said.

"Very well, what do we do now?" asked Harold. "I'd like to talk to Melanie if she ever regains consciousness. Do you think she was unconscious because of blood loss, or did she have other injuries?"

"We don't know yet," said Sam. "Nobody has elected to tell us her precise condition."

"Crumb," said Harold. "I don't know what to do. I suspect the baby Roy found on my doorstep this morning was Melanie's, but how do we find out? And will Melanie be in trouble for abandoning her baby if it *is* hers?"

Shaking his head, Sam said, "Too many unknowns at this point. Want to take another trip up to your cousin's room before we leave?"

Harold thought about it for a second or two and said, "Yes. If you don't mind coming with me."

Sam and I exchanged a glance. Accurately deciphering Sam's expression, I said, "Don't mind at all."

So the three of us trekked up to room 215 once more. As we walked, Harold asked, "Is failure to report a crime really against the law?"

"Sometimes," said Sam.

"Big help," I said.

"If you see someone commit a murder or run over someone in the street and take off without helping and you don't report it, you might be guilty of misprision of a felony."

"What the heck does misprision mean?" I demanded.

"It's the deliberate concealment of personal knowledge of a felony or a treasonable act," said Sam.

"Huh. I've never heard the word before this. I don't think I've ever read it in a book or anything."

"I suspect most folks haven't," said Sam. "I imagine it's most often used by people in the judicial, governmental or police systems."

"Interesting," I said.

We were approaching room 215 again, so we stopped talking and quietly walked to the room. Sam, being the authority figure among us, silently opened the door. We all walked inside.

Melanie Robinson lay on her back now, her head propped on a white pillowcase. She appeared drawn and tired, but she was awake. She turned her face toward the three of us and whimpered.

Harold hurried to her bedside. Sam and I hung back. "Melanie!" whispered Harold. "Melanie, what the heck happened? Are you all right?"

"Oh, Harold, I'm so sorry," the girl whispered. Tears ran down her cheeks. "I'm s-so sorry."

"About what? Melanie, please tell me what happened to you. Oh, and was that your infant on my doorstep this morning?"

"Y-yes!" More weeping. "I'm so sorry!"

After heaving a huge sigh, Harold said, "It's all right, Melanie. Your baby girl is fine."

"Y-you didn't give her away, did you?" asked Melanie after a long bout of tears.

"No," said Harold. "She's safe and secure in an upstairs bedroom in my home. I've hired a nurse to care for her, and she's already been examined by a doctor. He proclaimed her to be a fine specimen of baby humanhood. Or whatever I mean. Please stop crying, Melanie. I'll help you if I can."

"You've always been so kind to me, Harold," snuffled Melanie. "That's why I made Jimmy take me to your house. I put a note in with the baby. Didn't you find it?"

"The only thing we found in the basket was the baby wrapped in a blanket. Neither my houseboy nor I found a note."

"Oh. I wonder why."

"So do I," said Harold. "If I'd known the kid was yours, I

wouldn't have been in quite so much of a panic. Maybe. No. I'd still have panicked. I presume you didn't want your parents to know about her?"

The girl nodded miserably. "I ran away when I told them I was pregnant. They didn't like Jimmy. Jimmy said he'd...he'd...take c-care of me." She resumed sobbing.

"Who is this Jimmy person?" asked Sam, walking closer to Melanie's bed. "Is he the father of your child?"

Melanie gave a visible start and turned her head to stare at Sam. Guess she hadn't realized Harold had come with outriders. "Who are *you?*" she choked out in a horrified voice.

"These are two of my friends, Melanie," Harold said quickly. Guess he didn't think Melanie would react tamely to Sam's police identification badge. I suspect he was correct. "Daisy and Sam Rotondo."

"Yes. I'm Daisy Rotondo, and this is my husband Sam," I said as I walked up to the bed to stand beside Harold. I attempted to give Melanie an encouraging smile.

"Daisy came to my house to help with the baby," said Harold. "She's my second-best friend. We help each other when we can."

I'm only guessing, but I think Del Farrington was Harold's first best friend.

"Th-that's kind of you," Melanie said softly. "But I don't know why you didn't find the note."

"I have a feeling I know the answer to that puzzle," said Sam.

"You do?" I stared at him.

So did Harold and Melanie.

"The father of your child is the fellow you call Jimmy, right?" said Sam.

Melanie nodded. "Yes."

"But he didn't tell the hospital staff his name. Rather, he pretended you were a stranger whom he found bleeding on or near a street corner. He hasn't attempted to see you, has he?"

Her face scrunching into a mask of misery, Melanie shook her head. "No."

"You might have to face the unpleasant fact that Jimmy has

abandoned both you and your child." Although Sam's voice was soothing, his words must have stung like a scorpion. Tears streamed relentlessly down Melanie's pale cheeks.

"Listen, Melanie," said Harold. "Try not to worry about this Jimmy character—what's his last name anyhow?"

"Smith," whispered Melanie.

"Jimmy Smith?" Harold shot Sam and me a disbelieving glance.

"Yes."

"Well, try not to worry about your baby or Jimmy Smith right now, Melanie. Your baby girl will be very well cared-for. If this Jimmy Smith character has run out on his responsibilities, you're better off knowing it now."

Another torrent of tears and a watery, "No!" came from poor Melanie.

"Harold's right, Miss Robinson," I said, sensing a chance to educate. I know, I'm *such* a pain in the neck. "Men have been taking advantage of women for centuries. It's always the woman who pays for untimely pregnancies." Shoot, I'd almost said "unwanted," and although I meant it, I sensed Melanie might take umbrage after she got over the worst of her mental and physical agony.

"I will attempt to find Mr. Smith, Miss Robinson," said Sam.

"Do you want him found?" I asked the ragged woman on the bed. "If he cares so little about you and his own child, you'll probably be better off without him."

"Daisy!" whispered Harold. "Melanie doesn't need a lecture right now."

"Right," I said, chastened. "I'm sorry, Miss Robinson." Then I shut my mouth and swore I wouldn't open it again until after we left Melanie's room.

"Melanie," said Harold. "If Jimmy Smith gets in touch with you, please telephone me and tell me about it. Will you do that?"

"Wh-what for?" she asked.

"If he's the father of your baby, he should be responsible for her care and upkeep, although so far he sounds like a fairly irresponsible individual." Harold stopped speaking for a minute, and I nearly broke my vow of silence. At last, he said, "I must admit, however, that it will almost certainly be better if he doesn't get in touch with you. I don't want to hurt your feelings, Melanie because you've been hurt enough already, but he doesn't sound like the kind of guy who'd be a satisfactory husband or father. Did he ever ask you to marry him, by the way?"

Soft weeping from the bed finally gave way to a weak and shaky, "Y-yes. Sort of."

"'Sort of' doesn't sound like a firm proposal," said Harold. "All right, let's just assume he's out of the picture. You might not want to assume that yet, but I'm sure you will eventually. In the meantime, don't worry about your baby. I'll continue taking care of her. And don't worry about your hospital charges either. I'll pay for your care here too."

Melanie slowly lifted a hand and grasped Harold's sleeve. "Thank you, Harold. I'm so sorry."

"Just do what the nurses tell you to do and get better, all right?" said Harold.

"I will," she whimpered.

We got out of there and out of the hospital. I needed to piddle again, but I figured I'd wait until we got home.

ELEVEN

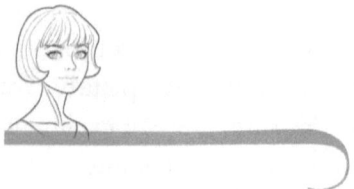

Harold walked with us to our Hudson. "Whoo boy," he said when we got to our car. "Poor Melanie."

"Yes," said Sam. "Poor kid."

"What do you suppose will happen now?" I asked the air, expecting one of the men to respond. When neither did, I said, "Sam? Harold? What will happen now? Do you know?"

Harold heaved a big sigh. "I have no idea," he admitted. "I'll take care of Melanie's hospital expenses and I'll continue to have Hazel take care of the baby, but I can't be the long-term solution to this problem."

"No," said Sam. "That's true."

"How old is Melanie?" I asked Harold.

"Hell, I don't know," he said, sounding cranky. "She's in her teens. I don't think she's more than fifteen or sixteen."

"She's so young," I said, feeling intensely sorry for Melanie Robinson.

I'd married my first husband at the tender age of seventeen, right after my high school graduation. I now know from experience that the seventeen-year-old Daisy Gumm had been far too young to make such a life-changing decision. My hand strayed to the lumpy quartet of "charms" I always wore on a gold chain around my neck. Included among them was the wedding ring Billy had given me. Tears stung my eyes and made me glad the days got dark early in the autumn.

"And her precious Jimmy Smith doesn't sound like a prince either," said Sam. "But I suppose we ought to try and find him."

"Why?" I asked.

"Yeah," said Harold. "Why?"

"He should be made to pay for the baby's care," said Sam. "And Miss Robinson's too."

"Nertz," I said. "He'll only complicate things. If Melanie's lucky, he's already taken off for Timbuktu."

"I thought you wanted men to be responsible for the babies they help make," said Sam, squinting down at me.

"I *do*," I said. "But this precious Jimmy fellow sounds like a cad and a bounder. He didn't even leave his name at the hospital when he took Melanie there. The hospital staff made it sound as if he and she were strangers. I'll bet he was the one who removed Melanie's note from the baby's basket, and he did it because he didn't want anyone to link the baby to him. I doubt he'll help Melanie if you *do* find him. He'll only add to her burdens."

"I'm sorry she ran away from home. Her parents are nice people. They wouldn't have kicked her out. At least I don't think they would," said Harold musingly. "I don't know them well, but they always seemed like loving, caring parents. Of course, if they voiced opposition to Mr. Smith, Melanie might have become huffy and run off with him."

"I think she was scared to death," I said. "And she feared bringing disgrace to her family." I heaved a big sigh.

"Well, we can't do much about it now," said Sam. "We need to get home and let Daisy sit with her feet up on an ottoman. She's not supposed to be on her feet a whole lot."

"Oh, that's right. I forgot you're about to foal, too, Daisy," said Harold.

"I'm not a horse, Harold Kincaid," I told him.

"Of course not," he agreed. "Although you're about as big as one."

"Pony," corrected Sam. "She's no way as big as a horse."

"Thanks," I snarled.

"But I'm going home," said Harold. "Can you come by again tomorrow, Daisy?"

"Tomorrow's Sunday," I reminded him. "I have to sing in the choir at church. Then Aunt Vi always expects us to take dinner at Ma and Pa's house."

"Lucky you," said Harold. "I think it's about time your aunt retired from cooking for my mother and stepfather. She's much too good for them."

"Harold! That's not nice!"

With a chuckle, Sam said, "It isn't, but Harold's correct. Your aunt doesn't need to be on her feet all day any more than you do."

"That's true," I admitted. "When is your mother coming back home again, Harold?"

"With any luck, she and Algie will be in Santa Barbara until after Christmas."

"Excellent," I said. "I really don't want her calling me every five minutes in a tizzy of one sort or another." I had another thought. "And after Christmas, I'll be a new mother, so she'll go easy on me. I hope."

"If it's any comfort, she hasn't been tizzying as much as she used to now that Stacy's shuffled off this mortal coil," said Harold.

"Ugh. I'm glad of that anyway," I said, giving an involuntary shiver.

I only voiced the "Ugh," because I'd been partly responsible for Harold's ghastly sister Stacy plummeting into the Nether Reaches of Hades where she belonged. Stacy had been a dreadful person. She'd tried on more than one occasion to kill me, as a matter of fact. I may not be a perfect person and I know I'm not universally loved, but darn! I didn't deserve to be murdered for being an imperfect person. Heck, everyone's imperfect.

Harold opened the passenger door to the Hudson, and I squished myself in. "See you soon, Harold," I told him.

"You'd better," Harold said. "And Sam, what do you think you'll do about finding Melanie's so-called lover?"

"Don't know yet," said Sam, getting into the Hudson on the driver's side. "Jimmy Smith isn't an unusual name. If he has a brain, he's probably already left town for Timbuktu, as Daisy said."

"The miserable owlhoot," I muttered.

Oh, "owlhoot" is another word I learned from Mr. Prophet. It means, as you've probably deduced, a bad man.

Sam and I watched as Harold walked to his Mercedes. His shoulders were slumped, and there was no bounce to his step.

"Poor, Harold," I said.

"Yes," said Sam. "He's in a real pickle."

"Pickle," I said, Sam's words having bumped my thoughts away from Melanie's baby and onto another path entirely. "I really want one of Vi's dill pickles."

"We have a cellar shelf full of them, don't we?" Sam said as he started the Hudson.

"Maybe half a shelf," I said. "I've been craving pickles recently."

"I've heard women crave certain foods when they're pregnant," said Sam. "I thought it was an old wives' tale."

"I'm not *that* old," I said. "And I want a pickle. And some more of that soup if there's any left."

"Soup for dinner sounds good to me," said Sam.

"Good." Then my thoughts veered back to Jimmy Smith—if that was his real name—and I added, "Do you have any idea how to find Jimmy Smith?"

"No," said Sam. "Put out bulletins at bus stations and the train station for whatever good that will do. It would help if we had a photo of him."

I heaved a sigh. "I hope he stays lost."

"You do?"

"Yes! I expect he's a wife-beater or a criminal or a deadbeat. That would be worse for the poor girl than if he just abandons her and his child."

Sam turned his head and eyed me for a second. "The girl *must* have more choices than those."

"This one does, thanks to Harold. Can you imagine what awful choices an impoverished girl would have in the same circumstances?"

"Don't have to imagine them," Sam said grimly. "I've seen them first-hand."

"Here in Pasadena?" I asked.

"Here in Pasadena," Sam confirmed. "Pasadena's a nice place, but people are people."

"True. Silly me." My mind veered to several months ago when a detestable young man had taken bets on how many young women he could seduce. He'd even impregnated one girl and then denied he'd done it. "Life can be awfully hard on some people, can't it?"

"After saving Flossie Buckingham's neck, I'm surprised you even asked the question."

"You're right. And Marianne Grenville. And her mother."

"And they weren't impoverished," Sam reminded me.

"Nor was Mrs. Bannister."

"I'd prefer not to think about her at all," said Sam.

"I understand," I said. It was true. Sam had been shot and nearly killed while he and I (pursuing vastly different paths) were solving the Bannister case. "Life can be *so* grueling for so many people."

"Yup. And that's even when they all play by the same rules," said Sam.

Couldn't have said it better myself, although I could have delivered a lecture or two on the subject. For the sake of Sam's sanity and domestic harmony, I didn't.

Did I hear a faint "Halleluiah" from someone reading my journal? Fiddlesticks. You shouldn't be reading my journal if you don't like lectures.

Just kidding.

When Sam pulled the Hudson into our driveway, I saw Mr. Lou Prophet sitting on the front porch of our house with his mangled orange cat on his lap. As I squinted at the scene under the porch light, I thought I saw Spike resting beside Mr. P's chair. When Spike leaped up and began barking joyously at Sam and me, my identification of the porch's occupants was confirmed.

Yuyu, who didn't like anyone who wasn't Mr. Prophet or Spike, gave a hiss I could hear from inside the Hudson and ran off, leaping over the porch fence and racing like an odd orange streak to Mr. Prophet's cottage at the rear of the property.

Sam opened my car door then the porch gate, and we both walked up the few steps to the porch. There I gave Spike a thorough petting and apologized for Sam's and my absence. "We had to help a friend," I told my wonderful dog. "Sorry we took so long."

"Where you been?" asked Mr. Prophet, standing and grimacing. I think he only grimaced because Yuyu had a habit of launching himself from his lap by using his claws for leverage. When the gnarled old man rubbed the thigh of his left trouser leg, my thought was confirmed. "Damn cat always stabs me when he's tryin' to get away from intruders."

"This is our house," I reminded him. "We're not intruders. We own the place."

Sam, who knew from experience when not to butt in, only chuckled.

"Yeah, I know that and you know that, but Yuyu has his own ideas. Where you been?"

"And a pleasant good evening to you, too," I told the old scoundrel.

"It ain't pleasant, and I wanted to talk to you. Where you been?"

"It is too pleasant," I argued.

"We went to see Harold Kincaid at the Castleton Hospital," said Sam, cutting our squabble short. I'm sure it was for the best.

"What's the matter with Harold?" asked Mr. P.

After giving Spike a few pets and pats of his own, Sam opened the front door and gestured for me to go in. So I did.

"Nothing," I said over my shoulder. "The hospital called and asked him if he could identify a woman who was found unconscious and bleeding near Fair Oaks and Walnut. The woman had just given birth, and the hospital people said she had Harold's name and address in one of her pockets. They wanted Harold to identify her if he could."

"Cripes," said Mr. Prophet. "Could he?"

"Yes," said Sam. "But come in, Lou. Daisy wants some soup and a dill pickle or two. You want some too?"

"Sure. Thanks. You eating pickles a lot these days?" Mr. P. asked me.

"Yes. Tons of pickles. Dill pickles."

"I heard women who're carryin' sometimes crave different kinds of foods. Pickles are better'n clay, I reckon."

"Clay?" I asked. "Pregnant women eat *clay?*"

"Some of 'em," he confirmed.

"I've never heard of anyone eating clay," I said.

"You probably never been to some o' the places I been. You live in the lap o' luxury here," he said.

I stared at him, trying to discern any hint of sarcasm or fibbage (I don't think that's a word either) on his leathery countenance. Couldn't. "You're serious, aren't you?"

"Yes, I'm serious! What do you take me for?" grumbled Mr. P.

I took him for an often-grouchy old man living far from his natural element. I didn't say so. What I said was, "Want some soup?"

"Yeah, I can handle some soup. You make it?"

"Aunt Vi made it," I retorted.

"Daisy, you should sit down," said Sam. "I'll heat the soup. Lou, you gather some plates and bowls will you? Daisy's been on her feet too much today."

"Sure," Mr. P. said. He didn't grumble at Sam I noticed.

"Did you see that doc at the hospital?" Mr. Prophet asked as he went to the pantry and selected some plates and bowls.

"What doctor?" I asked from my perch on a kitchen chair. Because Sam had brought me another chair, I put my feet on it. I knew the rules by this time. Sam was taking care of me, sweetheart that he was.

"The doctor you met today, o' course!"

"There are lots of doctors in hospitals you know," I said. Then I remembered the monologue upon which I'd eavesdropped. "Oh, you mean Dr. Vialargo?"

"Who the hell else would I mean?" snarled Mr. P.

"Dr. Benjamin," I said. "Dr. Greenlaw. Dr. Dearing—"

"Dammit. I don't care about any o' them other doctors," hollered Mr. Prophet from the pantry. "The only doc I'm interested in is the one who was at Harold's place this morning. Cripes. You already know that. Why're you bein' a damn mule about it?"

So far in approximately two or three hours, I'd been compared to a horse, a pony and now a mule. Interesting.

"Calm down, you two," Sam suggested, a hint of humor in his voice.

"Cripes. How do you stand it, Sam?" muttered Mr. Prophet, clumping into the kitchen from the pantry.

"Daisy's not so bad, Lou," said Sam. "In fact, she's pretty darned good most of the time. She does like to lecture every now and then."

"Every now and then?" grunted Mr. Prophet. "Hellkatoot."

Because Vi had stayed behind to clean the kitchen after Sam and I left for the hospital, the kitchen was clean as a whistle, as was the oilskin covering the kitchen table. Mr. Prophet laid plates and bowls at three places and went to the silverware drawer.

I took pity on the old goat. "We didn't see Dr. Vialargo at the hospital," I told him.

"Huh," he said, tossing me a squint.

TWELVE

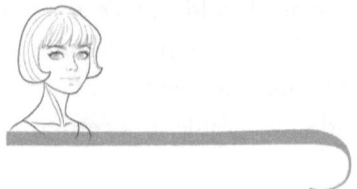

W hen Sam had filled bowls with Vi's delicious butter bean
and ham soup, opened a new jar of dill pickles, and cut
some bread slices for us to eat with our soup, I reluctantly removed
my feet from the chair Sam had positioned for me. We began eating.
Because I didn't see the butter dish on the table, I shoved my chair
back in order to rise and get it.

"What do you need, Daisy?" asked Sam sharply. "You don't
have to get up. Just tell me what you want."

"Butter," I said. "I'm not helpless you know, Sam. I'm only with
child."

"True, but I'll get the butter anyway," he said and rose to do it.

When he came back with the butter dish, I said, "Thank you."

"You're welcome," he said.

"Huh," said Mr. Prophet.

Once we'd had a few bites of our soup and bread and I'd
gnawed my pickle down to a stub, I looked at Mr. Prophet. His head
was bent over his soup bowl, and I could tell he wasn't in the mood
for conversation. As that had never stopped me before and I didn't
see any reason for it to stop me now, I said, "Why are you so interested in Dr. Vialargo?"

Lifting his head and giving me a hideous scowl, Mr. Prophet said, "No partic'lar reason."

"Applesauce." I retorted.

"Don't got none on the table," he said.

"You know what I mean," I said. "When you were introduced to Dr. Vialargo, you almost suffered a spasm, and you've been in a rotten mood ever since. What's rattled you about the new doctor?"

"None o' your business, snoopy."

"Fiddle, it is too my business. Ever since Dr. Vialargo showed up at Harold's house, you've been ugly to me. All day, darn it," I said.

"Ain't," he said. "Neither of us've been here all day."

"That's true, Daisy," said Sam. "I don't suppose you'd allow Lou to eat his supper in peace, would you?"

"Pooh," I said, but Sam had a point. "Oh, very well."

"Thanks," said Sam, attempting to stifle a laugh.

"Yeah, yer givin' me a bellyache," said Mr. Prophet.

"Fiddle-faddle," I said, loath to give up my probe. "Something about that doctor bothered you, and I want to know what it was."

"Why?" asked Mr. P. "Ain't none o' yer business."

"It might be eventually," I said. "You're probably going to have to see him again, you know."

"How come?" said Mr. P.

Good question. "*I* don't know! But you probably will. Sam and I—and Flossie and Johnnie—will be having a lot to do with doctors in the near future." I thought of a brilliant excuse for him to spill the beans. Oh, all right, so maybe it wasn't precisely brilliant. I said, "If you know anything about Dr. Vialargo that Harold, Sam, or I should know, you should tell us. If you know he's a secret toper or used to kill people for fun in Tucson, you *need* to tell us!"

"That's going a little far, isn't it?" asked Sam, lifting his head and staring at me. "Did the doctor say or do anything that made you think he might be a wrong one?"

Drat. "No," I admitted. "But I've never seen Mr. Prophet shocked witless before either, and he was shocked witless when he met Dr. Vialargo."

"Weren't neither," snarled Mr. Prophet. "He jist looks like somebody I used to know, is all."

"Oh," I said, pleased he'd at least admitted something. "Whom did he look like?" I tried to sound innocent.

"Daisy," said Sam. "You really *are* nosy."

"Yeah," said Mr. P. "Ain't none o' yer business."

"Bother," I said, giving up. After thinking about it as I chewed another bite of pickle, I said, "You're correct. I was being pushy, and I'm sorry."

Even though I still wanted to know.

I didn't add that part.

Mr. Prophet sniffed meaningfully.

Sam grinned at me.

I ate another spoonful of soup.

After dinner, Sam washed up and ordered me to the living room. "You don't need to be on your feet anymore today," he said.

"Thank you, Sam," I said. "Spike and I can resume reading *An American Tragedy*, although it's a depressing book. I want to read Mr. Biggers' latest, but it's always out at the library. Not even Regina has been able to snag a copy for me, so I'm going to Grenville's Books on Monday and will just buy myself a copy."

"Extravagant," said Sam,

"Pooh," I retorted. "I love Charlie Chan, and this time Mr. Biggers has him in California!"

"Which time?"

"This time in his new book! It's called *The Chinese Parrot*. Mr. Biggers lives on Orange Grove right here in Pasadena!"

"Yes," said Sam indulgently. "You've told me so several times."

"Well, I think it's exciting to live in the same city as an author whose books I admire so much. Pa feels the same way about Zane Grey, but I don't like his books as much as the Charlie Chan books I've read."

"I see. I like Grey's books," said Sam.

"So does Pa," I said.

"They're stupid!" came Mr. Prophet's voice from the kitchen.

"You ought to write about your own experiences in the Wild West," I called to him. "They'd be realistic anyway."

"Nobody'd publish 'em," said Mr. P.

"How do you know?" I asked.

"Because they don't want the truth in them books. They want some make-believe place with make-believe people in 'em. Just like in the pictures these days."

All at once a thought niggled my brain—not unlike a curious worm. That sounds disgusting, doesn't it? But it suddenly occurred to me that Mr. Prophet might tell me some of his stories, I could write them down and maybe someone actually *would* publish an accurate western novel. I didn't voice the thought because it was even younger than the child I currently carried. Still, it was an appealing notion.

At least to me. Mr. Prophet would most likely scoff and rebel. Ah well. Back to *An American Tragedy*. I knew the book would end badly. Bah. I needed a new P.G. Wodehouse book. Along with *The Chinese Parrot*.

"Want to go to the library and the bookstore with me on Monday, Mr. Prophet?" I hollered.

"Library *and* a bookstore?" he said skeptically.

"Yes. I need to buy a book unless it's suddenly available at the library, and it probably won't be."

"Eh, what the hell. Sure," said the old reprobate.

I settled into a big, comfy chair in the living room, turned on the nearby standing lamp and patted what was left of my lap for Spike to sit on. Spike didn't instantly jump up. I gazed down at him. He gazed up at me.

"Oh, very well," I said. I moved my big tummy and the rest of myself to the sofa and turned on the lamp sitting on the lovely table at the fireplace end of the sofa. When I patted the space beside me this time, Spike was glad to oblige.

I'm not sure how long we read on the sofa, but Sam woke me up at about ten p.m. and said it was time for bed.

It was probably a good thing that he held my arm as we walked up the stairs to our bedroom, because I'd not realized how exhausted I'd become during the exciting—perhaps chaotic is a better word—day. Sam helped me out of my daytime clothes, unclasped my gold chain and laid it carefully on the vanity table so that none of the charms fell off. Then he made me hold up my arms so he could slide my nightgown over my head.

"You did too much today, Daisy," he said in a repressive voice.

"Yes, well, I didn't have much choice in the matter, did I?"

"I suppose not," Sam admitted. "But if anybody else calls about a baby left on a doorstep, call me before you do anything about it. I promise I won't instantly toss the baby into an orphanage."

I was just about awake enough to give him a small chuckle. "Thanks, Sam. You're a good man."

"I try to be," he said as he scooped me up—he was also strong; I must have weighed a ton by then—and settled me gently onto my side of the bed. I'm not sure, but I think I was asleep before Sam joined me in repose.

Sunday morning dawned, as it usually did, too early for my personal comfort. Mind you, until recently, I'd generally wake up refreshed and energetic most mornings. Not at this stage of my pregnancy. I felt like an overstuffed walrus out of the ocean. I "oofed" and grunted my way to the bathroom, where I washed and put on a very little bit of makeup. Then I galumphed back to the bedroom and made the bed. Sam had exited the bed before me. So had Spike.

I suspected both of my gallant protectors were downstairs in the kitchen. With luck, one of them was fixing breakfast so I wouldn't have to. I was such a slacker, wasn't I?

Nevertheless, I felt little guilt that morning as I peered into my overstuffed closet and selected a dress I'd made for myself in anticipation of my width to come. I'd searched through about five hundred patterns for expectant women at Maxime's Fabrics on Colorado Street, but most of them looked either uncomfortable or wildly impractical. When you have no waist, why would you want a dress with a belt, even a belt that fastened below your bulge? Or a top and skirt? True, the skirts had front panels one's stomach could expand into, but I'd finally decided to improvise.

The outfit I selected that morning looked like a skirt and top, but it was actually a top sewn onto what looked like the skirt. Take that, pattern makers! It was pretty too. The skirt part of the dress was a solid blue, and the top was a pretty blue-and-white flower pattern. I'd sewed them together using a strip of fabric hidden on what would have been the skirt's waist if it had one, which it didn't. I tell you, I was a marvelous seamstress, even if I wasn't much good at anything else.

The stores and patternmakers even tried to get women to wear maternity corsets, for heaven's sake! Why would a woman want to wear a corset that squished both herself and her baby? Phooey on corsets. I didn't even bother with my bust flattener in those days. My bulge stuck out so much, no one could see my bosoms. Anyway, if an inquisitive person wondered about my upper torso, I'd sewn a pretty V-neck collar in white with blue embroidery around the edges. I also wore low-heeled Mary-Jane pumps. And my hat was a tasteful beige cloche upon which I'd pinned blue flowers I'd created out of the skirt material.

You didn't want to know all that, did you? I'm sorry, but fashion designers seemed to have decided women in the 1920s were supposed to be pencil-thin and have no waists, hips or bosoms, and I resented it. Even when I wasn't pregnant, I had curves, darn it!

Ahem. Back to the bedroom.

After I'd arrayed myself to look as presentable as possible given the shape I was in, I went downstairs. Sure enough, I smelled not only coffee percolating but something frying! Sam was *so* good to me. I walked into the kitchen, prepared to thank him, when I saw not Sam but Mr. Prophet standing at the range, frying pieces of ham.

"I didn't know we had any ham," I said, which wasn't the most polite opening line I'd ever voiced. I should have thanked him for frying the ham.

He turned a squinty on me. "Yer aunt brought over some ham. Said it was left over from the soup she made yesterday."

"Thank you for cooking the slices for us." I glanced around the kitchen and still saw no Sam. "Where's Sam?"

"Outside pickin' chives. He aims to fix us all cheese omelets with chives in 'em."

"My goodness! I didn't know Sam could fix omelets."

"Anybody kin cook omelets," said Mr. Prophet.

"I can't," I told him.

"No surprise there," he said.

"True. Is Spike with Sam outside?"

"Yeah. Spike and Yuyu went off together, playin'. I suspect Spike'll come in when the food's ready. Kinda like his mistress."

"It's not completely ready yet," I said. "I think Sam was right and I did too much yesterday."

"Mebbe."

"You think I'm lazy and useless, don't you?" I said, feeling both miffed and guilty.

After he flipped another piece of ham and judged it to be at the correct degree of doneness, he used the spatula to lift it out of the frying pan and put it on a plate with a piece of brown butcher's paper on it to drain. I continued to watch him for a couple of minutes. He was much more adept in the kitchen than I, even after months of tutelage from my aunt. Clearly, he didn't aim to answer my question. Guess that was answer enough.

"You're good at this," I finally told Mr. Prophet.

"Had to be," he said.

"Is there anything I can do to help with breakfast without ruining it?" I asked humbly.

"You kin break a bunch of eggs into a bowl. Try not to get pieces of shells in with the eggs."

"Aha!" I cried happily. "I can do that."

"Huh," he said.

Mr. Prophet had about as much confidence in my cooking skills as had I. Nevertheless, I went to the Frigidaire, lifted out a bowl full of eggs, and set it on the kitchen table. Then I got a mixing bowl and started cracking eggs into it.

After cracking the fifth or sixth egg—I should have been counting them, but my mind wandered—I heard the back door open. Seconds later, Spike bounded into the kitchen, paid me a brief visit of welcome, and then charged over to the stove and sat at Mr. Prophet's feet. It figured. Spike loved me, but Mr. Prophet was cooking *ham*.

Shortly after Spike appeared, Sam strode into the room carrying a basket which I presumed contained chives along with some other garden produce.

"Morning, sleepyhead," he said cheerily.

"Morning," I said, trying to match his cheer. Didn't come within a mile and a half.

But as the morning progressed, I became happier, and that's only partly because I partook of a delicious breakfast I didn't have to fix myself. In truth, I don't think I *could* have fixed such delicious omelets. Sam said he'd teach me, which was almost enough to make my mood skid downhill again, but not quite.

THIRTEEN

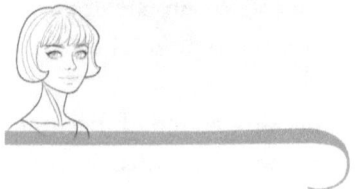

Because the day was chilly and lumbering up the street to church had become somewhat tiring for me, Sam drove my parents, aunt, and me to the First Methodist Episcopal Church on the corner of Marengo and Colorado. Mr. Prophet stayed home with the promise that he'd clean up the dishes if nobody forced him to go to church.

I don't think he was joking.

When we reached the church, Sam let me get out on the Marengo side of the building because that's where the entrance to the choir room was. I attempted not to waddle to the door of the room wherein we choir members kept our choir robes, music folders, and hymnals.

"Daisy!" cried Lucille Zollinger when she spotted me. "You're getting to be as big as a house!"

With a frown for her tactlessness, I said, "If you get pregnant, you'll be big as a house one day too, Lucy Zollinger."

"I'm sorry, Daisy. I didn't mean to be mean. I hope Albert and I will have children one day. We just finished moving into our new home on Holliston, and I plan to decorate a nursery for any babies to come." Her cheeks turned a fiery red, and I knew she was embarrassed to be discussing such things.

"How nice, Lucy," I said sweetly. "We have a nursery upstairs. Sam said he's going to build a baby gate at the top of the staircase so the little fellow won't fall down the stairs when he begins to toddle." I didn't say the next thought I entertained, which was that they'd best get that nursery fixed soon because her precious Albert was already old enough to be their baby's grandfather. Sometimes, I'm malicious as a riled rattlesnake. I try not to let the rattler out too often.

"What a good idea," said Lucy, her cheeks fading to their usual pallid ivory.

I gave her a big smile, and we were friends again. I swear, people drove me crazy.

To be perfectly candid, women as far along as I didn't generally show themselves in public to all and sundry. We pregnant women were supposed to stay home with our feet up and do nothing. Nertz to that, I say. I love to work in the garden and I love to sing, and I wasn't about to give up either one of those activities just because I was going to have a baby in Pasadena, California. I'm sure women who worked on farms in, say, Fresno, wore tents and still tilled fields, harvested crops, and took care of their other children.

Ahem. Didn't mean to get distracted.

I put on my choir robe, which was large and generously proportioned so it didn't look silly. For instance, I didn't look any more bulky than one of our lesser sopranos, Mrs. Finster. Her husband, Mr. Finster, was one of our basses. Neither he nor Mr. Warden, another bass, had as good a singing voice as Sam. I hadn't yet persuaded Sam to join the choir. He claimed his duties might call him away at inconvenient times. I think that was just an excuse.

Then I got my hymnal and took my place in line so we could process into the church after Mrs. Fleming's organ prelude. I sat in the front row of the choir stall beside Lucy, although she was a soprano and I was an alto. Because we were often made to sing duets together by our choir director, Mr. Floy Hostetter, he had us sit together. For the last couple of Sundays, he'd been eyeing the two of us as if we might be *Mutt and Jeff*. Lucy was tall and skinny, and I was shorter—five feet, four inches more or less—and not at all skinny. Still, he hadn't made me sit in a back row yet. He hadn't made Lucy and me sing any duets for a while either. Hmmm…

Never mind that. After Mrs. Fleming gave us a rousing introduction and Mr. Hostetter pointed his baton at us, we choir members walked onto the dais and into the choir section singing "Rejoice, the Lord is King." I liked the hymn because it had a wonderful, happy-sounding tune.

I consider myself a good Christian girl—well, woman now—but I still preferred lively tunes to slow and lugubrious ones. Don't tell anyone, but I don't like "Silent Night," which I think is considered sacrilegious, but it's so *slow*. I'd rather sing "Good Christian Men Rejoice" than "Silent Night" any old day, including Christmas.

The Reverend Merle Negley Smith greeted the congregants and one of our lay speakers read some announcements, led us in the Call to Worship, and had us bow our heads as he read the invocation.

After that the congregation was asked to rise and sing "Be Still my Soul." Which makes me take back my earlier words about not caring for slow hymns. I guess it depends on the music. "Be Still My Soul" is lovely, although I still think "Silent Night" is boring. I'm sure I must be wrong, but I can't seem to help it.

Another lay speaker led us in the Affirmation of Faith, after which we sang "Gloria Patrie," and we got to sit again for the offering plates to be passed. Before people could pass them, of course, Rev. Smith prayed for the offering.

By then I wasn't paying a whole lot of attention. My mind kept straying to Harold's cousin's baby and what the heck we were supposed to do with her. I'd run through prospective parents in my head, and I had actually wondered if Lucy Zollinger and her husband Albert might be a good choice. It sounded, however, as if Lucy aimed to give birth to her own children if they ever got around to having any. Besides, I thought Albert was a trifle old to be starting a family. By the time the kid got to kindergarten, he'd be a senile old man.

Unkind yet again, Daisy. What was the matter with me? Harold claimed my uneven moods were caused by fluctuating hormone levels. As I don't even know what a hormone is, I can't comment.

Then I considered Mr. and Mrs. Homer Fellowes. I'd gone through school with Gladys Pennywhistle Fellowes, and she was a nice person if rather stiff. She'd been the class brain. She'd even loved *algebra*, which astonishes me to this day. Her husband, Dr. Homer Fellowes, taught something incomprehensible to most of us mortals at the California Institute of Technology, so he was clearly smart too.

But no. The Felloweses were good people, but they already had a young child. Besides, I imagine any kids of theirs would be expected to excel in everything. Great expectations were fine and dandy, but I think—feel free to disagree with me—they're some-times more apt to stifle a sensitive child than encourage him or her.

I stopped thinking when Mr. Hostetter rapped his baton quite sharply against his music stand and startled me back into paying attention. Good thing, too, as we were supposed to stand again and sing the Doxology. He gave me a frown when he announced the next hymn, "Master, Speak! Thy Servant Heareth," which I hadn't been doing. Hearing, I mean. In spite of my inattention, the congre-gation and choir plowed through the song and we choir members got to sit again. In those days, I liked sitting a whole lot better than standing.

Again my mind wandered as Pastor Smith asked the congrega-tion if they had any special joys or concerns. Some of them did, but I wasn't paying attention. Again. If I could have, I'd have asked everyone to pray for Harold, his cousin's baby and his poor cousin, but nobody connected with the problem would have thanked me for it. However, I bowed my head along with everyone else and kept thinking about what I'd been thinking about since yesterday morning.

When Lucy nudged me with her elbow, I gave a start and lifted my head. Crumb, I'd almost missed standing for the anthem! As I stood, I vowed to pay attention to the rest of the service.

Fortunately, our anthem that day was one of my favorites, "O

For a Thousand Tongues to Sing." I'd known the alto part since I was in the children's choir many years earlier. It's always the first hymn in any Methodist hymnal perhaps because it was written by Charles Wesley who, with his brother John, founded the Methodist Church.

Then came the sermon, and my feckless brain wandered back to the baby again. I swear, I was useless that day.

I can't say I was sorry when the minister gave the benediction, and the choir and congregation stood and sang, "God be with You Till We Meet Again." Because Mr. Hostetter required it of us, we exited the choir area in an orderly fashion. Once in the choir room, though, we bumped into each other as we disrobed, hung our gowns on the rack, and stuffed our hymnals and music folders in their assigned cubby holes.

When I managed to shove my way out of the choir room, my family, except for Sam, had gathered on the church lawn on the Marengo side of the building. We'd already decided to skip cookies and tea (or coffee) in Fellowship Hall in favor of Sunday dinner at my parents' house.

"Where's Sam?" I asked.

"Gone to get the car," said Pa. "He thinks you're doing too much, Daisy." He said it with a twinkle in his eye, but I knew he agreed with Sam.

"Bunkum," I said. "Yesterday was a busy day, but most of the time I don't do much."

"That's right," said Vi. "You went to see Harold at the hospital, didn't you? Is the lad all right? Was he injured or sick?"

"Harold?" said Ma. "What's the matter with Harold?"

Both women appeared worried. As I taxed my brain to come up with an excuse for Sam and me going to the hospital to see Harold the prior afternoon, my benumbed convolutions were saved by Sam, who pulled his Hudson to the curb near us. I hurried to the machine and slid into the front passenger seat because Sam had opened the door. My parents and Vi took their places in the backseat when Sam opened their door.

Pa wasn't pleased by my failure to answer his question I guess, because he asked the same question of Sam once we were all seated.

"A cousin of his had been rushed to the hospital," said Sam. "Harold said he needed Daisy to go to the hospital and hold his hand and give him comfort."

"That's not what he said," I objected.

Everyone else in the car laughed, so I guess it didn't matter.

"True, but he did want you to deal with his—Was she a niece or a cousin? I can't remember," said Sam.

"I think we figured out she was a cousin. Maybe a cousin once removed. I don't know how all of those relationships work."

"Why did Harold need you?" asked Ma, always practical. It was a good question. I didn't have a good answer. Or even a bad one.

Again Sam came to my rescue. "His cousin or niece"—Sam turned his head to wink at me—"had just lost a baby. She was sad and discouraged, and Harold thought Daisy might give her some comfort."

"Oh, the poor thing," said Vi.

"I shouldn't think she'd appreciate seeing a healthy pregnant woman after just losing a child of her own," said Ma, being practical again.

"She was asleep when we got there," I said, finally prodding my brain into gear. "She didn't even see me. You're right though, Ma. She probably would have been unhappy." I frowned. "It was silly of Harold to ask me to go there."

"Now, now," said Vi. "Harold is a kind and sensitive fellow. He probably didn't even think about your...uh..."

"Shape?" I offered.

"Yes, your shape when he asked you to be with him. He only knew you too are a kindhearted person. The good Lord knows you've been giving his mother comfort and compassion for a million years or so."

"Valid point," I said.

"Yes, I guess it is," said Ma. "You haven't talked much about Mrs. Pinkerton lately, Daisy. Is she still mourning that awful daughter of hers?"

"Probably," I said. "I don't think she ever understood how truly evil Stacy was. But she and Mr. Pinkerton went to Santa Barbara for a couple of months."

"That's right," said Ma. "Silly of me not to remember. After all, Vi's been home every day for a couple of weeks now."

"I'm thinking about retiring," announced Aunt Vi.

"You are?" came a tuneful quartet from the car's other passengers.

"I am." Vi sounded not merely firm, but happy about her decision. "In fact, I *know* I'm going to retire. I love to cook, but my feet are getting bad from standing all the time. Besides, we don't really need the money I bring in any longer, do we?"

This was a sound question to ask. As the women in my family had been the primary breadwinners for years, *did* they need Vi's contributions any longer?

Sam pulled up to the curb in front of my parents' bungalow, right across the street from Sam's and mine as silence reigned. Then it was Sam who answered Vi's question.

"No, you don't need to rely on Vi's contributions any longer."

He exited the driver's side of the car. Ma, Pa, Vi, and I all looked at each other. Finally Ma said, "What does he mean by that?"

"I don't know," I said. When Sam opened my door and I heaved myself out of the Hudson, I said, "What do you mean, Sam?"

Ma, Vi, and Pa exited the backseat of the car when Sam opened their door.

"I know what he means," said Pa. "And he's right." He smiled at everyone.

"About what?" asked Sam.

"About not needing Vi's earnings any longer," I said.

"Oh," said Sam. "That's easy. Right, Joe?" He grinned at my father.

"Right," said Pa.

"Wait until we get into the house and tell us all about it, please," said Ma. I thought she ought to be able to retire too, but I didn't have a single clue about my parents' financial situation.

"Good idea," said Sam and Pa together.

We walked across the grass verge and the sidewalk and up to the big front porch of my parents' bungalow. Pa unlocked the front door —we'd never bothered locking doors until a couple of years before when it seemed as if every villain in Pasadena was trying to kill me —and ushered us all inside.

Rosebud greeted us with happy yaps and leaps. Her tail going like a fan, she relayed her joy at having her people home again.

"We were only gone for an hour and a half, Rosie," I told her.

She leaped on me. Good thing I was prepared for her. Mrs. Hanratty had taught those of us who had taken our dogs to her obedience classes to lift a knee if a dog jumps on one. The dog will bump the knee, bounce backward and then the human with the knee can kneel or shake a finger or whatever so the dog will learn not to jump.

I think this maneuver works better with some dogs than with others. For instance, Rosebud didn't seem inclined to learn anything she didn't want to learn. My Spike, on the other hand, had come in first in his class at the Pasanita Dog Obedience Club and was prob-ably the best-trained dog in California. He never jumped up on visi-tors to our house unless they asked him to.

"Very well," said Ma once we were all in the house, which smelled like roasting leg of lamb. Glorious aroma! "Why don't we need Vi's money? I think you should retire too, Vi, if you're able to."

"Sam and I talked a few years back," said Pa, still smiling. "He brought his financial portfolio over when he asked me if I'd approve of his courting Daisy."

My gaze paid a visit to the ceiling. *Such* an old-fashioned notion. Asking for permission to court a girl? Positively Medieval.

"And nobody told me," I said grumpily. "I thought Sam had taken up with Linda Killebrew across the street, because he kept going over there when I was laid up."

"I kept going over there because I wanted to buy the Killebrews' house," said Sam as if I ought to have deduced that on my own. He gave me a whole lot more credit in the deduction department than I deserved. Besides, I'd just been hit by a car and was in horrible pain.

Amid general laughter—I didn't join in—Pa said, "Anyhow, Sam and I came up with a sound financial plan for the family. We're not exactly rolling in dough, but we have sufficient plenty invested to make it possible for Vi to retire any old time she wants to."

"How wonderful!" said Ma.

"And you can too, Peggy," said Pa, reaching for her hand.

"Oh, my!" said Ma. "You mean I won't have to be head book-keeper at the Hotel Marengo any longer if I don't want to?"

"That's exactly what I mean," said Pa.

My generally undemonstrative mother threw her arms around my father and gave him the biggest hug I'd ever seen.

Sam, Vi, and I looked upon this display of affection gladly. In fact, I got kind of teary-eyed, but I think that was just because I was about to foal. In Harold's words. Then Vi said, "I'll go get dinner on the table."

"I'll help!" I said.

Sam said, "You'll do no such thing. You'll sit down in the living room and relax. I'll help Vi. You too, Joe and Peggy," he said to my parents. "You and Daisy just sit down and put your feet up while Vi and I set dinner out."

My parents and I didn't need to be commanded twice. We grinned at each other and walked into the living room. I didn't precisely put my feet up. Rather, I sat on the piano bench and riffled through the sheet music already on the piano stand. Then I selected a piece and began playing "The Toreador Song" from Bizet's *Carmen*. I forgot to mention playing the piano as something I loved to do, didn't I? Luckily I could still reach the pedals on my parents' upright piano and on the baby grand piano Sam had bought for me, which resided across the street in our own bungalow.

I'd just finished the piece when Sam came into the living room to tell Ma, Pa, and me that dinner was on the table. We rose, went to the dining room and sat.

We were almost halfway through the meal before the telephone rang. I gave a start. A telephone ringing in my parents' house always used to mean that Mrs. Pinkerton was in a dither about something and needed my instant presence to consult the tarot cards, use the Ouija board or conduct a séance. I glanced around the table to find everyone else seated at attention, Pa and Vi with forks suspended in midair. I suspect everyone present was recalling those the not-so-good old days too.

"I'll get it," said Sam, rising from his chair next to mine and walking to the kitchen, where the telephone hung on a wall.

"Oh dear," said Vi.

Couldn't have said it better myself.

FOURTEEN

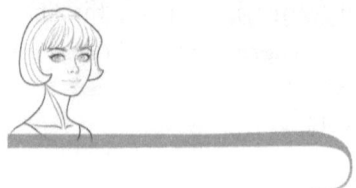

A s things turned out, the telephone call was for Sam so it was a good thing he answered the 'phone. We all stopped chewing, swallowed and listened to him speaking on our end of the wire. Sam's voice was deep and it traveled well, although some of his words weren't as clear as they might have been if we were all in the same room. I thought I heard the word "Kincaid" once, but I wasn't sure. After he hung the receiver on the hook, though, I think we all heard his heavy sigh.

When he appeared in the doorway, he glanced first at me. "I have to go to the scene of a crime," he said.

"Can't you finish dinner first?" asked Vi.

After frowning for what seemed like six hours, but was probably a split-second, Sam nodded once, hard, and said, "Yes. By golly, I *can* finish dinner." He walked over and took his seat beside me again.

"Must be an important crime, if they scouted you out here," I said.

"You sound like Lou, Daisy," said Sam.

"Piffle. You know what I mean," I said.

"Yes, I do. And yes, it's an important crime."

"Are we allowed to know anything about it?" I asked him.

"No," said Sam, spearing a piece of lamb and sticking it into his mouth.

"Don't pester the policeman, Daisy," said Pa with a smile in his voice.

"Listen to your father, Mrs. Rotondo," said Sam after swallowing.

I gave a sigh of my own, but I knew when I was beaten. Besides, I could quiz Sam about the crime later, in our own home. Whether he'd answer my prying questions was anybody's guess.

Because of my condition, nobody would allow me to wash up the dishes after dinner concluded. I was beginning to think pregnancy had several advantages, except that it was tiring and toward the end, a woman felt like a bloated penguin—not that I know how bloated penguins feel—and you ended up with a baby when it was all over. And that was only if you were lucky.

Then again, poor Melanie Robinson'd had a baby, and the birth hadn't been lucky for her. Which just goes to show yet again that everything in this life depends on one's circumstances, and one's circumstances can be iffy. I mean, running away from home with a fellow to whom she wasn't married didn't sound like a wise decision to me, but I had a wonderful family. Perhaps Harold had been mistaken, and Melanie's home life hadn't been as blissful as he'd assumed.

As usual when we dined at my parents' home, Vi packed a couple of containers full of leftovers for Sam and me to take home. "How nice. You won't need to cook again today, Daisy."

I hadn't cooked even once today, but I didn't think Vi needed to know it. "Thanks, Vi." I gave her a kiss on the cheek. "We both appreciate everything you do for us."

"Yes, we do," Sam confirmed.

"Oh, go along with you both," she said. It was one of her favorite sayings. Even though I'm not sure how it came to be or why, Sam and I both knew what it meant. Therefore, we smiled at her, and Sam carried the small cardboard box she'd packed for us.

Sam drove me home, which would have been a silly thing to do because we lived directly across the street from my parents. That Sunday it wasn't silly, though, because he then had to drive to the scene of a crime after dropping the food and me off.

"What crime is it that you have to investigate, Sam?" I asked as he pulled into our driveway.

"Murder."

"Good heavens! That's a pretty nasty crime"

"Yes. Won't know how nasty until I get to the scene and look."

"Where is the scene?" I asked.

"You don't need to know that," he said, blast it.

"Will you tell me about it when you get home?" I asked pleadingly.

"As ever, I'll tell you as much as I can about the matter," he told me.

I huffed. "All right. I hope you *can* tell me."

"We'll see," said Sam as he exited the driver's side of the Hudson, walked around it and opened my door for me.

Sam then opened the porch's side gate—there was another gate in the front—and walked me to the door. We both heard Spike's joyful yips of greeting. When Sam opened the door, the two of us knelt—well, I bent over some—to give Spike our own joyful pets and pats. Then Sam had to haul me to my feet again.

Sam, Spike and I walked to the kitchen, where Sam unpacked the cardboard box and began transferring its contents to the Frigidaire. "We can take the box back to Vi when we return the dishes," he said.

"Good idea. Then maybe she'll refill it for us," I said.

"You've been cooking some mighty good meals lately, sweetheart."

"Thanks, Sam." I appreciated his comment. Still didn't enjoy cooking, however.

Spike was intensely curious about a large tinfoil-wrapped package containing sliced lamb. I unsealed it and broke off two little bites of lamb. We had to be careful not to allow Spike to get fat because dachshund backs are so long. If you allow a dachshund to get too fat, his or her back will go out. Sam and I, however, couldn't allow Spike to go through this day without at *least* a tiny slice or two of lamb. He'd already smelled it, and it would be cruel to withhold it all from him. I made him work for his treat, though.

"Spike," I said, holding a scrap of lamb in my fingers and looking upon my precious hound with love. Well, and lamb. "What's one plus two?"

He knew this game. He started barking. After his third bark, I moved the little finger on my right hand, and he stopped barking. I told him he was a good boy and tossed him the first bite of lamb, which he swallowed happily.

In order for him to get his second treat, I said, "*Gesundheit.*"

Instantly, Spike sneezed. I gave him the second bite of lamb. "I don't like speaking German to my dog," I told Sam as I turned and washed my hands at the kitchen sink.

"He already knows the word, so you're stuck with it," Sam reminded me.

"I should have taught him 'God bless you' instead of the stupid German word. Germans killed my Billy." It was an old and bitter grievance, but it still haunted me.

"I know. But Germany is paying a stiff price for Kaiser Bill's war," said Sam, his voice gentle. He'd been Billy's best friend during Billy's life, and we both mourned him yet.

"They *should* pay," I said viciously. "After what they did."

"The Treaty of Versailles imposed huge fines and reparations on Germany. Or the Weimar Republic, I guess is what they want to be called now. By the end of 1923, something like forty-billion marks were worth the equivalent of one of our American dollars. It probably wouldn't be difficult for a smooth-talking dictator to convince most of the German people to follow him. I'd hate to see that happen."

"How come?"

"When people are so downtrodden they can't feed their kids, they're liable to fall for any scheme, good or bad, if it promises them a sufficiency of food."

"Are Germans really starving?" I asked, not quite aghast. It still hurt my heart even to *think* about Teutonic anything-at-all. I went so far as to call Spike a "liberty hound" rather than a dachshund when introducing him to people. Anyhow, Spike isn't German. He and Rosebud both were born in Altadena, California.

"The everyday people in Germany starved during the war years because Germany spent all its money on warfare. What with punishments handed out after the war, I suspect some of them are still starving. Don't forget that the Allied countries set up a powerful blockade to prevent the Central Powers from getting supplies, including food."

"I didn't even know they had a blockade. More power to us," I said. Not nice of me. But darn it, Germans had killed my husband, they'd killed Aunt Vi's only child, and they'd caused Johnnie Buckingham, Billy, and thousands of other American soldiers and sailors to suffer hideous shell shock. Maybe some Germans suffered too, but I didn't care about them.

"You might want to soften your attitude before Junior's born," said Sam, grinning and patting my belly. "If Germany rebounds and holds a grudge, we'll probably be fighting another war in twenty years or so."

"Don't say that, Sam!"

"Only giving a gentle reminder, sweetie. I don't want any child of mine to have to go to war. I got my draft notice, but I was never called up. I'm glad of that now, but I felt like a slacker then."

"I wondered about that when you and Billy were such good buddies. I resented you because you were well and whole, and Billy was a shattered wreck." It hurt to admit this, but it was true.

"Figured as much," said Sam. "But we made it up, didn't we?"

"Yes," I said, attempting to hug him. He helped by shifting to one side so my belly didn't poke him.

"But I've got to go. I promise to tell you whatever I can when I get back home."

"Thank you. I wish they wouldn't call you on Sundays." My voice was wistful.

"So do I, but it's my job," said Sam.

And, with one last peck on the cheek, Sam left Spike and me to rest for the remainder of the afternoon. Before we took our places on the living room sofa, I let Spike out back to do his duty as a dog. He did it admirably, so I grabbed an old newspaper. Followed him outside to pick it up and tossed it in the trash. Darned near toppled over when I bent to retrieve Spike's deposit. *Bend your knees, Daisy*, I told myself. *You can't bend from the waist any longer.*

Not having a waist was becoming awkward. I hoped our son would be born early-ish. Not so early that it would put either of us in peril, but early enough so that I could get rid of my ponderous protuberance soon.

Spike and I were making our way to the living room in order to take a nice nap when the telephone rang. Staring at it with loathing, I nevertheless answered it.

"Hello," I said, attempting to sound cordial.

"Good God, Daisy, do you know what's happened now?" At least Harold hadn't yelled into the mouthpiece this time.

"Don't have a single clue, Harold. And a good afternoon to you, too."

"It's not a good afternoon! I don't think I'll ever have a good day again in this lifetime."

"For heaven's sake, what's the matter now? If somebody else dumped a baby on your doorstep—"

"No, nobody's deposited another baby on our doorstep, but something almost as bad has happened. I'm surprised you don't know about it already."

"We've been at church and then at my parents' house for dinner," I said. Then I recalled the telephone call Sam had received and his recent departure. "Oh dear, it's about the baby though, isn't it?"

"Yes, dammit! At least I think it is."

"Sam was called out to the scene of a murder," I said. "I hope the victim wasn't Melanie. I hope she's not the killer either."

"It wasn't Melanie in either role," said Harold. "She's still in the hospital. But now a man has been found, apparently stabbed with a thin-bladed knife."

Interesting, but I didn't see what it had to do with Harold. "I don't know what that has to do with you, Harold."

"He had a driver's license in the name of James Smithfield in his wallet, along with a crumpled note with both Melanie's and my names on it! *That's* what it has to do with me!"

"Well, I didn't do it, so you needn't scold me," I said tartly. "Oh dear, do you think that's Melanie's…whatever he was?"

"The father of her child? The so-called Jimmy Smith?"

"Yes. I couldn't think of his name. Do you think the dead guy is him? He? Whatever it's supposed to be?"

"I have no idea, but I fear Melanie's going to have to identify the body. If she does, I'll have to be there to hold her hand. And *you'll* have to be there to hold *my* hand!"

"Nertz. Sam will have a cow."

"You're the one about to give birth. You have to go with me, Daisy. Anyhow, Sam will want to know who the guy is. And it makes sense to have you there to help Melanie during her ordeal."

"Who's going to comfort *me* during her ordeal?" I snapped.

"Sam and I will be there with you and Melanie."

"Thanks heaps," I said. "But Sam just left a few minutes ago to go to the scene of the crime. I'm not going anywhere until Spike and I take a nap, Harold Kincaid."

"Crumb," muttered Harold.

"Did the police telephone you when they found your name in the fellow's pocket?" I asked, thinking this story was taking on complications I hadn't anticipated.

"Yeah. Mind you, this note didn't have my address on it as had the one Melanie kept in her own pocket yesterday. This note merely mentioned the two of us."

"There has to be more than one person named Harold in the area, and maybe more than one Melanie. Why'd they think of you?" I said.

"One of the cops with a few more gray cells than his brothers in uniform connected the two names. Also, I guess this Smithfield character was found near Fair Oaks and Walnut, about where Melanie was scooped up off the sidewalk."

"That's a dreadful way to put it," I said.

"Feel free to edit my words," he snapped.

"Melanie didn't write the note to you? I mean, she didn't write 'Dear Harold' or anything like that at the beginning."

"I don't know. I haven't seen it yet. I'm supposed to go to the police station this afternoon and tell them if I can identify Melanie's handwriting. Which I won't be able to do, because I can't recall ever seeing it."

"Not even on Christmas cards or anything like that?"

"How the devil should *I* know?" Harold bellowed into the telephone's mouthpiece.

I jerked the receiver away from my ear. "Stop hollering at me, Harold Kincaid! I thought maybe you'd get Christmas cards from her or something."

"Sorry I yelled," said a contrite Harold. "Del and I get hundreds of Christmas cards and birthday cards, and we both get letters all the time. I don't recall if Melanie or her family ever sent us any correspondence. If they did, I suspect her mother addressed the envelopes."

"I see. Well," I continued, "I'm still not going anywhere for a while. I'm exhausted and need a nap. I hope the authorities don't suspect Melanie of dumping her baby on your doorstep. Abandoning a newborn must be some kind of criminal act."

"Gawd, I don't want Melanie to get into trouble," said Harold. "She's just a kid. Too young to know anything about the big bad world."

"She managed to get pregnant. That in itself implies at least some knowledge of the world."

"Untrue, Daisy Gumm Majesty Rotondo. You, of all people, should know that. For all I know, the father of Melanie's baby kidnapped and ravished her! Or told her he'd marry her."

"Of course," I said, penitent. I might have given this same lecture to Harold or Sam. Or Mr. Prophet. "But I can't join you instantly. When Sam comes home, we'll telephone you. Will that be all right with you?"

"I guess," said a sullen Harold. "Just hope the cops don't come to arrest me before then."

"How can they arrest you? Unless Melanie's blabbed, nobody

except you, Sam, Mr. Prophet, Hazel, Dr. Vialargo, the Buckinghams, and I know you have her baby in your house. Melanie may well be a morally weak person, but she's also physically and emotionally unfit to testify to anything right now."

"I suppose you're right," said Harold.

"I think I am," I said.

We both hung up our 'phones. Then I considered taking the receiver off the hook while Spike and I napped, but that would have been irresponsible of me so I didn't. I did, however, pull the living room draperies closed so if anyone came to the door, they wouldn't be able to tell if I was home. Just then I needed rest, not social interaction.

FIFTEEN

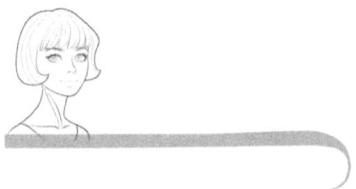

As luck would have it, the telephone didn't ring at all during the approximately one or two hours Spike and I napped. Nor did anyone ring our bell or knock at our door.

In fact it was Mr. Prophet who eventually nudged us awake. In truth, it was Spike taking a flying leap off the sofa and barking happily that awoke me. When my eyelids popped open, I managed to catch a glimpse of his happy short-legged run to the kitchen. I don't know if you've ever watched a dachshund from behind when it's racing like the wind, but it's a sight worth seeing. They have the most adorable doggie butts, especially while in motion. If you're sad, go find someone walking a liberty hound and you'll cheer up instantly.

That's what I think anyway.

I shoved myself to a seated position on the sofa and rubbed a couple of eyes. Mr. Prophet walked into the living room talking softly to Spike as he did so. When he saw me, however, he stopped walking and said, "You're just loafin' all the time these days, ain't you?"

Frowning and testing my body for fitness before attempting to rise, I said, "*You* get pregnant and see how frisky *you* are. Oh, that's right, you *can't* get pregnant, can you? You just play around and never give a thought to the consequences of your irresponsible actions, don't you?"

"Huh," he said. He sat on a chair near the sofa and patted his lap for Spike to jump up and sit on it. Spike, whom I'd never considered a traitor before that instant, did as requested.

I scowled at both of them. "What do you want? Did you interrupt my nap merely because you think I'm lazy? Of *course*, you did! What a silly question."

"Cut it out. I didn't mean any such-a thing," said Mr. Prophet.

"I don't believe you."

"I didn't mean it," he said again.

"I still don't believe you," I growled, annoyed with the miserable old coot. This was probably because *I* thought I was being lazy and slothful in recent days too, even though my body craved rest as it had never done before.

"Cripes. I need to talk to you about something. I'm sorry you was nappin'. I know ladies in your condition need take it easy."

"Oh yes? Precisely how many pregnant women have you been around with in your God-only-knows-how-many years on this earth?" I asked, still grumpy.

"One. You," he said. "I never been around a pregnant woman before you. I... Aw, hell." He clamped his jaws and didn't continue.

By then I'd managed to wake up. I also decided I felt better for having taken a nap. Still, I resented Mr. Prophet seducing Spike onto his lap. I also felt guilty for having snapped at the old rascal. Then again he no doubt deserved snappage for some reason, even if I didn't know what the reason was.

Therefore, I rose from the sofa and opened the draperies again. The late autumn sun poured in through the windows and made me glad. I loved our home, and the sun shining on our baby-grand piano cheered me instantly. I didn't tell Mr. Prophet about my change in mood, being pretty sure he'd come into the house in order to ruin it anyway. My mood, I mean.

"Then why'd you come in?" I asked him, sitting on the piano bench instead of the sofa. I had to sit pretty close to the middle of the bench because I feared tipping it over, thanks to my extra tonnage. Every time I visited Dr. Steindorf, her nurse weighed me and although I'd gained only thirteen pounds so far, I didn't want to take any chances. I also needed to use the toilet, but I wasn't going to say so in front of Mr. Prophet, darn it.

I'd been working on "Maxim" from *The Merry Widow*, although I didn't feel swell about doing so. After all, Franz Lehar was an Austro-Hungarian composer. Austro-Hungary sounded frightfully close to Germany. However, *The Merry Widow* entered into being in 1905, so I suppose it was safe for a bigot like me to play music from it.

To be fair to myself, I didn't hate all Germans any longer. I'd learned a difficult lesson a couple of years back and had actually saved a German woman's life. Then she'd saved mine. See? Anyhow, it's not us normal, everyday people who start wars. It's old men who can't get along with each other who start them. Then they send young lads to die for the old men's prideful mistakes.

"Well?" I prodded. "Why'd you come over?"

"Cripes. Nothing," said Mr. P.

I eyed him from the piano bench. I'd just straightened the sheet music to "Maxim" on the piano stand. "What is it? Spit it out."

"It's nothin'," he said again.

Swiveling on the piano bench—carefully so as not to upset it or me—to face him, I snapped, "It's not nothing. It's something. Just go ahead and tell me what it is!"

"Hellkatoot."

"And don't swear at me either."

"Hell, that ain't swearin'."

"Fine then," I said, swiveling myself back to face the piano once more. "I'll just practice my music."

I played the opening chord to "Maxim" and decided I needed to call the piano-tuner. After sending another sideways glare at Mr. Prophet and finding him staring off into space and petting Spike, I settled more comfortably on the bench and started "Maxim" again.

After approximately thirty-or-forty seconds' worth of piano music, I heard a loud, "I gotta talk to you!" from Spike's kidnapper.

Abruptly lowering both hands, I produced a hideously discordant sound on the piano. I lifted them just as abruptly and swiveled to face Mr. Prophet once more. "About what?" I asked.

"About that doctor."

"What doctor?" I only asked the question to be contrary. I knew about whom he was talking.

"You know what doctor," he growled.

I *really* had to piddle and I didn't feel like beating around the bush with this wrinkled old sinner. "You mean that tall, blond, handsome doctor who looks like Louisa Bonaventure? *That* doctor?"

The scraggly lines on Mr. Prophet's face wrinkled into a mask that might have done credit to a dried apple doll. "What the hell do you know about Louisa?"

"Only what I read about her in the same yellow-back novels in which I read about you." I lifted my chin and added, trying not to sound as guilt-ridden as I felt, "Besides, I heard you talking to Yuyu about her. You're afraid Dr. Vialargo is your son, aren't you?"

"Dammit, you listened when I was talkin' to my *cat*?"

"I was in the backyard picking oranges, I didn't spy on you or anything," I said. "I didn't deliberately eavesdrop." That was a big fat lie, but I didn't intend to tell him so. Anyhow, he knew it already.

"Cripes," he muttered. "Yes! Yes, I want to know if that doctor is my son. And Louisa's." He gave me a hateful look. "Happy now?"

"Not especially," I said. "How do you want to go about discovering his parentage?"

"Discovering his what? Talk English, will ya?"

"I was speaking in English," I said coldly. "How do you intend to find out if he's your and Louisa's son? I recommend asking the fellow, but I'm not you."

"That's fer damn sure," he muttered.

"Have a better idea?" I asked.

Mr. Prophet shifted his gaze from me and settled his attention on the huge pepper trees lining Marengo Avenue. I loved those trees, even though they were messy. But they formed a canopy over the street and I often pretended I was heading to a fairy-tale castle when I drove on Marengo.

At last, just as I was contemplating the merits of a race to the bathroom or a resumption of the piano piece, he said, "No. I don't have a better idea."

"Well then?"

"I dunno. I jist…jist…I jist don't know." Returning his gaze to me, he said, "You never heard where he was from or anything? Anything at all?"

"I met the man about two minutes before you did. I didn't even know he existed until we gathered in front of Harold's house yesterday morning."

"Shi-oot. I was afraid o' that."

"Why don't you telephone his office and make an appointment for yourself?" I suggested. "You can not only get a physical examination—which you probably need—but ask him where he's from. After that, you can ask more questions if his answer satisfies your curiosity. Why do you want to know where he came from, anyway?"

"Because he sounds like…well, like a relation of Louisa. Louisa's family come from Nebraska. Her folks was murdered by the Handsome Dave Duvall gang after the war ended."

"The what? *What* gang?"

Scowling at me, Mr. Prophet said, "The Handsome Dave Duvall Gang. Don't blame me. I didn't name the bastard and his crew of killers."

"I see. And the war about which you're talking is the Civil War, right?"

He blew out a breath. He didn't approve of calling the Civil War the Civil War. Too bad for him. "Yeah. That's the one. I know Louisa had a nasty aunt who still lived in Nebraska when Louisa and I was together. She was—I'm talkin' the aunt here—she was a mean ol' cow."

"Is the aunt 'Ol' Starchy Pants'?" I asked, revealing more of my eavesdroppery.

"How the hell do you know that?" He snarled. "You *are* a damn snoop, aren't you?"

"Not intentionally," I lied. "I didn't know you were grousing to your cat when I got to the orange trees." It was almost the truth.

No. It wasn't. I should have been ashamed of myself. I wasn't.

"Cripes."

I finally gave up pretending I didn't need the toilet. "I have to use the powder room. Be right back." I lumbered off the piano bench and hurried down the front hall to the half-bathroom at its end, hoping Mr. P. would still be in the living room when I returned.

He was! I felt twice relieved, if you know what I mean.

Deciding conversation was more interesting than practicing "Maxim," I sat on the sofa and said, "Why do you think Dr. Vialargo might be from Nebraska?"

"Because he sounds like it, o' course," said Mr. Prophet.

"Ah," I said.

"But I don't know how to find out if he's from Nebraska and was...is...Louisa's kid."

"He's not a kid anymore if he ever was one," I pointed out, feeling sorry for orphans everywhere. "Apparently he received enough of an upbringing so as to be able to get through college and medical school. Neither college nor medical school is cheap."

"Yeah, you're right." Mr. Prophet sounded downright morose.

"Perhaps he's quite bright and earned scholarships," I mused aloud.

"What's a scholarship?"

"Money given to an exceptionally good student so the student can go to college if he or his parents can't afford to send him there. There are probably scholarships to medical schools too. I've never thought about the possibility before."

"And if he got one o' them things, he's smart?"

"Don't get bigheaded yet," I advised him. "You don't even know his story. Anyway, if he *is* your and Louisa's son and is bright, he probably got it from his mother."

"Hellkatoot."

We both sat up straight when we heard Sam's Hudson pull into the drive and park beside the front porch. I shoved myself up from the sofa, and Spike leaped from Mr. Prophet's lap. After grunting in pain, Mr. Prophet also arose. I expect Spike had kicked a kidney with one of his back paws when he leaped.

Spike and I got to the door before Sam did, and I opened it and tried to greet him with a kiss. I succeeded in knocking him askew with our baby. That's only because he was carrying a load of paperwork as well as his briefcase and wasn't looking where he was going.

"Oh, Sam!" I said as he staggered back a step or two. "I'm sorry!"

When he lifted his head and peered at me, he had a big smile on his face, so I guess he wasn't annoyed. "It's all right, Daisy. Wasn't watching where I was going."

"You're on your own front porch," said Mr. Prophet from behind me. "Miss Daisy's big enough to knock anybody sideways."

"Am not!" I said in my most dignified matron's voice. Joshing.

"Don't fight, you two," said Sam, chuckling. "Let me in please. Yes, Spike," he said, observing our faithful hound executing a welcome-home dance at his feet, "I love you too."

"You're carrying too much stuff," I told him. "Give me your briefcase or some papers or something."

"I'm fine," he said, walking into the house. "But we'd better go to the kitchen. You know I don't like to blab about my cases, but I'm afraid this one is going to involve Harold, which almost certainly means it'll involve you too." He kissed my forehead and led Mr. Prophet, Spike, and me down the hall, through the dining room, pantry and into the kitchen, where he plopped his briefcase on the table and stacked the loose papers on the briefcase.

"The crime scene you were called to involved a man whose identification papers said he was James Smithfield, wasn't it?"

Frowning, Sam stared at me, his eyebrows soaring like larks ascending. "How the devil do you know *that*?"

SIXTEEN

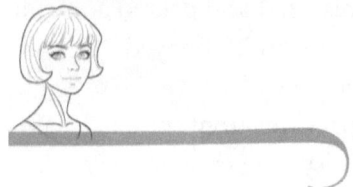

I flumped onto a kitchen chair. I hadn't meant to blurt it out like that. "Harold telephoned. He said the Pasadena P.D. called him because the dead man had his and Melanie's names on his person. Or on a piece of paper on his person, I mean."

"I should know better than to assume you're ever unaware of a murder in Pasadena, shouldn't I?" Sam sounded put out.

"That's not fair. I don't know about most murders committed in Pasadena. The Smithfield murder involves my best friend and a relative of his. Maybe two relatives."

"Two?" said Mr. Prophet.

"Melanie and her baby," I said.

"Uh, that's right. Fergot about them two being related."

"Melanie and her baby?" I asked.

"Harold and the baby," grumbled Mr. Prophet.

"Anybody want a cup of tea or anything before I sit?" asked Sam.

"No thanks," I said.

Mr. Prophet shook his head.

Sam sat and shuffled through a few of the papers on his brief-case. He selected one and said, "The station received a report at

136

one-thirty this afternoon about a man lying near the corner of Fair Oaks and Walnut. The caller, a male, said he didn't know if the man was alive or dead."

"Fair Oaks and Walnut is where the police station is," I said. "Someone could walk outside and check on the body." What I'd just said surprised me. "In fact, the coppers might have scooped up Melanie!"

"True," said Sam. "But it wasn't on our particular corner. It was west of us, and we're in the back of City Hall. Oliphant had to walk across the street and look." He grinned a grim grin.

"Poor Oliphant. Did he take his camera with him?" Officer Oliphant had taken photographs of several other crime scenes with which I'd been involved. Or, if not exactly involved, at least on the periphery thereof.

"Of course he did," said Sam

"Poor Oliphant. I wouldn't like to be stuck taking pictures of dead people all the time."

"It's not all the time," said Sam. I sensed he wanted to say something more about me forever stumbling over bodies but didn't quite dare. Anyhow, I hadn't stumbled over anything recently. Well, except my own two feet, but that's only because I couldn't see the ground and felt rather like an elephant forced to stand on its back legs. Awkward. That's how I felt.

"I suppose not. Do you think the late Mr. Smithfield was the father of Melanie Robinson's baby?"

"Don't know yet," said Sam. "Miss Robinson will be taken to identify the body, but she's not well enough yet."

"That's what Harold said. He said he'd have to be with her to hold her hand, and I'd have to be with him to hold *his* hand."

"Hmmm," said Sam. "Think I'll call the hospital and find out how Miss Robinson is doing."

"Good idea."

"Do you expect that doctor will be there?" asked Mr. Prophet.

Sam had just put the papers he'd been holding back on the stack on top of his briefcase, but he glanced up at Mr. P's comment. "What doctor?"

A tremendous grimace from Mr. Prophet prompted me to answer for him. "He wants to find out if Dr. Vialargo is his son. He thinks he might be."

"Oh, yes?" said Sam, although I'd reported the conversation I'd heard between Mr. Prophet and his cat. Or Mr. Prophet's monologue into Yuyu's battered, furry ear, I suppose is a more accurate description.

The telephone rang. I made as if to rise, but Sam put a gentle hand on my shoulder and said, "I'll get it."

So I let him. I drummed my fingers on the kitchen table. Mr. Prophet bent sideways and scritched Spike behind his ears. Spike loved it when people did that to him.

Both Mr. Prophet and I sat up straighter when we heard Sam say the word "Harold." I glanced at Mr. Prophet, who glanced back at me. I tilted my head toward the hallway. He shook his head. I frowned at him. He scowled back at me. Very well then, I'd just wait for Sam to report on the telephone call and not go to the hall and listen in.

A few seconds later, Sam strolled back into the kitchen and said, "Don't have to call the hospital. Harold has just been given a full report on Miss Melanie Robinson's condition."

"Is she going to be all right?" I asked.

"They aren't sure yet," said Sam grimly. "She lost a lot of blood, and she's weak as a kitten."

"Oh dear. She hasn't yet been told about Mr. Smithfield's demise?"

"No," said Sam. "Anyhow, we don't know yet if Smithfield and Smith are the same person." He shook his head in what looked like frustration. "And if they are, who's the other guy?"

"What other guy?" asked Mr. Prophet.

"The one who killed Smithfield," said Sam.

"Is it a confirmed murder?" I asked. "I mean, he didn't just collapse and die on the sidewalk for some reason?"

"The knife wound in his back indicates he had help with his demise."

"Oh," I said.

SPIRITS ADOPTED

"I'll know more tomorrow. That's when the doctor will perform a post-mortem exam on the fellow."

"Dr. Benjamin?" I asked, Dr. Benjamin was my family's long-time physician and good friend.

"Dr. Dearing is on the job tomorrow."

"He's nice," I said.

Mr. Prophet gave me a *look*. "You know all the doctors in this damn city?" he asked, sounding grouchy.

Letting go a huff of irritation, I said, "No, but Dr. Dearing and his family live across Maiden Lane from Mrs. Bissel, and I've met him on several occasions."

"Huh," said Mr. Prophet.

"Anyhow," said Sam, "Harold plans to visit his cousin at the Castleton again tomorrow. He said he'd like you to go with him, Daisy. Do you have anything else planned?"

"Library and a visit to Grenville's Bookstore to pick up a copy of *The Chinese Parrot* if they have one. I hope they do. It's a best seller, so I hope they stocked up. Especially since the author lives in Pasadena."

"But you can visit Harold after that?" asked Sam.

"I should think so." I shot a look at Mr. Prophet. "You want to go to Harold's with me, or would you like me to drop you off at home before I visit the bookstore?"

"Huh. Mebbe I will. Mebbe that doctor will be there."

"Maybe he will be, but it's more likely that Dr. Fred Greenlaw will be, if any doctor is. He's Hazel's brother, and he's Harold's usual doctor."

"Huh. I s'pose I'll go with you anyhow," Mr. P. grumbled.

"Golly, thanks," I said.

"Don't mention it," said the old curmudgeon.

"When you go to the hospital, will you please ask Miss Robinson the names of any of her and Mr. Smith's friends?" said Sam. "Jot them down or something. Or if anyone she knew didn't like one or both of them?"

"Sure, I can do that. Melanie might not like it."

"Too bad. I doubt if she'll be accused of this fellow's murder, but the location where both victims were found makes me almost certain the two cases are related."

"Sounds like it," I said, thinking poor Melanie was going to be showered with more grief than she'd already suffered. "Melanie's just a kid, Sam. Harold doesn't think she's older than fifteen or sixteen."

"If today's dead man is the father of her baby, guess he can't be charged with statutory rape. Difficult to charge a dead man with anything," said Sam with a sigh.

"What's statutory rape?" I asked, never having heard the term before.

"When an adult has intimate relations with a person under the age of...well, in California, the age of consent is eighteen."

"I married Billy when I was only seventeen," I pointed out.

"Your parents gave their consent to your marriage," said Sam. "Billy didn't just snatch you off the street. Or seduce you out of a seventh-grade classroom."

"Do men really have...sexual relations with children?" I asked. Then I smacked the side of my head in disgust at my lousy memory. "Never mind. I just remembered Dr. Wagner and Mr. Bannister and all of those disgusting, perverted, so-called adult males."

"Unfortunately, some men do prefer youngsters," said Sam.

"They make me sick," I said.

"Me too," said Sam.

Glad we were in agreement on the subject.

The four of us sat quietly for a little while (I'm including Spike in our group). It was Mr. Prophet who broke the silence.

"Got anything fer supper?"

"Leftover lamb, some of Vi's delicious rolls and some jelled salad with pineapple and celery in it."

"What the hell's a jelled salad?" asked Mr. P.

"It's a salad made with Jell-O and celery, shredded carrots, canned pineapples and chopped pecans. Vi said you can't use fresh pineapple because the Jell-O won't set if you do. I don't know what flavor of Jell-O Vi used. I suspect orange, because it's orange."

"Never heard of a salad like that."

I peered at him across the table for a few seconds. "I'm not surprised."

"C'n I make myself a lamb sandwich?" he asked.

"Sure," I said. There's mustard in the cupboard, and the lamb's in the refrigerator. It's the tinfoil package. I put the Jell-O salad in a container and covered it with waxed paper. The rolls are in the breadbox."

"I'll fix the sandwiches," said Sam. He heaved himself up from the table. "Anybody else want a sandwich?" he asked.

I consulted my stomach. No dice. It was still full of dinner. It was also quite big enough, thank you.

Sam said, "You don't want a sandwich, Daisy?"

"No thanks."

"You should probably eat something."

"Why? I'm as big as a house and still full from dinner."

"Yeah," said Mr. Prophet. "She's fat enough already."

I looked down at my faithful hound. "Spike, bite him."

Alas, I hadn't taught Spike such a helpful command. Both Sam and Mr. P. laughed, though, so that's something I suppose.

"I'll make you a sandwich and wrap it in waxed paper," said Sam. "You'll probably get hungry before bedtime."

"I'm tired enough to go to bed now, so I wouldn't rate your chances as likely," I told him.

"Cripes," said Mr. P. "You been sleepin' all afternoon."

"One of the joys of pregnancy," I said, frowning at him. "I'm always tired and always have to use the restroom."

"Coulda happily lived forever without knowin' that," said Mr. P.

"Yet one more reason you should have been more careful in your wild youth," I said, snarling.

"Yeah, yeah, yeah," said Mr. P. "You told me that already."

"It bears repeating," I said.

"Cripes," said the former bounty hunter. "You gonna have more kids after this one, Sam? She's liable to go after you with a knife one o' these days, she's so cantankerous."

"I'm only cantankerous with you, you wrinkled old villain," I told him. "You bring out the worst in me."

"Likewise," he said.

"Calm down, you two," said Sam, laughing at the both of us.

"I'm going to read in the living room," I told them both. "Spike?" I studied my formerly faithful canine companion and could tell he had no intention of coming with me. Not when there were people handling food in the kitchen. "Traitor," I said.

"Spike's not a traitor. He just likes food," said Sam.

"Well don't give him too much," I reminded him. "If he becomes obese and his back goes out, I'll tell Mrs. Bissel and Mrs. Hanratty it was *you* who killed him."

"Kee-rist. She's getting' downright vicious," Mr. P told Sam.

"I don't mind," said Sam. "She deserves to grouse. After all, she's right about so many men not having to pay the price of dealing with unwanted children."

"You're not one o' those," observed Mr. Prophet.

"You're correct," I said as a stab of guilt pierced me. "I'm sorry, Sam. Thank you for making a sandwich for me. And save some salad too please."

"Will do."

I clumped out of the kitchen to the living room. There I sat in one of the comfortable upholstered club armchairs after tugging the ottoman close to the chair. Then I grabbed one of the extra pillows on the sofa, placed it at the back of the chair, pulled the chain of the lamp standing behind the chair, picked up *An American Tragedy*, and resumed reading.

I'm not sure how much later Sam woke me up and asked if I was ready for my sandwich, or if I'd rather go straight up to bed.

Groggily, I said, "Bed, please," and darned if he didn't pick me up—along with our unborn son—and carry us up to the bedroom.

The next morning I felt quite rested. Small wonder.

SEVENTEEN

At eight-thirty Monday morning, Mrs. Rattle knocked at our front door and Spike and I let her in. As she stepped into the hall and I helped her off with her coat, she said, "How are you feeling, dear." She eyed my protuberance. "It won't be long now."

"It won't?" Stupid question. I knew how far along I was.

"I can tell the baby is settling into birthing position."

"You can?" That was more than I could do.

"Of course. This is your first so you don't recognize the signs, but I'd wager you don't have more than four or five weeks yet to go."

"Golly, that sounds great to me. I'm tired of carrying this gigantic wash tub in front of me all the time."

After I hung her coat on the rack and she put her hat on the shelf, she eyed me critically up and down. "Late November or early December is what I'd wager."

That day I wore a dress I'd made of navy-blue cotton that had white bias tape sewn around the yoke. From the bottom of the yoke, the gathered skirt could grow as much as I needed it to. I'd made three dresses in different colors from the same pattern, by gum.

And lest you think I wasted all my time sewing clothes for

myself, I'd already laid in a supply of soft flannel baby dresses—although "dresses" doesn't sound right when you're talking about a boy baby—for the infant. From there I'd sewn enough clothes to last until he was two at least. Plus which, I'd sewn my mother, my aunt, my sister, and my sister-in-law lovely rayon lounging pajamas for Christmas. Lounging pajamas were all the rage at the time.

The telephone rang. I heaved a sigh, Mrs. Rattle patted me on the shoulder in a consoling gesture, and I sat on the telephone table's chair.

"Hello?" I said.

"Daisy," said Harold. "When can you come over here?"

Every nerve in my body went taut with apprehension. "When?"

"Yes!"

"Very well, but if you recall, I promised to take Mr. Prophet to the library. Then I need to visit Grenville's Books."

Because he didn't instantly yell that he needed me *now*, I allowed myself to relax a trifle.

"Can you pick me up a copy of a book called *The Book of Baby Mine*? If it comes in different colors, get me a pink one please. I'll pay you back when you get here."

"You want a baby book? Is that why you telephoned?"

"Yes, I want that particular baby book, and no, that's not why I called. But I figured whoever adopts this kid—or maybe Melanie—would like a record of its first few days."

"That's thoughtful of you, Harold. Good for you." In actual fact, we had a baby book for our soon-to-be-born son. Its cover was blue leather.

"Yeah, I'm such a thoughtful guy," said a sarcastic Harold. "But why I want you to come here as soon as you can is because I called the Castleton Hospital this morning. Melanie will be fit enough for me to take her to the morgue and identify, or not identify, the dead fellow they found yesterday. You need to come with me. I'm not good with dead bodies. Or babies. Wish we could find an adoptive family soon."

"It's only been a couple of days," I pointed out.

"We still need to find someone to adopt the kid fast. Del is about to have a heart attack, he's so worried bank patrons might learn about the situation."

"Is Hazel still on the job as the baby's nurse?" I asked. "And speaking of Del, why aren't *you* at work?"

"I'm not at work because I have to take care of a damned baby! Hazel is here and seeing to the infant beautifully. Another nurse comes in and watches the kid at night. Her presence doesn't let me off the hook, however. Del is a bundle of nerves. As soon as we get this problem solved, I'll return to work."

Harold worked as a costumer for different motion picture studios in the Los Angeles area. As he already had enough loot to provide a living for several families for a century or more, he didn't technically *need* the job, but he enjoyed it.

"Very well, I'll look in Grenville's for the baby book. In pink. You said it's *The Book of Baby Mine*, right?"

"Right," confirmed Harold.

"Good." I wrote down the title of the book on the telephone table's notepad, just to be safe. "I expect Mr. Prophet will be with me."

"Okay by me," said Harold. "Try to hurry."

"Of course," I said with a sigh.

Because Spike had stayed with me and hadn't followed Mrs. Rattle to the utility room, I petted him, told him he was a good boy, and wished I could just stay home with my dog for the remaining weeks of my pregnancy. Too bad for Daisy and Spike, huh?

Spike and I made our way to the kitchen where Mrs. Rattle was already busy cleaning counters. She smiled at us. "Will you be going out today, Daisy?"

"Yes," I said. Then I scolded myself for sounding disappointed. "I'm about to see if Mr. Prophet is ready for a trip to the library. It opens at nine. Then I aim to pay a visit to Grenville's Books. After that, I promised Harold I'd visit him to see his latest acquisition." Wow, that wasn't even much of a lie!

"You're such a busy woman," said Mrs. Rattle. "Why don't I prepare a casserole dish for your supper tonight? It will save you from being on your feet, and I love to cook. Your basement is stocked to the gills with preserved chickens and so forth."

"Thank you, Mrs. Rattle. That would be extremely kind of you. And it's thanks to Aunt Vi that our basement is so well stocked." Then I recalled yesterday's lamb. "Oh, but there's lamb in the ice box, if you want to use that."

"Oh, lovely! I can make a shepherd's pie. And I'm sure you do your part," she said.

"I enjoy gardening, so I'm responsible for filling some of our basement's bottles and jars, but it's Vi who's the cook and canner in the family." I heaved another small sigh. "I still don't much like to cook, although I hate to admit it."

"Nonsense," said Mrs. Rattle with energy. "We all have our special gifts. From what I've seen, you're a marvelous seamstress, gardener, and pianist. Your aunt has been given the gift of cooking."

"Thanks, Mrs. Rattle. I appreciate your perspective." I didn't believe it and continued to feel guilty about being such a lousy cook, but I didn't bother telling her so. She already knew.

As Spike and I were about to head out and find Mr. Prophet, he thumped through back door and into the kitchen.

"Ah," I said. "There you are."

"You been lookin' for me?" He scowled at me for some reason known only to himself.

"No. I was just about to see if you're ready to go to the library."

"Mornin' Elvira," he said to Mrs. Rattle.

"Good morning, Lou," she said to him, smiling sweetly.

There had been a time when he was terrified of sweet Mrs. Rattle. He vehemently denied it when accused, but he had been. I remember it well. He'd believed she'd had an amorous eye on him. As the woman had been happily married for years by then, he'd imagined her interest. Well, I'm sure she *had* been interested in him because he was a colorful fellow, but her intentions were purely investigative. As far as I knew, Mr. Prophet was the only former booze-swilling, womanizing, gun-happy bounty hunter in the city of Pasadena.

"I'm ready to go as soon as you are," Mr. Prophet said to me.

"All right. I'll get a sweater." I eyed my dog and made another decision. "And I'll call Pa and ask if he wants Spike to be company for Rosebud while we're gone."

Mr. Prophet grunted something and sat in a kitchen chair. I returned to the telephone table and called my father. He said he and Rosebud would be delighted to have Spike stay for a while. After I donned my sweater, therefore, I got Spike's leash from the utility room. Then I fetched both Spike and Mr. Prophet from the kitchen, said good-bye to Mrs. Rattle and went to the front door. There I plucked my navy blue cloche hat from the shelf, and stuck it on my bobbed hair. Mr. Prophet gathered the books from the table beside the front door, and the three of us marched across the street.

Spike and I had already taken a walk with Pa and Rosie earlier in the day, but they were both delighted to see us again.

"Any special requests from the library?" I asked my father.

"Just the usual. Any westerns or Edgar Rice Burroughs' books. Any mysteries or detective stories you think your mother and aunt would like."

"Gotcha. Thanks, Pa," I said as I picked up the already-read books from the table beside their front door.

"Don't carry those, Daisy!" he said in a scolding tone.

With my arms full of books, I looked up at him, surprised. "Why ever not?"

"You're about to give birth to a grandchild of mine, and I don't want you to damage yourself before you do it," said Pa.

"Oh. All right then."

I don't know why everyone was so worried about me. Except that I wanted to nap all the time and had to use the bathroom a lot, I felt fine. Ish. I guess I didn't feel as lively as I had before I got pregnant, but still. I'm sure farmers' wives still had to do all the chores around their houses, including cooking and baking. And maybe even milking cows. Did *they* have helpers for their everyday duties?

Hmm. Maybe they did. But only if they were lucky.

Fortunately for me, I was lucky. After Pa deposited the books in the book-return laundry basket I kept in the backseat of the Chevrolet, I said. "Thanks, Pa," and went around to the driver's side of the machine. After Mr. Prophet got into the machine, he and Pa gabbed for a couple of seconds. Then I started the car and very carefully backed it out of the driveway. I wasn't a topnotch backer-upper, but I managed to get the car onto Marengo and drive north.

"What're you going to get at the library?" I asked Mr. Prophet.

"Dunno. I'll probably look at the history section and maybe the biographies."

"No western books?" I asked innocently.

"Hellkatoot."

"Guess that means no," I said.

"Might look at the western history section," he said grudgingly. "Even those don't tell the truth very often."

"I suppose there are as many different stories about the American West as there are people who lived in it," I said, feeling philosophical.

"You live more west than I ever did until I come here," he pointed out.

"I guess you're right," I said, admitting defeat. Didn't bother attempting further conversation with my passenger.

A car drove out from a parking space in front of the library into westbound traffic on Walnut just as I pulled up and was looking for a place to park. That was easy. So far, the day seemed to be going my way. Of course, most of it hadn't happened yet, but I decided to be happy until something awful cropped up.

Because there weren't many books in the laundry basket, Mr. Prophet split them into two piles and we carried a pile each. A polite library patron opened the door for us, and we both thanked him. That is to say, I thanked him, and Mr. Prophet grunted, so it amounted to the same thing.

Regina Browning, my special librarian friend, stood at the returned-books end of the library's front counter when we walked in. She gave us a huge smile and waved at us. I'd have waved back, but my arms were full of books. Because we were in the library, we didn't speak until we reached her.

"How are you today, Daisy and Mr. Prophet?" There had been a time when Regina was frightened of Mr. Prophet. Most people had that reaction. He did appear rather unsavory upon first encounters. The guy was old, he'd lived a wild and woolly life, and the results of those things had etched themselves onto his countenance. He was no more dangerous than your average grizzly bear, however.

That's a joke.

"We're fine, Regina," I said, smiling back at her. "How are you and Robert?"

"We're doing well, thanks. I have some books tucked away for you," she added. Then her smile faded. "I haven't been able to snag *The Chinese Parrot* though. That's what I was doing when you walked in: looking at the returned books, hoping someone had turned in a copy. But they hadn't, so I wasn't able to get one for you."

"That's all right," I said. "Mr. Prophet and I are going to Grenville's Books after we leave the library, and I'm going to buy myself a copy!"

"Extravagant," said Regina with a chuckle as she, Mr. P., and I walked to her reference desk near the book stacks. As she reached for the books she'd put on a shelf under her desk, Mr. Prophet wandered off.

"Goin' to the history section," he mumbled.

"Have fun," I said.

He grunted. Such an affable fellow.

"Sorry I couldn't snatch a copy of *The Chinese Parrot*," said Regina. "But I've still got quite a haul for you."

Boy was *she* right! We had a pleasant whispered conversation as we waited at her desk for Mr. Prophet to rejoin us. "I'm so glad Mrs. Christie has a new book out," I told her.

"I am too," she said. "And I'm sure your father will enjoy *Thundering Herd* by Zane Grey and *Tarzan Twins* by Mr. Burroughs."

"He asked me specifically to look for books by Grey and Burroughs."

"These are both new, so he should be happy," said Regina.

When Mr. Prophet and I finally left the library and headed to Grenville's Books, Regina helped us carry our books to the Chevrolet. I carried *The Murder of Roger Ackroyd* by Mrs. Christie, the Grey and Burroughs books, and *Whose Body* by someone named Dorothy

L. Sayers. Regina carried *Corkscrew* by Mr. Dashiell Hammett, *Marazan* by Mr. Nevil Shute, and some *Father Brown* stories by Mr. G.K. Chesterton.

Mr. Prophet carried his own (and Sam's) selections, but he opened the back door of the machine for us. Regina and I handed him our books, which he then neatly piled in the laundry basket.

It was a happy Daisy Rotondo who started the Chevrolet once more, waved to Regina and carefully put the car in gear and eased out onto Walnut Street. I turned left on Fair Oaks and took another left onto Colorado Street. Then I drove to Colorado and Oak Knoll and parked almost in front of Grenville's Books. I was lucky with parking that morning, by golly.

EIGHTEEN

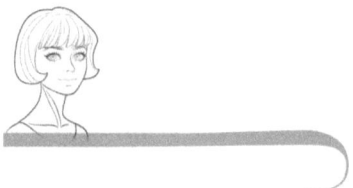

W hen I walked into the store via the front entrance, I was
surprised to see Marianne Grenville behind the counter.
Generally, her husband George manned the counter. He was probably around somewhere.

"Good morning, Marianne," I said, smiling at her.

"Good morning, Daisy," she said. Her attention was fixed on
something behind me and she seemed alarmed, so I stepped to one
side and said, "Marianne Grenville, please allow me to introduce
you to Mr. Lou Prophet. Mr. Prophet hails from Arizona—"

"Georgia," he growled at my back.

"Mr. Prophet originally hailed from Georgia. He now works as
caretaker at Sam's and my place."

"Howdy," said Mr. Prophet, keeping more to the Arizona theme
than the Georgia one.

"Good morning, Mr. Prophet." Marianne's alabaster brow wrinkled. She was a lovely girl. Well, she wasn't a girl any longer, but she
hadn't been able to get out much when she was growing up, and I
guess she still didn't. Although she'd endured horrors during her few
years on this earth, she still came across as an innocent.

"I'm looking for a copy of *The Chinese Parrot*, by Earl Derr Biggers, Marianne. I hope you have one."

"We do," said Marianne, giving me a wobbly smile. Her eyes filled with tears.

What the heck?

"Marianne, what's the matter? I hurried up to her, reached across the counter and put a hand on her shoulder. "Are you feeling unwell? Is it George? Your mother?"

She shook her head hard, grabbed a hankie from her pocket and wiped her cheeks. "No. Everyone is fine. I'm sorry, Daisy."

"There's no cause to be sorry. Something *is* wrong," I said. "Otherwise, you wouldn't be crying. Please let me help you." Again. I didn't add that word.

"Daisy!" said a jolly voice from the back room behind the counter. "It's good to—Marianne, what's the matter?" George Grenville appeared with a smile for me. His smile vanished when he saw his wife in tears. "Oh, Lord. I'm sorry, Marianne, so sorry."

As I watched in confusion, George wrapped his arms around Marianne and gave her a big hug.

"What's wrong with them?" Mr. Prophet whispered from not far behind me.

I shrugged. "I don't know."

"Here, Marianne. Let me help you into the back room. You can rest there." George guided his emotionally overwrought wife to the back room and shot me a speaking glance. Too bad I didn't know what language he was speaking.

"What do we do now?" Mr. Prophet wanted to know.

I shook my head. "I have no idea."

As long as we were there though, I decided I'd just go find myself a copy of *The Chinese Parrot*. Grenville's Books had been around for almost as long as I had, so I was familiar with its layout. I figured so popular a book would probably be on a display at the end of a shelf with its cover facing out. And I was correct!

"Oh, I'm so glad I found you!" I told the book, hugging it to my bosom.

"Cripes," muttered Mr. Prophet.

"Pooh on you," I said. "You don't know how long I've wanted to read this book."

"How long's it been?"

"Almost a year!" I said, horrified that during a whole twelve months, I hadn't found the time to visit Grenville's Books. Then again, the year had been a busy one, what with ghosts both ancient and modern to exorcise and so forth.

The bad news is that I'm serious.

"Daisy?"

When I heard George Grenville's voice, I turned to find him looking troubled and gesturing for me to join him at the counter. "Sure George," I said as I walked to the counter. "Is Marianne all right? I hope nothing I did upset her."

"Well," He said, "It did, but it isn't your fault."

I tilted my head, hoping to gain insight by exposing a different set of convolutions to the riddle. Didn't work. "I don't understand, George."

"I know. But... Listen, can you come into the back room for a bit? I'll have to keep an eye on the store, but it's early and not many people are here yet."

"Certainly. Let me just tell—"

"Go on," said a gruff Mr. Prophet. "I don't like to see wimmin cry. Tell her to dry up. I'll watch the counter."

"Um..." George was clearly uneasy about leaving a man who looked like one of the Old West's more dangerous outlaws in charge of his counter.

"It's all right, George. Let me introduce you to Mr. Lou Prophet. Mr. Prophet, this is George Grenville, owner of this fine bookstore."

"How do you do?" asked George, tentatively holding out a hand for Mr. P to shake.

"Fine. You?" said Mr. Prophet, shaking George's hand.

"Uh...all right, I think. Do you mind if I take Daisy to the back room for a few minutes?"

"Hell, no," said the old sinner.

I rolled my eyes so far back in their sockets, I'm surprised I couldn't see the heels of my shoes. "Cut it out," I told him sharply.

"Huh," said Mr. Prophet.

"It's all right, George. Take me to Marianne. I'm sorry to have upset her. But all we did was walk into the store."

"That's all it took," said George not unkindly.

As already mentioned, I was familiar with the layout of this particular bookstore. Almost too familiar, actually. You see, several years back I'd been responsible for rescuing Marianne—whose last name at the time was Wagner—from an untenable position as a forlorn runaway. I'd deposited her in the little cottage behind Grenville's Books. That's how George and Marianne met. Shortly thereafter, they'd fallen madly in love and were married.

"It's my baby, isn't it?" I said softly to George.

He stopped before entering the back room and whispered, "Yes. Marianne has always wanted children, but...well, you know. We can't have children."

I said. "I know."

And then I was almost blinded by a truly brilliant idea. Or maybe it wasn't, but it felt brilliant. Rather than blurt it out as I generally did after having a brilliant notion, I trod carefully. "Have you and Marianne ever considered adopting a baby, George?"

"All the time," said George. "And Diane is encouraging Marianne and me to adopt"—Diane was Marianne's mother—"but adopting a baby isn't as easy as it sounds."

"It's not?"

"No. Adoption agencies require adoptive parents to be investigated these days. They're more rigorous about the investigation if a baby is involved. Older children are easier to adopt, but we want a baby."

"Why would an investigation into your... Oh."

"Exactly," said George. "Oh."

"Shoot," I muttered as understanding hit me like a rock.

George continued, "Anyone responsible for placing an infant in a good home would definitely not approve of us."

"I see," I said. "Let's go talk to Marianne."

George and I finally entered the back room. There we found Marianne sitting in a chair and attempting to calm herself by taking in deep breaths and letting them out slowly. I'd recently read in an article in the *Saturday Evening Post* about this deep-breathing technique for helping a person relieve taut nerves.

"Marianne?" George whispered as he approached his wife. "Marianne, Daisy's here."

"I know she is," said Marianne, letting her last breath go in a huge gust. She opened her eyes. "I'm sorry, Daisy. It's just…it's just that… Well, I haven't seen you for several months, and I didn't realize you were g-g-going to have a b-baby. So soon. Oh, bother!" She began crying again, poor thing.

"It's all right, Marianne," I said. "I didn't have any idea. I mean, I understand, but I'm sorry to have upset you."

"It's not all right," said Marianne vehemently. My experience with Marianne had led me to believe she had about as much backbone as aspic, so her fervor surprised me. "I've been doing better lately. That's why I'm at the shop!" She sucked in a deep breath and let it out again. "We all thought that if I had more interaction with the public, I'd be able to overcome this tendency to…to… Oh, God."

"Marianne," I said softly. "You can't help what happened to you. But all isn't lost yet."

"It's not?" Gazing up at me with drippy eyes, Marianne said, "Why not? I mean, I've been helping George for a couple of months, and you're not the first mother-to-be I've seen in the store. But none of them hit me like you did. Well, you know what I mean. I'm so happy for you, and I'm so miserable for George and myself. That doesn't make any sense, does it?"

"It makes all the sense in the world. All the other mothers-to-be weren't well known to you, and I am."

"Yes," she said. "But it's not your fault."

"I know that, too," I said with a smile. "And Sam and I are happy we're going to be parents."

"I'm s-sure you are." Her voice wobbled.

"But I might know of a way to help you," I said, daring to voice a smidgeon of my brilliant idea. I didn't like to see women crying any more than Mr. Prophet did.

"You do?" Marianne gave an incredulous chuff. "Nobody in his or her right mind would allow a baby to be adopted into *my* family! For heaven's sake, Daisy, you know that as well as I do. And I wouldn't blame them. *I* wouldn't allow a child of mine to grow up in my family!"

"You and George have created your own family now, Marianne," I said, trying to keep my voice gentle. This woman had already endured too much in her life; it would be mean to me to shake her shoulder and tell her to toughen up. "Try to calm down. I'll pay for my book, and then I need to visit a friend who might—don't get your hopes up too far—be able to help you."

"How?" George and Marianne asked the one-word question at the same time.

"I recently read an article in the *Los Angeles Times* stating that almost seventy percent of adoptions these days are so-called 'private' adoptions. That means they go through an attorney rather than an adoption or government agency."

"Really?" said George. Marianne only blinked at me a couple of times.

"Really," I said. "But I can't stay here any longer. I'm sorry to leave you in such distress."

"I'm not as distressed as I was," said Marianne. She even managed a little smile. "I was just shocked to see you, was all. When is your baby due?"

"Probably the end of November or early December," I said, recalling Mrs. Rattle's words to me that morning.

"I'm happy for you, even though I know I don't look happy," said Marianne, gaining a little strength.

"Thank you," I said. "But let me pay for my book, and I hope I'll be able to talk to you more in a few days."

"You know a lawyer who takes cases like this? Baby-adoption cases?" said George.

"Yes," I said. It was a huge lie, but Harold knew tons of attorneys, and he had a newborn baby he'd *love* to see adopted into a family like that of the Grenvilles. Harold had been involved in the rescue of Marianne too. "But try not to despair."

"Thanks, Daisy," said Marianne in a small voice.

"Here, Daisy, let me help you with your book," said George.

"Thank you both," I said. Then I added, "Try to buck up. I might have some good news for you, although don't hold your breath."

George and I left Marianne to gather her courage in the back room and walked into the bookstore. There we found Mr. Prophet leaning against the counter, glaring at people who tried to enter through the front door. The store remained empty, so I deduced he'd scared any prospective customers away. His appearance was daunting.

"Thank you, Daisy," said George when I'd laid *The Chinese Parrot* on the counter and reached for the little purse I'd shoved into my pocket that morning. George took the book, wrapped it in brown paper, and returned it to me.

"How much do I owe?" I asked, taking the parcel.

"Nothing," said George. "It's on the house. If it weren't for you, my Marianne would have perished by this time."

Dramatic, but more than likely true. I was *so* lucky to have the family I had.

"Try to keep her spirits up," I told him. "And please take care. Marianne and her mother have both been through so much."

"Yes," said George drily. "They have. I didn't even know people like Dr. Wagner existed until I met Marianne. The man deserved to be murdered by his children, even if that means Marianne and I won't pass an inspection."

"Forget the inspection," I told him, perhaps unwisely. "Well, don't worry about it, anyhow."

"I'll try," said George with a grateful smile. "Thanks, Daisy."

"Thank *you*," I said, holding up my copy of *The Chinese Parrot* in its brown paper wrapper.

When Mr. Prophet and I got back to the Chevrolet, he growled, "What the devil was *that* about?"

After I started the car, I told him the whole miserable story.

When I stopped speaking, I realized he'd begun staring at me, an expression of disbelief on his wrinkly face. "Is that really *true?*" He said at last.

"Yes. Every word."

"Hellkatoot."

NINETEEN

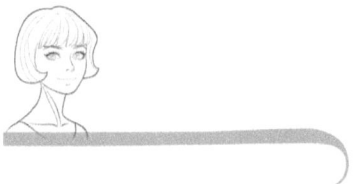

W hen we arrived at Harold's home in San Marino, two other automobiles already sat at the curb in front of his house. One was a shiny red Marmon Wasp, and the other was...

Oh heck.

"Brace yourself," I told Mr. Prophet as I opened my door.

He'd opened his door, but he turned to frown at me. "Fer what?"

"I think that Chevrolet Roadster belongs to Dr. Vialargo, the man who is possibly your son."

I heard him whisper an awful word that began with S-H and ended in T.

"Well golly," I said. "You wanted to know about him. This might be a great opportunity."

Again he whispered the bad word.

"And don't use that kind of language around Hazel, the doctor, or the baby," I scolded.

He said it again.

I shook my head in despair and exited the Chevrolet. He did likewise on the passenger side of the car, only without the head shake. For some reason beyond my comprehension, he seemed angry. As if *he* had anything to gripe about!

The front door of Harold's house opened with a flourish, and we saw Harold standing in the door frame looking haggard. Poor Harold. He was such a good man; he didn't deserve the problem deposited on his doorstep.

"It's about time!" He said as Mr. Prophet and I traversed the walkway to his home.

"I told you we had to visit the library and the bookstore," I snapped. "So just hush up."

"Bother," said Harold. He stepped back so Mr. Prophet and I could enter his grand home. "I'm sorry. It's just so nerve-wracking to have a baby in the house. She cries all the time, and it scares me. Hazel is a gem, but my God, how do people *stand* babies?"

"I imagine most people with babies have had considerably more time to prepare for them than you did," I said.

"They couldn't have much less," muttered Harold. "Morning, Lou," he said to Mr. Prophet.

"Mornin'," said Mr. Prophet.

"Is that Dr. Vialargo's machine out there?" I asked Harold. Then I shot a look at Mr. Prophet, who had resumed frowning.

"Yes," said Harold. "He's upstairs examining the infant." He ran his fingers through his hair. "Should I give the thing a name? I hate just calling it 'the baby'."

"Why don't you allow her adoptive parents to give her a name?" I suggested gently. "Which is something I want to discuss with you."

"You want to talk about baby names? The one upstairs is a girl and yours is a boy. Or will be a boy."

"Yes, Harold, I know that. It's not, however, baby names I want to discuss with you. I saw George and Marianne Grenville at the bookstore this morning."

"I already know you went to the bookstore," barked Harold. More politely, he asked, "Did you pick up a pink copy of *The Book of Baby Mine.*"

"No, but—"

"Dammit, Daisy! *I* can't go into bookstores and buy baby books!"

"I don't know why you can't," I said. "But there's a good—"

"I'm not about to slip up and let *anyone* know I've taken in a stray baby!" Harold now looked not merely haggard but seriously annoyed.

"Stop interrupting me! You're in a foul mood, aren't you?"

"Yes," said Harold, tugging tufts of hair on either side of his head. He was still a wreck, poor guy. "I'll probably be in a foul mood until the damn—darned baby is gone. Del is about to move out."

"No," I said. "You don't mean that. Do you?" Incredulity, thy name was Daisy. Well, you know what I mean.

"I do mean it. He's about to book a suite in the Green Hotel for the duration."

"Oh my goodness, why?" I said.

"Don't blame him," muttered Mr. Prophet. "You say the doc's upstairs with the kid?"

Evidently startled by the sudden swerve in the subject under discussion, Harold shook his head. Then he nodded. "Uh, yes. Dr. Vialargo is upstairs. Why?"

"Gotta talk to him," said Mr. Prophet, heading for the staircase.

"Oh." Harold said, understandably surprised.

Harold and I watched the old man ka-thump to the foot of the stairs. He stood there for a few seconds, taking in and releasing big breaths. Then he held tightly to the banister and began limping up the steps.

"What's the matter with Lou?" asked a bemused Harold.

"Long story," I said. "And one of the reasons I didn't get your book. But you'd better come with me. After we see the baby, I need to talk to you about adoption."

Letting go of his hair and walking with me to the staircase, Harold said, "You and Sam aren't offering to adopt the kid, are you?"

"Good Lord no!"

"Then what's all that about adoption?"

"Later, Harold," I said. "I already said I want to talk to you. But I want to see the doctor and Mr. Prophet first. I don't want any punches to fly."

"*Punches*? Why in thunder are you talking about punches?"

"I'll show you," I said. "Just shut up and follow me."

"Yes ma'am," said Harold.

We walked up the stairs and turned right to get to the baby's temporary quarters. There we encountered Mr. Prophet, who hadn't yet dared to open the door to the room. He appeared pale and frightened, which wasn't at all like the Mr. Lou Prophet I knew.

"What's the matter?" I asked. "Afraid of the doctor?"

"Ain't afraid," he snarled. "Jist…jist… Aw hell."

I gave him a gentle shove to move him out of my way, then knocked softly on the door and opened it. The picture thus revealed was a sweet one: Dr. Lawrence Vialargo smiled at Hazel Greenlaw. Hazel sat in a comfortable chair, held Melanie's baby in her arms with a bottle of formula, and returned his smile. The doctor and the nurse glanced up to see who had invaded their privacy. I guess they weren't being too private together, because both smiles turned our way and neither disappeared. Their smiles, I mean.

"How is the baby?" I asked as I entered the room, Harold hot on my heels, Mr. Prophet still in the hallway.

"She's thriving," said Dr. Vialargo in a satisfied-sounding voice. "I'd been a little bit worried about her because when babies suffer extremely early traumatic events, they sometimes fail to thrive. But this little girl is doing well."

"What do you mean, they 'fail to thrive'?" asked Harold, sounding worried once more.

"Just what I said. Sometimes, a baby—or a puppy or kitten or calf or any other baby animal—will have a negative reaction to birth trauma and will fail to thrive. That's the name of the condition: failure to thrive."

"Oh, my," I said. "I've never read about that. I'm glad this baby isn't failing to thrive."

"She's downing formula like a champ," said Hazel. "She's

already sleeping well, and her… Well, the rest of her functions work well too."

"Are you referring to poop?" I asked, having read about that part of caring for infants in one of the three thousand baby-rearing books people had given me.

"Exactly," said Hazel with a chuckle.

"I'm so glad," I said. Then I looked through the open door to the hallway and realized Mr. Prophet still hadn't dared enter the room. Therefore, I took matters into my own hands. Pushy, wasn't I? Turning to the doctor, I said, "Dr. Vialargo, what state do you hail from?"

He lifted an eyebrow, which gave him a haughty expression. "I'm not sure you could say I hail from any particular state." His voice had taken on a haughty edge too. "Why?"

I swear, men were such pains in the neck sometimes! I decided to forge onward. "Because Mr. Prophet thinks you might be his son."

Dr. V's right eyebrow lifted to match the left one. Unless it was the other way around. "Does he now?"

"Good gawd," said Harold in an undertone.

I kept my attention on the doctor. "Yes, he does, and he's petrified. I figured since he's too afraid to come into this room and face you, I'd ask for him."

"Ain't afraid!" said Mr. Prophet, who now stood in the doorway. The wrinkles on his weathered face had shaped themselves into a ferocious glower. "It's because you look like Louisa."

"Louisa, eh?" said Dr. Vialargo. His eyebrows resumed their normal position, although he didn't look appreciably less haughty.

It didn't sound to me as if either the doctor or Mr. Prophet aimed to make this easy on any of us.

"Oh, for pity's sake, please just let the old villain know," I pleaded with Dr. V. "He doesn't deserve to know, but I'd appreciate it if you'd just tell him where you come from and put us all out of his misery. *Please*."

"Difficult man is Mr. Prophet?" asked the doctor.

"You have no idea," I said. "But he's also useful once in a while. For instance, he's saved my life at least twice. I appreciate that and so does my husband."

"He has, has he?"

"Oh Larry, just tell them," said Hazel. It sounded to me as if she was as tired of this masculine to-ing and fro-ing as was I. "He was born in Nebraska," she went on. "And if you're his father, Mr. Prophet, you should be ashamed of yourself."

"Shame and Mr. Prophet don't often go hand in hand," I said acidly.

"Hellkatoot," muttered Mr. Prophet. "If you're Louisa's and mine, I'm *sorry*, all right? Miss Daisy here's been lecturing me for however long we've known each other about how terrible men are for playin' around with wimmin and never stayin' to face the consequences."

"And has she convinced you of the truth of her lectures?" asked Dr. Vialargo. "Do you understand yet why she might look upon 'loose' men the way most of society looks upon what they call 'loose' women?"

I must say, the doctor's eyes were quite startling. At the moment, it looked as if they were shooting blue flames at Mr. Prophet.

"Cripes," whispered Mr. Prophet. "You *are* Louisa's son, aren't you?"

"Louisa?" asked the doctor, who clearly didn't want to let Mr. P. off the hook so easily.

"Yeah," said Mr. P. "Louisa Bonaventure."

"Interesting name," said Dr. V. "And you think I look like this Louisa Bonaventure person, do you?"

Mr. P dropped his gaze to the carpet at his feet. "Yeah." His voice was almost inaudible.

The doctor didn't speak. Hazel and I exchanged a couple of exasperated looks.

I finally behaved like the well-bred and delicate mother-to-be I was and stamped my foot. "Darn it, you two, just get it over with!" I didn't yell in deference to the baby. If it had just been Hazel, Harold, Dr. V, Mr. P and I, I'd have hollered.

"Yes, Larry," seconded Hazel. "Just tell him!"

After giving Hazel a thick slice of his frown, Dr. Vialargo finally said, "I am Louisa Bonaventure's son."

"You are?" Mr. Prophet sounded like a bullfrog croaking.

"I am. No thanks to you or my mother, I managed to grow up and thrive in spite of you both. I'm sure you're my father because my aunt used to talk about you. Not kindly."

"Would that be 'Ol' Starchy Pants'?" I asked, curious.

Dr. Vialargo strove not to smile and managed to keep his amusement to a slight quiver of his lips. "I expect so. I wasn't allowed to call her anything but Aunt Prudence."

"Hellkatoot," croaked Mr. Prophet. "It *is* Ol' Starchy Pants. *She* brung you up? Cripes, I'm *really* sorry now."

"And you're how old?" asked the doctor.

"Older'n you," muttered Mr. P.

"I'm thirty-three," said Dr. Vialargo. "It never occurred to you that you might have children sprinkled here and there, as Mrs. Rotondo might put it?"

"Not until recently."

"*Now* do you believe me?" I asked Mr. Prophet, my own voice hard as ice crystals. "You men get off *so* easily in this stupid life."

"Not all of them are irresponsible swine," said Hazel. "Harold's a good man, and this baby isn't even his."

"True," I said.

"Your husband is a good man," Hazel went on. "My father and yours are good men."

"Yes they are," I said unwillingly. "The swine are the ones who toast my toes though." I don't think that's an actual expression; I think I just made it up.

"Mine too," said Hazel.

"Well, this has been fascinating," said Harold in a let's-get-this-party-started tone of voice. "But I want to know why you're so fascinated with George and Marianne Grenville, Daisy. I don't give two hoots about Dr. Vialargo—nothing against you, Doctor—or Lou, but I want you to tell me your news."

"I think George and Marianne Grenville might want to adopt

the child," I said. "Marianne took one look at me and burst into tears when we went to the bookstore today. George said it's because I'm pregnant, and Marianne can't *get* pregnant."

"Really?" Suddenly Harold beamed at me and looked as if a thousand-pound weight had been lifted from his shoulders. I almost feared he might take flight and bounce off the ceiling a time or two.

"Really," I affirmed. "But there are issues needing to be dealt with."

Coming down to earth with a thump, Harold said, "What issues?"

"If you go through a government agency or an adoption agency, they will investigate the adoptive parents' backgrounds to see if they're suitable. They look especially hard at people who want to adopt babies."

"What's the matter...? Oh."

"Exactly," I said.

"Is there a problem with the two adoptive parents?" asked Dr. Vialargo, his attention swerving from his probable father to Hazel, Harold and me. "If there's anything sketchy about them—"

"There isn't," I said, interrupting.

"Well, then, why are you worried?" he said, clearly puzzled.

"Marianne's father was murdered by his sons. Before they killed him, he used to beat Marianne and her mother. He also..." My voice came to an abrupt stop.

Hazel took up the gauntlet. "He raped his daughter, she got pregnant, and then he gave her an abortion that rendered her unable to have children."

"Good Lord," said Dr. Vialargo, stunned.

I smiled brightly. "Yes, although I doubt the good Lord had much to do with Dr. Wagner. But see? There are worse fathers than Mr. Prophet in the world!"

"I had a worse one too," said Harold, acting as the Greek chorus to Hazel's and my act.

"In fact," I said having thought of the Buckinghams, "Mr. Prophet is like a great-uncle to the three-year-old son of some friends of mine."

"Is that so?" asked the doctor, haughty once more.

"Well, maybe a great-great-uncle."

"Hellkatoot," said Mr. Prophet.

TWENTY

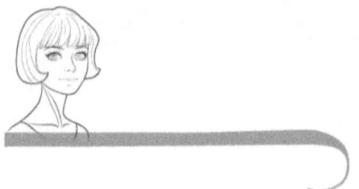

Harold herded Dr. Vialargo, Mr. Prophet, and me out of the baby's room and downstairs to his gracious hallway. He said, "Let's talk about this in the living room. We'll give Hazel time to put the baby down."

"Put the baby *down*?" I was horrified for a second. "Oh, you mean put the baby in its crib."

"What else would I have meant?" asked an understandably touchy Harold.

"Just for a tiny moment there, I thought you meant euthanasia," I admitted.

"Good God," said Harold.

Mr. Prophet remained silent.

I think Dr. Vialargo chuckled softly.

Harold's living room, as you have no doubt already guessed, was a large and lovely room with fresh flowers in vases here and there. Over the fireplace hung a picture of a modern young woman wearing a gold-colored cloche and dress sniffing a red, red rose. It was absolutely beautiful, and I'd never seen it before.

"Harold, that picture is gorgeous. When did you get it?"

"Last month," said Harold, distracted for a moment. "The artist is Andrew Edovard Marty, and its title is *The Scent of Roses*. Had it shipped from France. I had one picked out for you, but you're having a boy and the one I wanted is of a girl."

"How do you know Mrs. Rotondo is carrying a boy?" asked Dr. Vialargo, surprised out of his thoughts.

Oh boy. Could I tell this doctor I knew I carried a boy because I was told so by a Tongva shaman? Harold and I swapped looks, and I said, "Just a guess."

"Hmmm." Dr. Vialargo stared at my belly for entirely too long. Then he shook his head. "You do know, don't you, that there's really no way of telling until the child is born? I hope you're not buying everything in a special color because you think you'll have a boy."

"No," I said. "Nothing like that. But we need to discuss the Grenvilles adopting Harold's baby."

"It's not *my* baby," said Harold indignantly. "It was born to my niece—or maybe she's a cousin—Melanie."

"We're pretty sure she's the mother anyway," I said because we couldn't be absolutely positive the baby upstairs came from Melanie Robinson's body.

"If what you told me about the…Grenvilles? Is that their name?" asked Dr. Vialargo.

"Yes. George and Marianne Grenville," I confirmed. "They own Grenville's Books on Colorado and Oak Knoll."

"I've been there," said the doctor, sounding surprised. "But if everything you told me about them is true, how can they ever hope to adopt a baby?"

"They're not responsible for her father's evil deeds," said Harold. "Just as I'm not responsible for impregnating Melanie or for ruining my father's bank, which my father tried his best to do."

"Your father has a bank?" asked the doc, confused.

"No. He tried to ruin his bank. Del, my roommate, saved it. My father's in prison at the moment, and I trust he'll stay there until he croaks."

Appearing vaguely shocked, Dr. Vialargo said, "My goodness. We're not talking about your father, however, but about the

Grenvilles. Do you honestly believe they'd be appropriate parents for the tiny bundle upstairs?"

"Yes," I said firmly. "George and Marianne are great people. Marianne's been through a lot, but she's weathered all of life's slings and arrows so far."

"That may be true, but is she fit to be a mother?" asked the doctor candidly. "How could she have learned to care for children if she was never cared for herself?"

"Her mother is a saint," I said, perhaps exaggerating a bit. Not much though.

"I thought you said she was beaten by her husband." The doc squinted disapprovingly at me.

"I did, because she was, but her only fault was in accepting the hand of Dr. Everhard Wagner in marriage. She didn't know he was the devil incarnate until after they tied the knot." I frowned back at Dr. V.

"Why did she stay if he was so bad to her and her daughter?" asked the doc.

"Because she'd have had to divorce him, of course!" Me.

"Isn't divorce better than having a husband who beats you and rapes your daughter?" Dr. V.

"Have you ever tried to get a divorce as a woman?" Me.

"Of course not." Dr. V. Superciliously.

"Then you don't know what you're talking about." Me.

"You tell me then," said Dr. V, scowling hideously.

"He had the money and adult sons. Diane Wagner had nothing of her own, except two sons who treated her abominably and a daughter she tried her very best to protect," I told him. "It's only recently that women even got the right to *vote*, for pity's sake! Do you honestly think a male judge or a panel of male jurors would listen to, much less give credence to, a woman who claimed her husband was a monster? Especially when the man was a *doctor*? Poor Mrs. Wagner—she ultimately changed her name back to her maiden name, Chapman—had been beaten down so many times, she almost believed she deserved it! She's recovering now, thanks to George and Marianne—"

"And you," Harold chucked in.

"I suppose so," I admitted. To Dr. V, I said, "Have you ever even *considered* the abuse some women have to suffer at the hands of their spouses? Ever? Before now, I mean?"

My voice had risen as had my temper. Dr. Vialargo's blue eyes widened as I hurled words at him.

Bless Harold for a saint, he said, "Yes, Doctor. What Daisy said is the absolute truth. If you don't believe it, ask the Buckinghams at the Salvation Army. Mrs. Buckingham is the person who saved Mrs. Bannister's life after Mr. Bannister beat her almost to death."

"Ugh," I said. "I'll never forget that episode."

"Nor will I," said Harold with a bite to his voice.

Mr. Prophet, a hangdog expression on his face, sat in a chair far, far away from the rest of us. I'd almost forgotten he was there until we all heard a rusty, "Yeah. Men like that don't deserve to live. I might have been a lousy father, but I never beat a woman."

"Well, there you go," said Dr. V. "A sterling endorsement from an impeccable source."

"Stop it," I told him. "You may *not* judge the Grenvilles. Harold and I know them well, and we both know them to have sterling characters. And so does Diane, who lives with them and will be a great asset in caring for the baby. Both Diane and Marianne are wonderful women who were vilely abused. Their abuser is now dead, and the three sons of Mr. Wagner are tucked safely away in a prison far, far away."

"I don't know…" Dr. V's voice petered out.

"We do, so you don't have to think about it," I retorted.

"But if what you say is correct, how do you expect them to pass an investigation into their past?" At least Dr. V didn't sound as annoyingly condescending as he had earlier.

"Because we won't go through an adoption or government agency!" I said triumphantly. "Harold knows all sorts of attorneys, and the adoption can be private between Melanie and the Grenvilles. Or Harold and the Grenvilles. Or the lawyer and the Grenvilles. No other entity needs to be involved in the adoption."

"I might speak up," said Dr. Vialargo.

I stared daggers at him. "Why? Why would you do that? Would you prefer to see the infant upstairs put on one of those despicable orphan trains? They're still legal, you know. Or dumped in an orphanage? Children have even fewer rights than women in this supposedly enlightened country."

After an extended spate of silence, Dr. Vialargo finally admitted, "No. Those two options are terrible."

"I won't see Melanie's child thrown into an orphanage," said Harold, his voice hard as steel. "You have nothing to say about this, Doctor."

"I should have a say," muttered Dr. Vialargo.

"Why?" I asked. "We don't need your permission. If a doctor's statement is required, Harold and I both know many other doctors. You're not the only physician in town. In fact, you're a newcomer. Besides, if you're still waffling about the Grenvilles, ask Hazel! She knows all about them. Believe me."

"Crumb," said Harold. "That's right. She had a run-in with Dr. Wagner too, didn't she?"

"What?" Dr. V cried. "Miss Greenlaw? That man abused her too?"

"Yes," I snarled. "And she's taking care of the baby right this minute. Do you want to go upstairs and snatch the kid away from her?"

"Cripes," muttered Mr. Prophet from his far-away corner.

"No," said the doctor with a hard shake of his head. "Miss Greenlaw is an excellent nurse. She would never hurt a child."

"Neither would Marianne Grenville," I said.

"Well..." But Dr. Vialargo seemed to have run out of steam.

"It's the truth, Doctor," said Harold. "But Daisy, we have to pick up Melanie and take her to the morgue to view the body."

"What's this about a *body*?" Dr. Vialargo, shocked again. "What sort of place have I moved to?"

"Pasadena, California," I snarled. "It's a beautiful city with a low crime rate. But there are villains around in spite of its beauty. Look at Dr. Wagner. Oh, that's right. You can't because he's dead."

"Are you telling me the young woman whom you believe to be

the mother of the infant upstairs has to identify a dead body?" He was even more shocked now.

I sent Harold an incensed look. "Yes. A murder victim who might have been the baby's father."

"I don't understand any of this," said the doctor.

"You don't have to," I told him. "All you have to do is go on about your business. Harold and I will tackle the ugly side of life, so you don't need to." Sarcastic brat, wasn't I? I mean bwat.

"Cripes," said Mr. Prophet. "Guess I'll have to go with you." He, on the other hand, sounded relieved.

"Better a murdered man than your son, eh?" I said, feeling almost as peeved with him as I was with the doctor.

"Dammit," said Mr. Prophet.

"What time is it anyway?" I asked anyone who might care to answer.

Harold shook his sleeve down and peered at his wristwatch. "Eleven-thirty."

"No wonder I'm hungry," I said. "It's almost lunchtime."

"Let's get Melanie's part of the day's problems taken care of first," said Harold. "Do you mind terribly? I don't think it'll take much time for her to tell us if the body is that of her lover or that of somebody else."

"Good Lord," said Dr. Vialargo. "I'll be on my way." He stood, shuffled around a bit and said, "First, I'll check on the baby one last time."

"Want to make sure Hazel isn't smothering it?" I asked. Was I in a mood or what?

"Nonsense," said the doctor. He turned stiffly and went to the staircase.

"Let's get out o' here," said Mr. Prophet.

"Let me put on my jacket first. And brush my hair" said Harold, who never went anywhere unless he was neat and shiny.

"And I'll use the powder room," I said.

"I'll take us all to Mijares after we finish with Melanie," said Harold as he ran up the stairs to his room.

"That sounds good," I said.

"Yeah," said Mr. Prophet.

"You're going with us?" I said.

"Well, yeah. Guess I'll have to. Won't I?"

"I suppose so." I took off for the downstairs powder room.

After I'd relieved myself and washed my hands, I surveyed my face in the mirror. It wouldn't hurt to un-shine my nose and renew my Tangee Natural lip rouge. I retrieved my pretty Richard Hudnut powder compact from my small handbag, patted neutral powder on my nose and brushed off the excess. Then I dabbed a tiny bit of the lip rouge on my cheeks and used my fingers to give myself a little color. Lastly, I used the lip rouge on my lips, washed my hands, and left the powder room to join Harold and Mr. Prophet.

They'd gathered in the hallway at the front entrance, along with Hazel and Dr. Vialargo.

"I called the hospital," said Harold. "And I also called Sam. I figured he'd want to be there for the identification of the corpse."

"Excellent idea," I said.

"My pleasure." Harold gave me an exaggerated bow.

"Where's the baby?" I asked, hoping as I did so that Hazel hadn't actually smothered it or done anything else of a drastic nature.

"Roy's watching her for a few minutes," said Hazel. "He's extremely gentle and good with the wee thing."

"And he's another person *you* wouldn't allow near a baby, isn't he?" I said to the doctor.

"God, don't tell me *he* was abused by that dead doctor too?" Dr. Vialargo looked and sounded distressed. "I always thought Pasadena was a civilized city."

"It is," I said. "But people don't like to admit what goes on behind closed doors anywhere, even in Pasadena."

"That's the truth," said Hazel. She patted the doctor's shoulder. "It's all right, Larry. You've been a medical doctor long enough to know the truth of Daisy's statement."

Dr. V gave Hazel a rather fond smile—which surprised me— and said, "You're correct, of course."

"Very well," said Harold. "If we've trodden that ugly subject into the ground, let's go. I'm hungry too, and I'm looking forward to some Mexican food."

"Me too," I said.

"Uh," said Mr. Prophet. I think he was afraid to speak lest I drive him up to Sam's and my house and dump him off at the curb.

"Mexican food?" said Hazel, her appropriately called hazel eyes twinkling. "Are you going to Mijares? I love that place!"

"Yes," said Harold. "After we visit the morgue."

"Sounds like a pleasant afternoon," said Hazel with a laugh.

The doctor cleared his throat. "Um, perhaps you would take dinner there with me, Miss Greenlaw. After work."

"Good idea," said Harold brightly. "The night nurse arrives at seven. Mijares is open until nine, I think."

"I think you're right," said Hazel. She gave the doctor a brilliant smile. "I'd love to dine with you, Larry."

Dr. Lawrence Vialargo, stuffy and upright illegitimate son of Mr. Lou Prophet, bounty hunter, and Miss Louisa Bonaventure, the so-called Vengeance Queen, blushed like a schoolboy.

TWENTY-ONE

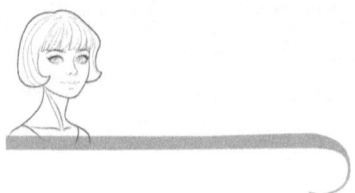

"Did you see the good doctor turn red when he asked Hazel to have dinner with him?" I asked Harold as he settled behind the wheel of his Mercedes.

"Yes, I did," said Harold, chuckling.

"Don't act like any son o' mine," grumbled Mr. Prophet from the backseat.

"I suppose not. He at least attempts to be a man of honor, unlike some other men of my acquaintance." There I went, being bwatty again.

"Shucks," grumbled Mr. Prophet.

I glanced into the backseat, surprised by Mr. P's innocent comment.

The Los Angeles County Morgue had an office in Pasadena, in the basement of the city hall. The city hall, along with the Pasadena Public Library, was scheduled to be replaced in February of 1927. The police department was also located in City Hall. The P.P.D. would get its own special building when Pasadena's new Civic Center, including the library, city hall, and courthouse were opened. I'd miss the present library, but not the present city hall and its over-stuffed departments.

First, though, we had to visit the Castleton Hospital. Because we didn't want Melanie to be any more terrified than she already was, we told Mr. Prophet to stay in Harold's car. Mr. Prophet's hygiene was fine, but he still looked like a desperado.

When Harold pulled up to the curb and he and I walked to the hospital, Melanie Robinson was waiting for us, along with an attendant whom I presumed to be a nurse, in the lobby of the building. Melanie looked pale and frightened, and I felt sorry for her.

"Are you able to walk, Melanie?" asked Harold.

"Yes," she said in a tiny voice.

"Daisy and I will walk on either side of you, so you'll have our support if you need it," Harold told her.

"Thank you," whispered Melanie.

With assistance from the nurse, Melanie managed to stand. She didn't appear sure-footed yet but Harold took one arm, I took the other, and we slowly guided her to the hospital's front door. Glancing back at the nurse, Harold said, "We'll bring her back soon."

"Yes," said the nurse sternly. "We will expect you to return in less than forty-five minutes."

"That will be plenty of time," I said.

When we walked outside, I noticed Melanie suddenly squint in the bright sunshine, and her footsteps faltered. Harold and I held her up and allowed her time to adjust to the altered lighting.

"Oh my," she said. "It seems like forever since I've been outdoors."

When she opened her eyes and turned her head to look at her surroundings, she shut them again quickly and let out a gasp. She'd been through an ordeal and a half in recent days. Come to think of it, it had undoubtedly been an ordeal of several months.

"Just come with us to the car, Melanie. You'll be able to see better when your eyes adjust."

"Yes," she said softly. "I'm so sorry, Harold."

"It's all right," Harold told her, although nothing was all right about Melanie's situation. I mentally applauded his attempt to make the kid feel better.

If the body in the morgue turned out to be the louse of a man she thought she loved, however, I didn't think her better mood would last long. I couldn't even imagine having to identify the body of my husband or aunt or anyone else whom I loved. Such a thing would surely crush a sensitive soul. I didn't think Melanie had much strength of character left, if she'd ever had any at all. I'd seen first-hand how a brutal, cruel man could devastate a woman's spirit. I'm only fortunate the men in my life had so far been good ones, starting with my father.

"Melanie," I said as we approached Harold's Mercedes. "Don't be alarmed by the fellow in the backseat. His name is Mr. Lou Prophet, and he's a friend of Harold's and mine. He isn't as disreputable as he looks. He's only old and worn out."

"Daisy," said Harold, sounding as if he were reproving me for my candor.

"Harold," I said, "he does look kind of scary."

"I don't mind," said Melanie.

"Still, you sit in the front seat along with Harold. I'll sit beside you. Mr. Prophet will remain in the backseat."

"I'll introduce you. He's not as rough as he looks," said Harold.

"Not quite," I equivocated.

Harold opened the front door of his Mercedes. We both helped Melanie get in. She seemed to be in some pain. From having given birth? From having been abused? Who knew? I sure didn't. I knew it was painful for a woman to give birth, but I didn't know how much recovery time she needed. Guess I'd find out soon enough.

Mr. Prophet grunted a "H'lo" when introduced to Melanie. She didn't say anything but squeaked something that might have been a word. Couldn't tell.

A few minutes later, Harold found a parking place in the lot next to City Hall, and he opened the front door for Melanie and me. I helped her get out of the car, and then Harold and I again acted as use-as-needed crutches for the girl.

I was overjoyed when I saw Sam in the lobby of the police station. He rose upon our entry. "Miss Robinson," he said, and gave her a tiny bow.

"Are-are you a policeman?" asked Melanie, shrinking back a little.

"Melanie, this is my husband, Detective Sam Rotondo," I told her. "You might not remember, but the two of you met in your hospital room a couple of days ago."

"Oh," whispered Melanie. She hesitated for a second then said, "I-I don't recall much from my first couple of days in the hospital."

"Perfectly understandable," said Sam. "Here, let me help you. We can take the service elevator downstairs to where you'll be needed."

He meant the morgue. Sam could be tactful when tact was called for. He guided us all to the big elevator where every now and then the odd unidentified body was carted to the morgue if the P.D. couldn't find family members to take charge and send the corpse to a mortuary. The elevator rattled a lot and didn't smell very good. The entire city hall carried a whiff of old-age and misery, which was odd since it hadn't been in operation for very long. Twenty-some years. But Pasadena kept growing and growing, and new quarters had become necessary. I didn't know if the city fathers aimed to tear down this building when the new, ornate and gigantic city hall opened. Maybe they'd use it for other purposes. It was one building I wouldn't mind seeing destroyed.

The basement area was cold as the grave, which was fitting, but which didn't help Melanie feel any better. She shivered, but nobody had thought to bring a wrap for her.

When we entered another frigidly cold room, we saw a long window on its other wall. The windows' draperies were pulled closed. Guess they didn't want to display any old cadaver, but waited until a specific one was required for viewing. Sam left us facing the window, took a couple of steps to his right and knocked at a door. A fellow in white cracked the door open maybe an inch and said, "Smithfield?"

"Yes," said Sam. He came back to stand with Melanie, Harold, and me.

"What happens now?" asked Melanie.

"We're going to stand here with you, and an orderly will pull the curtain back from the window. Be prepared to see the body of a man lying on a cot behind the curtain. The orderly will lift the sheet from the face. Please let us know if you recognize the man on the cot." Sam's voice was kind as he relayed the hideous message.

"D-do they think it's Jimmy?" asked Melanie, her voice thick.

"We don't know," said Sam. "We're hoping you might recognize him. I'm sorry you have to do this."

"It's all right," said Melanie. "I know it's my duty. I've been so stupid."

Because tears had begun trickling down her cheeks, I withdrew a clean hankie from my pocket and handed it to Melanie.

"Th-thank you," she murmured.

"Are you ready?" asked Sam.

Melanie nodded. Sam tapped softly on the window, and the curtain was drawn aside to reveal a dead man on a cot. The attendant did precisely what Sam said he'd do and gently pulled the sheet away from the dead man's face.

After Melanie gazed at the body and remained mute for several seconds, Sam asked, "Are you all right, Miss Robinson?"

"Yes," she said. "But I don't understand. I thought you said I'd be identifying Jimmy."

Harold and I swapped glances. Sam's attention was glued to Melanie. "This isn't Jimmy Smith?" he asked softly.

"No. Let me get a little closer, please."

Leaving Harold and me behind, Sam took one of Melanie's arms and slowly led her to the head end of the window. She leaned forward, cupped her hands to her eyes, and stared longer at the dead fellow. She dropped her hands and shook her head after several seconds.

"I don't understand," she repeated. "Where's Jimmy?"

"If this isn't Mr. Smith," said Sam, "we don't know where he is. Do you recognize this fellow at all? Have you seen him before?"

For the record, the deceased appeared to be a dark-haired young man, perhaps in his twenties. His face was ashen because he was dead, but I think in life he might have had a ruddy complexion. I also figured his eyes were brown, although I don't know why I assumed their color.

"It's Jimmy's friend," whispered a clearly bewildered Melanie. "I've met him several times with Jimmy."

"Ah," said Sam. "Do you recall his name?"

"Yes. I think so."

"Would you mind telling us who he is? His name?" asked a still-gentle Sam.

"No, no. I wouldn't mind. That man's name is Frank." She pointed at the body behind the window.

"Frank?"

"Yes."

"Did you ever hear his last name?" prodded Sam.

"Um, yes. I think so. It was like yours. Something Italian, I mean."

"Italian, you say?" Sam's eyebrows rose. There weren't a whole lot of Italians in Southern California. Yet. I'm sure they'd come eventually.

"Yes," whispered Melanie. She closed her eyes and, I presume, began to think.

Names are funny. Sometimes I'll hear a name and remember it forever. Other times, I'll hear a name and it's gone the next instant. I figured Melanie was sifting through her gray cells in an attempt to call the dead guy's name to mind.

"Oh," she said, opening her eyes. "I remember now."

"Yes?" said Sam.

"He was Jimmy's friend. This is Frank. Frank Pagano."

I nearly fainted on the spot.

"Frank *Pagano*?" Sam's voice rose on the last word, making Melanie wince. He cleared his throat. "I'm sorry, Miss Robinson, but did you say the man on that cot"—he pointed—"is Frank Pagano? You don't believe his name could be something that... well...*sounds* like Pagano?"

Puzzled once more, Melanie said, "What sounds like Pagano?"

"Um..." It was a valid question, and I saw Sam struggling. He, however, knew scads more Italian last names than I did, so I didn't offer suggestions. "Oh, like Palumbo. Or Donato? Repetto? Vigano? Gambino?"

Melanie looked up at Sam and shook her head. "N-no. No, I'm sure Jimmy said his last name is—well, was—Pagano."

After blowing out a big breath, Sam said, "Thank you very much, Miss Robinson."

"But...but where's Jimmy?" asked Melanie. She began leaking tears again and put my hankie, which was still damp from the first bout of weepage, to use.

"We don't know," said Sam.

T'was but the truth.

"I...don't get it," said Melanie.

"We don't get it either, Melanie," I said, my voice at purr-level. "From information found on this man's person, we thought he was James Smith. Or perhaps James Smithfield. But you're certain this fellow isn't your Jimmy?"

"No. No. That man is Frank. Frank Pagano."

"Very well," said Sam. "Thank you for your time, Miss Robinson. Mr. Kincaid and Daisy will take you back to the hospital now. I'm sorry about any mix-up."

"I'm not," said Melanie, sounding firmer than she had thus far in my acquaintance with her. "I don't want Jimmy to be dead."

"I'm sure you don't, Melanie," said Harold. "But the matron or whoever she was at the hospital will be expecting you back there in a few minutes, so we'd better get going now."

"I'm so confused!" Melanie cried weakly.

"Here, hold onto my arm," I said. "Harold and I will help you out to the car and take you back to the hospital."

"Thank you," said Melanie. She added, "I think."

Carefully turning Melanie, I helped her shuffle to the door leading to the hallway. I heard Harold say, "Sam, just a minute. I have to ask you something."

"Yes?" said Sam, not as gently as he'd spoken to Melanie. I could tell he was frustrated. I expect he was also furious, upset, outraged, and fit to be tied.

TWENTY-TWO

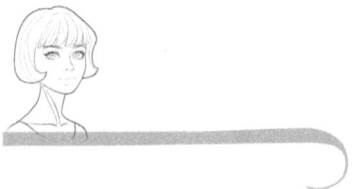

Frank Pagano was Sam Rotondo's no-good nephew! Melanie and I waited at the elevator. Sam and Harold soon joined us and we creaked and clanked up to the lobby floor of the station. We got Melanie to Harold's Mercedes, and I rode with Harold, Mr. Prophet, and Melanie back to the hospital. I waited in the car as Harold escorted his shaky cousin—second cousin?—to the hospital's front door.

Mr. Prophet, who didn't smoke as much as he did when I first met him, got out of the backseat and rolled himself a quirley—that's Western for a cigarette. He sucked in smoke and blew it out again. I'd never understood the appeal of smoking, but many young women who attempted to achieve the "flapper" image smoked in those days.

"Boy, was that a surprise," I muttered to Mr. Prophet when he regained the backseat.

"What was?" he asked.

"She said the body in the morgue wasn't that of Jimmy Smith but of a fellow called Frank Pagano."

"Pagano?" said Mr. P. "Ain't he the feller tried to knife you a couple o' years back?"

"The very one," I confirmed. "This time he knifed someone else, and he didn't miss. I think the guy he knifed was a friend of Melanie's beloved. Frank is the one who called himself Jimmy Smith. But Jimmy Smith isn't his real name either, evidently."

"Huh?"

"The driving license in the dead man's trouser pocket said he was a James Smithfield. I'm sure those papers belonged to the real Jimmy Smith. I'm also sure James Smithfield was the dead man's actual name. But Melanie said the corpse's name was Frank Pagano."

"Why you sure of that?"

"It would be too coincidental for a fellow named Smith and another one named Smithfield to be hanging out with Melanie Robinson in Pasadena at the same time. Especially if Smith or Smithfield palled around with Frank Pagano, who is a detestable person."

"Why would that be so dang coincidental?"

"Except rarely or in books by Charles Dickens, coincidences tend not to happen. And Melanie said her beloved, whose name she thought was Jimmy Smith, isn't the dead man but rather a close friend of his."

"Huh?"

"Yes," I said. "It's perplexing."

"I still can't figure out what you said," said Mr. Prophet.

"Completely understandable," I said. I couldn't figure it out either.

Shortly after returning Melanie to the nurse, Harold hurried back to the machine. "Jeez, I don't know what's going on. Melanie still claims the dead guy is Frank Pagano. But that corpse didn't belong to Frank Pagano, did it, Daisy?"

"No, unfortunately, it didn't. I suspect Melanie's precious Jimmy was actually Frank, and the guy in the morgue whom she thought was Frank was really Jimmy."

Silence filled the car. I got the feeling both men sharing space with me in the auto were attempting to disentangle my words.

"What a mess," Harold said after several seconds. "If that was the real Jimmy Smith—"

"Last name is Smithfield, according to his driving license."

"Cripes," muttered Mr. Prophet.

"Oh," said Harold. "Yeah. You're right, I guess."

Nobody spoke as Harold pulled away from the curb, drove to Fair Oaks, hung a right and headed to Pasadena Avenue and Palmetto Street. Palmetto was where Mijares Mexican Restaurant sat releasing tantalizing aromas into the air around it. I was surprised to see Sam's Hudson parked not far from the entrance of the restaurant.

"I told Sam to meet us here," said Harold, clearing my befuddlement before I could speak of it.

"Thanks, Harold. What a good idea," I said, happy to see my husband. And the restaurant. I was starving to death by then—not literally—and had to use the facilities. But that last part was only normal for me in recent weeks.

As soon as Sam saw us, he hurried to Harold's Mercedes and opened the door for me. He helped me from the auto, and I'm pleased to report my grunt was too soft for most people to hear. "I need to use the powder room," I told my patient husband.

"Figured as much. I've already asked where it is. Go in the front door and turn right."

"You're a saint, Sam," I told him.

"I'm not feeling saintly at the moment," he said.

I understood. Frank Pagano. Sam's nephew used to be merely a pain in the neck. His villainy had grown significantly, though, in a mere two years or so. He'd not only attempted my own personal life, but he'd demolished Harold's zippy little Kissel Gold Bug by driving it into a ditch. Since then he'd managed to succeed in killing someone. At least that's what I surmised after the morning's odd and unsettling visit to the morgue.

As I hurried as well as I could to the front door of Mijares, Mr. Prophet and Harold exited Harold's Mercedes and joined Sam. They followed me into the restaurant. When I'd done my business, washed my hands and looked in the mirror, I decided I wasn't too shiny. Therefore, I left the powder room to find Sam waiting for me. What a good man I'd married! And to think I'd hated him at first.

"Thought I'd better wait here to escort you to our table," he said.

"Thanks, Sam." Then I sniffled because I couldn't help it.

Alarmed, Sam said, "What the devil's wrong with you?"

"Nothing. I'm just so happy I'm married to you."

When Sam said nothing, I glanced up at his face. He appeared perplexed.

"It's true," I said. "You could have been a louse like your nephew or Dr. Wagner or Mr. Bannister, but you aren't. You're a good man. My Billy was a good man too. I'm fortunate to have found you both."

"If you say so," said Sam, sounding somewhat sarcastic. "I agree about Billy."

"Thank you." I saved further sniffles for later. I'd sacrificed my hankie to Melanie, so couldn't mop up my own teary cheek. Besides, crying would embarrass Sam, Harold, *and* Mr. Prophet. Although I didn't have a whole lot of sympathy for the elderly rogue, I figured he'd been embarrassed enough for one day.

Our booth wasn't far from the door, and Harold and Mr. P were seated already. Harold rose when he saw me. Mr. P didn't, but I didn't expect him to. What with his leg and peg and sitting at the wall end of the booth, he couldn't maneuver very well.

"Ain't been to this place for a long time," said Mr. P.

"I haven't either," I said, sitting and scooching myself across the padded bench so Sam could sit where the waiter would be. I picked up my menu and started salivating.

"Me neither," said Harold. "Not sure why. I like the place a lot. Del isn't so fond of it, but he likes his food rather plain." His brow wrinkled. "Although I don't know why. He comes from New Orleans, and they have spicy Cajun food there."

"What does Cajun mean?" I asked, lifting my gaze from the menu for a second and squinting at Harold.

It was Mr. Prophet who answered my question. "Cajuns are folks who live in the Louisiana Bayous. Lots of 'em in New Orleans. They're mainly descended from French Canadians."

"My goodness," I said. "They're a long way from Canada."

"Yeah," said Mr. P.

I resumed studying my menu.

"I'm going to get a couple of tamales and rice and beans," Sam announced, placing his menu back on the table.

"Sounds good to me," said Harold. "Only I want a taco too."

"I'll have a couple of tacos," I announced. "I want the ones with beef in them."

"Sounds good," said Sam. "Want rice and beans with your tacos?"

"Um…yes," I said at last, thinking about the effects beans have on the human body. We'd had beans and ham a few days ago, so eating beans today most likely wouldn't make for a more tuneful afternoon than I wanted. Anyhow, I aimed to nap with Spike, so it wouldn't matter.

"I'll have a couple of tamales and a taco. With rice and beans," said Mr. Prophet, who'd been eating Mexican food for decades. In fact, Mijares was one of the few things about Pasadena in which he actually took pleasure.

After giving the waiter our orders and requesting water for all of us, Sam said, "Do you think that poor baby was fathered by my lousy nephew?"

"Sounds like it," I said, likewise concerned for the infant in Harold's home. "I hope badness isn't inherited."

"It might be," said Harold. Then he said, "No, it couldn't be. Stacy and I had the same parents, and Stacy and I were about as alike as mud and air."

"True," I said. "If the Grenvilles are able to adopt the wee mite, they'll rear her properly. I don't remember if what little hair she has was light or dark. Do you know, Harold?"

"Nope," said Harold. "The kid has only looked red and bald since I met her."

"Same," said Mr. Prophet.

"But it seems my criminal nephew is back in Pasadena and spreading his degenerate ways through the populace."

"I thought you put him in jail the last time he was here," I said. "He sure committed enough criminal acts."

"I did. He got out somehow. I think Renata posted bond for him, and he skipped town. Renata lost that money, and her murdering son is out loose again. Damn him."

"Renata's still a pretty name, although your sister doesn't seem to have a lot of common sense."

"She doesn't," snapped Sam.

"Melanie lived in Eagle Rock, so he must have hung out there too. Wonder why they came to Pasadena," said Harold.

"My guess would be to find you and hope you'd give them money," I said.

"Cripes," said Harold. "If it were just Melanie and the baby, I wouldn't mind spending money, but I'll be damned if I'll support your lousy nephew, Sam."

"Makes sense to me," said Sam. "If I ever see him again, I'll arrest him for murder and abandonment."

"Can men be arrested for abandonment of their families?" I asked, intrigued.

"Yes. Of course, the same law applies to Melanie, although she's a minor, so I suspect Frank will get another charge added to his record because of that." His grin was downright wicked. Frank deserved it.

"I'd rather Melanie not get into trouble," said Harold. "Although I don't appreciate her using me as a dumping ground for her baby."

"Don't blame you on either count," I told him.

"Huh," said Mr. Prophet. "Mebbe you just oughta shove your nasty nephew in front of a trolley car if you ever see him again, Sam."

"Sounds like a good plan to me," said Sam. "But where the devil is he now?"

"You probably should have officers searching for him," I said.

"Not as easy as it sounds," said Sam.

"True," I said. "But you can post men at the train station, can't you? And have them pay attention at intersections and so forth. Heck, even places like the library are fair hiding places for people who don't want to be found. I'd bet you anything Frank's never been in a library in his life, so he'd never suspect other people go there on purpose. Same with churches."

"I suppose," said Sam. "Churches are a good idea. He was horrified when he found out my fiancée wasn't an Italian Catholic."

"I remember it well," I said, smiling. "He stole a silver cross from the Methodist Church."

"He damn near knifed you in that church too," said Mr. Prophet. "Cripes, if you hadn't moved your head just when you did, you'd'a been stuck to that bench forever."

"It's a pew, Lou," said Sam. "And I'd have detached her."

"Dunno why," mumbled Mr. Prophet.

"Pooh on you," I said in my most adult, sophisticated manner.

"You're right about the train station," said Sam. "I wonder if there's a telephone booth around here."

The waiter brought a tray full of water glasses then, so Sam asked him about the telephone booth situation. After blinking at Sam for a second, the waiter said, "*No sé.*"

Mr. Prophet proved his worth at last. To the waiter he said, "*Tienes el teléfono?*"

"Ah, *sí*," said the waiter, smiling at the old scoundrel. "*Venga conmigo, por favor.*"

"*Gracias*," said Mr. P. "Go with the waiter, Sam. He'll take you to the telephone."

"Thanks, Lou," said Sam, gratified. To the waiter, he said, "*Gracias, señor.*" He rose as the waiter distributed water glasses, then went with the aproned man to the front of the restaurant.

"Golly," I said to Mr. P. "You're good for something after all."

"Daisy!" said Harold, horrified.

"It's all right, Kincaid. I'm used to getting beat up by Miss Daisy."

"Fiddlesticks," I said, although I wished I hadn't said what I'd said. It wasn't very nice, was it? Ah well.

Sam returned to our booth about a minute before our food arrived.

"Ah, I'm glad you're back, Sam," I said.

"Me too," said Mr. Prophet. "Yer wife's bein' cruel to me again."

"It's true, Sam. She is," said Harold.

"I'm sorry," I said.

"Sure you are," said Mr. P.

"I am," I insisted.

"Well, you can both stop pestering each other now," said Sam.

"I suppose so," I said. "Did you call the station and ask for officers to patrol the Santa Fe Station?"

"Yes, and also for a couple of men to look in Catholic churches and the library," said Sam. "They still have a 'wanted' dodger for Frank, and Doan has photos he took of him."

"Good," I said.

"Ah," said Sam as the waiter showed up with a tray full of fragrant Mexican dishes. "Let's eat."

We did, and the food was delicious. I only recalled the casserole dish Mrs. Rattle aimed to prepare for us as I stuffed the last bite of beans and rice—smothered in lovely melted cheese—into my mouth. Then I said, "Oh dear."

"What's wrong now?" asked Mr. Prophet.

"I forgot all about Mrs. Rattle's shepherd's pie. She said she'd prepare it for us for supper tonight."

"It'll keep in the Frigidaire, won't it?" asked Sam.

"Yes, I do believe it will," I said, cheering up.

"Good," said Sam, leaning back in the booth and sighing. "We probably won't need another full meal today. They sure have good grub here. Can't get Mexican food in New York."

"It sure is," said Harold. "I'd take something home for Hazel and Roy, but I guess Hazel will be dining here with the good doctor, and Roy always has food if anyone needs it."

"Good doctor, huh," Mr. Prophet mumbled under his breath.

"He does seem to be a competent physician," I said.

"I reckon," growled Mr. P.

"You should be happy to have such a well-educated and capable son," I told him.

"Hellkatoot," he said.

I swear, I couldn't win with the man.

TWENTY-THREE

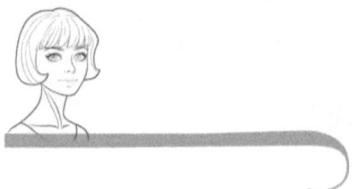

B ecause Sam had to get back to the station and coordinate teams to search for Frank, Harold drove Mr. Prophet and me to his house so I could fetch the Chevrolet.

"I have to pick up Spike," I said as I settled behind the wheel. "Then I'm going to go home and start reading *The Chinese Parrot*."

"Have fun," said Harold.

"She'll prob'ly nap," said Mr. Crotchet. I beg your pardon. Prophet.

"Good idea," said Harold, bless him. "She needs to rest. She's carrying a precious bundle, don't forget."

I stared at him for a second or two, but discerned no sarcasm, so I said, "Yes, don't forget it."

"Shi-oot," said Mr. Prophet. "A 'precious bundle,' is it?"

"Yes," Harold and I said together.

"Okay then," said Mr. P.

Harold waved us off.

I parked the Chevrolet in the driveway, and Mr. P. and I walked to the side entrance of my parents' bungalow. We were met by a deliriously happy Rosie and Spike. Pa wasn't far behind them. "Busy morning?" said Pa.

"Very," I said. "But I got *The Chinese Parrot*! And books for you, Ma, and Vi."

"Excellent," said Pa. "I think Rosie's worn Spike out." He laughed.

"Spike, did that brazen hussy wear you out?" I asked my dog, my voice oozing sympathy.

"Women tend to do that to a man," muttered Mr. Prophet.

"Not really," said Pa. "They've been good doggies. In fact, except for a couple of times when they went out back and played, they've been pretty much asleep since you left."

"Oh, good," I said. "Spike and I can practice more napping at home."

My father smiled and kissed my cheek.

Mr. Prophet said, "Huh."

Mrs. Rattle was long gone by the time I finally walked into our lovely home. I felt bone-weary, so after making sure everything in the house was as it should be—we had experienced a couple of unfortunate incursions in the last few months, and I didn't want a repeat—Spike and I went into the living room. I took *The Chinese Parrot* with me.

The book, however, rested on the coffee table after I pulled the curtains closed and lay on the couch with Spike. We were expert nappers by then.

My bladder woke me up. No surprise there. As I tottered down the hall to the powder room, I heard a key in the front door's lock and the door open. Spike had already jumped from the sofa and was in an ecstatic welcome-home barking frenzy.

"Hush, Spike. Isn't your mommy resting?" came Sam's voice as I opened the powder room door.

"It's okay!" I called. "We just woke up."

"Ah, good," said Sam.

I joined my husband and my dog in the hall. "Did you get people out searching for Frank?" I asked as I got on my tiptoes and kissed Sam's cheek, which was a little scratchy. He always shaved in the morning, and he was always scratchy when he got home from work.

"Yes. Even have a couple of motorcycles to patrol side streets."

"Do you think Frank will hang out on side streets?" I asked doubtfully.

"Don't know what the idiot will do," said Sam, sounding crabby. "I just don't want him anywhere near you."

"Me? Why me, in particular?"

"In case it's escaped your attention, my deplorable nephew has attempted to kill you on several occasions."

"Of course, it hasn't escaped my attention! But why's he still mad at me? I thought he only wanted me dead because somebody else hired him to kill me."

"According to sources, he holds a major grudge against you."

"Sources? What sources?" Frank Pagano had a grudge against *me*? "Why in the world should he hate me, in particular?"

"Don't ask me." Sam had hung up his coat on the rack and deposited his Fedora on the shelf. He now gave me as much of a hug as he could. "He disapproves of you not being a Roman Catholic. And you have to agree you're not Italian."

"Why should that matter to him? I figured he was just a despicable teenager when he had a fit about me not being an Italian Catholic. Well, attempting to kill me was more than having a fit, I guess."

"You're correct, and he's still despicable," said Sam, guiding me toward the living room. We sat on the sofa together, and Spike jumped up to join us. Sam seemed edgier than usual.

"There's more, isn't there?" I finally asked.

After letting out a huge sigh, Sam said, "Renata cabled me at the station."

This was a surprise. Renata Pagano didn't approve of me any more than her son did. "Why?"

"To warn me. If it's any comfort, I believe my sister has finally given up on her son."

"That's no comfort. I'd hate it if our son did such awful things as to make us give up on him."

"So would I," said Sam. "But to be fair, I think Frank had help in his race downhill. His parents were totally unprepared for his antics."

"What do you mean?"

"Prohibition has done a lot to foster the urge to drink in people who, I believe, never even thought about drinking alcohol before. Naturally, if there's a demand that can't be filled honestly, some people will fill it illegally."

"I know all that," I said. "What does that have to do with Frank and his parents?"

"According to Renata, and I have no reason to doubt her, Frank saw some of his friends strutting around, wearing expensive clothes and looking like dandies, and he wanted to be like them. Unfortunately for Renata and Frank Senior, those kids were runners for gangs in the neighborhood."

"The senior Frank told me the younger Frank had been dropped on his head when he was a baby," I said. "I don't know if it was supposed to be a joke or not."

"I have a feeling it wasn't a joke," said Sam. "Nobody else in the family, at least none I know of, is like Frank."

"Maybe Frank Junior was just born bad," I posited.

"Possible," said Sam with a shrug.

"I don't like to think that some people are born bad," I said.

"I don't either," said Sam.

Spike took a flying leap from the sofa and raced into the kitchen, his tail waving in the air like a fan, barking a happy welcome. Sam and I looked at each other.

"I think Mr. Prophet's come to call," I said.

Sure enough, a rusty voice came to us from the back of the house. "You two in here somewhere?"

"We're in the living room," called Sam.

I heaved a sigh. Then with Sam's help, I heaved myself off the sofa.

"Miss Li come to call this afternoon," said Mr. Prophet, limping into view. "She brought some noodle soup. There's a ton of it, so I thought I'd bring some to you."

"Noodle soup," I muttered, tilting my head to one side and contemplating the state of my stomach. It still felt full.

"It's got other stuff in it. Chinese, don'tcha know," Mr. Prophet elaborated.

"That was nice of her," said Sam, walking over to Mr. Prophet. "Thanks, Lou."

"Thank Miss Li," said Mr. Prophet. "She also had somethin' to tell me that I think you two should know about."

"That sounds ominous," I said, making my own way over to the former bounty hunter. He didn't appear as dangerous this evening as he sometimes did. Maybe my assessment was due to my body having had time to rest, or maybe he was in a mellower mood than usual thanks to Li Ahn. Maybe both.

"Might be ominous," said Mr. Prophet. "Come to the kitchen, and I'll put this pot on the stove."

"Thanks, Lou," said Sam before I could tell him not to bother.

The two of us walked to the kitchen, where we saw Mr. Prophet set a heavy cast-iron pot on one of the burners. Spike frolicked at his feet, understanding the meaning of that pot. It contained *food*. Spike loved food.

I plunked myself onto a kitchen chair as soon as I entered the kitchen. Then I rubbed my eyes. How long had Spike and I been napping anyhow? I glanced at the kitchen clock, which said the time was seven o'clock. "Good heavens! Spike and I slept the whole afternoon away," I said, mildly appalled at this behavior.

"You needed it," said Sam.

"We didn't get home till after four," said Mr. Prophet. "Even I took a rest."

Oh. Well then, our nap didn't seem as outrageous as it had when I'd thought we'd come home closer to one or two o'clock.

"You guys want any of this soup?" asked Mr. P. "It's good."

"I'm still full from lunch," I said.

"I'll have some," said Sam. "I didn't get to nap all afternoon." He winked at me, so I didn't slug him.

Joking!

"I'll put the leftover soup in a couple of jars," I said, "and it can go in the Frigidaire."

"*I'll* put the leftover soup in jars," Sam corrected me.

"Thanks, Sam. It can get cozy with the shepherd's pie Mrs. Rattle left for us. At least I think she did."

Mr. Prophet opened the door of the refrigerator. "She did," he announced.

"Good." It suddenly occurred to me that what with Mrs. Rattle's casserole and Miss Li's noodle soup, Lazy Daisy wouldn't have to cook on the morrow. I love days like that. I could get some sewing done!

Mr. Prophet dished out two bowls of noodle soup. It sure smelled good. I consulted with my stomach once more. It told me it didn't need more food in it. Dang. But I could have some soup tomorrow. Maybe even for breakfast, if I hurried. Mrs. Rattle had strict notions about what people should eat for breakfast, and they didn't include noodle soup.

"What did Miss Li tell you that we should know?" I asked as Mr. P. brought the bowls to the table.

He set one in front of Sam and one in front of his place. "Fergot spoons," he said and limped to the drawer in which our "everyday" flatware was kept. We had "good" flatware and china for all the parties Sam and I never hosted. I *had* to go through all my closets full of china and other paraphernalia Pasadena's rich ladies had given me and dole most of it out to my family and friends.

Another time.

"She said some slick-haired, hard-boiled lounge lizard was walkin' 'round the house across the street, lookin' in windows. Said he knocked at the front door, but nobody answered. He got in a machine and drove away."

"Uh-oh," I said, instantly identifying the intruder.

"Stay here," said Sam, rising from the kitchen table. "I'm calling the station."

"Do you really think he still wants me dead?" I asked hopefully, although my heart sank even as I spoke the words.

"Couldn't say, but I don't want to take any chances."

Mr. P. and I eyed each other across the table. "We think it's his nephew, Frank," I said.

"That's what I thought too," said Mr. Prophet.

"Oh dear," I muttered, thinking I *really* didn't want to be murdered before our son was born. Or afterward either.

The two of us listened to Sam talking to someone at the police station. Then he must have pressed the switch hook a few times because we heard him dialing another number. When he called the person who answered the wire on the other end "Joe," I knew he'd telephoned my parents to warn them about Frank's return to the neighborhood.

"No need for that," Sam said to my father. "Just keep your eyes open. I'm posting a team of officers to patrol this section of Marengo. He's dangerous, Joe, so be careful." Several seconds of silence ensued then Sam said, "Make sure one of the uniforms is at your place before you and Daisy take the dogs out in the morning." More silence. "Yeah," said Sam at last. "I'm sorry too." This time when he hung up the receiver, he left it there and joined Mr. Prophet and me in the kitchen.

"I'm glad you called my folks," I said when Sam sat again.

"Thought I'd better," said Sam.

"I'll be lookin' out for the curly wolf too," said Mr. Prophet. A curly wolf is Western for a villain.

"If he shows up here, sic Yuyu on him," I said, not quite in fun. If that cat went after Frank, I'd put my money on the cat.

"Don't want that joker anywhere near Yuyu," grumbled Mr. Prophet.

"And I don't want him anywhere near Daisy," said Sam. "You're not going out tomorrow, are you, except to take a short walk with the dogs *and* whichever uniform is with you?" he asked me.

"Except for walking Spike with Pa and Rosie in the morning, I don't have much to do. I'd rather stay home and do more sewing."

"Good," said Sam. "Stay home."

Then I thought about Harold. "Shoot, what about Harold?" I said.

"What *about* Harold?" asked Sam. "He doesn't need you. He's got two nurses to take care of that baby."

"I know, but the Grenvilles want to adopt the child, and Harold needs to retain an attorney to complete the process."

"That doesn't have to involve you," said Sam.

After thinking about it for a second or three, I said, "You're right! I'll call Harold tomorrow morning. He probably should know about Frank's continued presence in the area."

"Cripes, you're right," said Sam. "Better call him tonight. If necessary, Harold can hire guards."

"I can't imagine Frank wanting that poor baby," I said.

"I can't either, but Frank's Frank. He might make trouble with Harold for the hell of it."

"Oh Lord, and what about Melanie?"

"Damn," said Sam. "Maybe Harold can take Melanie to stay at his house for a while. We should keep all the people Frank has grudges against in as few places as possible."

"Yes," I said. "You're right."

Sam made another trip to the front hallway where the telephone table sat and dialed Harold's number. Mr. Prophet and I heard him tell Harold about Frank, ask if Harold could house Melanie Robinson for the nonce and request that he secure an attorney for adoption purposes. Harold must have agreed to all of Sam's wishes because Sam finally said, "Thanks, Harold." He hung the receiver on the hook, heaved a deep sigh and joined Mr. Prophet, Spike, and me in the kitchen once more.

Then I had a small bowl of delicious Chinese noodle soup because why not? Sam made me sit after dinner while he washed up the dishes. Keeping with the Chinese theme, Spike and I lounged on the couch with pillows at our backs, reading *The Chinese Parrot* until it was time for bed.

TWENTY-FOUR

When I awoke the following morning, I was surprised to realize it was only Tuesday. Seemed as though at least a month had passed since Melanie and (we think) Frank Pagano left their baby on Harold's doorstep. Spike and Sam were already up and about when I grunted myself out of bed. After a quick wash-up and a quicker brush of my hair, I donned one of my pretty, if tent-like, day dresses and waddled downstairs to join my two men in the kitchen.

"Smells good in here already," I said.

"Should," said Sam. "I'm heating some of Miss Li's soup, if you don't mind eating soup for breakfast."

"I was planning on having her soup for breakfast myself," I told him, pleased to know our minds were as one.

"An officer named Wright will be here before you and your father set out to walk the dogs," said Sam. "Don't leave the house—well, either house—until he's present. If he doesn't show up by seven-thirty, call me."

"Yes, sir," I said, saluting.

"Not funny, Daisy," said Sam. "Your life is in danger. And so is the life of our unborn son. I don't want to lose either of you."

"You're right. Sorry, Sam. Didn't mean to make light of the situation."

"Is tomorrow when your exercise class is supposed to take place?"

Bah. I hated that exercise class. Nevertheless, because I was supposed to lead the stupid thing, I said, "Yes."

"Well, call someone and tell her you can't be there."

"But I'm supposed to be the leader," I protested—not heatedly.

"Choose another leader. Until Frank is caught, you'd best stay home."

I couldn't suppress my smile. "I'm so glad!"

"You're glad a murderer is out to get you?" Sam set a bowl of soup before me.

"No, I'm not glad about that. I'm glad I have to stay home and not go to the exercise class. Thanks for the soup."

"Thank Miss Li. All I did was heat it up. Here are some crackers to go with it."

Sam laid a plate of soda crackers with salted tops on the table so we could both reach them.

"And here's your coffee." Sam put a cup and saucer on the table next to my soup dish.

"Thank you. I really like being waited on. I don't suppose you'd be willing to keep it up after Giuseppe is born, would you?" For the record, Sam and I had decided to name our baby boy Joseph, after my father. We hadn't decided on a middle name yet.

"No, I wouldn't," said Sam in a tone that made me believe his words.

"That's okay," I said, dipping my spoon into the soup and picking up a soda cracker. "Boy this soup is great. Wonder if Miss Li would mind sharing the recipe."

"Ask her," said Sam. Then, as if he'd made a deadly blunder, he added, "But not today! Or tomorrow. Not until Frank is no longer a threat."

"I didn't mean I'd ask her today. I know it's dangerous out there. When I married you, I didn't know you had criminals in the family."

"When I proposed to you, *I* didn't know there were criminals in my family."

I slipped Spike a couple of cracker crumbs.

"Be careful. If he gets fat, I'll blame you," said Sam, turning the tables on me.

I laughed. "Don't worry. Spike isn't going to get fat if I have anything to say about it."

"What's goin' on in here," came a creaky voice from the back door.

"We're having soup for breakfast," I said. "Want some with us?"

"Already ate breakfast." Mr. Prophet appeared in the kitchen, looking as old and battered as usual. "You know how to shoot a rifle, Miss Daisy?"

The question caught me by surprise. "A *gun*?"

"A rifle," he corrected me.

"Isn't a rifle a gun?"

"Don't give her any ideas, Lou," said Sam. He wasn't joking. Much.

"Be a good idea for her to be able to protect herself," Mr. P. said.

"I don't want to shoot a person," I told them both. "Not even Frank. Well, not unless he's outdoors. I don't want to get blood on the walls or furniture or anything. My father used to take Walter, Daphne, and me out to the desert to shoot at cans and bottles when I was little. It was fun."

"Were you any good?" asked Mr. Prophet.

"My aim was better than Walter's," I boasted. "Daphne didn't like to shoot because she feared getting dirty. And she didn't like the noise. I didn't like the noise either, actually."

"How'd she expect to get dirty?" asked a curious Sam.

I'd just taken a sip of soup, so I couldn't answer him until after I swallowed. "She's always been dainty and girly," I said. "She only liked to play dolls and pretend to keep house. She didn't like picking up the nasty cans and bottles and putting them on the dirty boulders."

Both men stared at me in what I considered a rather rude way. "Hey," I said. "I'm girly. Just because I'd rather play cards than dolls doesn't mean I'm not girly. I had dolls when I was a kid. And the only reason I used cards so much was because I was a spiritualist-medium. Starting when I was ten years old."

"If you say so," said Sam. "But Lou, I don't want guns in the house."

"You got two guns and a Bowie knife in the house every time I walk into it," Mr. P. reminded him.

"Yes, but you know how to use them," Sam pointed out.

"Besides," I added, "nobody looking at you would know you were armed."

"I kin put my Winchester '73 on a couple o' hooks over the fireplace. That's where most folks keep their shootin' irons."

"I don't want a rifle over the fireplace," I said. "We don't have to go outdoors and shoot our food any longer. Even if we did, I don't expect the people who own the dairies in El Monte would like it if we shot any of their cows." I wrinkled my nose. "And I wouldn't know what to do with a cow carcass even if I didn't have to kill it first."

"I'm serious," snapped Mr. Prophet. "That feller ain't goin' to leave you alone. Sam told me all about him, and don't ferget I met him. He's a no-good punk, and you need protection."

The doorbell chimed just then, making me give a start of alarm. I didn't rise, but looked at Sam, who did. Suddenly I was afraid. Darn it! I didn't want to be afraid in my own house!

Too bad, Daisy.

I rose from the table and tried to tiptoe after Sam. Couldn't do it very well, but I walked softly. I was glad to see him peer out of the peephole before unlocking the door, although I did hold my breath just in case Frank was out there aiming a gun at the peephole. I stayed in the doorway between the pantry and the hall when Sam opened the door.

"Good to see you, Wright," he said to the person on the porch. "Just stay on the porch for a while. Keep a watch on this house and the one directly across the street. The bungalow over there is where the suspect was seen earlier, but don't take any chances. The suspect is dangerous and probably crazy."

Oh my!

"Yes, sir," said the person I presumed to be Officer Wright.

"When you patrol, be sure to check in the backyards too. There's another house behind all the citrus trees in our yard. In fact, our yard is gigantic, so you and Garcia can take turns patrolling the area."

"We've already worked out a patrol plan, Detective, so we should be good."

"Great. Thank you."

"Best of luck, sir," said Officer Wright.

And he had a partner named Garcia? By golly, Pasadena was becoming more interesting by the day.

When Sam joined me at the door to the hall, he seemed surprised to find me there instead of in the kitchen slurping soup.

"The two of you scared me," I said. "I don't like being afraid in my own house."

With a sigh, Sam said, "You should be used to it by now."

"That's a sad commentary on our life, Sam."

"I know it is, but it's true."

"You're right," I said, downhearted. I guess Frank Pagano was better than having the ghost of an evil woman after me, although I'm not sure to this day.

Mr. Prophet sat at the kitchen table when Sam and I re-entered it. He'd poured himself a cup of coffee, loaded it with sugar and milk and looked grumpy.

"What's the matter?" I asked him. "Do you want some soup? I'd love to get the recipe from Miss Li."

"The matter is you don't want to take care o' yourself," snapped Mr. P.

"Because I don't fancy using a gun?" I asked, peeved.

"There's nothin' wrong with bein' able to protect yourself," said the old sourpuss.

"If it makes you happier, I nearly killed a man with Sam's cane once." I dipped my spoon in my soup dish again. Boy that stuff was good!

Mr. P. squinted at me.

"It's true, Lou," said Sam, who drank the last of his soup out of the bowl. We weren't formal in our house, and he had to get to work. When he finished, he took his bowl to the sink, tapped Mr. Prophet's shoulder and said, "Come with me. I'll introduce you to Wright and Garcia, if he's there. You fellows should get acquainted."

"Definitely," I said. "We don't want police officers to shoot you just because you look like an owlhoot."

"Cripes," grumbled Mr. Prophet, rising and going with Sam to the front door.

Suddenly my heart gave a huge spasm and I called after them, "Don't open the door until you're sure it's safe!"

"We're all right," Sam called back.

I heard the front door open and Sam introducing Mr. Prophet to a police officer. I should have known everything was keen on the front porch. If any creeping menace hovered there, Spike would have growled and snarled. But he still sat at my feet, gazing at me with eyes positively pleading for relief from famine. They dissembled, those eyes. In fact, as I peered down at him, I decided I had to be more careful with the snacks.

"Don't lie to me, Spike Majesty Rotondo. I can see that you're not the least little bit malnourished."

Spike wagged his tail at me. I loved that dog *so* much!

I rose, took my own bowl to the kitchen sink, rinsed out both bowls and realized Sam must have put the soup into jars last night, because there was no huge empty pot on the burner, but an empty jar in the sink. When I opened the Frigidaire and looked inside, I saw another jar with more noodle soup in it there. I loved my husband as much as I loved my dog, by golly!

A noise at the door to the pantry made me swirl around. Almost lost my balance, for pity's sake! There stood Sam and two uniformed policemen. I guess Mr. Prophet had stayed at the front door to act as lookout. Sheesh, our house had become like a castle besieged by the evil lord in the next village. Except our house, while Sam's and my own castle, wasn't nearly as big as any castle I'd seen in the flickers.

"Careful," said Sam, rushing up to me and putting a hand on my shoulder to steady me.

"My fault," I admitted, embarrassed. "I thought you were on the porch."

"I brought Officers Wright and Garcia in to meet you and Spike," said Sam.

He introduced Spike and me to the two policemen. They were polite young men, and even bent over when they saw Spike holding out his paw and shook it. I was proud of my dog. And the policemen were nice too.

"Have you met my father and aunt yet?" I asked the men.

Sam answered for them. "I'm taking them across the street now. Lou's staying on the front porch to keep a look-out."

What about the back porch? I didn't ask my question. The Pasadena Police Department was probably straining its budget by allowing Sam to use two of their men for the sake of me. Then again there was an added incentive, because everyone believed Frank Pagano to be the fellow who'd stuck a knife in the back of James Smithfield. I decided I needn't feel guilty about the P.P.D.'s largesse.

Naturally, I felt guilty anyhow. But I attempted to get over it. Then I hurried into the house and to the utility porch where I snabbled Spike's leash, clipped it to his collar, and the two of us set out across the street right behind Sam and the two coppers.

I think Rosebud's shrill bark startled the poor policemen. Spike had a low and manly bark. Most of the other dachshunds I'd met via Mrs. Bissel also had big barks. You'd think, if you couldn't see them, they were at least Doberman pinschers, if not Saint Bernards. Not Rosie. She sounded like one of Mrs. Frasier's squeaky miniature pinschers. Mrs. Frasier is one of the wealthy women for whom I conducted séances from time to time.

Oh, and miniature pinschers are little red dogs that look like tiny Dobermans. According to Mrs. Hanratty and Mrs. Bissel, the two most knowledgeable dog people of my acquaintance, miniature pinschers were bred years, if not centuries, before Doberman pinschers were even conceived of. I don't know how they learn these things. I sure never took any classes about dog breeds in school.

Come to think of it, if the school folks had offered me a choice between algebra and dog-breeding history, I'd have snapped up dog breeding. Not unlike Spike snapping at a scrap somebody throws him. I still got shivers when I thought about those long-ago algebra classes.

After Sam left for work, Pa and I took Spike and Rosie for a walk. Officer Wright accompanied us. Rosie and Spike were happy to have another human walking with us, and Pa and I were happy for his company. He seemed a nice fellow. Also, after we'd walked south on Marengo to Bellevue and turned left, on our way to Garfield Avenue, we happened upon Officer Garcia, so Officer Wright introduced him to Rosie, who barked at the poor man.

As we neared Cordova Street, where we'd have to turn left again in order to take us to Marengo Avenue, where we lived, I let out a huge sigh.

"What's the matter, Daisy?" asked Pa. "Are you tired? You're not having a cramp, are you? We can call Officer Garcia and have him get a police car to—"

"No!" I said, wishing I'd kept my sigh to myself. My father was almost as much of a fusspot about my condition as was Sam. "I'm only wondering what's going to happen to those of us who live on South Marengo when the Pasadena Civic Auditorium is built. Or starts being built. It's liable to be dusty and noisy for quite a while."

"Ah," said Pa, catching my drift. "And after it's built, I expect traffic to increase a good deal, and our quiet little street won't be so quiet any longer."

"Exactly. I love our house. I'd hate to have to move, especially since Sam has built the staircase ramp for Spike. And the arbor for our roses. I'll be sad to leave our first home together."

Drat my up-and-down emotions! I felt tears prickle my eyes, and I lifted a hand and pretended to scratch my nose. In reality, I swiped my eyes and lectured myself to stop being so…so…pregnant!

"Well, arbors and ramps aren't difficult to build," said Pa philosophically.

"I suppose not, if you're Sam. Both Sam and I like gardening, so we could create a new rose arbor I guess."

"Of course you can," said Pa in an encouraging voice. "The traffic is getting worse all the time. I suspect that's because Pasadena's growing so fast, and Colorado Street seems to get more crowded every day."

"You're right," I said after contemplating his words for a couple of seconds. "Maybe we could all move up to Altadena."

"Why Altadena?" asked Pa, surprised.

With a shrug I said, "I don't know. But it's nice there."

"It's nice here," said Pa.

"True. Pasadena and Altadena are both beautiful places to live."

"They are," agreed Officer Wright.

I expect Spike and Rosie would have added their approval had they been able.

TWENTY-FIVE

Mrs. Rattle had arrived at our house by the time we got back from our walk. Spike raced into the kitchen to greet her. I thanked Officer Wright for his company, hung my sweater on the coat rack, and put my hat on the shelf. Then I, more slowly than Spike, walked to the kitchen to greet our wonderful household helper.

"Lovely morning, isn't it, Mrs. Rattle?"

"It is indeed, my dear," said Mrs. Rattle. "Spike loves his walkies, doesn't he?"

"He sure does. I do too, and so do Pa and Rosebud. It's nice to get out into the fresh air on these crisp mornings."

Mrs. Rattle eyed my belly. "That's a charming frock, dear. It's loose but doesn't look unfashionable."

"You think so?" I asked, surprised. "I think it looks like a tent."

Mrs. Rattle's peal of laughter startled me because I didn't expect it. "Daisy, you couldn't create a dress that looks like a tent if you wanted to. You're much too clever a seamstress for that."

"Oh." I knew I was good with the old sewing machine, but I hadn't expected this praise. "Really?" I glanced down at my dress. I could only see the lower part of it, but I knew (because I'd made it) that the bodice was a solid rust-colored cotton. The part I could see (the skirt) was made of a fabric decorated with a swirl of fall colors. I guess it was pretty.

"Thank you," I said at last.

Shaking her head, Mrs. Rattle said, "You're too modest, Daisy."

"Don't tell Mr. Prophet or Sam that. They might set you straight, and that would be embarrassing," I said.

Another burst of laughter from Mrs. Rattle. If I didn't know better, I'd think she'd been nipping at the sherry or port or something else alcoholic. Not that we had any in the house. I just smiled and said, "Think I'll retire to the sewing room now, Mrs. Rattle."

"Of course, dear. I'll begin with the dusting."

"Thank you," I said. "Would you mind answering the telephone if anybody calls? I expect any caller would hang up before I could make it to the 'phone in my current condition."

Another laugh—I had no idea I was so funny—preceded Mrs. Rattle's, "I'll be happy to answer the telephone, dear. You just take it easy."

"Thank you, but if anybody I know calls, please holler up the stairs, and I'll slide down the banister."

"You'd *never!*" cried Mrs. Rattle appalled.

Her reaction taught me a valuable lesson: I shouldn't try to be funny. My jokes fell flat on their faces. Apparently I was funny enough without trying. I'll never figure it out.

"Just kidding, Mrs. Rattle. But if, you know, Harold or Flossie or Sam or any of my family call, I'll be happy to talk to them. I just can't get to the telephone quickly."

"Of course not, dear."

As a re-jollied Mrs. Rattle made her way to the utility room to fetch dust rags, mops, buckets and other housecleaning paraphernalia, Spike and I went upstairs. Little did Mrs. Rattle know that I was in the process of sewing up a perfectly splendid set of imitation silk lounging pajamas for her.

Christmas should be especially fun this year, because we'd have a new little baby Rotondo to spoil! Well, not *spoil*, but we'd definitely welcome him to the family.

That's providing Sam's stupid nephew didn't succeed in killing any of us first. I had faith, though, primarily because Frank Pagano truly *was* about as stupid as a clod of dirt. My friends and family were all smarter than he was; we'd outwit him.

I hoped.

Spike and I were merrily sewing and singing—in truth, Spike was napping—when Mrs. Rattle called up the stairs to me.

"Daisy! It's Mrs. Buckingham on the 'phone."

Piffle. "Thanks, Mrs. Rattle. Be right there!" I hollered back. Because I had just started stitching up the yoke of the pajama top, I plopped my pin-laden pincushion on the fabric so it wouldn't slip from the machine—rayon was *so* slippery—and went to the telephone. Spike followed me. I think he was disappointed that I stopped at the telephone table and didn't continue to the kitchen or the yard.

"Good morning, Flossie," I said. I heard no baby screeching in the background, so I presumed little Daisy wasn't being a bwat today.

"Daisy!" said Flossie happily. "Sam stopped by today to tell Johnnie and me about his horrible nephew being loose in Pasadena again, and I wanted to volunteer to lead the exercise class for you."

"Flossie, you're a gem of a woman!" I said, meaning my words absolutely. "That's *so* kind of you. Even when I'm not big as a house, I hate that class."

With a laugh, Flossie said, "I'm only volunteering for the interim, you know. I can't do it forever."

"Darn," I said with a fake sigh.

In a more sober tone, Flossie said, "Sam brought us a photograph of Frank, so we'll keep on the lookout for him. Johnny gets out a lot more than I do, but you know him. If he spies Frank Pagano on the street, he'll probably march the band over to surround him and have the tambourine ladies jangle him to death."

We both laughed. The scenario she presented sounded *so* much like Johnnie, it honestly wouldn't surprise me. However...

"He'd better not, though. Frank has taken to stabbing people with a knife. Sam told me it was most likely a switchblade, which I guess is a folding stiletto-type knife."

"Don't worry. Sam told us the same thing. Johnnie won't do anything stupid."

"I'm glad. I expect Frank will do any number of stupid things, though, so try to stay away from him. Well, unless you can sneak up on him and throw a burlap sack over his head."

"Johnnie's band doesn't carry burlap sacks with them these days," said a chuckling Flossie.

"I miss you, Flossie. Wish I wasn't confined to the house. I'd visit you and the kids."

"How about I visit you after tomorrow's exercise class?" she suggested. "Not with the kids though."

"Perfect!" I said. "I'd love it. I can fix lunch for us." I hope Flossie didn't detect the doubt and terror in my voice. The kitchen and I, while on better terms than we used to be, still scared each other. In truth, I suspect the kitchen was indifferent to me. It still frightened me a whole lot.

"Don't even think about it," said Flossie, firm. "The church ladies love to fix food for Johnnie and the kids and me to eat. I'll bring sandwiches, and we can have an orange or two to go with our sandwiches."

"And dill pickles!" I declared, delighted. "Oh, Flossie, that would be *so* nice of you. I'm really much better in the kitchen than I used to be, but I still don't like cooking."

"Fear not," said Flossie. "Your lunch tomorrow is taken care of. Er..." After a moment of hesitation, she asked, "Are you fixed for today? I can—"

"No, you can't!" I told her vehemently. "I have a lovely shepherd's pie for lunch. Mrs. Rattle made it, and we ate so much Mexican food so late yesterday afternoon, we haven't even touched her shepherd's pie yet. Oh, and we still have some of the noodle soup Miss Li gave Mr. Prophet to give to us. I won't have to cook for another day, at least. I hope."

"Perfect," said Flossie, although I don't know why. I thought my fear of cooking verged on the idiotic. "See you tomorrow, Daisy!"

"See you tomorrow," I said. We both hung up our receivers.

It was a happy Daisy who first visited the downstairs powder room and then walked back to the foot of the staircase. As luck would have it, the telephone rang before I took my first step.

"I'll get it, Mrs. Rattle!" I said.

"Thanks, dear," she said.

I picked up the receiver and said, "Hello?" into the proper end of the thing.

"Daisy, I've hired not merely bodyguards, but a lawyer," said Harold. He sounded happier than I'd heard him since before last Saturday morning.

"Excellent! Have you explained the baby situation to the lawyer?"

"Yes, and he sees no problem with the adoption, although he'd like to interview George and Marianne first, just to make sure. And Marianne's mother, since she'll be caring for the baby too."

"I don't foresee a problem with any of them. Will Melanie have any involvement in placing her child?"

"No. The lawyer, Peter Altman, said it's best if Melanie doesn't get involved. She might be held accountable for abandoning her baby."

"Poor Melanie. What a predicament she got herself in to."

"True. But she's really only a kid, Daisy. I telephoned and talked to her at the hospital, and she told me this coming Thursday will be her sixteenth birthday."

"What? Oh my goodness, Harold. It's monstrous that Frank Pagano could seduce so young a girl."

"Happens all the time," Harold said drily.

"Yes, I know," I said.

"I don't think your friend Frank—"

"He's *not* my friend!" I blurted into the mouthpiece. "He's a conniving piece of snail slime! And he's dumb as a...a...I can't think of anything stupid enough."

"A slug?" Harold suggested. "I don't think slugs are very smart."

"That will do," I said graciously. "When will Mr. Altman speak to George and Marianne?"

"I'm not sure. He's going to telephone. I was hoping you could be in on the interview."

"I'd love to, but Sam's confining me to the house, and I can't go anywhere. He's even got two uniforms patrolling the neighborhood."

"Sam's wise to do that. I hope you're taking the matter seriously."

"Are you kidding me? Frank Pagano has already made attempts on my life. I'm taking the matter extremely seriously."

"Good."

And then I had what I consider a brilliant idea. Another one. By golly, I was having brilliant ideas by the bucketful. "Harold!"

"Still here. No need to yell," said Harold.

"Sorry. Didn't mean to holler in your ear. But perhaps Mr. Altman can interview the Grenvilles here, at our house. There's a perfectly good den in which he can conduct the questioning. Heck, we even have a big dining room with a large table, if forms need to be filled out or something."

"Did I know you had a den?" asked Harold.

"Well, we never use it. We generally yak at the kitchen table or read in the living room. The den is pristine, with a Louis the Whateverth sofa, sideboard, and chairs."

"Oh God, did my mother give you the furniture?"

"However did you guess?"

"She just loves those old Louies."

"Well, they look nice. I don't think I'd choose them for myself. I prefer the new Craftsman pieces, but your mother was exceedingly kind. I mean, those Louis the Whateverth chairs and sideboard must have cost her a fortune."

"I'm sure they did. But if you want to dump them and get some Stickley or other Arts and Crafts pieces, just give me a call. I have lots of friends with better taste than my mother."

"Would your mother have to know?" I asked, feeling guilty.

"How often has she been to your house?" asked Harold.

"Um...I don't think she's ever been here."

"Precisely. She'll never know."

"What do you think about interviewing people here? Before I replace all the Louies with new stuff?"

"I think it's a great idea. I'm not sure what to do with Melanie, though. This morning I asked if she wanted me to get in touch with her parents, and she burst into tears."

"Not awfully helpful."

"Not helpful at all," said Harold. "But I'll talk to Pete. I think he should be the one to interview the Grenvilles."

"Would you like me to give them some kind of warning first? I mean, if he just shows up at their house or at the bookstore, they might be alarmed."

"He will reach out to them by telephone first," said Harold as if I should have known that.

"Of course. I probably should have thought of that myself."

"Probably," said Harold. "Although to be fair, you haven't had as much experience with attorneys as have I."

"I've had no experience at all. Well, except for the time Mr. Millette and Mr. Grover tried to kill me, but I don't think most other attorneys do things like that."

"I wouldn't bet on it," said Harold grimly.

"By the way," I said belatedly, "how's the baby this morning?"

"Hazel tells me she's fine," said Harold. "I wouldn't know from personal experience, although I do pop in to view the infant from time to time."

"Does the baby look Italian?"

"Italian! She looks like a wrinkled tomato at the moment, Daisy Gumm Majesty Rotondo. She was only born three days ago, remember? Maybe four days."

"You're right."

"She has dark hair, if that helps."

"Not a whole lot," I admitted.

"Well then, there you go."

"I guess," I said.

"But I'll hang up now. Just wanted you to know the latest. I'm not sure what to do about Melanie."

"I'll think about it," I told him. "Although if she can't bear the thought of calling her family, I'm kind of stumped."

"You and me both," said Harold.

"Maybe you could call them? I mean, you're related and all," I suggested.

"They'd think it strange if I called out of the blue," said Harold.

"Perhaps, but you might do it anyway. We can think of an excuse. Maybe."

"Maybe," agreed Harold.

We both hung our receivers on their switch hooks.

Then I walked up the stairs and continued making Mrs. Rattle's Christmas pajamas. I'm happy to state that the pincushion did its job well, and the rayon didn't slide from the sewing machine's pointy jaws while I yapped on the telephone with Flossie and Harold.

TWENTY-SIX

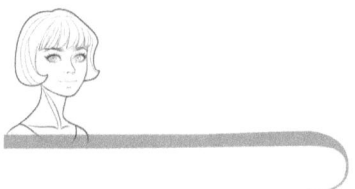

I'd just about finished sewing up Mrs. Rattle's Christmas present when an uproar from the backyard startled me into returning to the so-called "real" world. Sometimes I get so involved in sewing, my mind will wander. That day, it had been wandering down Christmas Tree Lane in Altadena—the rest of the year it was Santa Rosa Avenue—and thinking how much delight little Joey would take in the sight next year. This year, he'd be too young to properly appreciate it.

Rising from my sewing chair, I waddled across the hall and into the spare bedroom that overlooked the backyard. Peering out the window, I espied Mr. Prophet, Mrs. Rattle, Spike, the dilapidated orange-striped cat Yuyu, and none other than Pudge Wilson out there. They seemed to be having some sort of altercation.

Because it was quicker than trying to hurry downstairs and rush to the backyard, I pushed open the window and listened for several seconds.

"I don't care *what* you want to do," bellowed Mr. Prophet. "Get out and stay out!"

"But Miss Daisy is in peril!" Pudge declared. "It's my duty as a Boy Scout to protect her!"

"How the devil you gonna protect her?" asked Mr. Prophet. "With that bugle o' yours?"

"I can sound an alarm," said Pudge, hugging his bugle to his chest.

"Pudge, dear," said Mrs. Rattle, "I don't think—"

Neither male person paid attention to her. How typical.

"I *can* sound an alarm. Listen here!"

Very well, I had to take action. "*Stop!*" I hollered from the second-floor window. "Stop it this minute, all of you! Pudge Wilson, don't you *dare* play your bugle in front of Mr. Prophet!"

To be fair to Pudge, he was proud of his improved skill with the instrument.

To be fair to Mr. Prophet, the first time Pudge had practiced his bugle, we were seated on my parents' front porch steps and unaware of his presence. Then he made such a terrifying noise on that horn of his that Mr. Prophet thought we were under attack by a villainous mob and nearly shot the kid with his Colt .45.

"Miss Daisy?" Pudge glanced up to see me at the window. He looked hurt as if I'd crushed his feelings.

"I'm sorry, Pudge, but we have to be very careful," I said. "We can't call attention to ourselves."

"But I'd only play it in an emergency," pleaded Pudge.

"Thank you very much for your help, Pudge, but I don't—Wait a minute. Why aren't you in school?" It wasn't even lunchtime. Pudge Wilson should be peacefully ensconced in a class at George Washington Junior High School on Raymond Avenue.

Digging his shod toe into the dirt, Pudge hung his head and said, "I cut school."

"Pudge!" I cried, pretending to be aghast. "Your mother and father will be *so* disappointed in you for ditching school!"

"Nertz," muttered Pudge.

"And whatever would the Boy Scouts think? You're supposed to do *good* deeds, not cut classes!"

"Aw, Miss Daisy."

"Don't you 'Miss Daisy' me, Pudge Wilson! I'm going to telephone your parents right now," I told the lad. He'd always had a soft spot for me in his adolescent heart. It got annoying sometimes, although he meant well.

"Aw, Miss Daisy, *please* don't! They'll skin me alive."

"You should have thought about that before you decided to ditch," I said sternly. It was difficult to keep a straight face, but I knew it would be improper to laugh.

"What's going on back here?" came a commanding voice at the backyard gate, the one off the driveway. I swiveled my gaze left-wards and saw Officer Garcia unlocking the gate. Guess Sam had provided my guardians with keys. To be clear, Pasadena was a peaceful city—unless you were Sam and me.

I swear, Frank Pagano was a blight on the human species!

"It's all right, Officer Garcia," I called down to him. "Pudge Wilson was trying to help."

Scowling, the policeman walked into the backyard. He was greeted with enthusiasm by Spike and an angry hiss from Yuyu. Then Yuyu took off in the direction of Mr. Prophet's cottage at the back of the property.

"Why aren't you in school, young man?" demanded Officer Garcia.

"I...I...oh, heck."

"He ditched," said Mr. Prophet. "Decided he'd be good at protecting Miss Daisy."

"I *would* be!" cried Pudge. "I can sound an alarm. Listen!" And the kid blew such a blast on his bugle that everyone within earshot flinched. I expect most of them stuck a finger or two in their ears as well.

Spike let out a howl of anguish and raced for the back porch.

"That's enough of *that*!" said Office Garcia in an unfriendly voice. "Give me that bugle, young man. Are you trying to violate the noise-reduction ordinance?"

"No!" He uttered a cry of dismay when Officer Garcia snatched the bugle from his hands. He cast a beseeching glance up at my window. "Miss Daisy? I was trying to help. Honest!"

"I know you were," I said attempting a soothing voice, although that bugle blast had made every nerve in my body stand up and quiver in shock and consternation. Lord, that thing was loud. "But you're not helping, Pudge. Your main duty is to learn as much as you can in school so you'll make us all proud one day. If you cut classes, you'll only get Fs in everything and make your parents furious. And the Boy Scouts will probably kick you out if you do more things like this!"

"I'll drive you back to school, young man," said Officer Garcia. "We can talk to the principal, and he will telephone your parents, I'm sure."

"Oh no!" said Pudge, sounding pathetic.

Too bad.

"You deserve no praise, Pudge," I said severely. "It sounds to me as if my parents or Sam warned you about the recent danger in the neighborhood, yet you ditched school and came here anyway. Not smart, Pudge. The Boy Scouts would *not* be pleased with you. And neither are we."

Mean, Daisy. But if it'd save the kid's life, appropriate.

Hanging his head, Pudge muttered, "I'm sorry."

"Don't do it again, Pudge," I said, still being stern. And I heard the telephone ring. Curses.

"Is that the 'phone?" asked Mrs. Rattle.

"I'll get it," I told her. "Why don't you and Officer Garcia escort Pudge off our property and be sure to lock the gate."

"I certainly will," said Mrs. Rattle. "And you, young man," she added for Pudge's benefit, "should be ashamed of yourself for frightening us all like that."

"Yes'm," said a sorrowful Pudge.

I heard no more, because I hurried to the staircase and, holding the banister, descended it as quickly as possible. The telephone table was pretty much right there at the foot of the stairs, so I wasn't panting much when I answered it. "Hello?"

"Mrs. Rotondo?"

"Yes, this is she," I said, my heart sinking. I recognized the voice as belonging to a down-the-street neighbor, Mrs. Longnecker. Mrs. Longnecker was a fusspot.

"Did you hear that horrible noise a few seconds ago?"

"Yes, I did. It was awful, wasn't it?"

"Do you know what made it? You haven't taken up playing the tuba, have you? Or teaching bird calls?"

"Neither of those things, Mrs. Longnecker," I assured her. "It was…" Oh, heck, I wasn't going to tell on Pudge. "It was an unfortunate incident."

"I should say it was unfortunate!" she sniped. "It sounded as if someone had trodden on a donkey's foot."

Interesting. I told her the truth: "I've never heard what that sounds like, Mrs. Longnecker."

"Fiddlesticks. I know it came from your place. If anything goes awry in the neighborhood, it always has to do with you."

Because this was the regrettable truth, I didn't argue. "It won't happen again, Mrs. Longnecker," I said instead.

She didn't answer at once. I think she really wanted to know what had made the noise. I didn't fill her in and eventually she said, "I should hope not!" and hung up on me.

"Old cow," I muttered as I headed to the powder room. I heard Mrs. Rattle and Mr. Prophet enter through the back door, Spike leading the way.

As soon as I finished in the powder room, I walked to the kitchen where the two older statespersons stood yakking. Mrs. Rattle smiled at me. Mr. Prophet still looked as if he wanted to murder someone. I suspect Pudge. Spike wagged and came over to tell me he'd missed me for the several minutes I'd been away.

"That kid's gonna drive me nuts someday," he griped. "He's turnin' into one o' them—what do they call 'em? Juvenile something-or-others?"

"A juvenile delinquent?" I asked.

"Yeah," he said. "One o' them."

"Oh, no, Lou," said Mrs. Rattle. "Pudge Wilson is a darling boy, if a trifle misguided sometimes."

"Misguided, my ass…foot," the old reprobate snarled.

"He pulled a stupid trick today," I said mildly. "But I expect his parents and the school will deal with him."

221

"He blows that horn 'o his at me again, he's gonna lose it," promised Mr. P.

I heaved a sigh. "Did he climb the fence to get in? It must have still been locked because Officer Garcia unlocked it when I looked out the window."

"Yeah, he climbed the fence," said Mr. P. "Damn—darned heathen."

"Oh, I wouldn't go *that* far," said the kindhearted Mrs. Rattle. "He honestly believed he was helping Daisy."

"Bah. He's a menace."

"How about lunch?" I said loudly, trying to sound cheerful. "Want a sandwich or something, Mr. Prophet? More soup?"

"I noticed you haven't touched the shepherd's pie I prepared for you." Mrs. Rattle sounded hurt.

Crumb. I forgot she'd have rooted around in the Frigidaire as she tidied up.

"We had a terrible day yesterday, Mrs. Rattle. We got home too late to eat it. I'm planning to have it for dinner tonight."

"Oh, good. I feared you didn't want it."

"No!" I said, appalled. "Good heavens, any time you want to feed us, please feel free. I'm...not comfortable in the kitchen yet."

"Huh," said Mr. Prophet. "You got somethin' fer lunch?"

"There's still some of Miss Li's delicious soup," I said. "And I can make toasted cheese sandwiches."

"I'll cut the bread," said Mrs. Rattle, understanding my struggle with bread knives and loaves of bread. "Why don't you cut some cheese slices, Daisy. And Lou, you go wash your hands."

"Cripes," said Mr. Prophet. But he headed for the downstairs powder room to wash his hands.

"I'll get the jar of soup out of the Frigidaire," I said.

"Is that what's in that jar?" said Mrs. Rattle. "I wasn't sure."

"Miss Li from down the street fixed some delicious Chinese noodle soup," I told her. "I want to get the recipe from her." I thought of something brilliant to say. "I still have the recipe for that chicken casserole you made for us before. I haven't prepared it yet."

"I'm so glad you enjoyed it," purred Mrs. Rattle.

"We did indeed," I lied. In truth, her prior chicken casserole had been burned to death by an evil ghost, but I don't think she'd have believed me if I'd said so. I understood; I didn't used to believe in ghosts either.

The telephone rang. As I was on my feet, I turned around and walked to the hall to answer it.

"Hello?"

"Just checking on you," said Sam. "We got a message about a bomb being set off in our neighborhood and I thought I'd better call you."

"Oh dear." I sighed deeply. "That was Pudge Wilson and his bugle. About scared the daylights out of Mrs. Rattle, Mr. Prophet, Officer Garcia, Spike, and me. Mr. Prophet's cat took off for shelter."

"What was Pudge doing blowing his bugle at this time of day?" Sam asked reasonably.

"He heard I was in danger and came to patrol. He said he'd sound a warning if anybody approached. Oh, and he cut classes in order to do it."

"Shoot," muttered Sam. "That kid's a menace."

"That's what Mr. Prophet said."

"The Wilsons aren't going to be happy about this."

"I don't expect the school authorities will be pleased either," I said.

"Probably not." After a couple of seconds during which neither of us spoke, Sam added, "Is it too late to rethink this baby thing?"

"I fear it is," I said.

We both laughed like hyenas.

By the time I got back to the kitchen, Mrs. Rattle had not only cut bread, but she'd sliced cheese and dumped the soup from the jar into a saucepan.

"There you go," she said happily. "Have a nice lunch. I'm headed for home now."

"Thank you *so* much, Mrs. Rattle."

"Yeah," said Mr. Prophet from behind me, startling me.

"It's a good thing I'm not holding the knife right now," I told him.

"Hellkatoot. You heard me comin'."

"Did not."

"Did too."

Giggling like a little girl, Mrs. Rattle took her leave of the two of us. I guess we *were* behaving like school children. Bother.

TWENTY-SEVEN

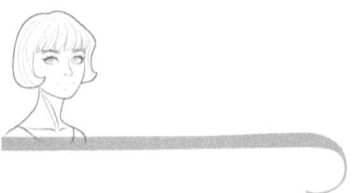

After an extremely satisfying lunch, I washed up the dishes and then decided I could finish Mrs. Rattle's Christmas present later.

"Let's take *The Chinese Parrot* out to the back porch, Spike. I'll read some more of it. Then I'll probably fall asleep in the porch chair."

Spike thought this was a wonderful idea. He trotted before me, his tail waving like a banner in a breeze. He waited patiently as I made a detour to the utility room. There I picked up three chair cushions and a lap blanket crocheted for me by Flossie Buckingham.

As soon as we cleared the back door sill, Spike saw his pal Yuyu, who'd dared face the back lawn once more now that it was boy-and-bugle free. Spike bounded down the porch stairs and streaked over to Yuyu, who instantly pounced on Spike. Spike rolled over, taking Yuyu with him, and the two raced off to what we call the Back Forty. That's where the two of them kept finding human bones earlier in the year. I always experienced a pang of fear when the dog and cat played back there.

If we decided to sell our wonderful home because of the Pasadena Civic Center being built right behind us, I hoped the house we chose wouldn't have any old bones or shamanic ghosts in it. Once was enough for that, thank you very much.

Maybe twice.

Oh, who's counting?

I pulled one of our cane and rattan chairs and its matching ottoman away from the wall and positioned them where I wanted them to be. Then I put a cushion on the chair's seat and one at the chair's back, dropped the third cushion onto the ottoman, maneuvered my bulk onto the chair and sank into the cushioned comfort of the chair, lifting my feet and snuggling them onto the ottoman.

Comfort and joy, by Jingo! With Flossie's lap blanket keeping me warm in the mild autumn air, I opened the book.

Not sure how long I slept, but the book sliding off my tummy and landing on the porch planks woke me up again. Blinking my gummy eyes, I wondered what time it was.

When Mr. Prophet said, "'Phone's ringin'," I glanced up to find him looming over me.

"Well, answer it," I said grumpily.

"Me? Ya want *me* ta answer your 'phone?"

"You're up and I'm not," I growled.

He held up his hands as if in surrender. "I'll answer it."

"Good." That wasn't awfully pleasant of me, was it? "Phooey, Spike," I said to my shiny black-and-tan liberty hound. "Remember when we didn't have telephones? Life was so peaceful then."

Because he wasn't around then, Spike didn't remember pre-telephonic Pasadena. He did cock his head at me and give me a tentative wag of his tail. I heaved a big sigh and let my feet plop to the porch floor. For a second I contemplated taking the cushions and lap robe indoors, but then decided to do it after I got off the telephone with whoever was calling. I'd picked up my book with a loudish grunt, turned and was about to re-enter the house, when Mr. Prophet said, "It's fer you. Harold."

"I'm coming," I said and carried myself and my book to the telephone table.

At my back, I heard Mr. Prophet say, "Huh."

226

"Hey, Harold, what's up?" I tried to sound cheerful when I spoke into the receiver.

"We're going to have to include Dr. Vialargo in our conference with the Grenvilles. Pete said he'd be more comfortable if a doctor signed off on the baby."

I didn't say anything immediately because I had to sort out those names. Pete? Ah. The attorney. Dr. Vialargo? Ah. Mr. Prophet's son and the new-ish doctor in town. Then I frowned.

"What do you mean, 'signed off on the baby'? What does that even mean, Harold?"

"Don't get grumpy with me, Mrs. Rotondo," said Harold. "I'm only telling you what Pete Altman told me. He wants the doctor to give the adoptive parents a health report on the kid and explain how she came to be adoptable. Makes sense to me."

"Sorry, Harold. Didn't mean to be a grouch. I just woke up from a lovely nap."

"Oh. Sorry I called when I called," he said, understanding the need for naps in a person's life.

"It's all right. I think the doctor's health report is a good idea, actually. I'm sure the Grenvilles and Diane will want a hale and hearty baby." I thought about Mr. Prophet and his relationship with Dr. Vialargo and my lips turned up in a wicked grin of their own accord. Bad Daisy!

"Yeah, I thought so too, although its parentage might be dicey if Sam's nephew is its father."

"Ew. You're right. But I don't think a baby can be born evil, do you?"

"We've had this conversation before, and I'll remind you again. Do you recall my late sister, Stacy?" asked Harold.

I did. "I do. But Stacy was a fluke. You're not evil, Harold!"

"Thank you," said Harold sarcastically. "But we had the same father, and he was definitely evil."

"I suppose he was. Heck, Harold, I don't have any idea if evil people produce other evil people, or if some kind of exposure when they're young makes them evil."

"I think I deciphered that sentence," he said. "But I don't know

227

if you're right. Frank Pagano, assuming he's the father of the baby upstairs, is definitely bad."

"Melanie's not bad," I pointed out.

"Neither is my mother, but she's a nitwit," said Harold.

"True. And to judge by Melanie's behavior in recent months, she might also win a nitwit contest. Or maybe she's just young and too innocent for her own good."

"Hell, I don't know," said Harold. "And I don't much care. I want the kid to go to a good home, and I think the Grenvilles will provide one. Still, we should be honest with them about her parents."

"I agree," I said. "Although Marianne is so thrilled with the baby idea, she'll probably ignore us about the parents."

"I expect you're right," said Harold. "Will Lou be there?"

"He'll either be here or in his cottage in the back," I said.

"I hope he's present," said Harold. I could virtually see his evil grin.

You can see why he and I are great friends, can't you?

"How about Thursday morning?" said Harold. "Would that be a good time for us to visit?"

"What time Thursday morning?" I cudgeled my brain for three seconds. "Tomorrow's Wednesday, isn't it?"

"It is," Harold confirmed.

"Sure. Thursday morning will be fine. Unless you want refreshments at the meeting. I'm still not good enough in the kitchen to bake things, although I'm sure I can make tea and coffee for people."

"Don't bother. I'll have Roy fix some delicacies for our mid-morning pleasure."

"Bless Roy's heart," I said reverently.

"What about *my* heart? I thought of it."

"Bless your heart too. In fact, you should be doubly blessed. First you took Roy in, and then you took that baby in, then you attempted—well, you're still attempting—to care for Melanie. Plus now you're facilitating the baby's adoption. I guess that should make you thrice blessed, by golly."

"And don't forget it," said Harold, laughing.

"Oh, crumb," I said, having thought about something.

"What's crumb?" asked Harold.

"Thursday's choir practice."

"That's at night, isn't it?"

"Well, yes, but I can't go, so I have to call Mr. Hostetter and tell him I won't be there. He doesn't appreciate it when his choristers don't show up."

"I should think he'd give you a pass," said Harold. "I'm surprised he's still allowing you to sing in the choir, as big as you are. Aren't ladies supposed to hide when they're in the 'family way'?"

"They used to," I said. "But I'll be darned if I will," I said, being firm with Harold who didn't deserve it. He wasn't responsible for society's stupid rules. They weren't on his side any more than they were on a pregnant woman's side.

"As long as Sam's stupid nephew is after you, you should probably stay home, even if you don't care about being pregnant."

"You're right."

"Why do you have to call the choir director? Why don't you telephone another choir member and ask her to apologize to the gorgon for you?"

As I'd just that second decided to call Lucy Zollinger instead of Mr. Hostetter, I said. "Brilliant idea, Harold! I'll call Lucy."

"Excellent. Go call Lucy, whoever she is."

"I shall," I said.

"Glad we got *that* straightened out," said Harold.

"I love you, Harold," I said.

"Yeah. Back at you," he said uneasily.

"As a *friend*," I clarified.

"What else would you mean?" he asked.

"I need to finish reading my book now," I told him.

"Maybe you should finish your nap first. Your brain's not firing on all cylinders."

"What's a cylinder?"

"Beats me. I think they have something to do with automobiles."

"Hey," I said in mock anger. "I may be as big as an automobile, but I don't run on cylinders."

"Right. See you Thursday. What time should we get there?"

"How about ten? Is that too early? Too late?"

"Ten o'clock on Thursday morning. Got it. Be prepared for the Grenvilles, Pete and me, Hazel and Dr. Vialargo. And I hope Lou shows up."

"Are Hazel and Dr. Vialargo stepping out with each other?" I asked.

"Looks like it to me. He's extremely polite to her, and she teases him. A match made in heaven if I ever saw one."

"If you say so."

"Bye," said Harold.

"Bye," I said.

After I hung up the receiver, the stupid 'phone rang again. Crumb. Even with Mrs. Pinkerton in Santa Barbara, we still got too many telephone calls.

"Hello?" I said sweetly.

"Hey, Daisy," said Pa. "Vi wants to know if you and Sam—and Lou if he wants to—can come to supper tonight."

"How nice!" Then I recalled Mrs. Rattle's shepherd's pie sitting forlorn and neglected in the Frigidaire. "But Mrs. Rattle made us what looks like a delicious shepherd's pie with the last of the leftover lamb. We were supposed to eat it yesterday, but yesterday got swallowed up by too much action and we didn't. I promised her we'll have it for supper tonight."

"Huh. Well, how about we go over there then?" said Pa.

"What a *wonderful* idea!" I said, happy. I loved my family, and I loved to entertain. It was the cooking part of entertaining that made me shy away from having people visit more often. "I can fix a salad—"

"You don't even have to fix a salad," said Pa. "Vi has a green salad already made. She won't dress it until we bring it to your place. And she has dessert, too."

"What's she going to dress it as? A witch?" Stupid joke, Daisy Rotondo, but Halloween was right around the corner.

"Ha ha," said Pa.

"Sorry about that one," I said.

"Don't be sorry," said Pa. "Halloween's a couple of weeks away though, so I think she'll just use the salad dressing she made up and put in a jar in the ice box."

"Wow, then please do come on over. I'll invite Mr. Prophet, and if all goes well in the city today, Sam should be home in time for dinner. Six-thirty all right with you?"

"Perfect," said Pa.

"Good. I miss strolling across the street and visiting. But until Sam's idiot nephew is captured, I guess we all have to be careful."

"You bet we do. We don't want anything bad happening to any of us, especially now, when we're going to have a new grandchild."

"Absolutely," I said and sighed as the two of us disconnected.

Glancing down at the dog at my feet, I said, "Spike, we're going to have company for dinner. That is to say, we won't eat the company, but they'll join us for dinner."

Spike thought that was a great idea and wagged to prove it. Glad at least one member of the family thought my jokes were funny.

Because people would join us for that evening's meal, I decided we'd have it in the dining room and use the good china. Mind you, thanks to the generosity of my many wealthy lady clients, we had about sixteen sets of exquisite china, but I decided to use the one *I* picked out, which was Shelley's Syringa Gardenia pattern. I think Ma was a little disappointed that I didn't select a china set with gold rims that looked fancier than mine, but I thought it was gorgeous.

When I entered the dining room, I realized I'd have to add another leaf to the table to enlarge it when I managed to pull the two sides apart.

Two sides.

Nertz.

I peeked at the hound at my feet. "Spike," I said, "Sam will kill me if I pull the table apart all by myself." Gazing then at my big belly, I added, "Besides, I don't think I can. Want to visit Mr. Prophet and Yuyu with me?"

In answer, Spike gave a happy yip and dashed to the back door. I followed him, not dashing. I was about to reach out and open the back door when I remembered the possible menace of Frank Pagano. Various people were supposed to keep him away from our house, but I wasn't sure we could trust them to be precisely where they needed to be precisely when we needed them to be there, if that makes sense.

I know it was the wrong season, but I said, "Bah, humbug," to Spike and peeked out the back door's window. All seemed as it should be so I slowly opened the door and saw Mr. Prophet sitting in a chair on the back porch reading a book, a rifle cradled in his arms.

"Oh," I said, surprised. "If I'd known you were there, I wouldn't have been so scared."

He turned his head and scowled at me. "You knew we was lookin' out for you, didn't ya?"

"Yes, but I didn't know how closely I'd be guarded."

With a totally unjustified eye-roll, Mr. Prophet said, "Then you're out o' yer mind."

"Thank you," I said stiffly. "I had aimed to walk to your cottage and ask you if you'd help me put another leaf in the dining room table."

"Why d'you want to put leaves on the dining room table?" he asked, still frowning.

"Not real leaf-leaves that flutter on tree limbs," I said. "But a shiny piece of polished wood that makes the table longer. Only we have to pull the two sides of the table apart in order to put the leaf in, so I need you to help me pull the table apart and stick in the extra leaf."

"Cripes," said Mr. Prophet, rising from his chair and shouldering his rifle. "I know what a leaf is. I been livin' a long time on this earth, you know."

"Why'd you ask me about putting leaves on the table then?" I asked, irked.

"Jest to rile you up some," he said, giving me a toothy grin and propping his firearm on the floor of the back entryway.

"Great," I said. "You'll be pleased to know your ploy worked."

"Good. Now where's this leaf o' yours?"

I showed him where the extra table leaves were in the utility room. He picked up one and carried it to the dining room.

"Ya got somethin' fancy goin' on tonight?" he said as he scanned the room and noticed that I'd set out the box of "good" flatware and one of the Shelley Syringa Gardenia teacups I'd retrieved from the china cabinet.

"Ma, Pa, and Vi are coming to dinner tonight."

"Yeah? Well, that'll be good."

"Yes, and you have to dine with us too," I told him.

"You cookin'?" he asked as we each took a position on either side of the table and pulled it apart.

"No, I'm not," I barked. "Mrs. Rattle made a shepherd's pie for us to eat yesterday, but we couldn't. So we're having it tonight, and Vi's bringing everything else."

"I expect I'll come over then," said the cantankerous old curmudgeon.

"Thanks heaps," I said.

"Not a problem." He gave me another toothy smile.

It was clear I couldn't win a war of words with the man, so I just smiled back and said, "You may go back to your guarding duties now."

"Want me to help set the table?" he asked, surprising me.

"Thanks, but there's no need for that. I've got everything prepared."

"You gonna use a tablecloth?" he asked.

"Yes. Oh," I said, realizing why he'd asked. "It would be nice of you to help me put the tablecloth on the table," I admitted.

"Figgered. Where's the tablecloth?"

I got out the white tablecloth and an Irish lace topper to go over the cloth. I didn't feel like ironing the big tablecloth, so I hoped the lace topper would cover up any creases. Mr. Prophet and I each took an end of the cloth and marched—well, he limped—to the head and the foot of the table. Then we flipped it open and it sailed beautifully onto the shiny mahogany table top. We did likewise with the Irish lace topper.

"Boy, that worked really well," I said, surprised.

"Yeah. When's supper?"

"Six-thirty," I told him.

"See ya then," he said and prepared to limp back through the pantry and kitchen to the back door. I followed him. There he retrieved his rifle and resumed his seat on the back porch. I noticed he'd laid his book on his chair when he'd left it to help me.

"What are you reading?" I asked, curious.

With another smile, this one sardonic as heck, he said, "'*You Can't Win*', by a feller named Jack Black."

"I've heard of that book! It was written by a crook, wasn't it?"

"Yep," he said, still smiling. "It's good, too."

I just shook my head and returned to the dining room to set the table.

TWENTY-EIGHT

Dinner that night was lovely. We all enjoyed Mrs. Rattle's shepherd's pie, to which she'd added celery, chopped onions, and carrots. Vi's salad was delicious. She dressed it with what she called thousand-island dressing. I'd never heard of it before, but it was mighty tasty. Vi said it had chopped eggs and sweet pickle relish in it. That was all right by me.

Tapioca pudding for dessert! With whipped cream. With the pudding she also served up what she called sand tarts, which were a feathery cookie with ground pecans in the dough and confectioner's sugar sifted over them.

"This was a meal fit for a king," said Pa, rubbing his tummy after he'd popped the last piece of sand tart into his mouth.

"It was great," said Sam. "Did Mrs. Rattle give you that recipe, Daisy?"

"I'll ask her for it tomorrow," I promised. "She left me the recipe for the last chicken casserole dish she made for us. That's the one Stacy Kincaid's ghost burned to a crisp."

My parents and aunt stared at me as if I'd lost my mind. "Um, well, you know, we had a little trouble earlier in the year. Remember?" I said, attempting a light tone and a smile.

"That's all right, Miss Daisy," said Mr. Prophet. "We don't expect miracles from you."

"Thanks a lot," I grumbled. He'd been at Stacy's exorcism, darn it! My own spirit guide, the old Scottish guy I'd made up and named Rolly when I was ten years old, had actually gained reality and consigned Stacy Kincaid's soul to the heck. I didn't like to think about it.

"I vaguely recall something about ghosts," said my mother after a significant spate of silence.

She *should* recall Stacy's ghost! It had almost battered her to death with dried peppercorns from all the pepper trees on Marengo. Bother.

Deciding to change the subject, I said, "I love this china set. It's my best china," I told everyone proudly.

"I remember when you brought a teacup and saucer from this set and your other one home after Harold took you to Bullock's downtown," said Ma.

"You were hoping I'd pick a fancier one, weren't you?" I asked.

Ma smiled a little sheepishly. "Well, I'd looked at china patterns in magazines, and some of them are pretty spectacular. They have gold rims and swirls and all sorts of lovely patterns on them."

"I had to be careful about selecting the cups," I said truthfully. "A lot of the new china patterns have pointy handles on the cups, and neither Sam nor Mr. Prophet could get their big fingers or thumbs through those small spaces. I doubt Pa could have either."

"You chose your china pattern because of our fingers?" Sam sounded incredulous.

"Well, yours and Pa's," I said. "It wouldn't be fun to pick up a hot teacup by its bowl and burn your fingers, so I had to get teacups with big enough handle holes."

"That's mighty kind o' you, Miss Daisy." Mr. Prophet, on the other hand, sounded as though he aimed to burst out laughing as soon as my back was turned.

"You're welcome," I said, not meaning it. I *loved* my Shelley Syringa Gardenia china! "But Ma, do you have a favorite pattern?

236

I've been given so many different china sets that I want to give one to you and one to Flossie Buckingham."

"My goodness!" said Ma, surprised. "How nice, Daisy."

"It's going to be one of your Christmas presents," I said. It was the truth. "But I was thinking maybe you'd like to see the different sets I have and choose the one you like best." To my aunt, I added, "I have enough sets to give one to you too, Vi, if you want one."

"You have three extra sets of china, and you want to give them away?" Vi didn't believe me; I could tell.

"I'll take you to the basement and show you if you want me to," I said. "In fact, we should all go down to the basement. There are at least four complete sets of dinnerware in boxes down there. I honestly don't think I need another four sets. I mean, you know how much I cook, right?"

"Right," said Vi. "But I don't really need or want one, Daisy. It's kind of you to offer, but why don't I help Peggy pick out one for her and Joe, and I'll just use that one."

"That's okay with me," I said. "If you want a dessert set, a tea set, a hot chocolate set or a luncheon set, I have some of those too."

"They got special dishes for desserts and tea?" said Mr. Prophet, lifting his fuzzy gray eyebrows. "Cripes. Don't people have nothin' else to spend their money on?"

"Not some of the people I know," I said drily.

"Must be nice," he said.

"I guess," I said, "But I'd rather be me than, say, Mrs. Pinkerton."

Nobody argued.

My mother and I cleaned up the dinner dishes while the men and Vi moseyed to the living room to chat. After the dishes were washed, rinsed and put away, Ma and I also tootled to the living room.

"Why don't you play the piano, Daisy?" said Pa, who liked to sing almost as much as I did.

"Sure. If you want me to. I've been practicing a couple of pieces. I'll try them out on you guys. The piano's a little out of tune, but we can get that fixed as soon as we're freed from the threat of Frank Pagano."

"Yeah. Play something for us," said Mr. Prophet.

I squinted at him, thinking this was an odd request from the source, but I shuffled the music on the piano stand and decided to play "The Toreador Song." It was dramatic. I played it better than I'd done so far, and when I hit the last chord and removed my fingers from the keyboard, everybody clapped. Surprised me. I rose, therefore, from the piano bench and attempted to take a bow, forgetting for a second that I no longer had a waist.

"I'll be so glad when this kid is born," I grumbled.

Eyeing my middle like an expert baby-caller, Vi said, "It won't be more than a couple or three weeks now, Daisy. Be patient."

"How can you tell?" I asked her.

"Has the baby been kicking recently?" she said.

"Not much," I admitted. "I asked Dr. Steindorf about that, and she said it was normal for the infant not to move so much during the last month or so. Not enough room."

"True," said Vi as if she were an expert. She'd only had one son, and my mother'd had two daughters and a son, but she didn't offer any salient additions to Vi's prediction. "Your bump has lowered, too, which is an indication."

"It's *lowered*?" I said, alarmed.

"Perfectly natural," said Vi. "The baby has to get into the proper position for birth."

"Good grief. Dr. Steindorf said something about breech births, but she said I didn't have to worry about one of those because she said the baby is in its proper position." She'd poked and prodded me so much I figure she could have drawn a picture of the baby, in fact.

"There you go," said Vi, as if I'd just confirmed her prediction.

"What's a breech baby?" asked Mr. Prophet.

I decided I could answer this one because I'd been to see Dr. Steindorf a mere week prior. "The baby's head is supposed to come out first. In a breech birth, the feet come out first. Even worse—it sounded worse to me anyhow—is a transverse position. That's when the baby is turned sideways. Unless the doctor can reach in and turn the baby, it can't come out at all that way."

When I glanced around the room, I noticed everyone looking as if they'd rather not hear any more tales of baby-birthing. This irked me a little bit because it wasn't *my* fault female anatomy was what it was.

"Everyone in this room was *born*, you know," I said. "And your mothers had to go through the pain and misery of it all." I pinned Sam with a stare. "You'd better be good to me, Sam Rotondo."

"I will be," he promised. His face looked a little greenish, so I believed him.

"Giving birth isn't fun," said Ma at last. "But the results are worth it." She smiled sweetly at me. "And this time when one of my children gives birth, I'll be right across the street and won't have to wait months or travel for miles in order to see my grandchild."

"It's a boy," I said, then wished I hadn't. My folks got perturbed when I talked about ghosts burning meals. I simply *couldn't* tell them a Tongva shaman had predicted the birth of a healthy son before I barely knew I was pregnant. "That's what Mrs. Rattle says anyway," I said to make up for my bald statement.

"People say they can tell," said Ma. "But I've had three babies, and I didn't know what they were until they were born. Their sex, I mean." Then she blushed, "sex" not being a word people bandied about, even back then when morals seemed to become looser by the day.

Mr. Prophet had started out the evening looking almost jolly. As the talk turned to babies, I noticed him withdrawing. Guess he was pondering his lost love, Louisa Bonaventure, and the son she and he created together: Dr. Lawrence Vialargo. In my opinion, he deserved to feel at least a little bit ashamed of himself. Women can't create babies by themselves, but—as I've mentioned far too many times already—they have to bear all the consequences.

I was darned lucky to have Sam.

"Well," said Pa after a brief silence in the living room. "We'd probably better get going. Thanks for a swell evening, Daisy and Sam." He stood and stretched. "Rosie's probably missing us."

"She's missing you, anyhow," said Ma. "I don't think that dog cares about Vi or me."

"Oh, she does too," I said. "She's just a little fickle." That didn't make any sense.

"We're glad you could come," said Sam.

"Yes, we are," I confirmed.

"But let me check the front porch first. The evening shift should be here by now." Sam shook down his shirt sleeve—we didn't dress formally for meals, even when we used the good china—and peered at his wristwatch. "Yes, they should be. It's a little after eight o'clock."

Thus reminded of the danger lurking somewhere in Pasadena, the assemblage's general happy mood slid downhill. Nevertheless, we all pretended to be happy because... Because Frank Pagano was a lousy excuse for a human being, and he had no right to scare decent people like us, darn it!

"All clear," Sam called from the front door.

We got up and marched to the front door. Another policeman in uniform, this one named Branigan, smiled at us. Then he escorted my parents and Vi back to their house across the street.

I felt a little melancholy as I watched my family traverse the front walkway and step out from the pepper-tree-lined sidewalk and onto the street.

"It's all right, sweetheart," said Sam, putting an arm around me. "Frank is as dumb as a box of rocks. We'll find him soon."

Because I couldn't precisely turn in his arms—baby tummy—I tilted my head and laid it on his shoulder. That is to say, it was still attached to my neck, but...

Oh, forget it.

"I'll be goin' now, too," said Mr. Prophet. "Thanks for supper. It was good."

"Thanks, Lou," said Sam.

"We'll walk you to the back door," I said. "Spike needs to go outside and have a final piddle for the day."

We did. Spike galloped out the door, down the porch steps, and gleefully visited every bush and chair leg in the backyard. He didn't sniff anything out of place. We could tell, because Spike is a champion guard dog. He's also a mighty hunting hound. He's chased all sorts of interloping birds, cats (except for Yuyu), and gophers from the yard. Well, he did something considerably worse to a couple of gophers, but that was all right with Sam and me, although I did feel a little sorry for the gophers who were only doing what gophers did. We just didn't want them to do what it was they did in our flower and vegetable beds.

Sam, Spike, and I stayed up a little longer after my family and Mr. Prophet left. I finished *The Chinese Parrot*, and it was a great book! Only the parrot died. I don't like it when animals die in books. People can die with reckless abandon since they cause all the problems in the world. But animals are usually just going about their business. Of course, if no one had captured that particular parrot and caged it, it would still be flying free in some tropical jungle. Maybe.

The truth is that people (including me) tend to anthropomorphize animals. Mountain lions kill pretty little fawns all the time up in the San Gabriel Mountains. At least I expect they do. But I don't like to think about unpleasant things.

Yet one more reason I'd be *so* glad when the menace of Frank Pagano was dealt with. Oh dear, I see I've ended a sentence with a whatchamacallit. I'm sorry.

TWENTY-NINE

Wednesday morning arrived along with a grumpy gray sky and drizzles. We didn't get a whole lot of rain in Pasadena during the autumn months. Winter was our rainy season, if we could be said to have a rainy season. Or any seasons at all, come to think of it.

I'd called Pa first thing, and we decided it would be stupid of us to take the dogs for a walk on a rainy day when Frank Pagano was after us, although Frank was an afterthought. We were mostly concerned about dragging dogs through puddles. I tried to explain the matter to Spike, but his tail drooped anyway. When, however, Sam and I got to the kitchen, he perked up again. If there was anything Spike liked better than a walk, it was food.

Fortunately for everyone wanting toast that morning, Sam cut slices from the loaf. I manned the fancy toaster somebody had given us as a wedding gift, stacked toast on a plate, and took the plate to the table while Sam made coffee. He was much more skilled in the kitchen than I was. I tried not to feel like a failure as we ate our breakfast.

Didn't work.

Never did.

The day still appeared overcast and drippy when I glanced at the kitchen window over the sink. "Take your umbrella when you go to work," I told Sam.

"It's already in the car," he said, lowering the morning newspaper to peer at me. "Will you need anything in particular today? I mean, I can stop at a store or something."

"Thanks, Sam. That's nice of you, but I don't think I need anything. Flossie is coming over and bringing lunch." Then I remembered Frank the menace. "Is it all right if she visits?"

"Don't know why not," he said, going back to his paper and picking up his coffee cup. "She doesn't look like you. I don't think even Frank could mistake you for her or vice versa."

"True. Say, have you found the crossword puzzle yet?"

"Oh," he said, surprised. "Yes. I took out the page and then forgot to give it to you." He picked up the folded newspaper sheet lying beside his coffee cup and handed it across the bowl of oranges in the center of the table.

"Thanks."

"Did you find someone to direct the exercise class for you?" he asked.

"Flossie said she'd do it. Crumb, I forgot to call Lucy and tell her I won't be at choir practice tomorrow night."

We both heard a key turn at the back door. I glanced up, Sam lowered his newspaper again, turned his head, and we both saw Mr. Lou Prophet ka-thump into the kitchen. Spike, who had been snoozing under the table—we'd both finished eating, so nobody was dropping crumbs any longer—jumped to his feet and bounced over to greet him.

"Hey, Spike." Mr. Prophet's voice sounded particularly raspy this morning.

Spike wagged at him and accompanied him to the kitchen table.

"Morning," I said.

"Mornin'," he said.

"Morning," Sam said.

We were a creative bunch, weren't we?

Guess I was a little nervous, because when the telephone rang, I nearly jumped out of my skin. Ew. That would have been disgusting, huh?

Sam said, "I'll get it. This early in the morning, it's probably for me."

The call was and it wasn't for Sam. Someone had thrown a brick through one of the windows at my church! Well, our church.

"It was probably Frank," I said, hoping the window could be repaired or replaced easily. All those windows were stained glass, and they were beautiful.

"It probably was," agreed Sam. "But the church will be closed today, according to Doan, so your class won't meet anyway."

"Well, doesn't that just figure?" I said, irked. "The one day I can't go, the class won't take place anyway. I'd been *so* looking forward to getting out of that stupid class, but now my not attending isn't special any longer."

Sam and Mr. Prophet stared at me, both looking confused, but I knew what I meant.

"There's one good thing about it though," I added, having just recalled a salient fact. "Flossie can come over earlier than we'd planned. And since she's not going to lead the exercise class, she might be able to bring little Billy and Daisy with her."

"You want her to bring the kids?" asked Mr. Prophet, frowning.

"Well…" I commenced thinking for the first time that day. My thoughts weren't happy.

"She probably shouldn't," said Sam. "Just to be on the safe side."

I heaved a sigh. "You're right. I'll give her a call… What time is it anyhow?" The clock was on the kitchen wall behind me, and I didn't feel like turning my head.

"Eight," said Sam. "I'd better get going." He walked around the table and kissed the top of my head. "See you this evening."

"See you," I said in return. "Be careful."

"You be careful," he said.

"Will do. Now that I can't go anywhere, I'm glad Flossie's coming here. I miss people."

"Huh," said Mr. Prophet. "Mind if I make myself some toast?"

I waved a hand in the air. "Feel free. There are oranges, too, as you can see. And there are eggs and bacon in the Frigidaire, if you want some."

"I think toast will do," Mr. P. said.

The doorbell chimed, and Sam said, "That's probably the early shift. I'll check."

"Be careful," I said again.

"Don't worry about me," he said.

"Can't help it," I told him. It was but the truth.

"It's all right," Sam called from the door. "Officer Wilde is here."

"Ask him to come in for coffee," I said.

"His duties remain outside, watching the neighborhood," said Sam.

"It's all right, Mrs. Rotondo," came Officer Wilde's voice from the front porch. "I'm fine out here. You have a nice covered porch, and it's not raining hard. I'll take a cup of coffee if you have any to spare."

Sam's the one who came to the kitchen, poured coffee for Officer Wilde and took the cup out to him. Okay by me.

As Mr. Prophet fixed his toast, I worked the crossword puzzle. I loved doing crossword puzzles and was glad they'd begun publishing them in the newspaper every day instead of once a week.

A jar of Vi's plum jam and jar of her orange marmalade already rested on the kitchen table, so when Mr. Prophet's bread was toasted, he brought over his plate and sat.

"Whatcha doin'?" he asked as he reached for the butter dish and commenced buttering his toast.

"The daily crossword puzzle," I said.

"Ah. That's one o' those grids where you fill in letters from the hints they write on the side?"

I glanced up at him and blinked, somewhat taken aback that he knew about crossword puzzles. "Yes," I said. "That's exactly what they are."

He nodded and glanced at the two jam jars. My own breakfast had consisted of an orange, two pieces of toast (one with plum jam and the other with marmalade), and a cup of coffee. Mr. Prophet reached for the jar of orange marmalade, dipped a clean spoon into it and withdrew a big glob of marmalade.

I approved of his selection, which I'm sure would come as a thrill and an honor to him. Yes, I'm lying. I went back to my crossword. Spike decided to sit beside Mr. Prophet's chair since food would more likely be dropped by him, as the only human eating.

After Sam had gone upstairs to brush his teeth and get his suit jacket and briefcase, he descended them again. As soon as I heard him step from the stairs and onto the hall runner, I also heard the telephone ring. Sam was there already; he could get it. He did.

I heard him talking, but didn't hear what he said. I did hear him utter a curse word, which made me lift my head and frown. Sam cared about the environment in which our son—and any future children—would be reared, and he ordinarily didn't swear out loud. Then I heard him replace the receiver on the switch hook. And that's all I heard. I was about to get up from the table and see what was going on, when footsteps approached the pantry and headed for the kitchen, so I stayed put.

When Sam walked into the kitchen, he looked unhappy. This worried me.

"Sam, what's wrong?" I lifted my bulky body from the kitchen chair and took a step toward him. He hurried to me and took my hands, alarming me. A lot.

"Daisy. I'm not sure how to break this to you gently, but Melanie Robinson has disappeared."

"*What?*" I stared up at him. "What do you mean, she disappeared?"

"She's not in the hospital any longer. She didn't check out officially, and she wasn't released by a doctor."

"Oh dear. Do you think Frank has her?"

"I have no idea. That was Harold on the telephone. He said the hospital called him to say that Melanie was in her room last night, but she and her few belongings were gone this morning."

"Good Lord, I hope she's all right. I also hope she's not with Frank. But she shouldn't be alone either. Darn her!"

"We don't know what happened yet. Save your condemnation until you know she deserves it."

"You're right of course. I just hope somebody can find her."

"If Lou agrees to go with you, maybe you and Flossie can drive around the hospital neighborhood and search for her. I don't think she had any money with her, do you?"

"I doubt it," I said. "But that's a good idea." I turned to the lone diner at the kitchen table. "Mr. Prophet, would you and a couple of your firearms be willing to hunt down a girl with Flossie Buckingham and me today? Only don't shoot her if we find her. You may shoot Frank if you see him."

"Better not do that either," said Sam with a grin. "He deserves it, but he hasn't been tried and convicted yet."

"Sure," said Mr. Prophet, somewhat to my surprise. He usually argued at least a little bit when asked to help me.

Rather than say so, I said, "Thank you."

"Okay. I'll send officers out to search too," said Sam. "But I've got to get to the station now."

"I hope nothing awful happens in Pasadena today," I said.

"It probably won't. It usually doesn't," said Sam. "See you."

We shared a kiss and Sam took off for the front door. He opened it to reveal Mrs. Rattle on the porch smiling at Officer Wilde. She lowered her umbrella, shook it out, and set it under the awning to dry as she said good morning to Sam and the officer. Then she wiped her feet and entered the house. We greeted each other happily.

Another day had begun, by Jupiter.

I decided to call Flossie. I needed to tell her that there would be no exercise class. Also, if Johnnie wasn't already walking the damp streets with the Salvation Army Band, she could ask him to look out for Melanie too.

"Oh dear, the poor girl," said sweet Flossie. "I'm sure she's totally confused and doesn't know what to do with herself. I've been in that position before, and it's not fun. At least I didn't have to give a baby away."

"I know, Flossie. I just wish she'd stayed in the hospital. Leaving in the middle of the night sounds thoughtless to me. Unless she was coerced. I hope Frank Pagano didn't sneak in and take her."

"Yes," said Flossie. "There's that too."

I explained to her what Sam had suggested. "Would you be willing to go on a Melanie hunt? Mr. Prophet will come with us and be our guard."

"Absolutely!"

Flossie, Mr. Prophet, and I left the house, Spike, and Mrs. Rattle at about ten a.m. Officer Wilde escorted us across the street to get the Chevrolet. After we greeted Rosebud, Pa, and Vi, I drove south on Marengo and to the Castleton Hospital. Then, with Flossie and Mr. P. assiduously staring out the windows—I had to keep my eyes on the slippery streets—I drove around several more blocks.

"Anything?" I asked at one point.

"We'd tell you if we saw her," grumbled Mr. Prophet.

"I know, I know. I'm just worried about her." My statement was true, although even truer was that I was tired of hunching over the steering wheel and guiding the auto through sloppy streets. Any time we crossed a street with trolley tracks the car tended to slide, which was scary, darn it.

Suddenly Flossie said, "Wait a minute. Daisy, can you park?"

"Um…" We were on Green Street, an east-west street not containing trolley tracks. It did, however, contain automobiles parked on both sides of it. "No, I'm afraid there's nowhere to park here," I said at last.

"She just turned north on Euclid," Flossie announced.

"You mean left?" I said to make sure.

"Yes. Take a left on Euclid. North," Flossie confirmed.

When I came to the corner of Green and Euclid, luck was on my side and I was able to make a left turn.

"By golly, you're right, Flossie!"

Not sure why I sounded so surprised. Melanie Robinson, soaked through and wobbling slightly, was indeed making her slow way up

Euclid Avenue. She might have been heading to Colorado Street, but the Rolly spirit within me—Rolly sometimes rears his head and always startles me—said she didn't know what she was doing or where she was going.

She just wants to get away from everything, Rolly said in my brain. I mentally said something unkind about Melanie. Rolly tut-tutted. Still and all... "I can't pull over, because there are too many—"

"I'll just go fetch her," said Flossie. As the Chevrolet was almost stopped, she opened her door and got out! Made of stern stuff, Flossie. Well, she'd had to be in order to survive so long, given her circumstances.

"Be careful!"

Mr. Prophet and I didn't sound awfully musical together, but we bore the same message. Flossie didn't need our instructions. She hurried right up to Melanie Robinson, took her arm, and made her stop walking. Although the girl was startled at first, Flossie spoke soothingly to her—I know she was soothing because I know Flossie. Her words seemed to calm Melanie, who staggered a step or two then more or less collapsed against the wall of the Euclid Hat Shop on the corner of Colorado and Euclid.

"Fiddlesticks," I muttered. I glanced at the street behind the Chevy, didn't see traffic, set the brake and got out to help Flossie with Melanie.

So did Mr. Prophet, although I didn't know it until he limped over to the three of us.

"She all right?" he asked, his raspy voice sounding critical. As my own thoughts had been quite critical, I didn't think badly of him.

"No!" Melanie whimpered. I think she was attempting to speak loudly.

"Melanie Robinson, what the heck are you doing out of the hospital?" I asked, not kindly.

"I...I...I didn't know what to do," she said between sobs.

She had a knack for selecting the person most likely to give her some slack, I guess, because she turned in Flossie's arms and sobbed on her shoulder, thoroughly soaking Flossie in the process. If she'd tried such a move with me, I'd have held her off. Not sure what Mr. Prophet might have done, but I doubt he'd have been as sympathetic as Flossie.

"Let's get her into the car," I said, still unsympathetic. "We can take her...somewhere."

"No!" Melanie tried to wail, but she only sounded whiny.

"Let's go to the Salvation Army. I know precisely what to do for her. Come along, Melanie." Flossie, who had been a hard-as-nails gangster's moll at one time, now sounded like a ministering angel. A firm ministering angel. Which she kind of was. You know: One of those "angels unaware" the Bible talks about.

"Oh, please," said Melanie, although she didn't say anything else, so we didn't know if she was pleading to go to the Salvation Army or somewhere else. Therefore, Flossie and I huddled her over to the Chevrolet. Mr. Prophet opened the back door. Flossie and I shoved Melanie into the car.

"Don't even think about getting out of this car, Melanie," I said as I released the brake and resumed driving north. "Why did you leave the hospital?"

No answer. I was about to growl some more when Flossie said, "Let's wait until we get warm and dry, Daisy."

I didn't want to wait. I wanted to scold the girl some more. Patience isn't one of my more conspicuous virtues. In fact, I'm ashamed to say I have maybe a teaspoon or two of patience. I needed to practice the art for when little Joey came into our lives.

"She can't get out anyhow," said Mr. Prophet.

His words made me feel better, which was unusual.

THIRTY

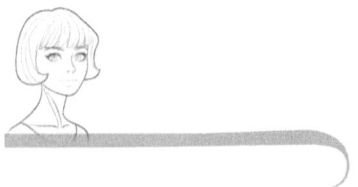

Because the streets were still wet and I didn't fancy slithering all the way to the Salvation Army on trolley tracks, I turned right on Colorado, made a left on Los Robles then took another left onto Walnut Street. Walnut didn't have trolley tracks, thank heaven. When we got to the Salvation Army, which sat on the corner of Walnut and Fair Oaks, I pulled to the curb on Fair Oaks.

Flossie, Mr. Prophet, and I all accompanied Melanie Robinson to a back entrance and made sure she got into the building. Slumping, limping, and silent, Melanie accompanied us, meek as a lamb.

"Come with me, Melanie," Flossie spoke sweetly into Melanie's ear. "Let's get you warm and dry. Then we can go to the kitchen and chat."

"Oh no," whimpered Melanie. But she made no escape attempt.

"Come along," said Flossie. "Daisy, will you take Mr. Prophet to the kitchen and make some hot cocoa? We'll be along as soon as we can be.

Me? Make cocoa? I could do that. At least I thought I could. I led Mr. Prophet to the Buckingham's little home at the back of the Army's headquarters and took him to the kitchen. "Have a seat," I said, pointing at the kitchen table and four chairs. Apparently one of the church ladies was watching the children.

I made a visual tour of the neatly organized shelves and discovered a tin of Hershey's Cocoa Powder. Taking a deep breath for courage, I plucked it off the shelf. Fortunately for me—and anyone else planning to create a heated chocolate beverage—there was a hot cocoa recipe printed right there on the box! I loved it when manufacturers didn't assume all their users were championship cooks.

By the time Flossie and Melanie—cleaned up, hair washed and shining, and with fresh clothes culled from Salvation Army donations—arrived in the kitchen, I had a pot of darned good hot cocoa ready for everyone to drink! I'd have been proud of myself if making hot cocoa weren't so easy and the Hershey's box didn't have the recipe printed on it.

"Let me see if I can find the marshmallows I made the other day. I should have some left. The kids aren't tall enough to open the cupboards yet," she said with a laugh.

I stared, amazed. "You *made* marshmallows?" I said.

"Yes, they're easy to make. Just use some gelatin, sugar and water. You have to beat them a lot to make them fluffy, but they're easy as pie."

Easy for you, maybe, I thought. *And I don't know how to make pies, either.* What I said was, "I didn't know you could make them at home." Truth, by golly.

"Yes, you can. They're not expensive to make. I can show you if you'd like me to," said Flossie, happy and chirpy.

"That's all right," I said with a smile I hoped looked genuine. "I don't use marshmallows very often."

"Wait until your baby is born," said Flossie with a laugh. "You'll probably use them more often then."

Then I'll buy some. I didn't say that either.

"Thanks for making the cocoa, Daisy," said Flossie.

"Sure," I said.

Melanie sat slumped in a chair at Flossie and Johnnie's kitchen table. She appeared sick and miserable, and my harsh judgment of her lessoned an iota or two.

"Why did you leave the hospital, Melanie?" I asked as gently as I could.

She lifted her head and gazed at me with bleary blue eyes. Shaking her head slowly, she said, "Jimmy said he was coming to get me. I...didn't want to go with him."

"You didn't?" I said, amazed.

Shaking her head, Melanie said, "No. I had a lot of time to think while I was in the hospital."

"Here's some cocoa with marshmallows, Melanie," Flossie said sweetly, placing a cup before Melanie on the table. Flossie also put a teaspoon into the cup in case Melanie wanted to stir the melting marshmallows.

"Thank you," Melanie said mechanically.

"What did you think about while you were in the hospital?" I asked Melanie, wishing Flossie would sit down and shut up.

She did, and I felt guilty. Naturally.

"I..." Melanie stopped speaking and sipped at a teaspoon full of cocoa. "This is good. Thank you. I...haven't eaten much recently."

I believed her. She was skinny as a pencil lead.

"But I thought about Jimmy making me put our baby in a basket," Melanie continued. "We left her on Harold Kincaid's front porch, because I know Harold a little bit. He's always been kind to me. I figured he'd be kind to our baby. Jimmy said we couldn't k-keep her."

"Why was that?" Asked Flossie gently. She handed Melanie a clean napkin, with which Melanie wiped her eyes.

"B-because we weren't married. He said we'd get married if I ran away with him, so I did. But every time I asked him about getting married, he got mad. He got mad at me when I told him I was going to have a b-b-baby, too." Melanie completely lost her composure and sobbed into her napkin.

"Were you afraid that Fran—that is to say Jimmy would come to the hospital and make you leave with him?" I asked, barely stopping myself from calling her former beloved Frank.

The poor girl nodded.

"And you didn't want to be with him any longer?" I asked.

After a few seconds, Melanie said, "No. I thought and thought and thought while I was sick in bed. Jimmy didn't call or come to see me for the first few days, but you did and Harold did. Then, when that detective made me look at the body of Frank, I...I... Oh, God, I don't know what I thought. I started wondering why Jimmy had dumped me at the hospital after making me give away the baby. He didn't even come inside with me." She swallowed hard and took another sip of cocoa, her face a mask of woe.

"I'm sorry, Melanie," I said. Couldn't help myself.

"Did you like living with Jimmy?" asked Flossie.

Lifting her head for a second before bowing it again, Melanie whispered, "No. I thought we were in love. He said he loved me, but I don't think he really did. Men who love women don't leave them for days with no food or money. At least I don't think they do."

"They don't," I said.

"Not often they don't," amended Flossie. "Did he work at a job?"

I think Melanie shrugged, although it was hard to tell what with her drooping as she was.

"Well?" asked Mr. Prophet, startling me. "Did he work? Why'd he leave you for days without food or money?"

Melanie too seemed startled. "I...I don't know. He'd come back after a few days and bring me a sandwich or something. I began worrying about the baby. I feared she wasn't getting enough nourishment."

"If you ever need anything when you're in a pickle like the one you were in, the Salvation Army is the place to go," I told her kindly. "As you just learned from Flossie, they help everyone who comes to them in need."

"It's true," said Flossie. "But I don't think we need to know more about your life with Jimmy right now."

Dang! I wanted to hear everything. Flossie however, being the tender and nurturing angel she was, knew better than to force the adolescent Melanie to tell us more of the horrors she'd endured with Frank Pagano, no matter how snoopy I was.

"What we need to dos," Flossie went on, "is figure out what you should do now."

"D-do?" whispered Melanie. "I don't have a dime. Or clothes. Or anything."

"You needn't fret about that right now," said Flossie. "The first thing we need to do is get you healthy again. Do you want to return to the hospital?"

"N-no," she said upon a sob. "Jimmy knows I was there. That's why I left."

For a second, I contemplated telling her she could stay at Sam's and my house, but fortunately, I recalled that no one was safe there and didn't speak. Then I considered Harold. But that wasn't a good idea either. If Frank couldn't get to Melanie at the hospital, he might besiege Harold's place. Harold had bodyguards and lots of money, but Frank was sneaky.

Besides, I really didn't want Melanie to see her baby. I'm not being unkind, honest. If she saw the baby, she'd want to keep her, and she wouldn't be able to care for a baby properly. Heck, she couldn't even care for herself. Melanie was only fifteen, for the love of God! And I had no idea how her family might react. I decided to clear up the latter issue.

"Would you like us to arrange a telephone call to your parents, Melanie?"

Boy, *that* question straightened her spine. She sat as upright as a tetherball pole and said, "No! No, please. I-I don't want my parents to know any of this."

"Did you leave them a note when you went away with Jimmy?" Flossie asked.

She nodded and started oozing tears again. "I told them I was running away, and they shouldn't try to find me. I said that Jimmy and I were g-getting married and leaving California. I don't want to bring misery and shame on them. I l-love them."

And there she went, bowing her head and sobbing to beat the band.

Flossie, Mr. Prophet, and I shared a few glances. Great. I crooked a finger at Flossie and jerked my head toward the small utility room off the kitchen. Then I heaved myself to my feet and Flossie and I went there.

"What do you think?" I asked. "Do you think her parents will disown her or anything? Will they want the baby? They might do one of those swap-type things and pretend the mother had the baby and Melanie is its sister. *Her* sister, I mean."

"Yes, I know people try that one all the time," said Flossie caustically.

Taken aback by her tone I said, "You don't think that's a good idea?"

"It's a bad idea," she declared. "I've seen people do it, and it only confuses the child, makes the real mother miserable, and the mother of the real mother resentful. That's not to say Melanie's mother won't still love both Melanie and Melanie's daughter, but situations like that seldom works out well in my experience. And Johnnie's too. We've talked about it quite often."

"Oh. Well, you both know more about these things than I do," I said, giving up instantly. Truth to tell, what I'd propounded sounded like a rotten idea to me too. I doubt that growing up as a lie is good for a child or anyone else in the child's family.

Flossie pursed her lips together and thought for several seconds. At last she said, "I don't know what's best for Melanie and her family at the moment, but she's right about Jimmy—I mean Frank —finding her at the hospital. If he gets his mitts on her again, I doubt she'll live through it."

"Same doubt here," I said glumly.

"Tell you what," said Flossie. "A wonderful woman named Mrs. Ted Forrest—her first name is Janet—is one of our most helpful members. She already has two unwed mothers living with her. The Salvation Army is paying for them to acquire the skills they'll need in order to live in the world. The Forrests are quite well off and have no children of their own. Johnnie and I check up on the girls regularly, and they seem to be thriving.

"What skills are they learning?" I asked, fascinated.

"At the moment, one of them is finishing high school at John Muir Technical High School. The other one is taking a secretarial course at Pasadena Junior College."

"Do their parents know they're here in Pasadena?" I wondered.

"One girl's parents know. The parents of the other girl disowned her."

"Poor thing," I said. "I can't imagine disowning a child. Well, unless it turns into someone like Frank Pagano."

Chuckling, Flossie said, "That's the trouble with children. You can rear them beautifully, but they'll always find ways to do things you don't want them to do."

"That's depressing, Flossie." I didn't want our little Joey to grow up doing horrible things.

"Yes, but everything is not always lost. With luck there can be reconciliations, if the parents aren't too stiff-necked and the children aren't too stubborn. We live in curious times. Life isn't as strict as it used to be in most places. Not where I grew up, but here in Pasadena."

That's because Flossie had spent her early years virtually parent-less in one of New York City's grubbiest and most crime-infested slums. She'd told me a few things about her childhood, and I honestly don't know how she survived to grow up.

"That sounds like the best idea so far. Frank might come looking for her here, too, if he figures out that Sam and I are friends of yours."

"He already knows we're friends," said Flossie. "Remember Mrs. Bannister?"

"How could I *ever* forget Mrs. Bannister? That was a frightful mess. Sam almost got killed."

Nodding, Flossie said, "I recall it well. But why don't I telephone Mrs. Forrest now and find out if she's willing to take in another lost soul?"

"Sounds like the best idea anyone's had all day," I said.

That's what Flossie did. When Mrs. Forrest, a large, pink-faced, jovial woman showed up in Flossie and Johnnie's kitchen, she pretty much adopted Melanie on the spot. Melanie was actually smiling slightly when Mrs. Forrest mother-henned her away from Flossie's kitchen and to her own home, which was in South Pasadena. South Pasadena is a beautiful community just south—in case you hadn't already guessed—of Pasadena.

Mr. Prophet and I were fed a great lunch by Flossie, and then he and I went home. There we again met Officer Wilde, who was munching a chicken sandwich prepared for him by Mrs. Rattle. She'd also cut up an orange for him and had been feeding him cookies and coffee all morning long, according to the officer.

"I'm gonna get fat if I have to guard your place much longer," he said after he'd swallowed a bite of sandwich.

"Mrs. Rattle is a kind woman," I said as I opened the front door and Spike raced to meet Mr. P. and me.

"Yeah," said Mr. Prophet who, as mentioned earlier, had once been afraid of Mrs. Rattle, "Elvira's a nice lady."

Mrs. Rattle left shortly after we got home.

The first thing I did was telephone Harold to tell him what Flossie and I had done with Melanie.

"I know Mrs. Forrest!" Harold sounded shocked.

"You sound shocked. Do you not approve of her?"

"*Approve* of her? I think she's the greatest thing ever to happen in Pasadena."

"South Pasadena," I said.

"Wherever she lives, I didn't know she took in waifs and strays."

"Well, she does. And Melanie is now in her keeping. Should somebody call her parents, do you think? Melanie doesn't like the idea, but if a child of mine disappeared, I'd definitely want to know what happened to him or her."

"Same here. I honestly don't know, Daisy. We can ask Pete and the Grenvilles tomorrow and maybe we'll come up with an answer."

"Sounds good to me."

Harold and I disconnected.

Spike and I marched upstairs to take a nap. I was bushed.

THIRTY-ONE

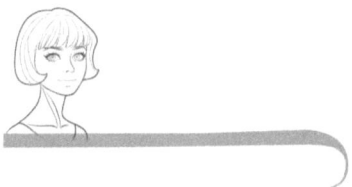

W hen Spike and I were again awake and aware, I remembered to place a telephone call to Lucy Zollinger.

"You're not coming to choir practice?" Lucy asked, although I thought I'd expressed myself clearly.

"No. It's becoming too hard for me to get around." That was true, if not the entire truth. "And I was afraid to call Mr. Hostetter."

"I don't think he'll be too upset," said Lucy. "He was looking at you last week as if he wondered why you were there."

"True. I remember it well. I think it's because these days, women don't feel it necessary to hide themselves away from public view during the last few weeks of their pregnancies."

"I think you're correct," said Lucy demurely. She didn't think I should walk around with my huge tummy declaring my condition either. She always had been a prude.

Rather than say so, I just said, "Thanks, Lucy. With any luck, I'll be at church on Sunday."

"Are you getting close to your delivery date?" she asked.

"Yes. A couple of my older lady friends who claim to know such things think I only have three or four weeks left. I'll be glad when it's over. Of course, babies are a lot of work."

"So I've heard." Lucy sounded wistful.

"That's right. You and Albert want to have children, don't you?"

"I'd love to have at least one child," Lucy said. "We've prepared a room as a nursery, but Albert's not so sure. He thinks he's too old to be starting a family."

As I thought so too, I didn't quite know how to answer her. I pried anyway. "How old is Mr. Zollinger?"

"He's forty-one."

"That's not too old!" I said. "My father was at least in his early forties when I was born, and he's the best father anyone could have."

"Really?" Lucy's voice registered interest and relief.

"Really. And you and Mr. Zollinger are well set up in the world."

"Yes, I suppose we are. And Albert does have a life insurance policy."

Huh. I wondered if Sam had a life insurance policy. I know we had insurance on the house. "Well, there you go. Of course, if anything happened to either of you, it would be difficult to rear a baby alone. If anything happened to Sam or me, my family would swoop in and take care of the baby. And Spike."

"What a melancholy conversation," said Lucy.

"You're right. I'm sorry I started it."

"Don't be silly," said Lucy. "You're thinking a lot about babies these days."

"That's for sure." And one of the thought-about babies wasn't even mine. "Thanks, Lucy."

"Happy to do it," said Lucy. "I don't like calling Mr. Hostetter either. He gets grumpy when one of his choir members doesn't show up. But he's less annoyed if they call in advance."

"Yes indeed." We both hung up.

The next morning, no walk for Spike or Rosebud for the second day in a row. Only this time, the rain wasn't my excuse. The people coming to the house at ten a.m. were my excuse.

When Mrs. Rattle arrived, I asked her to begin with the den. "We don't use that room at all, but this morning, some folks will be coming for a meeting."

"Oh my," said an excited Mrs. Rattle as she hung up her sweater and put her hat on the shelf. "Will you have snacks and so forth? Would you like me to prepare coffee or tea or anything?"

"Um... I don't know, to tell the truth. Harold's bringing edibles, so I guess coffee and tea would be nice. Thank you."

"Happy to help. I'll also prepare some fresh orange juice. How many folks will be here?"

"Hmm. Let me see." I lifted a hand and commenced counting people on my fingers. Darned if I didn't need both hands! "Wow, that's a lot of people," I said.

"Eight people will fit comfortably in the den," said Mrs. Rattle confidently. "I'll make sure the furniture is placed appropriately so that the seating is arranged for conversation and drinking coffee or tea, and the food and drinks are laid out on the sideboard."

"Nothing daunts you, does it, Mrs. Rattle?" She amazed me.

"Don't be silly, Daisy! You're a wonderful hostess, and that room is lovely. I'm glad it's getting some use. What about flowers? Aren't there chrysanthemums blooming in the yard?"

"Yes! What a brilliant idea," I told her.

"You find a couple of large vases, Daisy, and I'll go out and cut the flowers. I know you like to garden, so you have secateurs and a garden trug, don't you?"

"Yes. All the gardening tools and so forth are in the utility room."

"Excellent. I'll get some flowers for the den and the living room. You want the draperies opened, don't you?"

"Yes. I'll open them. Thanks, Mrs. Rattle."

I waddled to the den. It was truly a lovely room with light-salmon-colored walls. The Louis the Whateverth chairs and sofas were upholstered in dark green. I'd found pretty salmon-colored and green pillows to place here and there. A chandelier with little flame-shaped light bulbs lit the room when it was dark, but the day was bright and sunny, so I pulled open the green draperies—they had a pinkish design on them—and tied them with sashes. Harold had found brass lamps for the tables and the sideboard.

"Oh, my, this is such a lovely room!" exclaimed Mrs. Rattle when she came in with her trug filled with russet, yellow, and orange chrysanthemums.

"Those chrysanthemums will look splendid in here, Mrs. Rattle," I said. "Thank you! Let's go find a couple of vases and decide which china to use for the guests. I have far too many china sets. If you want to take one off my hands, please just let me know."

With a laugh, Mrs. Rattle said, "Kind of you, dear, but I have my own china. It was a wedding gift when Mr. Doan and I married." She looked a little dreamy for a second or two. "My goodness, that was thirty-five years ago! When Mr. Doan passed, I didn't think I'd ever marry again, but then I met Mr. Rattle."

"I know exactly what you mean. I felt the same way after my Billy died. I went into a terrible decline. Don't know what was wrong with me, but I must have lost fifty pounds. Harold took me to Egypt. I was sick the whole time, and the trip was awful, yet I'd somehow recovered my spirits by the time we made it home again. Life is strange sometimes, isn't it?"

"It is indeed. But let's go find vases, and then choose the china you want to use."

"I know what china I want to use," I said, having just remembered it. "It's from Czechoslovakia and is hand-painted. It's called a luncheon set, and it has gold edging and red-orange poppies on it. I've wanted to use it for the longest time, but I've never had reason to do so until now."

This was becoming fun, by golly!

Mrs. Rattle and I visited the pantry where we chose vases for the beautiful flowers, and then I gently removed the box containing my Czecho-Slovak china from a low shelf.

"I'll give those a gentle wash," said Mrs. Rattle. When I opened the box, she gasped. "Daisy! These are absolutely *gorgeous*! Do you remember who gave them to you?"

"Harold. I swear, that man had more fun decorating my house

than I did. But he's got better taste than I have, so I don't mind at all."

With a jolly laugh and with Spike wagging along with us, we carried everything to the kitchen. There Mrs. Rattle washed the fabulous luncheon set, and I took the secateurs, the flowers and a couple of large vases to the utility room. Chrysanthemums are pretty good at arranging themselves, so it wasn't difficult to fix two vases overflowing with flowers. One of the vases was a cinnamon color, and the other was gray-green. Lovely.

By the time Mrs. Rattle and I had finished working in the den, I'd just about decided to commence using the room all the time. That was before I sat in one of the Louis the Whateverth chairs. Those stupid chairs were extremely uncomfortable. Oh well. At least my guests would be able to eat and chat in a pretty room, even if the chairs abused their bottoms and backs.

Perhaps I'd take up Harold's suggestion to replace the furniture with more comfortable Craftsman-style pieces. Thanks to Sam and his family's jewelry store empire, we had money. Still, I didn't like throwing Sam's money away, so I'd discuss the matter with him before Harold set me loose in a furniture store.

At approximately nine-fifteen, the telephone rang. When I answered it, Harold said, "Are you ready for us?"

"Yes, and hello to you too."

"Piffle. How many people are you prepared for?"

"Eight. Did I count correctly?"

"Yes. Roy made cheese straws, ham sandwiches and chicken sandwiches for the savories and tiny cream puffs for the sweets. And there will be carrot and celery sticks, radishes, figs, and grapes. Can you provide coffee and tea?"

"Good grief, that sounds like a major luncheon! I didn't know you'd bring so much food."

"I know all about you and cooking, Daisy. I figured you can save the leftovers and have them for supper. And lunch. What about the beverages?"

"Sorry. I was so overwhelmed with your menu, I forgot all about beverages. Mrs. Rattle will make coffee and tea, and we will have fresh orange juice, if anyone prefers juice."

"Excellent. You don't mind if Roy comes over to make sure everything's plated properly, do you?"

"Good heavens, no I don't mind! I'd love to have Roy accompany you with his creations. They'll make me feel guilty, but since I always feel guilty about my culinary misadventures anyway, it won't matter."

"You really ought to get over being afraid of the kitchen, Daisy. You can hire a cook if you need one. And then there's your aunt, who lives right across the street. I hope she's going to retire soon. My mother doesn't deserve her."

"Harold! That's…well, it's the truth, but it's still not nice to say so."

"Bah," said Harold.

"Wrong season. Anyhow, I think Vi is aiming to retire almost instantly after your mother and stepfather return from Santa Barbara."

"Good for her!" said Harold, and I could tell he was pleased for Aunt Vi. "Roy, Pete, and I are leaving San Marino now. We'll have a duet of armed guards in two other cars en route. We don't need to feed them. They'll stay outside as we converse with the Grenvilles, Pete, and Larry."

"What about Melanie?" I asked, even though I knew I shouldn't.

"Unfortunately, Melanie doesn't have much say in this instance. If she acknowledges this infant as hers, she could be arrested and jailed for abandoning the kid. I'm glad you found her yesterday and am doubly glad she ended up with Jan Forrest."

"So am I."

"As to her involvement in the baby's adoption, I think we should rely on Peter Altman to guide us through the labyrinth of red tape."

"Excellent idea."

"Good. See you in a few minutes."

"Looking forward to it," I said. Darn Frank Pagano! I felt lonely, being unable to get out of the house. I liked getting out and about and seeing people, darn it! And the library. I missed going to the library and chatting with Regina.

I reminded myself that I'd only been confined to the house for a couple of days. Still…

Frank Pagano was a living, breathing disaster. I almost hoped he wouldn't be breathing for much longer, but I knew the thought to be sinful. I, as a good Methodist Episcopal woman, should be above such horrid thoughts.

Sometimes I despaired of myself. I couldn't cook, had no patience, wished ill upon others and would rather grow vegetables than preserve them for the winter. Some kind of mother I'd be. Ah well. At least my children would be well-dressed. And able to read. Small comfort.

Before I could sink into abject melancholy, the telephone rang again. As I was right there, I answered it.

"Daisy, it's Flossie. I wanted to give you a progress report on Melanie."

"There's a progress report already? She didn't run away again, did she?"

"No, no, nothing bad. Jan takes great interest in 'her' girls, as she calls them, and she wanted to let me know that Melanie, although shy with the other girls at first, got over her qualms almost at once."

"Wow, I'm impressed."

"I think Melanie was delighted—and amazed—to know she isn't the only girl in the world who's managed to get herself 'in trouble', as the saying goes."

"I wish the boys would get in trouble too," I said, snarling slightly.

"As do I," said Flossie with a chuckle. "But life isn't like that, as you and I know all too well."

"Yes, I do know. I'm so lucky to have Sam."

"And I'm eternally thankful that you threw me at Johnnie. I'd probably be dead by now if you hadn't."

"I didn't *throw* you at Johnny!" I protested hotly. And there I went, fibbing again. My poor but well-dressed and well-read child would be reared by a lying, impatient, evil-thinking, lousy cook of a mother. I hoped Sam's many good traits would overwhelm all of my rotten ones.

"You did and you know it, and both Johnnie and I love you for it. Is the group of people who are going to decide about the baby's future meeting today? Sam said something about them all meeting at your house."

"Yes. We have a meeting scheduled for ten this morning. Harold has an attorney pal named Peter Altman, and if the Grenvilles and Marianne's mother Diane pass muster with him and the baby's doctor, the child will be on its way to adoption. I truly think the Grenvilles will be great parents. And Diane will be thrilled to have a grandchild. Her two sons are serving time in a penitentiary somewhere, and her evil husband is dead." I stopped talking. The description of the family into which we were plunging a six-day-old baby sounded ghastly.

"Doesn't sound exactly perfect when you lay out the bare facts, does it?" said Flossie, reading my mind and amused.

"No, it doesn't. But honestly, Flossie, I think the Grenvilles and Diane will be excellent parents and grandparents. Grandparent. Anyhow, George has kin too, and I'm sure they're swell people."

"I'm sure you're correct," said Flossie, humoring me. "Please let me know how it goes."

"I will. Thanks, Flossie. I wish Melanie had gone to you in the first place."

"If I recall correctly, she couldn't go anywhere because she was unconscious at the time she was found on the street."

"Details, details," I said.

We both hung up our receivers after sharing another laugh. I loved my friends.

THIRTY-TWO

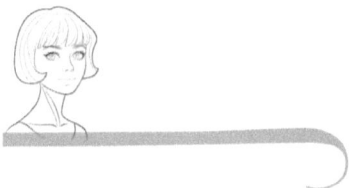

I gazed upon the den in our house with complacent joy. I didn't deserve to be complacent, although my joy was okay. After all, Harold and his mother had furnished this room. All I'd done was put some flowers in a couple of vases and adjusted tables and chairs. In spite of me, our den looked positively splendid and I loved it.

Harold, Roy, and Mr. Altman arrived not long after Mrs. Rattle and I had set out the last poppy-painted piece of china on the sideboard. We just stacked the plates, and I'd kept the two serving platters in the kitchen for Roy to fill however he wished.

"How do you do, Mrs. Rotondo?" said Mr. Altman when Harold introduced us.

"How do you do, Mr. Altman?"

"Oh, for gawd's sake, it's Daisy and Pete," said Harold.

He and a chuckling Roy walked into the kitchen with a couple of cardboard boxes filled with edibles. As I'd eaten a good breakfast of scrambled eggs with toast—I didn't burn the eggs *or* the toast—with Sam earlier in the day, my tummy didn't rumble with hunger pangs. Because my stomach was already obviously *there* and impossible to ignore, I was glad it had been placated.

"Aha!" cried Harold from the kitchen as Mr. Altman and I stood in the hall, "you're using the Czech poppies!"

I nodded to Mr. Altman—I mean Pete—and we both smiled and walked toward the kitchen. "Yes," I called back. "First time. I love them!"

"So do I," said Harold, sounding satisfied. As well he should.

"Wow, you brought a ton of food," I said when I'd made it to the kitchen. There Roy, Harold, and Mrs. Rattle were skillfully filling platters with sandwiches after first lining the platters with doilies. Roy had made really small cream-puff shells and filled them with either ham or chicken salad. I thought that was about the cleverest idea I'd ever seen.

"I'll fill the sugar bowl," said Mrs. Rattle. "Better wait until the guests arrive before I fill the creamer."

"Good idea," I said, clasping my hands behind my back and looking on uselessly.

We all helped carry the foodstuffs to the den, and Mrs. Rattle set out the sugar bowl. Harold had either brought or found some straight white vases or jars, into which the celery and carrot sticks sat. He settled radishes, olives and so forth on a tray and added a small jar containing toothpicks and a tiny pair of kitchen tongs. I guess he added the toothpicks and tongs for people who didn't want to pluck up radishes or olives (or pickles) with their fingers.

It occurred to me that I should be taking notes, in case I wanted to do this again on my own.

Then I told myself not to be idiotic. I could no more prepare a food scene like this than I could fly to Mars.

And *then* I told myself that I could hire somebody to set everything out on the beautiful homemade tablecloths I'd make along with their accompanying napkins. Perhaps I wasn't totally, irretrievably useless. Maybe.

At any rate, the rest of the invitees began arriving shortly after the sideboard was declared to be perfect by Mrs. Rattle and me. Harold still tilted his head and appeared dubious, but it was too late to fix anything now. As I greeted guests at the front door, Mrs. Rattle scurried to the kitchen to prepare coffee and tea. We'd already squeezed enough oranges to fill three pitchers, so I figured we were set.

Marianne, George, and Diane were excited and worried when I ushered them into the den.

"Please help yourselves to refreshments," I said. "We'll be bringing coffee and tea in a minute, and there's fresh orange juice if anyone wants it."

"This is magnificent," said Diane, looking captivated. "Oh, my, will you look at those darling sandwiches!"

"Lovely," said Marianne, clinging to George's arm. It didn't look to me as if she aimed to turn loose of it (George's arm, I mean) any time soon.

Just as the doorbell chimed, Mrs. Rattle and Roy bustled into the den carrying coffee and tea pots along with a pitcher of cream (or maybe it was milk). I said once more, "Please, help yourselves to anything. Roy prepared enough food to feed an army."

When I answered the door this time, Dr. Vialargo and Hazel Greenlaw smiled at me.

"Come in!" I said cordially. "We're meeting in the den. And please, eat something! Roy fixed enough food to keep the entire city of Pasadena fed for days."

"Ha! Roy is a marvel," said Hazel.

I hadn't actually known she'd be here, but what the heck. There was enough room, not to mention enough food, for four of her along with the rest of us. I walked the two newcomers to the den. I was pleased to see that the attorney, Peter Altman, had broken the ice, so to speak, on the fabulous spread set out on the sideboard.

"This is beautiful china, Daisy," said Hazel, picking up a hand-painted poppy bedecked coffee cup.

"Isn't it wonderful?" I said. Then, because I hadn't meant to sound stuck up and prideful, I added, "Harold gave us that as a— I can't remember. It was some kind of gift for some kind of occasion. I love it, but this is the first opportunity I've had to use it."

"It was a Christmas present, Daisy," said Harold reproachfully. "I swear, I hope your memory improves after you drop that hippopotamus you're carrying."

"Harold!" said Pete Altman, laughing. "You shouldn't be set free on room full of innocent public."

"Huh," said Harold. "The public is about as innocent as Jack the Ripper."

"Harold!" I said. "People aren't *that* bad. Not most of them anyway."

"I suppose," said Harold. He didn't believe me; I could tell.

After that, everyone relaxed, filled plates with goodies and sat in the various sofas and chairs placed around the room.

We were all having a jolly time when suddenly silence fell, kind of like a huge boulder, upon the assorted visitors. I'd just popped an olive into my mouth, but I turned to see what everyone was staring at.

And there he was: Mr. Lou Prophet, former bounty hunter, gunman, womanizer, boozer, all-around tough guy and, in all probability, the father of Dr. Vialargo. He'd dressed in a good suit and his neutral expression transformed into a scowl as he surveyed the company.

I would have leaped to my feet had I been able, but I wasn't. I shoved myself up, but Harold got in before me.

"Lou!" Harold said with every indication of delight. "So glad you could join us. I think you know everyone here except for Diane Chapman—she's Marianne's mother—and Pete Altman, the attorney who's going to draw up the adoption papers."

"How-do," said Mr. Prophet, doing his best to bow. If he'd still had the use of both of his legs, he'd have accomplished it. What with his leg and peg, he still did a creditable job. Silly, I know, but I was proud of him.

"Would you like me to fill a plate for you?" I asked after having struggled to my feet. "Roy and Harold brought a wonderful selection of edibles, and there's tea, coffee, and orange juice."

"Thanks, Miss Daisy. Think I can fill my own plate," said Mr. Prophet grimly.

Chiding myself for thinking of possible broken china, I managed to smile and say, "Wonderful. Everything's delicious."

Then I glanced across the room where Dr. Vialargo and Hazel

sat on the Louis the Whateverth sofa. They'd been chatting happily until Mr. Prophet hove into view. Now Hazel still looked happy. Dr. V. didn't. Fortunately for all of us, Diane Chapman—Marianne's mother if you'll recall—had taken the third cushion on the sofa, and there were two empty chairs available for Mr. Prophet, who could choose for himself.

While Mr. Prophet filled a plate for himself and set it on a piecrust table next to one of the empty chairs, conversation started spluttering uneasily to life again. Mr. P. filled a cup of coffee for himself and settled it too on the little table. Then he eased himself onto the uncomfortable chair, frowned, shoved himself back a little, shook his head—there was no way to get comfy on one of those chairs—and started munching.

I swear it was as if we'd all been holding our breath, but after no disasters accompanied Mr. Prophet settling himself, everyone resumed normal chattering. Whew!

Mrs. Rattle acted as maidservant during the initial—chewing—stages of the adoption meeting. She wiped up spills, filled cups and glasses, made sure everyone's plates were as full as they wanted them to be, and generally kept everyone happy without anyone but me seeming to notice her skills. I aimed to give her a big bonus after the baby-adoption dilemma was solved.

When Mrs. Rattle carted off the last dirty plate and Roy removed the platters with their remaining contents—which looked like they'd serve admirably as dinner for Sam, Mr. P. and me—Harold cleared this throat and stood. He even clapped his hands in order to get everyone's attention.

I'm *so* glad he took over the meeting. I sure didn't want to do it.

"All right now folks, listen up," said Harold.

Shufflings here and there. No one spoke.

"Here we have George and Marianne Grenville, a lovely married couple. The two of them wants to adopt a baby. As luck would have it, I have a spare baby needing a family."

"That's a little flippant, Mr. Kincaid," said Dr. Vialargo, the sober-sided son of the least sober-sided person I'd ever met in my life.

"Bushwa," said Harold. "The baby was left in a basket on my doorstep. I *really* don't need a baby in my life. The Grenvilles, however, do." He scowled at Dr. V., who opened his mouth and then shut it again, although he clearly didn't want to.

"Do you know who the parents of the child are?" asked Diane timidly. "I mean, have you found that out yet?"

After the slightest hesitation, Harold said, "Yes. We'll explain after Pete and Larry are finished asking questions of you."

Conversation continued. Pete Altman took notes as Marianne and Diane's backgrounds were explained.

"It sounds so sordid," Diane said at one point. "But it's virtually impossible for a woman to get help in a situation like that. I know it sounds insane—"

"Not to me it doesn't," said Pete, interrupting Diane, but for a good cause. "Believe me, Mrs. Chapman. I've seen tragedies like yours happen in my own family." He looked bleak for a second.

I wanted to ask for details but restrained myself. I was *incredibly* lucky to have Sam and to have had Billy. Billy's last years had been rough, but he was a good man. I heaved so loud a sigh, people swiveled their heads to peer at me.

After Diane, Marianne, and George had told their stories, George said, "We have Daisy to thank for Marianne and me meeting."

"And Harold," I said quickly.

"And Harold," George agreed. "We'll be grateful for the rest of our lives for what you did to bring us together."

"Don't be silly," I said, although Marianne's rescue had been terrifying and difficult for me. Harold had helped in the endeavor, although he hadn't had to flounder through as many perils and pitfalls as had I.

"I just handled the wardrobe," said Harold, telling the truth.

"Well, that's over now, and you seem to be a happy couple, Marianne and George." I took in a deep breath. "We still need to tell you something about the baby's parents, however."

And we did. At one point, George said, "You say the father's Italian?"

"We believe we know who the father is, and yes, he's Italian," I affirmed.

The adoptive couple shared a glance or two. Three, if you count Diane. Understanding more about prejudices rampant in our so-called "classless" society than most people, I was ready to do battle. Perhaps my smile, which felt tight on my face, clued everyone in to my strong feelings on the Italian matter.

"Your husband is Italian isn't he, Daisy?" said Harold, all innocence.

"He certainly is," I said. "He was my Billy's best friend and, while Sam and I didn't see eye-to-eye on everything in the beginning, we've come to value each other greatly. More than greatly. We adore each other."

So there.

"I see," said Diane, pushing herself back a little on the sofa.

"They're a dang good couple," rasped Mr. Prophet, from whom I hadn't expected to hear any words at all, much less words of a laudatory nature. "The two of 'em saved my sorry hide too."

So there again.

After almost three hours of talking, elucidation, tears, drama and ultimate relief and laughter, the Grenvilles had been cleared by Pete, Hazel, and Dr. Vialargo to adopt Melanie Robinson's baby, providing the baby agreed. In order to achieve this aim, George, Marianne, and Diane would visit the baby at Harold's home.

Which, of course, presented a big fat problem. Until somebody found and corralled Frank Pagano, there wouldn't be a whole lot of visiting going on among the folks gathered in the den.

Being optimistic by nature—I really am, even though it might not seem like it—I said, "Perhaps we can make an appointment for tomorrow, Harold. Would that be all right with everyone?"

"What about... Y'know," said Mr. Prophet.

"I feel sure we'll be able to visit Harold's house tomorrow. What time do you think would be appropriate, Harold?"

Harold squinted at me and said, "When pigs fly?"

"Harold, that's not awfully helpful," I said.

"When heck freezes over?" He mooted.

"It'll be okay," said Mr. Prophet, surprising all of us. At least he surprised me; not sure about the others. "We kin work it out."

"You think so?" asked a skeptical Harold.

"I think so too," said Pete.

"Whatever is the matter?" asked George, beginning to look uneasy.

"Just a little...logistical problem," I said, lying again. I swear, there's no doing anything with me.

"C'mere," said Mr. Prophet, gesturing at Harold and me. We got up and gathered around his chair.

"What? Frank Pagano is after *me*," I growled. "He hasn't done anything in Harold's neighborhood."

"Except drop off a baby," whispered a grouchy Harold.

"You'll have outriders," said Mr. Prophet. "You'll have the body-guards and everything. I don't think that Eye-talian feller will bother Harold none."

Harold and I eyed each other over Mr. Prophet's grizzled head. Then I shrugged.

"You may well be right."

"And if he's not?" said Harold.

"Bodyguards," I whispered.

Harold straightened. So did I. Bending wasn't something I did well at the time. After pondering for ten years—approximately five seconds, although it felt longer—Harold said, "Lou's right."

"Huh," said Mr. Prophet.

We agreed to meet at Harold's house at eleven a.m. on Friday. Whew!

Then I began worrying about whether or not Melanie's baby looked Italian. I hadn't seen it for a few days. Maybe its skin was taking on an olive cast. But what the heck! *George* looked like a Greek! Or maybe he didn't. I'd never met a Greek person before.

As I began escorting everyone to the door, Dr. Vialargo and Hazel stayed behind. I understood why when I glanced back and saw Mr. Prophet's gnarled hand clutching Dr. Vialargo's wrist.

Oh dear!

THIRTY-THREE

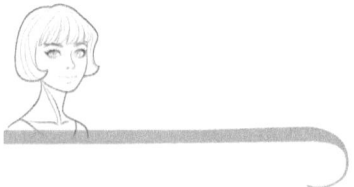

Turned out I needn't have worried. I didn't run back to the den to eavesdrop on a conversation that was none of my business although, as noted earlier, that had never stopped me before. Attempting to hide my antsiness, I said farewell to all but my two remaining guests.

Before returning to the den, I popped into the kitchen to see what kind of mess awaited me there.

No mess at all met my eyes! The wonderful Mrs. Rattle had already washed and dried the dishes, teapots and coffeepots and packaged up all the leftovers. She'd even stuck the covered tins of goodies in the Frigidaire. That settled it. I was giving Mrs. Rattle a raise as of that day.

After thanking her extravagantly—she claimed not to know why I was so grateful—I returned to the den. I mentally braced myself and made a side visit to the downstairs powder room. There I not only relieved myself, but I splashed water on my face to perk me up some as I'd started dragging almost an hour prior to that moment.

As I neared the den, I heard...what was that? Good heavens, it was laughter! Laughter! From the den! Surprised, I crept up to the door and peered in, fearing in spite (or because of) the laughter to

275

see Mr. Prophet dead on the floor. Or Dr. Vialargo in the same condition.

"C'm in, Miss Daisy," said Mr. Prophet from the same chair he'd been in before I left the den. He sounded downright happy. "These two have some news to share."

"You do? I mean, they do?" I walked into the den and sat on another one of the uncomfortable chairs.

"We do," said Hazel.

"Yes," said Dr. Vialargo. "I'm happy to announce that Miss Greenlaw has consented to become my wife."

"Congratulations!" I almost shouted in relief—I'd anticipated at least one dead body, don't forget. "What great news!"

"And this here son 'o mine don't hate me no more," said Mr. Prophet, positively gleeful in a rusty sort of way.

"Hate was always too strong a word," said Dr. V. to all of us. "I had no reason to doubt my aunt's assessment of my father, although as I grew older I realized she was one of those black-or-white people who allow for no shades of gray to interfere with their opinions."

"That's fer dam-durn sure," grumbled Mr. Prophet.

Hazel laughed. Dr. V. stiffened at first but then relaxed. He even smiled. I think Hazel was a good influence on him.

"When will the happy event take place?" I asked. "And where will you tie the knot?"

"We're not sure when. After Christmas sometime. I'm technically an Episcopalian," said Hazel. "My family has attended Episcopal services ever since they were conducted by Reverend Trew and met at Mr. and Mrs. Brown's house."

"That's where All Saints was built, isn't it? On Colorado and Euclid?"

"Yes. That's it," said Hazel.

For the record, she and Dr. V. were holding hands. I thought it was sweet.

"I've been to All Saints. It's a beautiful church."

"Yes," said Hazel. "It is. I don't attend regularly any longer, but that's where I met Harold."

"Interesting. Do you have a religious affiliation, Dr. Vialargo?" I asked.

"My aunt took me to the Baptist Church in Seward, Nebraska. I have no particular reason to seek a Baptist Church here in Pasadena."

"Episcopalians are more fun than Baptists," said Hazel.

"Fun isn't precisely the reason I attended church," said Dr. V. drily.

"Somebody told me the other day that Methodists—I belong to the Methodist Episcopal Church—are only Baptists who can read. I thought that was unkind," I said.

"There might be a grain of truth to it, however," said Dr. V, his lips quivering as if he wanted to smile but wouldn't allow himself to do it.

"It was Ol' Starchy Pants who hauled you to church, wasn't it?" said Mr. Prophet.

Cautiously, Dr. V. said, "Aunt Prudence took me to church, yes."

"You don't mind being married in the Episcopal Church, do you?" asked Hazel. "We can always get married at the new City Hall after it opens, I guess."

"The Episcopal Church will be fine," said the doctor.

I returned to the kitchen as the threesome continued chatting. Mrs. Rattle was just putting the last of everything away.

"Thank you so much for helping, Elvira." I said. "Well, you did it all, actually. I wasn't looking forward to cleaning the kitchen and putting all that food away."

"Don't be silly, Daisy. It was a pleasure for me to serve people such lovely food I didn't have to prepare. And on those magnificent *dishes*! I've never seen anything from Czecho... What is it again?"

"Czechoslovakia," I said. "Sam told me that when the Bolshies took over the region, they squashed two separate countries together. There used to be Czechs and Slovaks. At least I think that's what he said. I can never figure out Eastern Europe. I think of everyone as Russians, but Russia is only where the power lies. I think. It's too complicated for me."

Tilting her head slightly, Mrs. Rattle squinted and said, "It's definitely too complicated for me."

We were in the hall, walking to the front door.

"I met a Russian fellow once," I said, recalling my encounter with a former count or duke or prince or whatever he said he was. "He gave me a gaudy bracelet, but it was made from real gems. I mean rubies, sapphires, emeralds and so forth. I have it locked in a safe-deposit box at the bank."

"Wise woman," said Mrs. Rattle.

"I wasn't wise. Sam was wise. He's the one who told me the gemstones were real and not glass. He learned about that stuff in his parents' jewelry stores in New York City."

"Oh my. I had no idea," said Mrs. Rattle.

"I didn't either until that evening. The one with the count. Duke. Prince. Whatever he was."

Mrs. Rattle donned the sweater she'd brought with her, and I reached for her hat.

I sighed. I'd loathed Sam back then when he'd visit my parents' bungalow almost every day to play gin rummy with my father and Billy. Sam had made Billy's last couple of years almost bearable. For Billy.

I heard a small thump on the roof and stepped out on to the porch to see if I could espy anything up there. Mrs. Rattle heard it too and also looked. So did Officer Wilde, who'd been given many luncheon sandwiches along with carrots and celery, etc., by Roy. Roy'd used the everyday plates and cups for the policeman. I never thought I'd become a snob, but I felt like one when I saw the used plates and cups stacked on the porch railing.

Spike had heard the noise, too, and gave a couple of good-natured barks.

"What was that?" I asked of no one in particular.

"Don't know," said Officer Wilde. "Do you have squirrels around here?"

"I've never seen any," I said.

"Nor have I," said Mrs. Rattle.

"Might have been a cat," I mused, thinking of Mr. Prophet's Yuyu.

"Probably was," said Mrs. Rattle. "Or maybe an orange fell onto the roof. Or a crow might have dropped something."

"A crow?" I asked. "I thought crows were lightweights. Can they carry heavy things?"

With a laugh, she said, "They are small, but they carry things all over the place."

"True," said Officer Wilde. "I watched some crows throwing nuts onto our roof in order to crack them so they could eat the insides."

"My goodness," I said, suddenly enamored of crows. "I didn't know crows were so smart."

"Very smart birds," said Officer Wilde, nodding.

Spike had no opinion and there seemed nothing to bark at, so he went inside the house again.

"See you tomorrow, Daisy," said Mrs. Rattle, opening the front porch gate and treading down the steps to the front walkway.

"See you," I said. Then I said, "I'll take these dishes to the kitchen, Officer."

"I'll do that for you," said the nice policeman. "I dirtied them, after all."

We shared a companionable chuckle, and he took his dirty dishes to the sink. He even rinsed them off.

"Just leave them in the sink," I said. I was feeling too bushed to take care of them just then. "I'll wash them later."

"Thank you, Mrs. Rotondo. That was a delicious lunch."

"Glad you enjoyed it. I didn't have anything to do with preparing the food. My friend Harold's cook, Roy Castillo, fixed all the edibles."

"I should introduce him to my wife," said Officer Wilde in a pensive sort of voice.

"I've known Roy for a few years now, and his cooking skills haven't rubbed off on me," I told him. "Sorry."

"That's all right." The nice policeman sighed and sat in his chair beside the door again. I mentally wished him and his wife luck.

279

I re-locked the front door, sighed—I was exhausted—and walked back to the den. Darned if Mr. Prophet wasn't offering to show Hazel and Dr. V. his little cottage at the back of our property.

"I'm s'posed to be caretaker here, but I don't gen'ly do much," Mr. P. admitted to his son and future daughter-in-law. "If my cat's there, I'll introduce you to him too."

"Be careful," I warned the couple. "Yuyu's liable to hiss and scratch at you."

"He won't neither," said Mr. Prophet, offended. "If he hisses, it's only 'cause he don't know you yet."

"That's probably true," I said, attempting to mollify the old grump. "Yuyu and Spike play all the time. They're quite funny together."

"A dog and a cat play with each other?" Hazel sounded incredulous. Under the circumstances, her incredulity made sense to me.

"They do," I said. "Surprised me. I was terrified when they first met, fearing there'd be a bloodbath in our backyard. But they actually just stared at each other for a few seconds, and then began romping around the yard and digging up"—No, no, no. I wasn't going to go into the bone-and-ghost story with these two—"the backyard. Way in the back so you couldn't see the diggery—I don't think that's a word—from the porch." I finished.

"That's sweet," said Hazel.

"It is," I agreed. "And unexpected."

"I'll believe it when I see it," said a skeptical Dr. Vialargo.

"You probably won't see it today," I told him. "Spike and I are going to lie down for a while. We're bushed." I expect I was the only one bushed. Spike would probably have liked to play with Yuyu. I was mistress of the house though, however minimally, so he was going to nap with me.

Hazel, Mr. Prophet, and Dr. Vialargo left the house via the back door, and I moseyed to the living room where I flopped on the sofa and had a conversation with Spike.

"What do you say, Spike? Do we want to walk all the way upstairs to take a nap, or should we just stay here."

I may have patted the space next to me on the sofa. I won't say for sure because some people think animals should be kept off furniture, but Spike joined me on the sofa, and we snoozed. Not sure for how long.

THIRTY-FOUR

I dreamed of Rolly, my made-up spirit control, who occasionally manages to gain authenticity. Even in my sleep, I wished he'd go away and leave me alone, but would he? Of course not! Rolly kept telling me to wake up because something was wrong.

Think of the wee bairn, he said over and over. Rolly and I had supposedly been married and had five sons a thousand years ago in what is now Scotland. *Ye mun arise, m'love.*

I used to think it was sweet to have had a soul mate who called me his love and who had followed me through all my incarnations since the eleventh century. Mind you, I don't believe in reincarnation any more than I used to believe in ghosts.

Finally a big *thunk* from somewhere or other jarred me almost awake. "Spike, what was that?"

Spike jumped from the sofa, but he didn't answer my question. Rather, he turned in a circle on the living room carpet, stretched and yawned.

"Fiddlesticks," I muttered. "I'll see for myself."

I shoved myself off the sofa and gave myself a yawn and a stretch, although I didn't turn in a circle. Then I walked to the front door, peeked out through the peephole and saw Officer Wilde and

Officer Garcia yakking and laughing quietly on the front lawn. Nothing the matter there, so I opened the front door and looked outside. There was no Chevrolet Roadster parked at the curb, so I figured Dr. V. and Hazel had left. The two policemen and I waved at each other, and I went back indoors.

"Spike, why was Rolly such a fussbudget in my dream?" I asked my happy dog.

He didn't answer that question either. Nertz.

"Well, Spike, let's go see if Mr. Prophet is hanging out on the back porch. He's generally there with his '73 Winchester and Yuyu. Yuyu would probably kill Frank Pagano if he came anywhere near the house."

Don't know if it was the name "Yuyu" or the name "Mr. Prophet" that tickled Spike's fancy, but he trotted merrily down the hall and into the dining room. From there he'd go through the pantry and the kitchen and trot to the back door. Both Yuyu and Mr. Prophet were reachable from the back porch.

Smart doggy. I followed him, only to discover him at the back door, hackles bristling, growling and snarling for all he was worth at whatever was outside on the porch.

The door's handle turned and stopped. The door was locked, thank God. Whoever was out there—and I'm sure we're all expecting Frank Pagano at this point in the narrative—grumbled something I couldn't hear.

Oh Lord, what now?

My heart slammed around in my chest as if it were attempting to escape confinement. I knew just how it felt.

Spike let loose a frenzy of furious barks and jumped at the door as if trying to break it down or claw through it. I opened my mouth to reprimand him, fearing Frank would shoot him through the door, but then Frank kicked at the door in his own attempt to break it down.

Spike yipped in fright and backed off a bit. Not much.

Quick as a slowish flash I turned right, into the utility room. There I grabbed the mop Mrs. Rattle had used to clean the floors earlier in the day. Then, wishing I had a telephone in the utility room—only hours earlier I'd been moaning about the superfluity of telephones in our modern lives—I whispered, "Hush," to Spike, who had resumed his ferocious oral attack on the person on the other side of the door.

I don't think Spike heard me. I'm sure Frank didn't, because he said, "Shit! Shut up, you stupid dog!"

And then I'm not altogether sure what happened. Hearing that imbecile calling my brilliant dog stupid went into my ears, traveled to my heart, then to my brain, and something inside me snapped. The wretched man outside almost certainly held a knife. I knew from experience that he was good at throwing a large hunting knife, but a stiletto was more of an up-close-and-personal weapon.

Therefore, consumed by wrath, I grabbed Spike and shoved him behind me. I gave the hand signal to stay. He didn't want to stay but stayed anyway because he was a whiz-kid of a hound. Then I sidled to the other side of the back door, reached for the thumb lock, and pressed it, thereby unlocking the door. Then I turned the doorknob and drew my hand back instantly. I braced myself against the far wall and held the mop handle so it would have barred the door had someone been holding the other end of it. As things were, it wouldn't bar the door if anyone nudged it, but I was hoping…

Frank Pagano who had, as I'd suspected he would, backed up to make another lunge at the door, barreled through the door opening. He almost made me lose my grip on the mop handle when he stumbled over the mop, but didn't quite. He landed on the floor and skidded halfway to the kitchen. The skinny little knife he'd held flew from his hand as he hit the linoleum and skittered all the way into the kitchen.

"*Get him, Spike!*" I hollered.

By golly, Spike got him! I hadn't even taught him to do that. Frank had landed on his stomach, so Spike jumped on his back and started gnawing on his neck. As Spike attacked Frank's head, I bashed him with the mop on his legs and butt until he screamed for us both to stop.

"I *won't* stop, you stupid villain!" I screeched at him.

"*No!*"

"*Yes!*"

"*You're killing me!*"

"*Good!*"

"What th' hell?" Mr. Prophet's raspy voice sounded incredulous. I heard loud noises in my head. Or maybe just one loud noise.

"Shoot him!" I hollered. "*Shoot* him!"

"*No!*" shrieked Frank.

"Cripes," muttered Mr. Prophet. "Get off him, Miss Daisy. I'll handle this."

"I want to kill him!" I bellowed.

Another dreadful blast sounded in my head. Could we hear foghorns all the way from the Pacific Ocean to Pasadena?

"Don't blame ya," said Mr. Prophet, "but you better not."

"Then *you* kill him!"

"Cain't while you're in the way."

Mr. Prophet sounded so reasonable, my wrath rose. I hadn't believed it could do such a thing. How strange.

"Never mind!" I roared. "I'll kill him myself."

And yet another weird, loud noise smote my ears. Or maybe it came from inside my head.

"*Help!*" screamed Frank Pagano.

He sounded desperate. My heart filled with joy, thereby shocking me out of my terror-induced rage. When Mr. Prophet grabbed the mop and lifted it from my hands, I realized what I'd been doing and gasped.

"Stop it, Spike," I said. My voice was hoarse and unconvincing.

"What's going on in there?" came the voice of Officer Wilde. He sounded winded.

"Where the devil you been?" Mr. Prophet demanded of the police fellow. "Ya let this peckerwood get to Miss Daisy's back door. He'd'a killed her if her and her dog didn't kill him first."

I stood panting, my hands on my belly, staring at the prone form of Frank Pagano, still lying on his stomach near our kitchen door. The knife remained just out of his reach. And darn it, there was blood on the floor! Even without anyone using a firearm, there was blood on the floor. Blast!

285

Then I realized what Mr. Prophet had said, and panic shot through me.

"H-he's dead?" I whispered.

"Dunno."

I saw one of Frank Pagano's hands begin to inch toward the stiletto. Rage flamed anew in my body. As Mr. Prophet didn't seem to be doing anything to Frank, I sidled past both men and stamped on Frank's roaming hand.

"*Yow!*" he screeched.

"Don't you *dare* grab that knife, you filthy, despicable curly wolf!" I stooped over and, grabbing a kitchen towel first, snatched up the knife. I didn't do so carefully and it was pure dumb luck on my part that Frank hadn't pressed whatever he was supposed to press in order for the blade to appear. At least I hadn't ruined any fingerprints.

Still out of breath and puffing hard, I felt lightheaded when I stood up straight. Fortunately for me, the kitchen counter was nearby, so I leaned against it, panting like a grampus. Whatever a grampus is. I read it in a book somewhere.

"I'll take care o' this piece o' sh-garbage," said Mr. Prophet. "Gimme your handcuffs, Wilde."

"I should—"

"Give Mr. Prophet your handcuffs, dammit!" I snarled at the poor man. "You and your pal Garcia allowed this wretched creature to invade my *home*."

"Go call Sam, Miss Daisy. You ain't doing any good here."

Spike still danced around the flattened fugitive. He'd wagged at Mr. Prophet, but then he went back to snarling so ferociously that Frank finally covered his head. Guess he feared Spike would attack him again. *What* a good boy! Spike, not Frank.

"Call Sam," I repeated hoarsely. Boy, I'd sure yelled a lot. My throat was sore. "I'll call Sam."

"You all right, Miss Daisy? You ain't makin' much sense," said Mr. Prophet.

"I'm not making sense?" I repeated. The venom in my snarl shocked me into Daisy-hood once more. "Oh. Yes." I took in a

Pasadena-sized breath of air and let it whoosh out of my lungs. "I'll go call Sam."

"There ya go," said Mr. Prophet as if he were attempting to humor a madwoman.

Guess I had gone 'round the bend there for a little while. Fear and horror can do that to a person, even a usually mild-mannered one like me. Same thing happened when I'd believed a bad person had killed Harold Kincaid. That was the incident during which I'd broken Sam's cane. After the cane broke, I regret to admit I'd then attempted to stab the person I'd been beating.

It wasn't one of my proudest moments. Neither was this latest incident with Frank Pagano.

I walked to the telephone table, sat, picked up the receiver and dialed the Pasadena Police Department. As soon as the officer manning the front desk announced I'd reached the correct number, I said, "Detective Sam Rotondo, please."

A few moments passed, during which I wondered if my family had any Norse ancestors. Wasn't it the Norse folk who had warriors called berserkers? Those guys who went into a rage-induced trance and fought like demons? Pa had told me we had Scottish and Irish in our blood, and they were pretty fearsome warriors too. But did they go into a trance—

My musings were interrupted when the officer at the desk finally said, "I'm sorry, ma'am. Detective Rotondo isn't in the station at the moment. C'n I take a message?"

I shook my head hard in order to get my brain to concentrate on important matters. "What do you mean, he's not there? Where *is* he?" I guess a little berserker remained in me, because I pretty much barked my question at the poor man. "I'm sorry. Didn't mean to snap."

"That's all right, ma'am. I don't know where the detective is now. I'm sorry."

I sighed heavily. "It's okay," I said, not meaning it. I wanted Sam, and I wanted him *now*!

Too bad, Daisy.

I set the receiver gently back on the switch hook and contemplated the empty hallway. I loved our house. I'd hate to have to move.

My shock was genuine when I heard the front door being unlocked from outside. Fear zoomed through me again. I attempted to leap from the chair but couldn't quite make it. I did manage to stand and, with a hand pressed flat to the telephone table, remain upright.

When Sam pushed the front door open, I just about fainted. Maybe I did faint a little bit. I definitely found myself seated on the telephone table's chair again without quite knowing why or how I'd got there.

"Daisy!" cried Sam. "What's the matter?"

"It's Frank," I said in a gravelly whisper. "He's in the kitchen."

"Cripes."

Sam rushed past me and headed to the kitchen.

Why was Sam home? I didn't understand anything about anything. I sat, feeling depleted and exhausted, at the telephone table for another few seconds. Then I pushed myself up from the chair and followed the path Sam had taken to the kitchen. The tableau revealed when I got to the kitchen door didn't fill me with joy.

"Darn it, look at all that blood!" I said, pointing to a little red puddle on the floor.

Sam, Mr. Prophet, Officer Wilde, Officer Garcia, and Pudge Wilson stood in a clump, holding a bleeding Frank Pagano on his feet. Frank swayed in their grip as he muttered something about... I'm not sure what. I heard the words *Catholic, Italian, dog, German, bitch, Melanie,* and *fairy,* but not together in a coherent sentence.

What was Pudge Wilson doing here?

"Shut up, Frank," said Sam, shaking his idiot nephew.

Frank shut up. He appeared dazed. As well he should, the villainous peckerwood.

Oh. Perhaps Pudge had been responsible for the odd noises I'd heard whilst trapped in my berserker trance. Clearly neither Washington Junior High School nor his parents had confiscated his bugle, because it dangled from his right hand.

The stupid telephone rang. I turned and walked back to the telephone table.

"Hello?"

"You sound strange, Daisy," said Harold.

"I am strange, Harold. Frank Pagano just tried to kill me, but Spike and I foiled his plot. However, I do believe I went insane for a moment or two. I think we might have berserker blood flowing through our veins."

"What?"

I gave my head another hard shake. "Um…"

"Daisy, snap out of it! Are you all right?"

I wasn't sure I could answer that question. Sitting on the chair, I said, "Um…I don't think so."

"Did you say Frank Pagano tried to kill you?"

"Yes, I did. But he didn't. Spike and I got to him before he could get to us."

"How'd he get to you? I thought there were people patrolling the neighborhood!"

"So did I, but he somehow managed to get into our backyard. If Spike hadn't warned me, I'd have opened the back door and walked straight into Frank Pagano's switchblade knife."

"That doesn't give me boundless faith in the Pasadena Police Department," said Harold.

"Same here," I said. I felt a little numb now. Better than feeling enraged, I guess. "Um, did you call for a reason, Harold?"

"Yes, I did."

"Oh, what was it?" I managed to sound faintly interested.

"I went to visit Jan Forrest today and showed Melanie that photograph of Frank Pagano. She said his name is Jimmy Smith, and that he's the father of the innocent baby upstairs."

At those words I, who had been as slumped as an eight-months-pregnant woman could be slumped, sat up straight. "She *confirmed* it? That son of a—"

"Don't say it!" Harold ordered.

Fuming, I said, "Why not?"

"Because you don't use words like that," said Harold reproachfully.

"I can start," I said.

"Yes, but don't. We don't want you to turn into a bad-mouthed flapper."

His comment startled me. "Me? *I*? I'm not a flapper!"

"Precisely, and only flappers and men swear."

"Oh. Very well then. I won't swear."

"Thank you. I like the real you better than you attempting to be a flapper. Anyhow, we already knew Frank was the father of Melanie's baby, didn't we?"

"Yes. I believe we did know that." I cleared my throat as I attempted to decipher Harold's first sentence and finally gave up. "Frank might be held accountable for...some kind of rape. I don't remember what Sam called it, but I don't think Melanie will want to press charges lest her predicament gets spread all over the place."

"I agree. Say, is Sam there right now?"

"He's in the kitchen with two policemen, Pudge Wilson, Mr. Prophet, and Frank. Frank bled all over my kitchen floor, Harold!"

"I'm sorry. Is it possible for Sam to come to the telephone?"

"I think so. You want to talk to him?"

"Yes please."

"Okay. Just a minute." I laid the receiver on the telephone table, got up and walked back to the kitchen. There I found the aforementioned participants still doing what they'd been doing before the telephone rang.

Sam turned and frowned at me. Well! "What is it, Daisy?"

"Harold needs to talk to you," I said, even though I thought he'd been rude. Then again, my own recent behavior hadn't been above reproach.

"Harold's on the telephone?" asked Sam.

"That's a stupid question, Sam. Why else would I be here telling you he wants to talk to you?"

I saw the uncomfortable glance that passed among the two policemen, Mr. Prophet, Pudge and Sam, and my eyes narrowed.

"I'll be right there," Sam said in a hurry.

"Good."

When I saw the expression on Sam's face, I believed I might still have been behaving a trifle oddly. Therefore, I walked in front of Sam into the hall. From there, Sam detoured to the telephone table, and I continued on and into the living room where I decided to sit and be still for a little bit.

I woke up when somebody nudged my shoulder. "Hunh," I said.

"Daisy, sweetheart," I heard Sam say. "You might want to wake up now."

"No thanks, I really don't."

THIRTY-FIVE

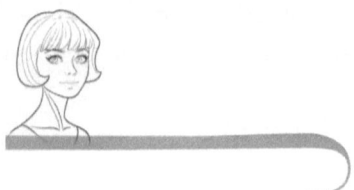

"You may nap after you and I discuss Harold's telephone call."
Sam sat next to me on the sofa, and I opened my eyes. They felt gummy, but I was pleased to see Spike on Sam's lap and wagging at me.

"Hey, Spike," I said to my heroic dog. "You did a great job on Frank Pagano."

"So did you," said Sam. He didn't sound as appreciative of me as I had of Spike.

Nertz. The preceding hour or so came flooding back into my formerly numb brain and I sat up on the sofa.

"It's not my fault," I said, wondering if I were telling the truth.

"I know that. I got a call at the station from Mrs. Longnecker, telling—"

"Why was that gossipy old hag calling *you*?" I demanded.

"She wanted to tell me she saw what she thought was a man climbing onto our roof via the camellia bushes out front."

"He climbed on to the *roof*?"

"According to Mrs. Longnecker, he did. And, since he managed to elude the patrols set out for him—and Lou Prophet, who darned near shot him with his rifle—I believe she was correct."

"Aha," I said. "That must have been what I heard. Frank on the roof."

"Guess so," said Sam.

"Why didn't she call me?"

"I don't know," he said.

"Hmmm. Interesting. I wondered how he got onto the back porch."

"From the roof, apparently," said Sam.

I recalled another part of Sam's statement. "Did that horrible felon squash our camellias?"

"I haven't looked yet," said Sam. "I was worried about you."

"Thank you, Sam. I, um, think I went a little crazy when I realized it was Frank at the back door. If Spike hadn't warned me, I'd have opened the door for him."

"According to Frank, you did open the door for him." Sam sounded perplexed. "But you seemed to have armed yourself first."

"Yeah. With a mop," I said, disgusted. "I'd headed to the back door because I wanted to make sure Mr. Prophet was out there, guarding the house. He wasn't."

"Ah. Lou said he'd been sitting beside the rose arbor reading when he heard the commotion. He said he was prepared to shoot Frank if he was causing the trouble, but that you and Spike seemed to be holding your own by the time he got to the door. In fact, he said he feared for a couple of moments that he might have to shoot *you.*"

Embarrassed, I said, "Hmm. I guess I got a little carried away there."

"I should say you did." Sam's perplexity seemed to be changing into humor. "You darned near killed my idiot nephew."

"I wish someone had," I said. "I'm sorry. That's not nice of me, is it?"

"You were provoked," Sam said soothingly.

"True, but I guess I'm not very ladylike, am I?"

"You're you, and I love you," said Sam.

"I love you too, Sam," I said, a lump in my throat.

"I'm glad, but let me tell you why Harold called."

"He confirmed that Frank is the father of Melanie's baby. What else did he tell you? And why did he kill Mr. Smithfield?"

"That Frank was calling himself Jimmy Smith, and that he took Miss Robinson to the hospital. And Frank hasn't yet told us why he thought he needed to kill Smithfield."

"Mr. Smithfield probably wasn't an Italian Catholic either.

"Probably," said Sam with a chuckle.

"Well then? What else do we need to know? Melanie isn't going to press charges against him, is she?"

"I doubt it, although she'd have every right. Harold said she's only fifteen years old."

"Yes," I said. "She won't be sixteen until tomorrow. Oh, wait! I think today is her birthday. Is there any way for a minor to remain anonymous when preferring charges against an evil man like Frank?"

"I'm honestly not sure. I'd have to consult an attorney, but I doubt it."

"Maybe Peter Altman can tell us," I said.

"Yes, Harold told me about Altman."

"Did Harold tell you we've arranged to have the Grenvilles and Mr. Altman visit the baby at Harold's house tomorrow at eleven-ish?"

"Yes, he did," said Sam.

"Will you go with us?" I asked, hoping he'd say yes.

He did! "Yes. I don't want to leave you alone for a while yet. You've been through too much recently, especially in your condition."

"Bother my condition! Frank is Frank, whatever my personal condition is. Why does he hate me so much anyway?"

"Would you believe me if I told you it's because you're not Catholic, you're not Italian, and you have a German dog?" Sam asked, smiling.

After thinking about his question for a few seconds, I said, "Yes. Yes, I would believe you. Frank is a dim bulb."

"That he is. I've been in touch with Renata and Frank Senior. Renata told me that the younger Frank fell off of a table when he was a baby and banged his head. She and Frank Senior think that's why Frank Junior has always been such a problem. None of their other kids is criminally inclined."

"Good grief. You mean that story about him hitting his head wasn't a joke?"

"No. It wasn't a joke. Renata asked me to apologize to you. At first, she blamed you for getting young Frank into trouble, but she no longer believes her son's behavior is your fault."

"That's big of her." Sarcastic, Daisy! "I'm sorry. I didn't mean to sound so nasty. But why did she think I was responsible for Frank's misdeeds?"

"Because Frank told her you were," said Sam.

"Crumb."

"Are you able to sit up and discuss a few things now?" Sam asked kindly.

"Yes. Thank you for being nice to me. I know I went off the rails today. I think I snapped when Frank called Spike stupid."

"That would do it, all right." Sam was still being kind.

"Where is your nephew now, by the way?"

"Wilde and Garcia took him to the police station."

"That's good. What's he being charged with?" Before Sam could answer my first question, I asked a second one. "Did Pudge Wilson actually blow an alarm on his bugle? I heard some awful noises when I was whacking Frank with the mop handle."

"Yes, he did. I have confiscated his bugle until Lou and I have a chat with his parents."

"He didn't cut school again, did he? That would be twice in one day."

"No," said Sam. "School was out, but he said he was worried about you, so he came to our back gate in order to stand guard."

"Good heavens."

"Something like that, yes," said Sam. "And Frank is being charged with attempted murder. As soon as we check the finger-prints on that knife of his, he may be charged with James Smith-field's murder. He's not going anywhere from here except to the electric chair."

"What a horrid person he is. What about Melanie Robinson?"

"What *about* her?" asked Sam.

"Does she have to know that the father of her baby is a murderer? I think she feels bad enough about her recent behavior without having Frank's villainy shoved in her face. She's only fifteen —well, maybe she's sixteen—after all."

"We'll probably have to talk to Dr. Vialargo about that," said Sam. "Perhaps Dr. Benjamin too."

"Does Pasadena have any psychiatrists or alienists? Maybe Melanie should see one of those."

Sam tilted his head to one side. "That might be a very good idea," he said. "I'll bet Johnnie or Flossie will know the answer."

"They probably will," I said. "They know more ways to help lost people than any other folks I've ever met."

"I totally agree," said Sam.

The following morning—our supper on Thursday night was leftover everything, and Mr. Prophet joined us—Sam drove Mr. Prophet and me to Harold's San Marino palace.

"This place is too big," said Mr. Prophet, eyeing Harold's home with a critical eye.

"Maybe if you had six or seven kids, it wouldn't be too big," I said.

"Still too big," said Mr. Prophet. As I already knew Mr. P. disapproved of lavish displays of wealth, I didn't argue.

"Looks like Dr. Vialargo and Mr. Altman are already here," I said, noticing the two nice-looking autos parked at Harold's curb. "Hope the Grenvilles and the baby like each other."

"Me too," said Sam.

They did!

For a story that began so murkily a mere week ago, this one seems to have had a happy ending. Or a happy second beginning, anyhow. Who knows how the story will truly end?

George and Marianne Grenville and Diane Chapman are still deliriously happy. I know it for a fact because I visit them occasionally. Also, Marianne brings little Holly to see Dr. Steindorf for check-ups, and we meet there every now and then.

As for Sam's and my little boy, Joseph Louis Rotondo, he was born at the Woman's Hospital of Pasadena on Tuesday, November 30, 1926. He weighed in at seven pounds, six ounces and was twenty inches long. He arrived at twelve-thirty p.m. after keeping me in agony for a mere eight hours. He had a head full of black hair, a perfectly formed face and body, and was the most handsome boy in the entire nursery ward. Not that I'm at all biased.

Mr. Prophet will deny this if asked, but when Sam and I told him our son's middle name was meant to honor him, he gulped twice and—I swear this is true—got a little teary-eyed. He still goes around armed, so I suggest you not confront him about it.

I've come to understand that being in labor for a mere eight hours is considered pretty much nothing to speak of when it comes to having babies. As soon as Joey was born, I heard horror stories about women who'd been in labor for days and days and whose babies were damaged or died shortly afterward. Sometimes, the mothers died too.

Neither Sam nor I, nor my parents and aunt, nor Harold and Del, nor Flossie and Johnnie, nor Robert and Regina Browning, had ever seen a more beautiful baby in any of their lives. I believed them when they said so.

My state of motherly bliss suffered only a minor dent when Sam's mother visited Pasadena for Christmas. She was actually extremely kind to me, even though I'm still neither Italian nor Catholic.

Little Joey hasn't begun walking yet, being only two months old, but I expect he'll be a good dancer eventually. After all, that old nursery rhyme says so!

Monday's child is fair of face,
Tuesday's child is full of grace.
Wednesday's child is full of woe,
Thursday's child has far to go.
Friday's child is loving and giving,
Saturday's child works hard for a living.
But the child that is born on Sabbath day,
Is bonny and blithe, good and gay.

The End

ROSY SPIRITS

A DAISY GUMM MAJESTY MYSTERY, BOOK 21

"What do you think, Joey? Isn't this a perfect place to go on a perfect day?"

"Baba, mama, dada," Joey replied. He was only eight months old, so his vocabulary was limited.

"I think so too. The only thing better would be if Spike could have come with us."

"Ike," said Joey. He adored my black-and-tan liberty hound, Spike, almost as much as I did.

"And, of course, your papa," I said, feeling guilty for not mentioning his father before mentioning Spike.

"Papa," said little Joey. I felt better after that.

"But the Busch Gardens folks told me they don't appreciate dogs piddling on their floral arrangements and statues. That applies to Spike and not your father."

"Gaga," said Joey.

"Of course, I'm not sure I appreciate the fellow who created these gardens, Adolphus Busch. He made beer, for heaven's sake. And his last name sounds suspiciously German." I recalled with whom I was talking and walking and said, "Forget I said that, Joey."

"Gehgeh," said Joey.

Now that I was the mother of a perfectly splendid and handsome boy, Joseph Louis Rotondo, I was attempting to be the kind of person I wanted to be, instead of the one I was. The one I wanted to be didn't harbor preconceptions about people based on their color, nationality or religion. As my first husband, Billy Majesty, was a casualty of the Great War, I still had trouble being impartial about Germans.

"That's right. But let's look over here. This is the Fairy Tale Garden. Not that I'd ever read those ghastly stories to you, Joey. The humans always lose in fairy tales, especially those by the Grimm brothers. You can learn about pain and suffering when you're out of diapers."

"Gaga," said Joey.

"Oh, look at these beautiful roses," I said speeding up slightly. Busch Gardens sprawled over fourteen miles and there were paved paths through most of it. It was much easier to push Joey's baby carriage on paved paths than dirt paths, although Joey sometimes laughed when he got bounced. Good-natured baby, thank goodness.

"These are so lovely," I said in awe as I gazed at the masses of rosebushes. "And they smell amazing. Just like our Cecile Brunner climbers at home."

"Ceecee," said Joey.

"And look at these beautiful hydrangeas, Joey." I had a soft spot in my heart for hydrangeas. A big clump of them grew beside the porch or the house in which I grew up, and Sam and I had recently planted some in front of our own porch. Our own porch sat directly across the street from my parents' home. Our dog, Spike, used to have a grand time chasing the neighbors' cat, Sampson, through the hydrangea bushes. Now Spike was best friends with a mangled orange cat named Yuyu that lived on our property across the street. I'd found his reaction to Yuyu astonishing at first, but now I was more or less used to it.

"Jaja," said Joey.

"Yes, indeed," I replied happily. "Hydrangeas." I spoke the word slowly, although I doubt if it made a difference. Joey was eight months old, for pity's sake.

"Jaja," Joey repeated. Then he said, "Ooook," and darned if he didn't point at something. I already knew my child was brilliant, but I hadn't realized *how* brilliant until that moment.

Charmed and impressed with my exceptional son, I said, "You want me to look at something, Joey?"

He continued pointing, but didn't repeat the word oook. Because his vantage point was considerably lower than my own—he was seated in his baby carriage and I was standing—I moved his buggy a little to one side and bent down to look. Something seemed odd about this particular clump of hydrangea bushes. Squinting, I knelt beside the carriage and stared harder.

Then I gave such a start of alarm, I nearly fell over backwards.

"Good heavens, Joey, that's somebody's foot!"

"Ooot," said Joey.

"And it's attached to a leg!"

"Egg," said Joey.

I stood up so quickly, my head swam. What on earth...?

Kneeling again, I decided to prod the leg, clad in what looked like brown plaid trousers. So I prodded.

Nothing happened.

"Oh dear," I muttered.

"Odee," said Joey.

I prodded harder.

More nothing.

Deciding it was my moral duty, even though the notion repelled me, I felt more of the leg. Finally got to a belt. The thick shrubbery was scratching my face, and I tried to shove aside branches and clusters of petals until I managed to see a face. Then I wished I hadn't. That's because most of it was gone.

"Oh my heavens, Joey, somebody bashed in the poor fellow's face!"

Available in Paperback and eBook from Your Favorite Bookstore or Online Retailer

ABOUT THE AUTHOR

Award-winning author Alice Duncan lives with a herd of wild dachshunds (enriched from time to time with fosterees from New Mexico Dachshund Rescue) in Roswell, New Mexico. She's not a UFO enthusiast; she's in Roswell because her mother's family settled there fifty years before the aliens crashed (and living in Roswell, NM, is cheaper than living in Pasadena, CA, unfortunately). Alice would love to hear from you at alice@aliceduncan.net

www.aliceduncan.net

 facebook.com/alice.duncan.925